Doctor Gavrilov

Doctor
Gavrilov

Maggie Hamand

To Carrie
keep
writing !
All the best,
Maggie

ccwc

First print edition
published in 2015 by
The CCWC
82 Forest Road
London E8 3BH
www.writingcourses.org.uk

ISBN 978-0-957694-45-3

A CIP catalogue record for this book is available from the
British Library

Printed and bound in Great Britain by TJ International, Padstow

Acknowledgements

With many thanks to all those people who helped me in my researches, in Vienna, Moscow and London. Special thanks go to David Kay, former Secretary General of the Uranium Institute and UN Chief Weapons Inspector in Iraq, Seva Novgorodsev of the BBC Russian Service, Zhores Medvedev, author of *The Legacy of Chernobyl*, Olga Fedina, Sveta Yavorsky, Christopher Long, and others who wish to remain anonymous, all of whom gave generously of their time to help me make the book as accurate as possible. I would also like to thank the late Julian Rathbone for his encouragement and belief in this book. Many thanks are also due to my eagle-eyed readers/editors, Gillian Paschkes-Bell, Andrew Rivett and Mary Flanagan.

'Why this is hell, nor am I out of it'
Christopher Marlowe, *Doctor Faustus*

Prologue
Vienna, 1992

IN THE LIGHT of the police spotlights Tim Finucan could see them dragging the corpse out of the Danube. Heavy with water and shrouded in a dark sack, it slipped from among the icy patches on the river and lay on the bank gleaming like a landed seal. An ambulance stood to one side, the blue lights flashing, creating a halo in the rainy air and shimmering on the wet ground. The paramedics stood ready with their equipment, but it must have been clear to them at a glance that this was a body that stood no chance of resuscitation.

Across the canalised river, half obscured by the rain, stood the tall, curved towers of the UN buildings; lights still gleamed in the upper stories. The rain turned to a fine, icy sleet, and Tim ran along the bridge to stand beside the cameraman. He couldn't keep the excitement out of his voice. 'This is great, terrific. We got the exact moment. How close in can you get?' Police cordons had prevented them from getting any nearer than the bridge, but the view was good enough from here. In the distance, alarm lights from a police car flashed in the darkness and they heard the whoop of the siren. Tim was anxious, impatient to be finished; they might be told they couldn't film and be cleared off the bridge at any moment.

'Can you just pan up to the UN buildings? It would be great to get them in the same shot – '

The cameraman had been at this job far longer than Tim and didn't try to hide his irritation. 'Shut up and pass me that next tape will you – it's about to run out.'

Each videotape lasted 30 minutes; in Tim's experience, they always ran out at the critical moment, either that or the battery pack needed replacing. He handed over the tape and the cameraman changed it over in a series of skilled, quick movements. On the concrete bank below them two men crouched over the body, passing a monitor backwards and forwards over it. The men wore protective suits and moved slowly, like spacemen, gleaming white against the darkness.

Tim felt a sudden chill. 'Shit,' he said. 'Do they think it's radioactive?'

Beside him his other companion, the American reporter Erwin Stone, inhaled deeply on the last of his cigarette and tossed the stub over the parapet. He hunched his shoulders and stamped his feet to get warm. 'Haven't you heard? The two men arrested yesterday were admitted to hospital this morning showing signs of radiation poisoning.'

Tim watched as they loaded the body into an unmarked vehicle which was standing by. The searchlights abruptly went off; the sleet stung his face like needles. 'Where's the hospital?'

'The Lorenz Böhler. It's not far from here. I'll direct you.'

They drove to the hospital but the staff were not giving out any information; a police guard in the entrance told them to leave. They set up the lights outside the main casualty entrance and Tim spoke his piece, putting his all into it while striving for an impression of seasoned casualness. Despite the icy rain, he made the cameraman shoot it twice; this was the first time Tim himself would appear on screen and he was anxious to get it right.

They packed up quickly and loaded the van with numb, slippery fingers. The American suggested a drink at the bar on the corner. It was dingy and empty except for a young couple lingering over their drink; in the background some Austrian folk music played quietly. The main thing was that it was warm.

Erwin went to the bar and ordered coffee and slivovitz; the cameraman slouched in the corner and looked meaningfully at the clock. Tim, however, wanted to thank Erwin for tipping him off about the body and pump him for any more information. Erwin had freelanced in Vienna for years; he'd told Tim that he knew better than to try to sell the story here and the paper he was a stringer for in the States had wanted only a couple of paragraphs, so he'd passed it on to Tim who could make more use of it.

Erwin took out his packet of cigarettes and laid them on the table while he searched in his pockets for his lighter. 'This is the third incident of nuclear smuggling we've had here this month . . . the first was just a few fuel pellets from an old Soviet-built reactor. The second was a laboratory sample, just a tiny quantity . . . this time it looks more serious.'

'But why all the protective clothing? Surely pure uranium isn't that radioactive? Even if it's bomb grade . . .'

'Well, there is no safe dose of radiation. And they might have got hold of some irradiated fuel rods . . . that could be highly radioactive. Or it could be plutonium this time.'

'Why should these guys take the risk?'

'Maybe they don't even know what it is they're handling.' Erwin lit up, tilted back his head and blew two thick columns of smoke from his nostrils. 'In any case, we're not likely to find out any more from the police. The Austrian authorities keep a pretty tight grasp over their media . . . It'll be hushed up.' He paused and added cynically, 'If we're lucky we might find out the nationality of the corpse.'

Tim looked around; the cameraman had nodded off in the corner. Erwin turned to him. 'You know, if you're doing a detailed report on this, the smuggling of nuclear materials is only the tip of the iceberg. Even more dangerous is the fact that there are plenty of nuclear scientists, out of a job, selling their know-how to anyone who will pay for it.' He glanced at Tim. 'You should follow this up.'

'I will.'

'Give me your address and phone number . . . I can send stuff on to you.'

Tim took out his card. 'I'll give you my home number but it's only temporary . . . I've got nowhere to live at the moment. I sold my flat first and then the place I was buying fell through . . . But you can always reach me at the office.'

Erwin drained his glass and slipped the card into his wallet. 'I might be able to help,' he said, unexpectedly. 'I ran into Michael Barratt yesterday, do you know him? He's moving to Delhi, he told me he was trying to find someone to take on his London flat. It's in Kilburn, not far from the subway. The house belongs to an old friend of mine who moved from Vienna last year . . . in fact you might even know her, she worked for the BBC in Bush House, Katie MacAllister, she was then . . .'

Though this kind of thing happened to him all the time, Tim was still astonished at this coincidence. 'Katie MacAllister? God, I used to know her quite well. She was in the German service, rather a stunning girl . . . I haven't seen her for years. Now I remember, she took a job here, Radio Blue Danube or something . . . didn't she get married?'

'Yes. Actually, twice.' He paused and looked Tim in the eye. 'Look, I'll give you her number. Give her a call. I'll ring her and let her know you'll be in touch."

Erwin wrote a number on a piece of paper and pushed it across the table to him. Tim folded it in half and clipped it safely into his pocket-file. He looked at his watch; it was nearly midnight. 'Look, it's been good to see you, you've been a great help . . . but I've got to get this edited and fed over to London . . .'

'At ORF?' Erwin was referring to Austrian state television.

'No, we usually use them but since this is such a sensitive story we've booked a studio at an independent facilities house . . . in fact, this is such hot stuff I'm not sure whether I shouldn't get straight back to London and edit it there . . . what do you think, Rupert?'

The cameraman opened one eye; Tim thought perhaps he hadn't been asleep after all. 'Suits me fine.'

Erwin went to use the phone and came back a few minutes later. He leaned forward over the table and spoke in a quiet, almost conspiratorial voice. 'I think your plan would be very wise. The authorities here have imposed a news blackout . . . in fact you'd better make sure your film doesn't get confiscated on the way out.'

PART ONE

1

DMITRY GAVRILOV knew at once that he was being followed. It had started yesterday. He had noticed someone watching him when he left the house that morning, and seen the same man again when he returned home from the tube at Kilburn. He had seen nothing that morning but now, as he walked up the Finchley Road, he saw the man in a black jacket coming up behind him at a discreet distance.

He stopped at the traffic lights. Cars rushed past him so fast that he felt dizzy. The autumn sunlight glanced off the glass and metal in sharp shards of light which hurt his eyes. He screwed up his eyes and glanced around, but the man was not there. Yet as soon as he started to walk, the sensation of being pursued struck him again. The lights changed, the traffic halted, but he was afraid to step forward, as if there were a gaping hole in front of him into which he might fall. His head felt light, as if it had swollen and filled with air like a balloon; it was as if everything around him was suddenly closer yet further away; he couldn't see properly, but couldn't say what was wrong with his sight.

He looked across the street and realised that there were specks dancing in front of his eyes, little points of nothingness as if holes were being torn in his vision. It was as if the reality of the world was being stripped away to reveal the void behind. Then he realised what it was; it was the beginning of a migraine. Though he'd experienced this before, it was still frightening; he saw a low wall and sat down on it, waiting for the aura to pass.

A black dog ran past him down the pavement, moving awkwardly, giving little darting glances across the road as if it wanted to cross. The sight of this dog with its curly black hair, lolling tongue and white-rimmed eyes filled Dmitry with an acute sense of foreboding. He felt some disaster was imminent, but was powerless to stop it. When the dog came to the crossing, it lurched forward into the road just as the cars began to move; he heard a high-pitched squeal of tyres on the tarmac as a car swerved to the left to avoid it, and then a grinding of metal as the car hit the van beside it a glancing blow. The dog, seemingly unaware, rushed across the road, along the pavement and out of sight.

The drivers got out, shouted at one another and exchanged details; traffic dammed up along the road. Car horns sounded loudly and people on the pavement stopped and stared. Dmitry sat still, his hand in front of his eyes, trying to blot it all out.

The man in the black jacket sat down on the wall beside him. Dmitry tried to ignore him, but after a few minutes he turned his head to look. The man's face was not clear; the little holes in Dmitry's vision had merged into one large central gap, a spherical emptiness where the man's face should have been. He saw only an impression of his skin, a doughnut shape of flesh, and the grey-brown hair sticking out around it. He could see the plump hands resting on the dark trousers, the black fabric of his jacket, and the large, polished tan shoes.

Dmitry looked to the left, catching out of the side of his vision an impression of a round, florid face. Then he looked away.

The man moved in a little closer, so that Dmitry could feel his breath stirring the tiny hairs on his own skin. The voice spoke softly next to his ear. 'You could make a lot of money, if you wanted to.'

The man spoke Russian. He spoke it like a native, but there was a hint of something else, some individual accent that Dmitry struggled to place. It shocked him both because he did not expect to be addressed in his own language but also because the man seemed to echo Dmitry's own thoughts, the thoughts he had just been having before he felt the onset of the migraine.

He turned to look at the man again, but the grey hole was still there. Flashing lights were now beginning to circulate around its edge, cogs within cogs, flickering and grinding without a sound. He screwed up his face, trying to bring the man's features into view.

'What did you say?'

'You heard me.'

'Are you offering me work?'

The man laughed. His fat fingers pulled a gleaming cigarette case out of his jacket and flipped it open. He drew out a cigarette and tapped it several times, before popping it into the space where his mouth should have been. He raised a lighter and snapped it, and then clouds of grey smoke drifted out of the missing face.

Dmitry put his hand in front of his eyes. It was a long time since he had experienced a full-blown migraine. He could not remember how long the aura lasted.

'You will be offered some work shortly. My advice is, take it.'

'What kind of work?'

'You will see.'

'Who are you?' It came out of Dmitry's mouth as if unbidden, and his voice sounded too loud, sharp as broken glass.

'Oh, I think you know who I am.'

Dmitry looked at him, at the round, soft, florid face, the little darting eyes, the curved mouth with cruel contours. He realised that the flashing lights, the migraine scotoma, had vanished, and knew that there would be a brief respite before the headache followed.

'It seems a pity,' said the man, 'To have all that knowledge and not use it.'

'What knowledge?'

The man looked at him, amused. Dmitry noticed that one eyebrow was thicker and higher than the other, and that this, in combination with the curved mouth made the man's face curiously lop-sided. He looked away, and realised that his hands were trembling.

The man inhaled again on his cigarette. 'There's no point in denying it. I know everything about you.'

'Not everything.'

'Well, perhaps not quite everything. I'm sorry, do you smoke?' Belatedly he offered Dmitry a cigarette.

Dmitry refused, jumped up from the wall and walked up the road. The man fell into step beside him. Dmitry walked faster; the man walked faster. He stopped, and the man stopped. It was intolerable.

Dmitry clenched his fists, stopped dead, spun around. 'Will you leave me alone!'

His head was hurting now, a tight band of pain forming around the temples. The man smiled, and bowed slightly. Again he offered the shiny cigarette case. 'Which brand do you like?'

'Nothing! I don't smoke! Fuck off, to the devil with you!' Dmitry made a gesture as if to strike him with his fist. Instantly the man backed off, still grinning inanely. 'Very well. We shall meet again, very soon.'

Dmitry watched the small, dark figure retreating down the pavement, and noticed that he was walking with a slight limp.

◆

At home, his wife Katie was walking up and down, with their baby, Alexander. They'd chosen the name because it worked in both Russian and English; but now he was only known by the shortened form, Sasha.

She glanced at the clock. As she paused for a moment in her jiggling motion, the baby cried louder. She held him tightly, talking in a soothing voice, her arms aching with the effort of holding him. Only ten minutes more of this purgatory, she thought, and she could go and fetch her daughter home from school.

Then abruptly, the baby stopped crying. His little body

stopped struggling, he opened his mouth to yawn, and fixed his blue eyes on her. As she rocked him, his eyes slowly shut and then his head flopped gently back against her shoulder. She sank down into the chair, adjusting him on her body, and gazed down at his tiny features, now perfectly composed in his pale, round face.

A long shaft of sunlight came in through the tall windows, lay in a bar across the floor, and illuminated the fuzz of hair on Sasha's head like a little halo. Katie sat there, savouring the silence and the sudden peacefulness in the room. She did not have enough of these moments. For a moment she was able to push all her worries to one side. Everything was getting easier. Her husband had some work, Sasha was sleeping better, and Anna seemed happier at school. In a few months she would be able to find some childcare and try to get back to work.

Consciously, she drew in deep breaths, unclenched her fingers, tried to shrug the tension from her shoulders and relax her limbs. Sitting here, in the bright warm sunlight, the memory of his crying was just a distant dream.

Her eye travelled around the room, fell on a letter on the table next to the jar of daffodils. Immediately her bright mood receded. Katie knew the letter was bad news. She had held the envelope up to the light and managed to read, I am sorry to inform you. That was all she had needed to see. He had not got the translating job he had applied for. Another rejection might be too much for him. They wouldn't be able to pay the bills.

It wasn't meant to be like this. She had been so independent, once, had worked hard at her career. She had worked in radio journalism, a job full of challenge and excitement. She could get back, when the children were a bit older, but it would be difficult, she'd lost most of her contacts. And she loved the children, she had wanted them so much, and she wanted to do her best for them.

She glanced at her watch. She stood up and gently placed the baby in the pram in the hallway; as soon as he touched the mattress he woke and started to whimper. She locked up and pushed the pram out into the street; once she was walking along his crying mercifully ceased. As she approached the school gates, she saw two mothers, Jenny, the mother of Anna's friend Charlotte, and another she didn't know the name of. They were talking about local schools. Katie wondered whether to stop and join in the conversation, but this subject irritated her. Jenny smiled at her, and she stepped forward, thinking of asking Charlotte round for tea, but then Anna came running towards her. Her face was bright, flushed with excitement. 'Mitya said he'd take me to the park.'

Katie saw Dmitry standing behind Anna, holding her coat and lunch-box. She turned and went towards him at once. Anna had been told she could call him Daddy but she never did. Perhaps she reserved a hidden place for her father in her heart, though she never mentioned him and never seemed to want to. Katie was both relieved and upset by Dmitry's offer. If Dmitry took Anna to the park, it would delay him knowing about the letter. But for her it meant another hour at home alone with the baby; it was too cold for her to go with them and sit and feed him in the open air.

She stood in the street, watching her husband. She could see from the stiffness in his neck, from the frozen expression of his face and its whiteness, that he had a migraine. She felt sorry for him, asked gently, 'Why don't you come home first and lie down?'

He looked up at the sky, over which grey clouds now formed a thin blanket. 'I don't want to lie down, I shall only feel worse. Don't worry, I've taken a pain-killer. I'd rather take Anna.'

◆

Anna let go of Dmitry's hand and ran ahead of him into the playground, her long, dark hair streaming behind her, her coat flapping. Dmitry followed more slowly and sat down on the bench. It was getting cold now and the sky had darkened; it was dreary, damp and bitter. Dmitry thrust his hands deep into his pocket and waited, his head throbbing distantly through the numbness the painkillers caused.

After a short while another man came into the park. He was alone, and stood there, watching the children play. After a few minutes he came and sat at the far end of the bench. He was quite young, had short, dark hair and an olive complexion, and he was wearing casual clothes, jeans, trainers and a leather jacket. He looked nervous and it crossed Dmitry's mind that he might be a child molester.

Dmitry smiled and waved at Anna as she called to him from the top of the wooden climbing frame. The man inched nearer, clearing his throat. He said, quietly, respectfully, in English, but with the hint of an accent, 'Dr Gavrilov . . .'

Dmitry went hot and then cold all over with something that was close to fear, a kind of shock, a recognition. He said, still staring straight ahead, 'Please go. I am not interested.'

'There would be a great deal of money involved.'

'I do not want your money.'

'My Government . . .'

Dmitry turned to him for the first time. 'Yes, who is your Government?'

The man hesitated for a moment. 'I do not need to reveal this at the present time. But your skills, your knowledge, would be very valuable to us. We would pay you highly for them.'

Anna came down the slide, ran over to Dmitry and asked him to tie up her shoelace which was trailing in the mud. Her eyes gleamed, her cheeks were flushed bright red, and her whole body was suffused and overflowing with energy. Dmitry sat her on his knee and retied the lace, tying it double and pulling it tight to make sure.

Anna pushed the thick dark hair away from her face, kissed him, and giggled. She adored him. Sometimes this disconcerted him; nothing in his life had prepared him for such absolute trust and unstinted love. Deprived of her own father, she had accepted

Dmitry at once and could, as Katie often observed, twist him round her little finger. He knew she made a fool of him, and he didn't mind; how could he do anything but love her when she looked so like her mother?

Dmitry pushed her off his knee. 'Go on,' he said gruffly, 'I'm getting cold. Five more minutes and then we'll go.'

'You have a very beautiful daughter,' said the man, his eyes following her as she ran. 'How old is she? Five? Maybe, six?'

At this Dmitry abruptly stood up. He walked away from the bench and turned his back on him. He idly read the sign in front of them and then, suddenly set alight with anger, he turned and pointed it out to the man.

'Can you read this sign? Adults are only allowed in here if accompanied by young children. Do you have a child with you? No. Do you want me to call the police?'

The man looked alarmed; Dmitry's size and strength and the sudden intensity of his anger must have frightened him for an instant. He said, 'Of course, forgive me,' and backed away, nodding his head, almost bowing in a sudden excess of politeness. When he had gone Dmitry walked up and down with quick, short steps, banging his hands together as if to warm them. After a few minutes he could stand it no longer. 'Anna!' he called. 'Anna, it's time. We have to go now.'

Anna turned and ran to him at once, smiling and holding out her hands.

◆

Katie heard Dmitry bang the front door shut, and the sound of Anna running up the stairs to her room. She looked up from changing the baby's nappy when she heard him come in.

At least now she had something positive to report. 'Oh, Mitya, I think I've got another tenant for downstairs. It's an old colleague of mine from the BBC and his girlfriend. They can pay the rent all right, and they can move in next week, if they like the flat, of course.'

'Good.'

The income from the flat downstairs was the main thing that kept them solvent. She had been ringing around all day trying to find someone she could trust who might want to rent it. Then she'd had the phone call from an old contact, Erwin Stone, saying he knew someone who was interested. When she'd heard it was Tim Finucan she'd rung him at once. At least she had good news about this before he opened the letter.

She'd better not put it off. 'There's a letter for you on the table.'

He tore open the envelope. There was a brief pause, then he turned away and dropped the letter and the envelope in the bin. He said nothing, and she didn't ask him. She sat down to feed the baby.

'Could you get Anna something to eat?'

She wasn't sure he had heard her. He crossed the room and stared out of the window at the rain. Katie wanted to go to him but she was unable to move, nursing her little son. As he sucked she felt the sudden wash of the let-down of milk and felt her body relax. She watched her husband move around the kitchen, making toast, scrambling an egg. The baby fed greedily, as if he were drawing all the strength out of her, and she felt her eyes droop; all she wanted now was to sleep. She was acutely aware that she and Dmitry were avoiding saying anything to one another. She wondered if he knew that she knew what was in the letter. She wondered how much longer they could go on living like this.

She looked at her watch. They would be coming shortly. She was intrigued to see Tim after all this time; she wondered what his girlfriend would be like. She and Tim had trained in the same intake at the BBC and she remembered the fun they'd had together. Fun. What a strange word that sounded these days.

'They're going to come this evening to see the flat and collect the keys if they want to take it.'

'Who?'

'The new tenants. I just told you . . .'

She looked up and saw that Dmitry was frowning, that he was staring ahead and that the egg in the saucepan was starting to catch. She could see that he was miles away.

◆

Tim's first thought on seeing Katie was that she had let herself go.

When she opened the door her dark hair was long and loose and tangled; her dress was smudged with spots of grease and she wore no make-up. She was thin, too, thinner than he remembered, though this suited her, emphasised the clean lines of her face. He glanced past her into the room. Damp baby clothes hung on a rack in front of the radiator and there were piles of plates and mugs stacked up in the sink.

Katie's eyes had a pink, dark-rimmed look of exhaustion and her voice was soft, almost hoarse.

'Tim, come in.'

'This is Ingrid.'

'I'm pleased to meet you.' Ingrid shook Katie's hand. Tim thought that it was strange to see them both together, the woman he had wanted so much, years ago, and his latest lover. Ingrid, as she stood there, seemed so tall, cold, awkward. Tim realised with a faint shock as he compared them that despite the years since he'd last seen her, he was still attracted to Katie.

Katie gestured to an old leather sofa which had two craters at either end. She took two wine glasses, faintly smeared, and put them on the table, took a bottle of white wine from the fridge and poured it carefully into the glasses, making sure there was the same quantity in each.

'Dmitry will be down in a minute; he's upstairs, working.'

'Oh, right. What does he do?'

'He's a translator. Technical and scientific stuff.'

'What language?'

'English to Russian. He's Russian; didn't I tell you?'

'Oh, I see.' Tim was surprised, slightly intrigued; he thought, trust Katie to do something out of the ordinary.

Tim sipped the wine; it wasn't very good. 'I was in Vienna last week, was interviewing this UN guy as background to these nuclear smuggling stories, when I got this tip-off, a Russian, dumped in the Danube, pockets stuffed with plutonium – ' He stopped abruptly, as Ingrid prodded his arm, and he realised that Katie wasn't listening. She had turned away from him, folding some nappies, tidying some letters on the table. She rummaged in the desk and brought out a letter which she handed to him. She said, 'Michael has said he's not coming back so you can have the place for as long as you need. This says all about the flat, the conditions and everything. You'd better read it. I'm sure everything will be fine but I think it's best . . .'

'Oh, much better to be on a business-like footing.'

'Come on downstairs and take a look.'

Their house was at the end of a flat-fronted Victorian terrace, on three floors. The entrance hall had been divided, with a door in to the main part of the house, and another door leading down to a semi-basement flat. It seemed light enough; there was one double bedroom at the front, a large living room, and a small kitchen and bathroom at the back. The furniture was basic but the place had been recently decorated and all the walls were white and bright. Tim looked at Ingrid and she nodded. He said he'd take it.

Katie opened the door into the garden. In the centre was a small patch of ragged grass. A few pale yellow daffodils poked up round the edges, but otherwise it had been abandoned completely to the weeds. A child's tricycle lay on its side on the concrete path and Katie picked it up and stood it upright. 'We share use of the garden. The patio bit here is yours . . . The rent is paid in advance and there's a month's rent as a deposit.'

A cold wind blew through Ingrid's shirt and Tim could see her shiver. They went in and Katie closed and locked the door and handed him the key. As he did so she touched his hand and he felt or imagined that she started faintly, and then she looked up at him with her grey-green eyes which he thought had a touch of pain in them. She turned and they followed her upstairs.

Tim signed the contract and handed it back to her, and then wrote out a cheque. Then they sat and sipped their wine awkwardly. There was no sound at all from upstairs.

Katie suddenly said, 'Excuse me,' stood up, and ran lightly up the stairs. In a few moments she came down. She said, 'I'm sorry, he's fallen asleep. He had a migraine . . .' Her whole face looked strained; she seemed awkward and uneasy. Tim had the feeling that there was something wrong. He stood up, turning to Ingrid. 'Oh, don't worry, we weren't going to stay. We'll move all our stuff in at the weekend, won't we, Ingrid?'

Ingrid turned her smooth, pale face to Katie and smiled, a knowing smile that seemed to indicate that she recognised her as a rival and was not afraid of her. Tim found to his astonishment that a violent emotion took hold of him, so powerful that he could not even remember feeling this before. It took him a moment to realise what it was; that suddenly he hated Ingrid.

◆

Dmitry woke up suddenly in the night with the terrible sensation of something sitting, crushing his chest, making him unable to breathe. For an instant he lay pinioned, then he sat up, drawing in breath. He was bathed in sweat and his heart was beating so vigorously he could almost hear it in the silent room. Katie lay beside him on her side, her hair a dark mat on the pillow, her hand outstretched. Dmitry staggered to the bathroom and splashed some water on his face.

The cold water made his head throb even more painfully. He reached up into the cupboard for his painkillers. He tipped up the bottle and they rolled into his palm. The thought went through his head that he could take them all at once and be out of his misery, but instantly he scooped them back into the bottle with the rim and swallowed two for the correct dose.

He stared at the bottle. For some reason that he couldn't understand, he thought of the black dog. It had been in his nightmare, he knew, although he couldn't now remember anything else about it.

They knew his weak point. They had so little money.

Of course he could make money so easily. The knowledge that he had was dangerous. He knew that people would kidnap, blackmail or even torture him to possess it. He had hoped to live here, hidden, away from risk, to start his life again, but he had no chance. They knew now who and where he was, and they wanted him, and knew that he was vulnerable.

He went back into the bedroom. Katie stirred, and as he slipped into bed he reached over and took her hand. He squeezed it and she smiled. He whispered her name but she didn't answer, and he realised that she was not awake. Happiness darted through him for an instant like a shaft of warm sunlight, and it gave him hope, that she still so loved him that when he touched and spoke to her she would smile in her sleep.

◆

On his way back up the Finchley Road, coming from the library where he was working every day on his ill-paid translation, Dmitry stopped and gazed into the window at the rich array of cakes in Louis' Hungarian patisserie. Chocolate bombes, cakes topped with chestnut purée, cheesecake, fruit flans, pretzels, cream horns, black forest gateaux, stuffed with white fluffy cream and glazed with light. As he stood and looked, he became aware of the reflection of a face looking in beside him. The hair was grey, the face pink, the eyes dark. He knew at once that it was the Russian who had approached him before.

The man cleared his throat. 'We meet again.'

Dmitry didn't answer, didn't even acknowledge that he'd heard him. He wondered what would happen if he assaulted the man, picked him up and hurled him against the plate glass window. Dmitry was nearly a foot taller than his tormentor, easily big enough to intimidate him . He glared at the reflection for an instant longer and then turned and walked rapidly away.

Again the man walked right beside him. He was smoking a cigarette. He had a swift, hurried walk and despite his limp seemed to keep up with Dmitry without any effort. An icy wind seemed to come from out of nowhere and tugged at Dmitry's coat, blew the cigarette smoke back into his face.

The voice suddenly piped up at his elbow.

'You wanted me to come. Don't you at least want to hear what I have to say?'

'Me? Wanted you?' Dmitry was so stunned that he stopped dead. He turned to the little man in astonishment and rage. A childish fury was whipped up in him in an instant, so that he wanted to kick him, strangle him, wipe the stupid idiotic smile off the plump, unpleasant face.

The man seemed oblivious of the effect he had on Dmitry; he drew deeply on his cigarette and went on in smooth, soft tones. 'Of course you wanted me. You want work, you want money, don't you? If you like, I can leave you now. But I think you would regret never knowing what it was I had to offer.'

2

A S THE MAN SPOKE, the first heavy drops of rain fell. They were standing right outside the Cosmo Restaurant. Through the windows Dmitry could see the crisp white table-cloths, the silver laid out neatly, the vases of fresh flowers, some people finishing a late lunch. He felt a sharp gust of wind and the rain came down suddenly in a downpour, soaking them instantly.

The Russian plucked Dmitry's sleeve. 'Come, let's have something to eat in here. Have you ever dined in this place? It's very comfortable, nobody bothers you here . . . Let me invite you.'

Dmitry, feeling himself becoming more drenched every second, allowed himself to be propelled into the restaurant. He wanted to resist, he had felt, standing in the cold wind on the Finchley Road, simply like turning and running, but he had not had the energy; all resistance seemed to have drained out of him. He felt like a stubborn child who wants to protest against going to school or the doctor or some other unpleasant experience but knows there is no point in putting up a struggle. He had to admit that the offer of a free meal was too much of a temptation.

They sat down at a table by the window. The waiter came and handed him the menu. Goulash soup, stuffed garlic mushrooms, chopped liver, rye bread and butter. Wiener Schnitzel, ragout of venison. Dmitry muttered that he would have some soup and ragout and listened while his companion, relaxed and unhurried, ordered the meal and selected a bottle of wine.

The man opened his napkin with a quick flourish, spread it on his lap and looked at Dmitry coolly across the table. His face seemed less crooked, less unpleasant than before.

Dmitry tried for an instant to meet his gaze but found that he couldn't. He turned and looked out of the window. People were scurrying along in the rain; the traffic was at a standstill; Dmitry didn't want to have to listen to what was coming. He felt so depressed at that moment that he could hardly force himself to speak; he wondered why he did, after all, he didn't have to keep up appearances in front of this man, he didn't owe him anything, not even politeness; he was just trying to make use of him in some way.

The soup came, the waiter fussing as he cleared a space on the narrow table. Dmitry turned back to his companion. He asked, 'Might I know your name?'

'What name would you like? Do you think it matters? Well, I suppose you have to call me something. I have a very old first name, Gleb. My father's name . . . it's the same as yours, actually. Or my family name, Rozanov.' He held out his hand, but Dmitry declined to shake it. Rozanov let the hand rest on the table for a few moments before he lifted it and started on his soup, lifting his spoon to his lips and slurping loudly with each mouthful. When he had finished he patted his pocket and drew out another cigarette.

'Have they approached you yet?'

Dmitry felt the hairs at the back of his head prickle.

'Yesterday. In the park. One man.'

'What did you say?'

'I told him to piss off.'

Rozanov tut-tutted and shook his head. 'Not wise, not wise,' he muttered.

Dmitry leaned forward across the table. 'Look, I can imagine who you represent. What is your interest in this? Why should it help you if I talk to them?'

Rozanov lit his cigarette, inhaled and turned his head sideways to blow the smoke away from Dmitry. 'You could get us information, very valuable information.'

'I don't understand.' Dmitry glanced at the calendar on the wall of the restaurant. 'Is this an April fool?'

Rozanov laughed. 'On the contrary, I have never been more serious. You are not meant to understand. You are just meant to take the money, and do what we ask.'

'I can't commit myself. I don't know who they are, but I can guess . . . It's too dangerous '

'Well, perhaps it is, Dmitry Nikolayevich. But perhaps it is also very rewarding. After all, it is a great pity that a man with your talent and knowledge should be messing around with these piddling little translations.'

'This was a conscious choice. I had decided I no longer wished to work in the nuclear sector. Anyway, I've thought about it already. If I do this even once, you will ask me again and again, and it will never end. It's not good even to talk to you people . . . I shouldn't be seen with you . . .' and instinctively he glanced around the restaurant.

Rozanov laughed. 'It's all right; we have checked it out; we are not under surveillance. Do you think I would be so foolish as to proceed if I knew we were being watched, Dmitry Nikolayevich?'

Dmitry stirred the cold remains of his soup with his spoon. He said, lowering his voice but much more strongly, 'Look, let's get down to specifics. What exactly do you want? How much are you offering me, and for what? Come on, let's have enough of all this mincing around . . .'

Rozanov spoke in a calm, even voice. 'We want you to meet these people, who I'm sure will approach you again, find out exactly who they are and what they want, see what they are offering you. You may be able to find out from them who else they have got, what facilities they have, who is supplying them . . . we are only asking you to meet them once, maybe twice, here in London . . . we would not expose you to any danger.'

'But even if I offer to go and work for them, they are not going to give me any information in return . . . not unless I show good faith by providing them with something myself, surely.'

Rozanov finished his cigarette. 'Supposing you do them a proposal. You could do it, Dmitry Nikolayevich . . . you can dream up some new technique for uranium enrichment which they might like to buy. You know the kind of thing . . . something cheap, something a little new and different, something the West hasn't got, they love that kind of thing . . .' – he gave a little chuckle – 'And preferably something that wouldn't work.'

Dmitry gulped down his wine; Rozanov poured another glass. Dmitry knew he would try to get him a little drunk; well, let him think that will work with me. It will do me good to drink and unwind; besides, it's good wine. For a moment he felt reckless; something about Rozanov's suggestion suddenly amused and intrigued him. He held his glass up to the light, admiring the deep colour. Why did he feel so worried; he had nothing to fear, they couldn't force him into anything, and it was good to be sitting here, eating good food, warm and sheltered, and speaking Russian.

The wine had gone straight to his head, perhaps because he was so tired. He was thinking what a shame it was that he couldn't afford to bring Katie to this restaurant; how, indeed, they never had money to do things like this together. Although it had recently been difficult between them, especially since the baby was born, he was sure that once their financial problems were solved that everything would get better. He thought of her now, her deep eyes, her smile, her naked body, and felt his body ache with desire for her. He didn't know why she affected him like this; but then could anyone explain the phenomenon of love?

'Do you love your wife?'

Dmitry dropped the knife he was fiddling with on to the plate with astonishment and stared at Rozanov. Could this man even know what he was thinking? 'What's that to you? I won't discuss her.'

'What is most important to you in your life, would you say? Your wife, your child, your work, your country?'

At that moment the waiter came with the next course, placing the dish of ragout carefully in front of him. It smelt delicious and the saliva poured painfully into Dmitry's mouth. As he raised a forkful to his mouth a phrase suddenly came into his head from nowhere: 'If you sup with the devil, you should use a long spoon.' It amused him for a moment to imagine Rozanov as the devil, with little horns hidden in the grey hair, and a tail tucked away between those ridiculous plump legs – so ordinary, unremarkable, yet probing gently as he talked, trying to find the right key to his victim's soul; money, women, ambition, patriotism . . .

Rozanov lit another cigarette and leaned forward across the table. 'Dmitry Nikolayevich, my advisors tell me that some years ago you put in a research proposal for some sonic device which would separate out uranium 235 from uranium hexafluoride gas. I believe this work was never funded . . . Can you explain this to me? Assume I know nothing.'

Dmitry looked up, startled. Rozanov was absolutely right, he'd had this idea; a brilliant idea, he had thought it; he had never been able to do any more work on it. He leaned forward over the table. 'You must know that uranium comes in two isotopes, the common U238, and the much rarer U235 which is needed for nuclear fission?'

Rozanov nodded.

'The uranium is converted to uranium hexafluoride gas through a series of chemical processes. This is not so difficult. The problem is the next stage. Fine membranes or centrifuges are needed to separate the lighter molecules containing U235 atoms from the heavier ones, and the complexity of these processes are the key block to developing nuclear fuel – or a bomb.'

Dmitry explained that he had thought of another way, which might be easier and therefore cheaper than the costly gas centrifuges. The idea had come to him one evening, standing in the shower, humming one line of a Beethoven string quartet to himself. If you stood a vibrating bar, a tuning fork, in an environment of gaseous uranium hexafluoride, wouldn't the vibration, at the right frequency, separate out the heavier and lighter isotopes . . .

He was lost now, remembering. He recalled with sudden clarity how he had stayed up all night trying to work out the basic physics of it, while Masha, his first wife, kept coming in to interrupt him, alternately angry and seductive, unable as always to tolerate it when he was not giving her his full attention . . . well, Rozanov had done his research, obviously. This had all been carefully set up in advance, planned, prepared, discussed at high levels. Dmitry felt suddenly trapped. The whole situation had a remorseless feel to it, as if he were playing a game of chess in which, despite his own spontaneous and unpredictable moves, his opponent already foresaw everything and pressed rapidly to victory.

Flustered, he pushed his plate away from him. The ragout suddenly seemed to have lost its savour; he did not feel hungry any more, in fact, the food slightly nauseated him. He could not keep track of his thoughts; he wondered for a brief instant if Rozanov hadn't drugged the wine. Now, as he looked at him, the crooked eyebrows in that smiling face suddenly irritated him beyond all measure, and the podgy fingers resting on the fork repulsed him, actually making him feel sick. He said, gathering himself together, 'You want me to sell them this? This is a crazy idea . . . I am not at all sure . . . of course it might even work.'

Rozanov smiled again. He offered a cigarette to Dmitry which he declined, and lit up his own. 'All right, assuming that it did

. . . how long would it take to get such a project off the ground?'

'Oh, I don't know. I only did some very preliminary work, purely theoretical. First I would need to go over all that, then you would need to build a small-scale model, then a small cascade . . .'

Rozanov waved his hand. 'Please, no technical details . . . I am not a scientist. How many years?'

'Oh . . . I should think . . . three, five, at a minimum . . . I can't predict. It would depend on the facilities, how many people were working on it, whether we were lucky or unlucky . . .'

'So there would not be any immediate danger?'

'No, of course not . . . but that is not the point.'

The waiter came and took away their plates. Rozanov ordered a coffee and leaned back, dabbing his mouth with the handkerchief.

Dmitry asked, without thinking, 'How much would you pay me?'

'Name your price.'

Dmitry could not imagine what to ask for. He thought of suggesting a fantastic sum, enough not only to get them out of debt but to pay off their mortgage; but then he was afraid that Rozanov would agree to it and the offer would be too tempting for him. The waiter brought coffee and Rozanov drank it swiftly, gulping and smacking his lips. Dmitry suddenly felt the whole thing was absurd, pointless; he wanted to get away. He said, 'Look, I have to get on. I will think about what you say very carefully . . . I will give you an answer in a few days. Where can I get hold of you?'

Rozanov suddenly began to laugh, a strange, muffled laughter which made his shoulders shake and seem to agitate his whole body. Dmitry looked over his shoulder but nobody seemed interested in them. Rozanov's laughter grew louder and more unpleasant; Dmitry leapt up from the table. 'What's so funny?' he demanded.

Rozanov didn't answer. Tears of laughter ran down his cheeks and he dabbed at them with his napkin. Dmitry could not believe it; he thought he had gone mad. He felt that he had been conned into the whole conversation by some madman or trickster; he was beside himself with rage. He took out his wallet, not wanting to be indebted to this man in any way, found to his embarrassment that it only contained five pounds, flung the note and some small change down on the table, and rushed out into the fresh air.

It had stopped raining. As he walked up the road the sun unexpectedly came out. A bright bar of light streamed across the street, but by some curious illusion he saw only the dark shadows it cast, like inky pools. He realised he was shaking. He wondered if he was cold, or if he was ill, perhaps going down with the flu, or whether it was another migraine coming on. He thought, what is the matter with me? Why should I let this man upset me so? Whoever he is, whatever he's up to, he can't really touch me. All I have to do is say no.

He looked at his watch. It was later than he thought; already after seven. The sun, which had come out from beneath a dark bank of cloud, was sinking behind the buildings in the west. He went to the bus stop. He thought, for a moment, as he stood and waited, of going home and confessing to Katie everything that was in his mind; his failed ambitions, his powerlessness in exile, his sense of isolation, the encounter with Rozanov and with the man in the park, his own precarious mental state; but he knew he would never do it. It would make her afraid, and it would admit too much weakness in himself, and he knew she depended on him, believed in him.

The meal had delayed him and he was again home much later than he had promised and intended. He opened the door; the living room was in darkness. Katie and the children were upstairs; he could hear the sounds of splashing in the bath and Anna's carefree laughter. He deliberately shut the door quietly and crept into the living room; he sat down on the sofa, on the side which didn't have so deep a hole in it, and leaned his head backwards, staring at the ceiling. He could hear Katie trying to persuade Anna to get out of the bath.

'I don't understand,' he could hear Katie's voice, exasperated. 'First you don't want to get in, and now you don't want to get out. All right, stay there and get cold if you want to.' Dmitry knew he should go upstairs and help her, but he couldn't do it; these days he rarely did.

Now he could hear the baby crying. Dmitry stood up and crossed the room, poured himself some stale, cold tea from the tea-pot on the table and looked to see if there had been any mail. There were three letters for him. He put on the lamp, trained it over the table and opened the first letter. In it was a small blank card, on which was written in untidy writing, Aziz Hattab, and a phone number.

Now that he was away from Rozanov it all seemed quite clear; he wouldn't have anything to do with this. He opened the second letter and stood there, frowning. He read through it quickly and was surprised to find that he didn't feel anything. Billennium, the publisher for whom he was translating the book, had gone into receivership. Two or three pages of details of meetings for creditors followed . . . he read the small print. He couldn't grasp it all but one thing was clear; he wasn't going to be paid.

The third was a letter inviting him to an appointment with the bank manager.

He looked up suddenly. Anna was scampering down the stairs. She said, 'Mitya, Mitya, are you home? Will you put on my pyjamas for me?' He said, 'Just wait a minute.' She must have heard the dullness in his voice, realised there was no use in pleading, and sat down on the floor and started to pull the pyjamas on herself, making heavy weather of it, putting the trousers on back to front. Dmitry softened. He said, 'Come here; let me help . . . Let's go upstairs and I'll read you a story.'

He picked her up and carried her upstairs. Through the open bedroom door he saw Katie sitting on the edge of the crumpled bed, her knees wide apart, her upper body leaning forward and the hair spilling over her face, and the baby lying across her lap, taking his bedtime feed. Katie was not looking at him, she was not looking at anything; her eyes had that distant, faraway look they so often had while nursing the baby. She did not acknowledge Dmitry's presence as he hesitated for an instant in the doorway. He said as he passed by, 'Billennium have gone bankrupt.' He didn't wait to see her reaction. He dropped Anna on to the bed and found a book to read, a long story about a crocodile who ate children; then he kissed Anna goodnight, tucked her in and went downstairs.

Katie was already there, sitting at the table, looking at the letter. She said, 'What are we going to do?'

He said, 'I don't know . . . I'll ring them in the morning. Perhaps there will be another publisher who'll take it on . . . maybe they'll pay up . . . I'll go and look at the contract . . .'

Katie said, 'We were relying on it . . . Tim's deposit will only cover the bills . . . how are we going to pay the mortgage?'

'We can borrow more from the bank. I'm going to see the bank manager tomorrow . . . don't worry, I'll sort it out.'

'We've already borrowed more from the bank. Mitya, we've been over all this . . . even with that money we were only just going to be able to manage . . .'

'Don't go on about it!' Dmitry snatched the letter out of Katie's hand and with an angry gesture stuffed it in among the other papers in his desk. He was angry with himself; time and again he came home to Katie wanting to please her, to help her with the children, yes, and show how much he loved her, but somehow when he got here it all turned to destructive and futile rows. He went over to the kitchen, opened the fridge, took out the vodka bottle and poured himself a drink.

Katie was talking to him; he heard her say, 'You're not listening to me.' She was talking in the low voice she always used when she was trying to be reasonable. Her face looked worried and pained. 'Should we try to sell?'

'Sell the house? How will that help us? You know it's already worth less than we paid for it . . . At least here we get the income from the flat and anywhere we rent is likely to be just as expensive . . .'

Dmitry stared down at the crockery piled up in the sink. For a moment he felt like smashing it. This whole situation was his fault; he felt he should have made more effort to find work to support his family, and it was because of him they had no safety net; until he got his permanent residency they were not able even to claim any state benefits, not even Katie in her own right. Katie rose from the table, took some potatoes out of the vegetable rack and threw them into a saucepan. Upstairs, the baby, who they had thought to be asleep, started crying again. At a glance from Katie, Dmitry went upstairs, sat on the edge of their crumpled bed and started to rock the cradle. He rocked it faster and faster, keeping up a regular rhythm, listening to the floorboard in the uncarpeted room creak and Anna talking aloud to her teddy in the next room. A wild thought came into his head; that perhaps Rozanov or the people he worked for had arranged for Billennium to go bankrupt. Or, much more likely, that he had known already . . . that could be why he had come today, it might have been in the morning's papers.

The baby's cries became more and more half-hearted and finally he fell asleep. Dmitry stopped rocking the cradle, sitting there tensely, expecting the baby to start up again; but there was only silence. Anna had gone to sleep; there was suddenly a great stillness in the room. Dmitry leaned over and looked at his son's small head with the fine down of hair, at the plump little hands resting on either side of it, and felt suddenly overwhelmed. What was there in his life that could possibly be as important as this tiny creature? As long as they had life and health did anything else really matter? He thought to himself, be grateful . . . remember to be grateful. Everything is not lost. He had better see what other work he could do . . . he would get on the phone tomorrow . . . surely there must be something . . .

◆

At three o'clock in the morning he sat up suddenly and found that he was wide awake, as if he'd never been asleep. The wind rattled the ill-fitting sash window; it was very cold. He began to think about that research proposal he had done all those years ago. What had he done with the notebooks? He would go and have a look in the attic tomorrow. He wouldn't have to go to the library tomorrow, there was no point now . . .

He turned over in bed and looked at Katie sleeping beside him. Her thick, wavy hair was spread out over the pillow. She stirred and put out her hand, touched him, and then, as if reassured, was still. He started to stroke her hair, her shoulder, then, moving down, her hips and thighs; she half woke and murmured, 'No, Mitya, don't . . . so tired . . . want to sleep.' He knew that if he carried on she would eventually respond to him, that she would enjoy it, she always did, but it seemed unkind, he knew how exhausted she was. He was acutely aware of the danger they were in, as if it were something palpable, nearby him; he felt a fierce desire to protect her and moved closer, pulling her against him, drawing her head in against his shoulder.

3

'HERE, take a look at these.'

Tim's editor tossed a pile of cuttings and a long screed from the wire service on to his already overflowing desk, hesitating only a moment in his swift passage across the newsroom floor, not stopping to hear Tim's response. Tim pushed his chair back from the computer screen on his long, semi-circular desk and looked at the cuttings. One reported on a survey which claimed that two-thirds of Russia's defence scientists wanted to work in the West now that their salaries were virtually worthless. Another piece pointed out that 30 tonnes of highly enriched uranium were due to be released annually over the next 15 years as Soviet warheads were scrapped. Two short items involved more cases of small quantities of nuclear material being intercepted in the West. Tim picked up the phone and dialled the extension in Rowley's office. 'What do you want me to do with these?'

'I think we should do a proper in-depth investigation into all this. I've spoken to our Moscow team, but in view of your interest in this subject I thought you could put it all together . . . do you fancy a trip to Russia?'

Yes! This was what he had been working towards. He said, as casually as he could, 'Of course.'

Rowley didn't waste any more time. 'Put down some initial thoughts as to how you'd go about it and we'll talk tomorrow.'

Tim finished work at around nine o'clock and stepped out into the Gray's Inn Road, breathing in the cold night air with relief. As always the pressure of his job left him reeling with a mixture of exhaustion and exhilaration. He took a taxi home; when he came in, the flat was just as he had left it; the furniture all over the place, boxes still lying about unpacked and clothes still spread out across the bed. In the living room, Ingrid was quietly working on her essay.

Tim tried unsuccessfully to hide his annoyance. 'Couldn't you have done some clearing up?'

'I have my essay to finish. I have deadlines as well, you know.'

Ingrid bowed her head over her work, and silence fell. Tim flopped on to the sofa and watched her. She was writing by hand, and as she worked, unconsciously, she twanged the rubber band she had wound round her fingers. The sound irritated him more intensely every moment, but he could not bring himself to say so. He knew that once he began a whole torrent of irritations and dissatisfactions would follow, so he kept quiet and picked up the newspaper; Ingrid continued to work as if he hadn't been there. Tim's irritation reached its peak and suddenly he found himself snapping, '*Must* you do that?'

'Do what?' She looked genuinely startled, not conscious of having done anything.

'Twang that rubber band.'

'Oh, I'm sorry.' She unwrapped it from her fingers and placed it carefully on the edge of the desk, arranging it in a neat circle. Then she turned back to her manuscript. Now, as she worked, she pulled out a long thread of hair and twisted it, round and round, with her fingers.

Tim tried to look away. Why did she have this effect on him? He couldn't be in the same room as her. After a few minutes he stood up, and took his paper through into the kitchen.

A few minutes later Ingrid came to stand in the doorway. 'Is anything wrong?'

'No.' He frowned, staring into space, trying to make it clear to her that he didn't want to be interrupted. He was aware that while he was sitting here he was trying to listen to the faint sounds from above, trying to see if he could distinguish anything from the footsteps and the faint murmurs of conversation.

Ingrid held out some sheets of paper, and asked, 'Will you read this essay me, Tim? Just to see if it makes sense to you. To correct the English for me.'

Tim felt guilty for being so short with Ingrid; he knew it was not her fault. He knew that it was because he was thinking of Katie; had barely ceased thinking about her, in fact, since taking the flat. He said 'Yes, okay Ingrid, if you'll give me some space.' He took the manuscript from her and laid it out on the table, angling the lamp on to it. He went to the fridge, pulled out a bottle of beer and poured himself a glass, then sat down and looked at the first page of Ingrid's essay.

She was still hovering in the doorway. Tim looked up at her and sighed. 'Take yourself off for a bath or something. Leave me alone if you want me to do this.'

She shut the door. Tim turned back to the essay and took a deep breath. It was on some new age theme, something about the New Alchemy and the quest for spiritual growth, and Tim scanned it impatiently; he had no time for this, and often made fun of Ingrid for her interest in this kind of thing. He flipped through the neatly handwritten pages, then turned back to the introduction.

'Alchemy is the process that was believed to transmute the base metals such as Lead into Gold. The Philosopher's Stone was endowed with the power of carrying out this transformation. The Stone was also called the elixir or tincture and was also thought to cause the prolonging of human life.

'The belief that the Philosopher's Stone could only be obtained by divine grace led to the development of the mystical alchemy, and ultimately it became symbolic of the transmutation of sinful man into perfect being through prayer and submission to the will of God. However, the experiments which were being carried out led to a greater understanding of some chemical reactions and led to the foundations of the modern chemistry.

'Practical alchemists were well aware that if they succeeded in making gold their lives might be in grave danger from avaricious and evilly disposed persons.'

There was a sudden loud noise from upstairs as a door slammed. Tim started and looked up; he heard heavy footsteps, Katie's husband's, he assumed, on the floor above. He listened for a moment, but there was nothing more; he turned back to the essay.

'Some who were suspected of succeeding had to disguise themselves and flee under false names. Hence they coded the records of their work to make them incomprehensible to others. So in this way there became the confusion between the spiritual alchemy and the practical alchemy.'

Tim put his pen through some of the redundant 'thes' and sighed deeply. He really didn't feel he could wade through any more of this. He realised he was hungry and wandered round the kitchen, but the contents of the fridge did not inspire him. He could hear muffled footsteps now, in the flat upstairs; he found himself musing, somewhat vaguely, about his assignment. Of course, he thought suddenly, Katie's husband was a Russian with a scientific background; maybe he would have something interesting to say on the subject. He might have some insights into the current situation in Russia which would be helpful.

He glanced at his watch. Quarter to ten wasn't too late, was it? He could hear that they were still up. Ingrid was sloshing around in the bath, so on impulse he ran up the stairs and knocked on the door to the upper part of the house.

Katie opened the door and smiled when she saw him; she asked him in at once. She said they had just eaten, were having coffee, and would he like to join them? He followed her into the living room. The television was on and he just caught the end of the news headlines which he'd been working on earlier – a campaign speech by John Major and the UN Security Council resolution giving Libya fifteen days to hand over the Lockerbie suspects or face a worldwide ban on air travel and arms sales.

As he walked in, Katie's husband looked up from the table, stood up, and turned off the news. He held out his hand and Tim shook it. He was very tall, well over six feet, with a large frame, and had slightly receding hair worn a little too long in the manner of some Russian intellectuals Tim had met. But it wasn't just his size that seemed to dominate the room; there was something about the way he looked at Tim that made him instantly feel small, awkward and out of place.

Katie ran a hand through her hair and brushed the long strands back from her forehead. 'Tim, this is Mitya . . . please, sit down.'

Tim sat at the other side of the table and watched Katie pour him a cup of coffee. She looked up at him and asked brightly, 'Is it all right? The flat?'

'Oh, yes . . . fine.'

'I saw Ingrid yesterday. She seems very nice.'

'Oh, Ingrid . . . yes.' Tim found himself uncharacteristically at a loss. Part of the reason for his unease was that Gavrilov, who said nothing, kept on looking at him, and neither smiled nor made any move to make him welcome. To fill the silence, Tim asked if they'd seen his piece on Channel Four news the other evening and Katie said no, she hadn't. Tim explained about his report from Vienna and said that they were now planning to look at the nuclear smuggling issue in more depth and that he was going to Russia shortly.

Tim now felt that Gavrilov's blue eyes were unquestionably cold and hostile, and bored into him with a ruthlessness which, in an English person, would have been considered unpardonably rude. Perhaps in his culture this wasn't so; Tim tried to give him the benefit of the doubt. He turned to face him, and said, 'Katie told me you had a scientific background. I was wondering if you could help me, actually, if you knew who I could speak to in Moscow . . .'

The atmosphere was suddenly very strange. Katie turned round and looked at her husband; he looked back at her, an expression Tim couldn't read on his face; there seemed to be a question in it. Tim felt uneasy; he could see that he had put his foot in something, though he didn't have the least idea what it could be. Katie said, sitting down opposite him, 'I'm sorry . . . Why do you expect Mitya to know anything about this?'

Tim was confused. He said, 'I don't know . . . I didn't mean anything specific . . . I just thought you might know, scientific institutions, organisations, government departments . . .'

Gavrilov asked, 'Don't you have a correspondent in Moscow? Don't they know these things?'

'Yes, of course, I'm going to phone them tomorrow. It was only an idea . . . I'm sorry, forget that I asked.'

Tim felt dreadfully uncomfortable; he wished he hadn't come. Ingrid, lying naked downstairs in the bath, suddenly seemed a much more inviting prospect. Katie, as if for something to occupy her, asked if Tim wanted more coffee, and to give her something to do, he said that he would. She poured it out. Dmitry helped himself to sugar, fiddled with the spoon, turning it over and over in his hand. He said abruptly, in a flat, uninterested tone, 'Well, you should try talk to someone in the military about the controls on materials from nuclear warheads . . . I think it is the Twelfth Chief Directorate which is responsible for transport and storage . . . Let me tell you in advance that you're not likely to get a great deal out of these types.'

Tim had taken out his pen and notebook, was jotting this down.

Gavrilov said. 'Of course, you must realise this case is a little exaggerated . . . the quantities picked up in Vienna were negligible, from the fuel rods of a reactor, not highly enriched at all, as some reports claimed. These people are small-time crooks, con-men . . . Russia is full of them these days.'

Tim said, 'Well, it's not so small-time . . . they are prepared to have people killed.'

'Of course. Why not? Drugs, arms, nuclear materials . . . it's the same thing to them . . .'

Tim asked, 'Well, what about the other risks? What about all the scientists, without jobs or on low pay . . .'

Gavrilov interrupted rudely. 'Ah yes; the scientists; all these lucky scientists who are going to be offered vast sums of money to go and work abroad. Of course, some might be tempted. Well, why not? Can you give me one good reason why they shouldn't go?'

There was a silence. Tim thought that there was something slightly wild, unbalanced in Dmitry's voice; in fact Tim wondered for a moment if he had been drinking. He said, 'I don't know. Apart from the moral issue . . . perhaps the KGB or FSB whatever it's called these days would try to stop them.'

'Ah; yes, that's good, that's very probable. Of course, what else are they there for these days? That is indeed very likely.' Dmitry got up from the table, walked across the room to stand by the mantelpiece and put a few lumps of coal on the rather miserable fire, and then walked back again. All his movements seemed too fast, slightly exaggerated, as if he was on the point of losing control. He began to walk up and down, to the window, to the table, and back to the fire. 'But then, who knows what these people might do. They might try to stop them, but then, on the other hand, they might try to encourage them. Well? Have you thought of that idea?'

Tim thought that this was so odd that he couldn't understand what might be behind it; he thought, there's something wrong with him, he's off his head. Katie was looking at the floor, clearly embarrassed; Tim felt sorry for her. She said, 'Mitya, please. I don't know what you're going on about. Can't we talk about something else?' Tim felt he ought to stop, for her sake, but he couldn't, he was fascinated. He said, 'No, it's all right, Katie, it's good for me to hear the other side like this.'

Dmitry sat down again. 'Actually, I am sick of reading every day in your newspapers about the danger of the leakage of nuclear technology from the former Soviet Union when everyone knows the West has done far more in this department than we have . . . why do they not criticise their own record? At least in Russia we hung on to our secrets, while the US passed them on to Israel, and from there to South Africa, and meanwhile the Germans trained – '

'Yes, but – '

'Please, let me finish. I want to ask you this: what makes you think there are more unprincipled Russians than there are Germans or Americans or even Britons . . . you have plenty of economic problems here I think . . .'

'I'm not talking about unprincipled, so much as desperate,' said Tim. 'It doesn't matter what your principles are if you don't have enough to eat or can't feed your family . . .'

'Look,' said Dmitry suddenly, lowering his voice. 'Try to look at it another way. The threat of nuclear war with Russia suddenly evaporates overnight. Why all this hysteria? We should be pleased, but of course for various reasons we are not. First, there is the whole defence industry . . . they are alarmed. Who will buy their armaments now? Then there are the intelligence services. In the absence of any real enemy, they have to justify their existence and find some other threat. But thirdly, perhaps more importantly, I think we ourselves cannot cope with the end of the Cold War. It's my belief that mankind psychologically needs the threat of imminent destruction. Now that we no longer believe in the day of judgement or in hell we have to believe in the possibility of a nuclear holocaust. It helps us to believe that we are living in the end times . . . it clarifies our minds so wonderfully.' He poured them both a glass of vodka and raised his in a toast. 'Well, to your story, Tim. No doubt you will write it the way you want it.'

◆

Katie lay in bed in the dark, unable to sleep. She was filled with an uneasiness which came close at times to panic. Everything seemed to be going wrong for her and Dmitry. She thought of how they first met, in Vienna, at her friend's funeral in the rain, and the instant attraction she'd felt for him. He had seemed so vibrant and strong to her then, so full of moral integrity. They'd been through so much together, she could not imagine the bond between them ever being broken. It pained her terribly to see him angry and cynical like this, consumed by financial worries and a sense of failure. Yes, she could understand his growing frustration, but she didn't know how to deal with it. And it was getting worse; there was no need for him to have behaved like that this evening. She had been glad to see Tim, it was good to have someone she knew living downstairs and she didn't want to fall out with him. After all, they didn't see many people; she felt Dmitry had spoiled things for them, had given a false impression to Tim. She understood that he was disappointed about the book, and that she should make allowances, but even so, it was too much.

She rolled over, unable to get comfortable. Dmitry put his hand on her thigh and she removed it. He said, 'Katie, what exactly have you told him about me?'

Katie was instantly defensive. 'As it happens, I have told him exactly nothing.'

'Then why did he ask . . .?'

'I don't know . . . it must be coincidence. Honestly, Mitya, I told him you were a scientific and technical translator and that was all.'

'I don't believe in coincidence. Don't ask him in again. I don't like him.'

Katie sat up on her elbow. 'Why not? That's ridiculous . . . I've known him for years, he's a bit arrogant, I know, but he's all right really.'

Dmitry said, 'He's a journalist. He's nosy. Besides, he fancies you.'

'Oh Mitya, whatever makes you think that?'

'I saw the way he looked at you. Besides, you are very beautiful. What man in his right mind would not want to make love to you?'

They lay for a moment in silence, then Katie rolled over and suddenly, hungrily, he began to kiss her. She responded eagerly, wanting him, needing to connect with him, wanting to dispel all the bad feeling between them so that they could feel close again. He was aroused, excited; she put down her hand guide him into her, and as she touched him he gave a moan of pleasure and opened his eyes wide to her.

And then the baby started crying.

The bank manager was young, a brash, eager man who made quick, jabbing movements with his hands to illustrate his points in a manner which annoyed Dmitry. He had a file open on the desk and looked through it, turning the pages with care. Dmitry had seen this technique before, used as a means of intimidation; it did not impress him. He sat, in his best suit and tie, and waited.

The manager cleared his throat. He said, 'Now, we seem to have a few problems with your account . . . it seems to be rather a long time since any money has been paid in . . . You informed us last month that there would be a reasonable sum of money coming in but this has never materialised . . .'

'I sent you a copy of the contract from the publisher. The rest of the money is payable on completion . . .' Dmitry could not bring himself to say that the publisher had gone bankrupt and the money wasn't coming.

'Yes, we have it here . . . but even this will mean you can barely make the mortgage payments and then there's the question of the overdraft, which is now up to the limit.'

The desk in the meeting room was bare except for the telephone, the in-tray, and the file. Dmitry looked at the sunlight gleaming on its polished surface. The bank manager was looking at him with something which was not exactly pity, though no doubt he would have felt pity had he had the imagination. Dmitry felt humiliated.

'You realise that you now can't make any more payments unless we renegotiate this overdraft. We've already extended this twice and we can't keep on doing this indefinitely when we can't see any money coming in . . . I'm afraid this time we will have to say no.' He sighed. 'Of course, I suppose this is all quite new to you. I don't suppose you are used to this kind of thing in Russia.'

Dmitry said, 'No, but now I believe we are beginning to enjoy all these new benefits of the capitalist system; unemployment, low pay, mortgage arrears, and bankruptcy.'

The manager, taken aback, gave a short, dry laugh. He glanced again at the file. 'Have you any ideas, yourself, how you would like to solve this problem?'

'Well, I have been offered a job, I don't particularly want to do it, but now, I see, I have no choice. Don't worry, I'll be paying in some money very shortly.' Dmitry could not help enjoying, for a moment, a secret sense of satisfaction in the knowledge that the manager would have felt nothing but abhorrence at being instru-mental in forcing him to do this dreadful thing. Dmitry slowly stood up; the bank manager shook his hand as he left. As the door closed behind him, Dmitry was sure he saw him shaking his head.

◆

The notebooks Dmitry had wanted were up in the attic, among dusty piles of papers and notes going back for years. He brought them downstairs and sat at the table, going through them. Soon he became utterly absorbed. When he looked up at the clock he and realised that it was nearly three-thirty; if he didn't hurry he would be late to pick Anna up from school.

On the way he stopped at a phone box and dialled the num-ber Rozanov had given him. A voice answered him and asked in English for his number. The woman said he would call straight back. Dmitry glanced impatiently at his watch; a train ran past on the viaduct, drowning out any sound. When the noise faded, the phone was ringing.

Dmitry turned instinctively away from the road so that no passer-by could see him, as if he half expected that somewhere there would be somebody who could read his lips or divine what he was doing. He knew as he did it that he would regret this; if anyone else had asked him if he should do such a thing Dmitry would have said, 'No, don't touch it, don't have anything to do with it.' He knew it was himself he was betraying, not a country or ideal; he could see that it would end badly. But it was too late; he'd made up his mind, he needed the money now and would deal with the repercussions later. He didn't waste any time introducing himself or on any caveats or justifications; he simply said: 'I'll do it.'

4

A T THREE in the morning, the baby woke again. Katie
stumbled from the bed, lifted him from the cradle, and put
him to the breast. The bed beside her was empty; she called out,
'Mitya?' softly, but he didn't reply. Sasha fed rhythmically, gulping the milk, his tiny hand gently stroking and kneading her
breast; Katie lay back on the pillow, staring into his eyes, losing
herself for a moment in the intensity of this experience. Only as
the feed came to an end did she find herself wondering where
Mitya had gone.

As soon as Sasha came off the breast she returned him to his
cradle and went to the top of the stairs. She could see the light
shining in the room below and started to go down, puzzled and
annoyed that what little sleep she would have had was now further disturbed. Dmitry was sitting at the kitchen table, sheets of
paper and notebooks in front of him, in the light of the lamp. He
was writing swiftly, his pen jumping from sheet to sheet, jotting
down figures and words in a hurried sequence. She noticed the
way that he wrote with both his hands, transferring the pen from
one to the other and making notes with both of them. His concentration was so intense that he didn't see or hear Katie coming
down the stairs and only looked up with a sudden start when she
came to stand right behind him. She put her hand on his shoulder and he put down the pen, put his hand to his forehead and
then rubbed his eyes, and said, 'Katie, why aren't you in bed? Let
me finish this.'

'But what on earth are you doing? It's so late.'

'I won't be long . . . Go and sleep.'

Katie hesitated. 'No, I'm awake now. I want to talk to you.'

'No, not now . . . please . . . this is not the time. I am in the middle – '

'But this is important.' Frustration welled up inside her; there never seemed to be a right time to talk.

'Katie, you know, when I'm working, I can't be interrupted. Now I have lost . . . Please, go back to bed.' He turned back to the papers on the table. Katie stood, watching him stare at them, now seeing that what was on the paper were strings and strings of calculations. The figures and the abstract symbols, together with his Russian scrawl, formed something so impenetrable and foreign that she felt herself completely shut off from him. For an instant she felt almost desperate. What was he doing? She had never seen him work on anything like this before.

'What is it you're working on?'

He didn't answer, held up his hand to silence her. She sat at the table opposite him, watching him. He was back in his stride now; sometimes his thoughts moved so quickly that his pen could not keep up, at other times he stopped and stared, frowning, crossed something out. Finally he looked up. He said, 'That's it, that'll do for now. Why are you staring at me like that?'

'I just wondered what this is.'

'Oh, nothing . . . just an idea . . . probably it will come to nothing.' He stood up, picked up the papers and crossed the living room, bending over to rake the embers of the fire. Katie watched him take some small pieces of wood out of the basket and put them on the glowing coals. He stood there for a long time, watching; when the wood finally caught he reached out and with a swift movement stuffed the papers into the flames.

Katie leapt up in astonishment. 'What on earth are you doing?'

'Burning it.'

'Why?'

'I've done it now. It's all in my head. I know how to do it again.'

Katie watched as the bright flames flared up and the papers charred and curled into snake-like shapes. There was something almost mystical, incomprehensible, to her about mathematics. Dmitry had told her that as a child he had been gifted, that he could work out complex calculations in his head. His memory, too, was remarkable, although she had often remarked how he could never remember to buy the milk or be on time to pick Anna up from school. Katie watched the flames die away and then Dmitry poke the fire, reducing the charred paper to tiny fragments. He said, 'Come on, let's go to bed. You're getting cold, standing there. Look at your feet.'

She tried again. 'Mitya, I wanted to talk to you.'

'I don't want to talk. You are looking so lovely like that, in your gown, with your hair loose, in the firelight.'

When he paid her compliments he didn't say them teasingly, he said them flatly, as if he were simply making an observation, stating something that was the indisputable truth. She couldn't help being moved. She crossed the room, put her arms around him and he turned and kissed her gently.

She knew he would want to make love to her, perhaps as a way of avoiding having to talk to her. 'Mitya, I wanted to talk to you about Anna's school. She's not happy – '

'The school is all right.'

'My mother said she would pay for a private school.'

'We can't accept it.'

'Why not?'

She could feel that Dmitry was angry; she knew his pride was hurt. Katie herself was torn on this issue, but she didn't want Anna to suffer; it was a rough school, and Katie felt she had been through enough.

'Your parents don't like me. I won't accept their money.'

'It's not for you. It's for their granddaughter.'

'Who is not my child. Is that what you were going to say?'

Katie felt herself harden. She said sharply, 'I didn't say that.'

'No, but you thought it.' He turned away from her and stared into the remains of the fire. 'Well, don't bother to consult me then. Do what you want.'

Katie sighed. 'They've invited us over on Sunday.'

'I can't come.'

'We'll have to see them some time. They'll think something's wrong.'

'Can't you tell them I have to work.'

'Yes, but what is this work?'

He didn't answer her. 'Anyway why should I see them. You know that they can't stand me. And they will just go on about the election next week and how wonderful this John Major is.'

Katie knew that she would get nowhere. She loved him, but he was so difficult. She was tired, was shivering with cold. She said, 'Come on, let's go up to bed.' She went up ahead of him while he tidied away the remaining papers. She wanted to make love to him to mend things between them but she was too tired, she couldn't keep awake; as soon as she lay down sleep overcame her like a dark curtain.

◆

At ten o'clock the next morning Dmitry left the house and walked down to the call-boxes by the underground station. As he reached the station, walking slowly, unhurriedly, Tim walked past, smiled cheerily and gave a little wave of his hand. Dmitry nodded his head in acknowledgement, forced himself to smile. But the sight of Tim had shaken him, made him feel transparent, vulnerable; it was almost as if Tim seemed to know what he was doing, as if his smile was mocking him. Dmitry looked all around him several times before going up to the call-box. The tiled walls of the tube station were grimy and streaked with nameless dirt; the phone smelt faintly of something unpleasant. He took the card Aziz Hattab had given him out of his pocket and rang the number. He didn't know if there would be any response at the weekend. It rang seven or eight times and Dmitry was just beginning to think with relief that nobody would answer it when a voice asked, 'Hello?'

Dmitry said, 'It's Dr Gavrilov.'

There was a pause. Then the voice said, 'Ah, yes. Please wait one moment. You wish to speak to Mr Hattab.' Another man came to the phone. He said, 'Dr Gavrilov, this is indeed a pleasure. You have rung to make an appointment?'

Dmitry muttered that he had.

Hattab suggested they meet at the Metropole Hotel. Would Monday evening be all right? say, at eight? They could meet in the bar. It would be possible to have a private conversation upstairs. Someone else who very much wanted to meet him would also be there. He hoped their meeting would be most useful to them both.

Dmitry hung up. He stared at the phone receiver and then picked it up. He rang Rozanov's number.

A woman answered and said Rozanov would call him right back.

When the phone rang Dmitry snatched up the receiver. He said, 'Eight o'clock. Monday evening.'

'So soon? Did you have to make it so soon?'

Dmitry sighed. He said, 'I can ring them back . . . but I would rather not have this hanging over me.'

'No, leave it as it is . . . But we don't have much time. We had better meet today, let's say, at three.' He gave him an address near Baker Street. 'You are calling on the same number as the last time.'

Dmitry glanced down at the phone. 'Yes.'

'Don't do that. Use a different phone each time. Till later, then.'

The line went dead. Dmitry looked at his watch; he had half a day to wait. He forced himself to go to the library to give himself something to do, and by three o'clock he was standing by entrance to a large mansion block. He pressed the brass bell and the door opened instantly. The lift was waiting in its ornate metal cage; Dmitry started up the staircase, his feet soundless on the thick beige carpeting. As he climbed, the lift glided past him all the way up to the fifth floor and as the door opened, he heard voices talking. On the landing he saw two doors; one of them was slightly open. Dmitry pushed it open with his fingertips.

He hesitated before entering.

Rozanov stood by the window, looking out through the net curtains. The flat was sparsely furnished, with a sofa, two chairs and a coffee table, a couple of pot plants, and a few cheap prints of impressionist pictures decorated the walls. Though it was clean, there was a faintly musty smell about it; it was clearly not a place that anyone lived in.

Rozanov cleared his throat. 'Where will you meet them?'

'At the Metropole Hotel, in the bar. Then we'll go and talk upstairs.'

Rozanov reached into his briefcase and put a batch of papers on the table. He said, 'This is some background reading for you. I'm sure you know something of this, but still . . . take a look.'

Dmitry flicked through the documents, copies of Libya's safe-guards agreement with the International Atomic Energy Agency, intelligence reports; information about the Tajura Research Centre; most of it he knew already. He pushed the papers away. So, they were from Libya. It didn't surprise him.

Rozanov handed him a pen. 'What do you think of this?'

Dmitry took it, examined it, offered it back. Rozanov did not take it. He pointed with his stubby, nicotine-stained finger. 'This contains a highly sensitive transmitter with a range of a mini-mum of fifty metres . . . we shall be able to hear the entire con-versation. You activate it like this . . . This is for your protection, you understand.'

Dmitry shook his head. 'It's too risky to carry something like this. Suppose they search me and discover it.'

'They will not search you . . . remember, you are a highly skilled scientist with exactly the qualifications they require and they are not going to find it easy to find another one. Why should they suspect you of anything?'

Dmitry was determined not to be placated so easily. 'But if they did . . . if they turned nasty . . . if they found – '

'Look, Dmitry Nikolayevich, don't concern yourself with this end of things. Leave that to us. I can assure you that they will not notice anything and that you will be quite safe. Just be very natural with them. It's expected that you will be nervous, just don't overdo it. Keep asking about the money. Remember it's the money which is important to you.'

Dmitry said, 'Speaking of this, I need some money in my account right now.'

'Of course, of course, it will be there on Monday. I think you will be pleasantly surprised.'

Dmitry took the pen, gave it a disgusted glance and tucked it into his jacket pocket. Rozanov grinned. 'Excellent . . . perfect. Now then, sit down. Let me just run through the things we would like you to ask . . .'

It was four o'clock when Dmitry stepped out into the street. Already he was uncertain how he could go through with this. The necessity of lying to Katie upset him. He was more and more worried about the unhappiness which seemed to have sprung up between them; he was already afraid that he had, after all, not been what she wanted, and that she was disappointed in him, and these feelings would only be a mild reflection of what she would feel if she knew what he was doing now. And now he had the weekend to get through. At least, he thought, he had not got to face her parents; Katie had agreed to spare him that.

◆

Katie's mother cut another slice of lamb and put it on her plate. 'Have some more potatoes, dear. You've lost weight . . . you look far too thin. Do you really think you should go on feeding that baby yourself?'

'Mummy, we've discussed this before. Anna, don't get down. You have to wait for pudding.'

'Can't I play with Sasha? He's unhappy.'

Katie glanced at her mother. Her mother nodded reluctantly and instantly Anna shot from her chair and went to torment Sasha on the carpet. Katie continued to eat, enjoying the expensive joint of lamb and the delicious new potatoes. Sasha cooed and then, as Anna started to lift him, began to cry. Katie turned to her in exasperation; an only child herself, she had no experience of sibling rivalry to help her deal with Anna's jealousy. 'Stop it!' she shouted. 'Stop it or we'll go home!'

Sasha only cried more loudly. Katie's mother went into the kitchen to fetch the apple pie, and Katie had to get up and walk Sasha up and down to calm him.

They ate the pie in silence. The clock struck two. Katie's father finished his plateful and still said nothing. Then he stood up and began the Sunday ritual of winding up the clocks.

After lunch Katie went into the kitchen to help wash up.

Her mother, as she had expected, started on her at once. 'Are you sure everything's all right? This is the third time he hasn't come.'

Katie would never have revealed to her that there was any problem in her marriage. 'It's just an opportunity to get some work done. It's hard, with the children . . .'

'You don't look happy.'

'It's just worrying about money.'

'Have you decided about the school?'

'Yes, I've decided to leave Anna where she is at the moment. She seems more settled . . .'

'We wanted her to go to the Catholic school.'

'I know. But I don't practise, and Mitya is an atheist – '

'He's not her father. It shouldn't be him who makes the decision.'

Katie decided to ignore this. 'It's just that I had to change schools so many times, I don't want the same thing to happen to her.'

Katie's mother's mouth formed a thin, hard line. 'That wasn't our choice. It was your father's job.'

'I know. I'm not criticising you.' She paused. 'I'm very grateful you've offered . . . it helps to know the money's there if we really need it.'

Katie's mother went on scrubbing the saucepan. 'Is he kind to you? Is he all right with Anna?'

'Mummy, I've told you, Anna adores him. It's all fine, really.'

Katie could not blame her mother; she felt her pain and confusion. She knew that her husband was not their idea of suitable son-in-law. Her father had been a diplomat, had found it hard to adjust to the end of the old world order and undo a lifetime's thought patterns; Dmitry as a Russian was still threatening to him. White-haired now, and stooped, her father made it clear he didn't understand his daughter and that her second marriage was anathema to him. Her mother, too, instinctively disliked Dmitry.

She was surprised and touched when, as she came to leave, her father pressed a fifty-pound note into her hand.

'Spend it on yourself,' he said gruffly.

Katie smiled and thanked him warmly, thinking with relief that it would feed them for a week.

◆

At a quarter to eight on Monday evening as Dmitry walked down the Marylebone Road the sky was clear, glowing a deep red colour, and the black outlines of the trees and rooftops stood out against it, like coals in a fire. As he thought of what he was about to do a sharp pang of despair suddenly pierced him, like a physical pain, and for an instant he felt like turning back. Why was he doing this? In the past he'd had to co-operate with the likes of Rozanov, of course, that was the system, but he had always made sure he had done so to the absolutely minimum extent necessary to keep him out of trouble; now he was free of all that, why let himself become enmeshed? He stopped, took a deep breath, and stared up into the sky as if he might spot something there which might save him or give him strength to fight what seemed to be his fate, but it was no good; the sky was already turning dark.

He crossed the road and entered the huge, ugly hotel. He walked to the bar, sat down, fidgeted, listened to the piped music. After a few minutes the young man, Hattab, who had met him in the park came up to him and said, 'Would you like to come upstairs with me? We are expecting you.' They went up to the tenth floor; in the lift they avoided looking at one another. When he entered the bedroom two men were in the corner, watching a pornographic film on the video. When Dmitry came in they turned the sound down but the shadows still flickered on the screen, distracting him. Then they turned it off. One of the men remained where he was, merely nodded a greeting. The second came to shake Dmitry's hand; he didn't give his name.

'I'm so pleased you could come, Dr Gavrilov . . . please, your coat. Sit down . . . a drink?'

Dmitry let him take his coat but did not sit down. The large bed with its blue counterpane seemed to dominate the room, and Dmitry walked nervously in the narrow spaces round the furniture, wondering how to begin, how to strike the right note. The two men were eyeing him, getting the measure of him; he felt awkward, inept. At any rate he must not have any alcohol to drink.

Hattab went to a tray of drinks on the table top; Dmitry shook his head. He said, 'No, thank you . . . look, let's not waste time, let's get to the point . . .'

The second, older man nodded, and began his obviously rehearsed preamble. 'My government finds itself in a very difficult situation. We have, as I'm sure you know, this excellent nuclear research centre at Tajura, which your country assisted us to build. We have a research reactor which uses 80 per cent enriched uranium . . . but because of the uncertainty in the present situation we are not sure that we will be able to guarantee the continuation of fuel supplies for the reactor and so on, which at present we get in a turnkey arrangement with the Kurchatov Institute. The way the West is behaving towards us at the moment we are very anxious to be self-sufficient in this and other areas, such as uranium enrichment technology.'

'You want me to design gas centrifuges for you.'

This directness was too much for them; they laughed nervously. The senior one gestured again for Dmitry to sit down; some coffee was brought on a tray. Dmitry took a cup and sat on the edge of one of the chairs; his host sat down opposite him. He said, 'I can see that you are keen to talk business . . . Well, why not. It is best that we understand one another. I am told this is your area of expertise.'

'Indeed.' Dmitry gulped down his coffee and placed the cup rather delicately on the edge of the table. He said, 'Tajura is regularly inspected by the International Atomic Energy Agency. Let me try to be absolutely clear what you are suggesting . . . would this initiative be reported to the IAEA or not?'

Instantly the Libyan became vague. 'Well, of course this would not be my decision . . . I can't say. But, I would imagine that, at this very early stage, this would not be considered necessary.'

They looked at Dmitry, waiting for his reaction. Dmitry did not react. He looked as if he was thinking, although in reality he couldn't think at all; he was mesmerised by the predictable awfulness of this conversation. He stared at the coffee table and his empty cup. The Libyan leaned forward and began again. 'You are concerned, of course, that your expertise will be used not for peaceful but for military reasons. I can only reassure you that is not our intention, Dr Gavrilov. We wish be able to continue our legitimate and peaceful nuclear researches without the intervention of hostile powers.'

Dmitry suddenly became impatient; he made a gesture with his hand as if to brush away all such distasteful matters. 'Yes,

yes, of course; there is no need for us to waste our time discussing this sort of thing . . . I am sure we understand one another completely.'

He saw the men exchange glances. He knew what they were thinking, what their glances meant; we've got him, he's going to go along with us. Dmitry felt hot, confused, he had to loosen his tie which threatened to choke him. He felt that he was playing a part, but that the part came only too easily to him; he took a deep breath and plunged on.

'Look, if you want information on gas centrifuges, I can provide it. But that will only be the beginning of your problems. First you will have to import parts and all of these, as you know, are on the IAEA trigger list. The intelligence agencies are much more shrewd about this sort of thing these days . . .'

'But this is not your end of the business, Dr Gavrilov. This would be for us to solve.'

'Most certainly. Of course, you are most likely not to succeed and then this would become my problem . . . because then I would not be able to continue with my researches and . . . well, possibly I would not get paid.'

He saw the Libyans look at one another again. He wondered if he was laying this on a bit thick. Perhaps wanting money alone was not sufficient motivation . . . perhaps they thought he must have other reasons.

Dmitry cleared his throat; they gave him some more coffee and he drank it down. As he did so he was aware that his hands were shaking slightly. He saw that they noticed it too and said, 'You understand . . . I am a little nervous. This is a big step for me to take. Look, let me explain . . . when I came here I did have something in mind. Gas centrifuges are all very well . . . but there are other ways to enrich uranium, ways which haven't been tried out in Russia or in the West and which would require equipment which might not be recognised by the relevant agencies . . . I could write you a proposal if you were interested.'

The Libyan was watching him, his eyes intent, shrewd. He said, 'Yes, indeed; I am sure we would be very interested.'

A silence fell. Dmitry stared gloomily at the carpet. So far he had failed to elicit any of the information on Rozanov's list; he must try harder. He said, 'Of course, I will need to work with uranium hexafluoride . . . only small quantities to begin with, of course, but I assume you have the facilities to produce this . . .'

The Libyan shrugged. He became instantly vague. He said, 'I'm afraid I don't know any of the technical details . . . these you will have to get from my superiors . . . But I am sure you will have everything you need. It will take a little bit of time, of course . . . Well. You must do us this proposal. How long will it take you? A week? Two weeks?'

'I don't know . . . it will take time to work it out . . . it depends how much detail you want . . . I imagine you will have to give it to someone at Tajura to assess . . .'

'Indeed, of course. You must put in as much detail as you are able.'

'Well then . . . I don't know . . .' When was he to do this? He plucked a figure out of the air at random. 'Perhaps two, three weeks.'

'Very good. You will send us this formal proposal . . . You will contact me when it is ready and we will arrange for its collection. A preliminary payment and a contract will be forthcoming as soon as the proposal is received and scrutinised and if it seems to be viable . . . In the meantime we would like to offer you a small retainer, for your work on this . . . there's no commitment, you won't have to pay it back. Would £5000 seem reasonable?'

He opened a briefcase; he had the money in cash, in crisp £50 notes which he counted out. Dmitry stared at it; the sight of all this money had a strange effect on him. He felt an over-whelming relief that it would enable him to settle the credit card debt. Of course, Rozanov would be paying him soon as well, but even so . . . he accepted it.

The Libyan shut the briefcase with a snap and gave a smile of satisfaction. 'It may be necessary to have another meeting, perhaps in Geneva. Once you have signed a contract, funds will be paid into a bank in Switzerland every four weeks . . . Of course, I don't need to remind you that this meeting must remain entirely confidential . . .'

Dmitry got to his feet, stuffing the money awkwardly into his inside pocket, surprised at how slim the bundle was. It was obvious there was no more to be said. He asked, 'But how may I contact you . . . I don't know your name.'

The man smiled. He said, 'My name is not important . . . Sometimes, you will understand, a certain delicacy has to be observed in such matters . . . You may contact me as before, through my friend and colleague here.' He held out his hand; Dmitry had to shake it. They opened the door and let him out.

He left the hotel, reaching inside his coat pocket to switch off the transmitter in his pen. Damn the thing; what was he to do with it now? It was now quite dark with a clear, starless sky and suddenly very cold; he shivered even in his coat. The traffic roared past over the viaduct and the fumes assaulted him, making him feel sick and dizzy for a moment. What to do now? He felt he had made a complete mess of the interview. This man he had spoken to was only an intermediary, he knew nothing. He had failed to find out anything of any use to Rozanov and had only succeeded in entangling himself, in making it seem as if he intended to do things he had no intention at all of doing. He should never have taken the money. He had a crazy impulse simply to take it and throw it in the bin.

He stopped with a jerk on the pavement for an instant, forced himself instantly to walk on again. It was no use thinking about it now; he should go home and try to forget. But how could he forget? He knew even as he tried to trivialise it to himself that he had done something terrible, that he was already committed and that the Libyans would not easily let go of him; that he had sold his soul and that only with the greatest difficulty could he buy it back again.

5

SOMETHING very odd had happened.

The previous morning, while Tim was lying in, Ingrid had come into the bedroom and said something to him. Tim, whose mind had been on his up-coming trip to Moscow, hadn't listened to what it was, and merely said, 'Right, fine,' and waved as she picked up her bag and went out. When she didn't come home in the evening, he had simply assumed she'd been telling him she'd gone somewhere for the evening. But she didn't come back that night.

The following evening there was no sign of her either. Tim was irritated with himself. He wished he'd paid attention to where she had said she was going.

On the third day he began to have an uneasy feeling while he was at the office; it occurred to him for the first time that she might not have told him she was going away at all, and that she might have been taken ill or had an accident. He wondered with a horrible, sickening feeling, whether he had not been completely irresponsible. He rang her college and left a message for her to ring him. She didn't call, and he rang and left a second message.

There was nothing much happening in the newsroom. After lunch he told Rowley that he had a lead he wanted to follow up and took a taxi home.

When he entered the flat he saw at once that it was different. A poster had gone from the wall and the candlesticks from the table. He strode into the bedroom and flung open the cupboards.

All her clothes were gone. He went into the bathroom. The jars of cream, the shampoos and conditioners, the skin-care products and make-up, had all vanished.

She hadn't even left a note.

Tim sat down heavily on the sofa. Then suddenly he started to laugh. He realised that he was relieved. He realised how long it was since they had really communicated with one another. He was lucky, too. Thank God she'd had the grace to go without making a dreadful scene.

As he sat there, laughing, the doorbell rang.

Tim ran up the stairs and opened the door and there was Katie. She looked harassed, flushed. She said, 'I saw you were at home . . . I have to go and get Anna from school and Sasha's just fallen asleep. Would you mind . . . if I leave him here and keep both the doors open, you would hear if he cried . . . You could go and sit upstairs if you wanted. I'll only be half an hour . . .'

Tim said, 'Of course, that's fine.'

She handed him the key to their door just in case it slammed shut. 'He's in our room . . .'

'It's all right. Don't worry.'

She turned and went out through the front door, banging it behind her. Tim stood in the hallway for a few minutes, then went through into their part of the house. It seemed too good an opportunity to miss. There was nothing much of interest in the living room, so he went upstairs, stepping quietly so as not to wake the baby. He checked Sasha really was asleep in the Moses basket at the end of their unmade bed, then looked round the room. He noticed the faded, ill-matched bedclothes, the bare, unpolished floorboards, and the dust which lay thinly every-where. In the corner there was a desk and bookshelves which Dmitry obviously used as his study. Tim went over and had a look. He glanced down the shelves of scientific books, which were mostly in Russian, at the conference reports and boxes of papers. He tried to decipher the script without much too much success, though he knew enough to see that many of the books were on nuclear physics. He saw a box of IAEA documents in English, which he flipped through quickly. He tried the top drawer of the desk; it was locked.

Glancing instinctively at the door in case anyone should be there, he picked up a notebook from the desktop, began to thumb through it. He could make no sense of the Russian, but there were pages of what looked like complex mathematics. He felt hot; his heart was beating; he was listening hard for any tiny sound at the door which might mean that Katie, or worse, her husband, were coming home. Then he heard a faint sound beside him which made him jump; the baby was stirring.

He ignored the sound, picked up another notebook. He tried the drawer again, hunted around the desktop for the key. He tried a little wooden box on the desktop, he searched the desk and then the drawers in the bedside table, he checked the windowsill and the shelf above the old fireplace. There was a vase on top of the chest of drawers; on impulse he picked it up, turned it upside down and a key fell out. He tried the key in the desk and it fitted. He slid the drawer open. In it he found their passports, birth and marriage certificates, national health cards, some foreign money; Austrian banknotes, some US dollars, and a wad of £50 notes. There were some letters, handwritten, personal correspondence, from Moscow. He flipped through this quickly, feeling increasingly uncomfortable. There was nothing here of any interest to him; he felt an instant's shame, knowing he had no right at all to be doing this.

He shut the drawer, wiped the key on his sleeve and dropped it back into the vase, and then wiped the surface of the glaze too. As an afterthought he did the same to the notebook. If there was a burglary and the police tested for fingerprints, he didn't want his turning up. This seemed as he did it an utterly fantastic possibility, but perhaps the thought was some measure of how outraged he knew Katie would be if she knew about his actions. The baby was crying loudly now, in frantic, anguished bursts. He glanced at his watch; Katie wouldn't be much longer. He made sure he'd rearranged everything exactly as it had been, leaned over the cradle and picked up the hot, red-faced, angry baby. He held the baby awkwardly, at arm's length. He looked like his father, Tim thought; certainly he was not pretty. He stared at the baby, and the baby stared back. He had stopped crying for a few moments, startled; then his face crumpled and he started bawling frantically again.

'All right, whatever your name is, Sasha, shut up, I'm not stealing you,' said Tim, carrying him downstairs. He went over to the computer, looked out of the window down the street, then put the baby down on a rug on the floor and ignored the piercing cries while he switched on the computer. It ran Windows but it was password protected.

The baby's face was purple with screaming. Tim exited hurriedly and turned off the computer. He picked up the baby and was juggling him rather ineffectually when Katie and Anna came in.

Katie took the baby from Tim gratefully and immediately the baby's crying changed to a whimper. She jiggled and soothed him, asked, 'Would you like a cup of tea?'

'Yes . . . thank you.'

Tim sat down. Katie balanced Sasha on her hip as she made the tea expertly with one hand. Anna went to the fridge and took out a yoghurt, unpeeled the top, and dipped a spoon into it, all the time staring at Tim. She looked a lot like Katie, with her thick, long hair and pale, sensitive face; he thought that she would grow up to be quite a beauty.

Katie said, pouring boiling water into the pot, 'Tim, I'm sorry about the other night . . . Mitya was in a terrible mood, one of the publishers he's working for has gone bust . . .'

'That's all right. Don't apologise . . .' He paused. 'You're not responsible for his behaviour.'

She didn't say anything. She put the tea on the table and sat down wearily. Tim asked, 'Where did you meet him?'

'Mitya? In Vienna.'

'He was working there?'

'Yes, at the UN.'

'As a translator?'

Anna was poking the baby; Katie told her to leave him alone. She seemed already to have lost the thread of the conversation; Tim thought how easy it was to avoid answering a question you didn't want to when there were children around. Katie poured out the tea, Russian style, into glasses with ornate metal holders and passed one to Tim. He tried again. 'What was he doing at the UN?'

He didn't know whether she was deliberate in being evasive. 'Oh, I don't know . . . it's just a hopeless bureaucracy. They spend their time writing memos and going to meetings . . .'

Tim pressed on, 'But he was at the IAEA?'

'What?' She looked at Tim, still distracted, then swivelled round to address Anna who had just hit Sasha with a rattle. 'Go upstairs! Go on! Now!' Anna went to the foot of the stairs and sat there; Katie, having won a partial victory, turned back to Tim with a sigh. 'It's hard for her. Did I tell you? She's not Mitya's child, she's from my first marriage.'

'And your first husband? Do you have any contact with him?'

Katie said, staring down at her tea, 'No, I don't.'

Tim didn't know if he could ask anything further, but he tried. 'Not at all?'

Katie looked at him and shook her head. 'No, not at all. I don't ever want to talk about it, Tim, actually, please don't ask me. I'm afraid I'm a rather private person.'

Tim was silent. Yes, I remember that, he thought, and that's one reason why I'm drawn towards you. He felt a sense with her of something hidden, held back, to which he would like to find the key. She was one of the few women he had really wanted who he'd never been to bed with; perhaps that was also what had kept his interest in her alive. He wouldn't ask her anything more, not now, anyway. He must tread carefully. It was not just she who intrigued him, either, but the whole situation; her rather odd, mysterious husband, who he was sure she couldn't really be happy with, and who might be useful for his work.

He sipped his tea. A silence had fallen between them, but it was not an unpleasant one. He said, 'Well, then, I promise not to ask you any more questions.'

As he spoke the front door opened and Gavrilov walked into the living room. He stopped, stared at Tim, clearly taken aback, and said, abruptly, 'What are you doing here?'

Tim looked at Katie to see what she would say; she pushed her tea way and half rose from her chair. 'Mitya, Tim was just looking after Sasha while I went to pick up Anna from school.' He could see that she was angry, but suppressed it. Gavrilov turned away and went to sit next to Anna on the sofa, put his arm around her, turned on the television and sat watching a cartoon. It was far too loud and the inane noise filled the room, making conversation impossible. Katie got up and took him a cup of tea; they did not exchange a word or glance.

She came back to the table. Tim couldn't help looking at Gavrilov; he could see the coloured light from the television flickering over his drawn face. Anna, clearly bored with the dreadful programme, slid to the floor and began drawing on a piece of paper; Gavrilov suddenly sat up and turned down the volume. He said, in a voice which was oddly sharp, 'Anna, what are you doing with that pen?'

'I found it in your pocket.'

'Well give it back. You'll break it.'

'I won't. I'm just . . .'

'Give it to me!' He held out his hand. The whole force of his will seemed directed at the child and she crumpled suddenly, as if she sensed there was something that she didn't understand; Tim too couldn't work out why the sudden anger. Anna threw the pen at him and ran out of the room and up the stairs; Gavrilov picked it up from the floor and put it in his jacket pocket; he leaned over and switched off the television, and a deep and uncomfortable silence fell over the room.

Tim felt it was time to go and stood up awkwardly. 'Look, I ought to be getting on. Thanks for the tea. If you need me again . . .'

Katie showed him to the door.

◆

In the morning Tim put a call through to their man in Vienna, Mike Warburton. He said he wanted to check if a Russian, Dmitry Gavrilov, now a translator, possibly trained as a nuclear scientist, had worked for the IAEA in Vienna in 1990 or 1991. He said he just wanted to know his background; it wasn't urgent.

Mike said cheerfully, 'OK, will do.'

◆

Rozanov appeared out of the crowds on the northbound Victoria line platform at Oxford Circus to stand beside Dmitry.

Although Dmitry had been expecting him, he almost jumped as Rozanov brushed his elbow. His voice half whispered close to Dmitry's ear; instinctively he stepped back, away from the platform's vertiginous edge.

'Well done. You were inspired. Perfect.'

Dmitry stared straight ahead. 'On the contrary, I got nothing out of them.'

'That doesn't matter. You'll get another chance. You were very good; very convincing.'

'They need a proposal. I'm working on it now. It's not too technical . . . I'm not giving anything away.'

'Excellent. We'll make your next payment when you meet them again.'

Dmitry handed Rozanov the pen-transmitter, anxious to be rid of it. 'It's no good. They want me to go to Geneva.'

'Geneva is very pleasant at this time of year, I believe,' Rozanov said mildly.

The wind had started to gather in the tunnel; the sign above them swayed and trembled and there was the distant tang of electricity. 'How can I go? I couldn't afford it. What excuse can I make? My wife is not an idiot – '

'This is no problem, Dmitry Nikolayevich. You can get very cheap fares to Geneva. You can say you need to visit the various agencies there to see if they have translating work . . . there's the UN, OPEC, the Intellectual Property Organisation . . . and then you will get the work and be amply reimbursed. We have it all worked out.'

Dmitry, thought, yes, of course you have. He felt completely exposed in front of Rozanov; felt that he predicted everything he said or did, and expected, was actually amused by, his muted, almost pathetic signs of protest. Rozanov slipped the pen transmitter into his pocket and turned towards the lights of the oncoming train. 'Of course, you must be careful what you say. Some wives are easy to deceive, and will not notice an infidelity when it is staring them in the face, while others can spot the first sign of it. What kind of wife do you have, Dmitry Nikolayevich?'

◆

Dmitry sat up late that night, writing his proposal. He had no idea what degree of detail was expected; he decided in any case he must keep it to the broadest possible terms. He translated his original proposal from years back, drew diagrams, made a summary; he could not believe that he was doing this.

He wrote:

This technique offers a low cost alternative for the enrichment of uranium and provides many advantages to existing techniques. Materials of construction are mostly available from the mass entertainment and military electronics markets.

Construction time would be shortened.

Power consumption would be minimised.

Costs – materially lower than for a centrifuge process.

There followed two pages of technical discussion about the new gas separation process. The major problem, he admitted to himself, would be, having separated the Uranium 253 from 258, how to remove them from the chamber separately. He decided to rather gloss over this difficulty; no doubt they would pick this up later. Probably their people at Tajura would turn the whole thing down as unworkable, and that would suit him very well. On the other hand, they might see him just to talk it over, and then ask him if he would be willing to pursue more conventional methods. Well, he would have to see. He couldn't look beyond this; he just had to take this step by step.

When he went upstairs Katie was still awake. He undressed and got into bed beside her and turned out the light. They lay together in the darkness; she moved towards him and said, 'Won't you tell me what you're doing?'

'I've been writing some letters. Katie, I think I'm going to go to Geneva. There might be some work from the UN there . . . I have some contacts, it sounds quite promising . . .'

Katie said, 'Yes, I see, yes, all right then. When will you go?' She sounded reluctant; he could sense she didn't want him to. Dmitry at once sounded vague, half-hearted.

'I don't know, exactly . . . perhaps I won't go. It was only an idea.'

As he expected, Katie changed her tone at once. 'No, I think it's a good idea . . . I think you should.'

Dmitry was silent, not knowing what to say. Katie said, 'Mitya, I was thinking . . . perhaps I should try to get some work.'

'What kind of work?'

'Well, I was a translator, too . . . I could ring up some of my old contacts . . .'

'But how could you? You're still feeding Sasha . . . you would have to pay someone to look after him and that would probably cost more than you would earn. Besides, you said you wanted to be at home with the children.'

Katie shifted in bed and then was silent for so long that he thought she must have fallen asleep. Then she said, 'I'm starting to go mad. I never see anyone and we hardly know anybody. I just don't think I was cut out to be a full-time mother; I'm no good at it.'

'No, that's not true. You are a wonderful mother. It's just the children who are difficult at the moment. It will get better, and when Sasha starts at school . . .'

'Well, maybe I could put some feelers out. I was talking to Tim and – '

He said, he couldn't stop himself, 'Oh, not Tim again.'

'Mitya, you're being impossible. What is all this about Tim? He's the only person who's ever offered me any help . . . You put me in a very difficult position. He was asking how we met and I had to go through contortions to try not to tell him what you did . . . why does it matter? If he wanted to know he could look it up easily . . . You've nothing to hide.'

Dmitry said, 'No, I'm sorry, I was being unreasonable.'

They were silent for a while; the conversation had gone round, and now they were back at the beginning. Katie said, 'Well, if I can't work, what can we do about money?'

He turned towards her, put his arm round her. 'But Katie, I've just told you, I'm trying to do something about it. Don't worry; I'll go to Geneva, and I'm sure I will get some work. Really, I'm certain.' He stroked her hair; he kissed the back of her neck, but she didn't respond to him; she suddenly turned away and started crying.

He said, startled, afraid, 'What's the matter?'

'I don't know . . . you've seemed so preoccupied, so unhappy, these last few weeks . . . It isn't me, is it? You don't regret . . .'

He sought at once to reassure her, relieved that for a moment he could give full and fervent expression to the truth. 'Regret? What, being with you? Katie, if you only knew . . . you're the one thing in my life I don't regret.'

◆

Geneva lay beneath a thick layer of cloud. Dmitry took the bus from the airport through the grey, aseptic streets to the bus-stop in front of the Palais de Nations, and then took another down into the town. The Libyans had offered to have someone meet him at the airport, but he had declined, preferring to make his own way to the hotel. He knew that he would probably be followed, he thought that Rozanov's men would surely want to ensure his safety, but he saw no evidence of it, which reassured him because he was sure that the men he was to meet would themselves be watching for any signs that he was under surveillance. And if they saw it, what then? He swallowed, tried to suppress the convoluted chains of thought which constantly overtook him and from time to time made him feel that he might go mad.

Sitting on the bus which ran from the Palais des Nations into the centre he was afraid, conscious of how alone and vulnerable he was in this foreign city. His meeting was at two, he had nearly an hour in hand; he got off the bus and wandered down towards the far end of the lake, where the Rhone flows out under a small stone bridge. He stopped to look over the parapet at the water sweeping underneath in a powerful torrent. Dmitry felt for an instant that he would like to dive into it; he was sure the shock of the rapid, freezing water would numb him instantly, and that, dressed in his heavy coat, he would instantly sink and soon drown. He could see himself rapidly borne, a dark blob in the water, swiftly out of sight.

He looked up from the bridge. While he had been walking, the weather had changed, and a cold, dry wind had sprung up. Lake Geneva lay before him, a deep, cold blue, the surface pulled into little stiff peaks like icing by the wind. This, he had been told, was the *Föhn*, which came down from the north off the mountains, scouring the air and throwing everything into a sharp focus. Across the lake the crisp snowy outlines of the Alps suddenly appeared as if revealed by the drawing back of a vast grey curtain. It was astonishing to see what had previously been invisible so huge and close at hand.

The wind was so dry that it seemed to scratch his face and the sun felt suddenly warm on his skin. He drew in a deep breath; the spray from the water seemed to invigorate him. He turned left and walked down the street, back to the side of the lake, where the *jet d'eau* rose in a huge plume ahead of him, and behind him, the sharp peaks of the mountains glowed in the sunlight.

The hotel seemed almost empty. It was modern, expensive, and the lobby was decorated in a dusky shade of pink. At the desk Dmitry said that he was expected by a Mr Ghesuda. The reception clerk asked for his name but Dmitry did not give it. He said that Mr Ghesuda would know who he was.

The clerk made a call and said, 'He will be coming down shortly. Would you like to sit down?'

Dmitry sat in a pink armchair by the window and waited. Two men came out of the lift, saw him, and came over; Ghesuda introduced himself and his colleague, Farzad, who was, he said, from the Ministry of Atomic Energy. Ghesuda was a small man with a mass of dark hair and an off-hand manner; the other man was older, with greying hair. He smiled much more warmly and shook Dmitry's hand.

Ghesuda said, 'We can talk here, in the bar, or if you prefer, we can take a walk . . . There is a terrace outside where we can be quite comfortable . . .'

It was sheltered out on the terrace, the wind felt almost warm; diluted sunshine lay in patches over the white metal table. The beer came cold in tall, frosted glasses and if it had not been for the company he was in Dmitry would have found it all very pleasant.

Farzad said, 'My superiors are very anxious to set this project up, Dr Gavrilov. They are expecting you in Libya. We would like to arrange this as soon as possible.'

Dmitry nearly choked as he swallowed his beer. He said, 'What about these sanctions, the air embargo . . . doesn't that make problems?'

Ghesuda shrugged. 'It would probably be best in any case if you did not fly by the direct route. What would you like to have as your cover? A trip to Moscow? You can fly London-Moscow, then on to some intermediate point – let us say, Bucharest, then Rome, Malta, boat to Libya. You can book the London-Moscow return ticket and we will arrange the rest for you. Someone will meet you at Heathrow airport in the departure lounge to hand you the ticket and we will have someone meet you off the plane from Malta to take care of you once you arrive there.'

This was going too fast for Dmitry, and it was not going to plan. Why had Rozanov assumed that he was likely to get the slightest scrap of information from them? Of course it was most likely that he hadn't; that he, Dmitry, had been set up; that Rozanov had intended, all the time, that he should go to Libya. He felt faint and cast around wildly for any way to slow this down. 'But there is a problem here . . . If I enter Russia I have to get an exit visa . . . my passport is an old one, a Soviet one . . . I have no idea how things are at the moment but this may be a problem.'

'Surely not if you are only in transit at Moscow airport? Well, we can look into this . . . we can always get you another passport, in another name, perhaps. And there are other routes. The journey will be a little exhausting, of course, but you will be well looked after in Libya, you will have plenty of time to recuperate, I assure you everything will be laid on to make your stay a very pleasant one.'

Dmitry made a soundless gesture of approval and drained his glass. They ordered another; Farzad said, 'Your proposal has created some considerable interest. The director of our research centre at Tajura is very anxious to discuss it with you.'

Ghesuda said, with a slight edge to his voice, 'I take it that you are still anxious to continue with this project?'

Dmitry said, 'Of course. I'm here, aren't I?'

'We have the contract for you to sign upstairs.'

'Contract?' Dmitry could only echo the word, stunned by his

own stupidity. The two men accompanied him in the lift to a bedroom on the sixth floor. The bland impersonality of these hotel rooms disgusted him; he thought the ante-rooms of hell would look like this. By the window stood a little desk and lamp and a gilded chair which one of the men pulled back for him. Ghesuda took a document out of his briefcase and laid it on the table. Dmitry's hand trembled as he took hold of it, and the letters blurred in front of his eyes. It was in English, setting out that he was contracted for a minimum of two years to provide services as an energy consultant to the Libyan government, to carry out research and supervision of the project outlined in his proposal of 14. April. The money – $10,000 a month – would be paid regularly into his bank account and there would be a terminal bonus. He turned the pages; he couldn't take anything in. He felt hot and clammy; of course, the room was heated, and he hadn't taken off his coat.

Ghesuda said, 'As you will see, there are regular payments but a large proportion of the money you will receive at the end of the two years . . . during that time you will be free to come and go as often as you like. We realise you have family commitments . . . we can't expect you to stay in Libya all the time.'

Dmitry said, 'This is rather awkward, with my family . . . I would like to consider it in more detail . . . The salary . . .'

'But, Dr Gavrilov, as you understand, we can't let you show this to anyone . . . it is quite straightforward. Please, read it now. We are in no hurry. If you are not happy with the salary, we can discuss this.'

Dmitry said, 'But I am not sure . . . until I have seen the facilities at Tajura . . .'

'I can assure you the facilities are excellent. You must be aware of this . . . with your contacts in Russia and at the IAEA.'

Dmitry swallowed. It sounded to him like a great gulp in the noiseless room. 'Yes, but I must be assured that you have the basic materials for me to work with . . . that you have the capacity to manufacture or import the parts I will need . . .'

'But we are quite confident of all this,' said Farzad, reason-ably. 'Otherwise we would not be offering you the contract.'

Dmitry picked up the document and read it through again, more carefully, but still absorbing only part of it. It was curious how easy it was to be pressured into signing something. It was expected of him; if he was what he pretended to be, what possi-ble excuse did he have not to sign it? The money was good, he had come this far. What should he do? Of course he could refuse, he could say he needed time to think, and then, in London, he could say he had changed his mind. He looked at Ghesuda's stone-hard face and instantly thought better of it. How was he ever going to get out of this? If he refused, he might never get out of this room. They might kill him. Or they might drug him and put him on a plane; he knew of such things. He did not know what meaning signing this document had; he did not understand anything about business, about contracts, still less about con-tracts to undertake work which must be illegal under interna-tional law.

He took a deep breath. He thought that to sign the contract in any case had no validity if he was doing it under duress, and of course he could argue, at least to himself, that he was; but this was playing games with himself. If he broke the contract, what agency would ever enforce it? Only the Libyans, and their enforcement might be an execution squad in some desert spot . . . He realised that he was sweating. He wiped his forehead and put the contract down on the table. He said, 'Yes, this all seems to be all right.' They held out a pen for him and he took it. He looked at them; at their expectant, wary faces, and knew they wouldn't understand such hesitation, that they would be sus-pecting that all was not as it seemed. He took the pen, and paused with it above the paper; his head swam; then he put the pen down again. He couldn't do this.

Ghesuda sat down on the chair opposite him. He said, in a low, threatening voice, 'There is a problem?'

Dmitry thought, I must explain myself, I must think of

something. But moments passed, and he could think of nothing to say. He stared at the paper, the pen in his hand, as if paralysed. Then suddenly an inspiration hit him. He said, 'Well, there is just one small thing . . . it is stupid, but . . . I understand that in your country alcohol is prohibited. I have a weakness for Russian vodka . . . I was wondering . . .'

Abruptly the atmosphere changed. They roared with laughter, and after a moment he joined them; perhaps they were, all of them, laughing with relief. Ghesuda said, 'This is no problem, no problem. Of course, we would not expect you . . . We shall fly in a personal supply . . .' He laughed again and then, looking at Dmitry, fell silent. His glance fell again on the contract, still lying on the table.

It was so easy now. With a flourish of the pen, Dmitry signed both copies. Ghesuda took his copy, folded it neatly and tucked it into the inside pocket of his jacket. Dmitry took his own; what could he do with it? He couldn't carry anything so incriminating, he would need to destroy it. He looked at the Libyans. Now they were all smiles, joking and laughing. Dmitry wasn't sure what they were laughing about, but he joined in with it. They patted him on the back. Farzad said, 'Now we will go to the bank. We have arranged to open an account for you.'

The wind was colder now as they strolled through the main streets. The windows of the shops were filled with luxury goods; jewellery, clothes, watches; gleaming dark chocolates and gilded antiques. They passed bars, restaurants, cafés. Dmitry passed by them as if in a dream. It reminded him of when he was a child, visiting Moscow, staring in through the windows of the elite shops and restaurants; he felt as barred from indulging in them now as he had ever been. A shudder went through him; Ghesuda took his elbow.

'Of course you know that the bank secrecy laws here do not mean that the police or security services can't investigate. We can open the account in your name; or, if you prefer, we can form a company for you in Liberia, which is registered in such a way that your name cannot be traced – '

Dmitry said, 'Is that really necessary?' He couldn't cope with this; he resisted any further complications. Ghesuda shrugged. He said, 'It is an option, if you are concerned about security, that's all.'

Dmitry now just wanted to get this over. They entered a private bank in the Rue du Rhone. The man they saw was pleasant, unctuous, welcoming his new customer enthusiastically; how different, Dmitry thought, from the manager in London. They went into an office and Dmitry was handed various forms. Details of the account were explained to him, though he could barely understand what they were saying. He was told that the account would be operated under the number 29690, and he should give an identification code – one word only would be fine – which he should quote with the number to make a withdrawal. Could he put the specimen signature here?

Dmitry signed twice, in Roman script and in Cyrillic. The code word defeated him for a few moments; he thought of putting 'bomb' or 'uranium' but this seemed foolish; as he sought for something that might be appropriate the word 'Faustus' came into his head, so that was what he put. It only occurred to him afterwards that Ghesuda might have been looking over his shoulder and seen what he had written, but it was too late to do anything about that. After a brief discussion he also signed a discharge for orders given by telephone or fax. When the transaction was complete Dmitry folded his copy of the papers and stuffed them deep into his jacket pocket.

They returned to the hotel. A waiter brought champagne and smoked salmon sandwiches. Dmitry had a glass; he felt he had to. It went to his head instantly; he wondered if they would try to get him drunk and then start asking him questions. He felt light-headed with relief that this was over, followed by a strange, half-mad desire to confess everything to them and beg them not to make him go to Libya. No sooner had this thought entered his head than he was struck with fear, a realisation that in his feverish, overwrought state he might actually forget himself. Instantly he wanted to leave; he looked at his watch. He said, 'I must be at the airport at eight.' They said, 'Of course, of course. We can organise a taxi for you . . . Please, do not worry about anything. From now on . . . trust us. You are in our hands.'

◆

It was midnight when he arrived home. He let himself in, quietly, thinking Katie would be in bed. He put his briefcase down on the living room floor. The television was on with the sound turned down low; a *Newsnight* discussion on Libya's failure to release the Lockerbie suspects by the deadline and the likely effect of sanctions. Dmitry didn't want to hear any of this; he crossed the room and turned it off.

The lamp was on; he saw that Katie was lying on the sofa, in her dressing gown, asleep. She had been waiting up for him; he was touched. She had made an effort to tidy the room; a bowl of delicate white narcissi stood on the table and the delicious smell faintly scented the room. Dmitry took off his coat, crossed the room, bent down, and kissed her.

She woke at once. Her eyes widened with pleasure, she smiled, she put her hand up and drew his head down to hers and kissed him again. She said, 'Your hair's wet.'

'It's raining outside.'

'Did it go all right?'

'Yes, fine.'

'Did you get some work?'

'Yes; it's a big report on nuclear disarmament. Look, I bought some things. There's some wine . . . I bought this dress for Anna, do you think she'll like it? And here . . . I got this for you. And some chocolates . . .'

She was laughing. He felt almost sick; here he was, lying his head off to her, and she noticed nothing wrong. She sat up, her hair loose, and embraced him. She was like a small child, at Christmas; she opened the packages he'd bought at the airport with such pleasure. She held up the scarf against her hair and turned her face up for him to kiss her. He smiled but inside he was in agony; she would never imagine the price he had paid to give her this small moment of happiness. Then he was aware of her looking at him. She asked, 'Mitya, what's the matter?'

'Nothing's the matter. It will be all right; we'll have some money . . . I will make you happy.' He kissed her lips and let his mouth linger on them for a moment; she responded warmly, reaching up her arms and wrapping them around him.

Her dressing gown parted and he slipped his hand beneath it, warming his hand on her smooth flesh and finding her moist already between her thighs. He ached for her fiercely and he could see how much she wanted him; she arched her back, slid her hips against him, was tugging at his clothes. He had the feeling then, for a moment, that she could save him. He could forget himself, momentarily, in the bliss of sex, in the softness of her body, in the depth of her eyes. But he knew even as he entered her and she began to moan, turning her head from side to side and asking him for more, yes, quickly, that afterwards he would have to explain to her that he had to go away, and he would have no option but to tell her more complex and corrosive lies.

6

THE WIND rattled the windows and it rained all night without a pause, which Dmitry knew because he had not had a moment's sleep to soothe the turmoil in his head.

Katie slept beside him, peacefully. At four, Sasha awoke; Dmitry picked him up, and went downstairs. He tried to pacify him, gave him a little water, walked up and down, up and down till finally the baby went to sleep; he sat down with Sasha on the sofa and sprawled there in a half-stupor. The baby was warm and comforting against his chest and he felt a sense of pride and achievement; this was the first time he had succeeded in settling the baby without resorting to Katie. He adjusted his position on the sofa and closed his eyes; but still he couldn't rest.

Katie found them there when she came down in the morning. She was still groggy, her hair tangled and uncombed. 'What's the matter? You look terrible.'

'I thought I'd let you sleep in for once.'

Katie smiled at him with gratitude and sympathy. She sat next to him and the baby stirred, as if sensing her presence; she took him and began to feed him. Dmitry went to make some coffee. His head ached; he felt dreadful, even worse because he knew he would have to go and meet Rozanov later on.

What had he done? There must be some way out of this; but what?

Katie said, 'Mitya, you look exhausted. Can't you go back to bed? You don't have anything to do today.'

'No, I have to meet someone . . . I'll feel all right later.'

'Who are you seeing?'

Irritation seized him; he couldn't help himself. What should he say; what idiotic lie could he think of next? He tried to keep his voice light and casual. 'Oh, some Russian contact, someone whose name I was given . . . I expect it will be a waste of time.'

Katie didn't ask any more; it was easy to deceive her, she never suspected for a moment, why should she? He might have concealed things from her in the past, but until now he had never had to lie to her like this. Lying made him angry, not only with himself, but curiously also with her for trusting him so easily. There was part of him that wanted her to ask more, to dig deeper, to challenge what he said, to force him to reveal himself.

He made the coffee and toast, and took some to her, called Anna down for breakfast; but when he tried to eat himself he couldn't; the food stuck in his throat.

Katie glanced at him, a worried expression on her face. He grabbed his coat and took Anna to school. She skipped along beside him, chattering away, while he paid no attention, fixed in his own dark thoughts. She didn't seem to notice anything was wrong; occasionally when she asked a question he said 'yes' or 'no' more or less at random and this seemed to satisfy her.

He kissed her goodbye at the school gates and took the bus to Chalk Farm, spending the morning in the library. At lunch-time he went to Baker Street; he found a delicatessen, intending to buy a sandwich, but in his anxious state felt unable to eat anything. Little dots kept appearing in front of his eyes as if he was about to develop a migraine but then faded away again. He wandered round the streets till nearly two, then went up to the flat.

Its soullessness struck him once again as he entered. There were two other men in the room, who Rozanov introduced, but Dmitry did not look at them and did not pay attention to their names. He refused to take off his coat and would not sit down. He told them what had happened. When he tried to explain his feelings he found he couldn't; it sounded feeble, hopeless. He said, spreading his hands wide, 'I'm sorry, I have gone as far as I'm going. We discussed this at the outset . . . We agreed I wouldn't go to Libya.'

Rozanov talked to him as if he were a small boy who had erred at school. 'Well, that is a little awkward, don't you think? If you felt like that, why did you sign the contract? You didn't have to sign it . . . you could have told them you needed to think it over.'

'I don't know . . . it wasn't like that.' Dmitry stood in the centre of the room, awkward, uneasy. One of the men took Dmitry's coat from him so skilfully that he was barely aware of parting with it and the other offered him a cup of tea; he found himself sitting down in one of the chairs opposite Rozanov, who added too much sugar and then stirred his own cup with a delicate silver spoon which tinkled loudly, trying to dissolve it. 'But, Dmitry Nikolayevich, I don't need to spell out to you how much value it would be to us if you did go. This will only be a short trip . . . then we will help you to extricate yourself.'

Dmitry cut him off, deciding to face the onslaught, whatever form it took; 'How will you do that? Once I'm there they'll have me . . . No, I'm not prepared to do it.'

Rozanov sighed. He didn't look at Dmitry; he looked at the table top, at his fat, stubby fingers which he pressed together. Dmitry found himself wishing they would snap. 'Look, Dmitry Nikolayevich, let me be blunt with you; you really have no choice. We have this excellent recording made with your help of you negotiating to sell your expertise to the Libyans . . . we could of course give it to the UK police, leak it to one of the Sunday papers . . .'

There was an absolute silence in the room. All three men were looking at him, waiting for his reaction; they had seen it all before, no doubt, dozens of times, and knew what people did. Some, perhaps became angry; others burst into tears; some probably pleaded and grovelled on the floor; perhaps a few became murderous. No doubt that was why the two men were here, to protect Rozanov if he turned nasty. Dmitry had known all along that something like this was likely to happen, but now that it had he was astonished at how violently he reacted. Foreknowledge of betrayal does not necessarily make it less painful, he thought. Did Christ feel less betrayed in the garden because he knew it was preordained? Did a man, who knew his wife had been unfaithful, feel less pain on finding her in bed with her lover?

His breath was taken away. A wave of anger swept through him, but he was not able to give it the slightest expression. He felt numb, completely dissociated from everything. He thought, perhaps they are bluffing, anyway. I must just see this through. He said, 'Very good, excellent. That is just what I want. Do you think I wasn't expecting this all along? I don't care if I am exposed or not . . . in fact, let me make it easy for you . . . I will telephone them now.' He got to his feet, crossed the room to the phone. All three men stared at him; he saw Rozanov give the slightest nod to one of the men, who went out of the room. Dmitry assumed that he had gone to disconnect the phone; he picked it up, but it was still working. 'Do you have a phone book? I will ring the Sunday Times. I will offer them an exclusive; I will tell them the whole story. Of course; why didn't I think of it before? I should be able to negotiate a good fee.'

Rozanov came over and laid a restraining hand on his arm. He was calm, soothing, utterly professional. He said, 'This is a very difficult situation for you. Come, take my advice, don't do anything foolish. Let's sit down and talk it over.'

Dmitry would not sit down. Rozanov went on in a calm, purring voice: 'Listen, let me tell you, if you did such a thing, you would be putting yourself at risk. What do you think would happen if you were named? Can you not foresee the consequences?'

Dmitry stared at Rozanov. He said, 'Yes, yes, of course I see them, I see everything, that is why I could not sleep last night.' He began to pace up and down, turning backwards and forwards, feeling all the helplessness of the fish dangling on the hook.

Then he said, in a low voice, 'Look, it's not much use threatening me. Do you think I care that much about my future? What kind of a future do I have, anyway? I am no use as a translator, as a serious scientist I am probably finished and now that I have got involved in this I haven't the slightest hope of ever rehabilitating myself . . . None of your threats have the slightest meaning for me. If I walked out of here into the street under a bus it would probably be the best thing that could happen to me.'

'But if you feel like that, Dmitry Nikolayevich, you don't have much to lose by carrying on with this. At least you will be doing something useful along the way, something of incalculable value, perhaps, for your country.'

'Useful.' Dmitry made a gesture of indecision, despair. 'And what would I tell my wife? She would never forgive me.'

'Oh, you can arrange a cover story. You might need another, longer trip to Geneva. You could go to Russia to see your family or perhaps you could say it is to find out about some project . . . de-enrichment of uranium from dismantled bombs or something like this. We can help you think of a good cover story. I'm sure your employers will understand your need for secrecy; all of this can be arranged, Dmitry Nikolayevich.'

Dmitry still fought against the inevitable; he knew how painful it would be to have to continually lie to Katie. 'I promised her when I left the IAEA that I would never work again as a nuclear scientist. Even to justify a trip to Russia would be difficult.'

'Why? If she objects because you might be helping to make bombs, how could she object if you tell her you are helping to dismantle them? Besides, is that a decision she should make for you? Who makes the decisions in your household, Dmitry Nikolayevich?'

Rozanov had miscalculated here; he had meant probably to shame Dmitry, but instead seemed to realise that he had provoked a violent anger and retracted at once. Dmitry stood, looking at him, rooted to the spot, hearing nothing. Everything in this room now had an aura of unreality. This cup, for instance, which he held in his hand, was just an ordinary cup, and yet he couldn't understand the shape or texture of it; all the things in the room were simple, ordinary things, a table, chairs, a lamp-shade, and yet he felt as if he had never seen anything like them before and couldn't work out what they were doing there.

He felt dizzy; there was a rushing sound in his ears and he realised he would have to sit down. He stumbled forward and half fell into the chair. Hot tea spilt across his shirt; the cup and saucer fell on to the floor and split into several pieces. He wondered if he had lost consciousness for a moment; Rozanov, an anxious expression on his face, was loosening his tie and swiftly undoing the top buttons of his shirt. He slipped his hand inside and held it there, so that Dmitry, for a moment, was forced to sit and stare into the eyes of this man he detested, feeling his cold hand pressed against his very heart.

'Is there pain?' asked Rozanov. His eyes were cold, calculating the extent of his error. Dmitry's heart, which had seemed to miss a beat, was pounding now and he felt the blood rush to his face.

'No,' said Dmitry, getting control of himself, quiet, sardonic, 'No, don't worry, you have not given me a heart attack.'

Relief flooded Rozanov's features. He took his hand away and shook his head at the man who, poised by the telephone, was no doubt about to call an ambulance. Dmitry wondered if this had happened to Rozanov before, if he had inadvertently killed someone in this way; he sensed from his momentary panic that it had. Dmitry leaned forward and put his face in his hands. If this incident didn't convince them that he was no use for this kind of job, what would?

Rozanov did not speak for some time; perhaps he was considering this very point. Dmitry wondered if he had reprieved himself; whether Rozanov would think he was too weak or unstable to continue with this venture; but Rozanov seemed unconcerned. No doubt spies, after all, saw human beings at their

weakest; blackmailed, deceived, breaking down and confessing
from some inner need or under threat of death or torture.

Rozanov asked, off-hand, 'Have you visited a doctor recently?
You don't have any problems with your blood pressure? Maybe
you should arrange to have a check-up.'

'I'm fine. I have migraines . . . I think that I am getting one
now.'

Rozanov shrugged. He said, 'Well, then, let's proceed. The
Libyans will make all the arrangements for you to go . . . we will
not need to be involved. Of course, when you are there it will be
better if you have no contact with our people in the embassy,
although your presence will be made known to them. Libya, as
I'm sure you are aware, is one of the most closed societies in the
world. You must understand that all telephones, houses and
hotels used by foreigners are bugged and monitored with the latest European technology. People are everywhere on the lookout
for anything strange which they will report to the security services. You will not be free simply to go off on your own . . . that is
why it is much better if you have no contact with us out there
but wait till you are back for your debriefing . . .'

'Yes, of course.'

'However, we will run through the procedure to make contact
in case there is an emergency. Please, don't make any notes. It
must all be in your head. If you have to write something down,
remember to conceal it in some way . . . For example, the name
of the person at the consulate you must ask for. Put it here, in
your diary, and then a Moscow phone number . . . of course this
person does not exist.' He ran through what Dmitry should do,
the procedures to be followed if he had to have a meeting, pass
any urgent information over. Rozanov went on; 'At Tajura, keep
your eyes and ears open. You may have access to material others
have been denied, places, persons involved in any parallel military programme. We can also give you a miniature camera so
that you can photograph any documents . . .'

Dmitry sat back suddenly in his chair. He said, 'No . . . no, I'm sorry. This is ridiculous . . . it is exposing me to too much risk. I'm not going to sneak around the place at night with a spy camera . . . if I am searched it would completely give the game away . . . besides, it is not necessary. I have an exceptional memory.'

Rozanov raised his eyebrows. 'Do you? I have heard this. It is in your file. Together with some surprising mathematical abilities too.' He turned to Dmitry and suddenly snapped, 'What are 698 times 143?'

After the briefest pause, Dmitry answered back, '99,814.'

One of the other men reached for his calculator. He raised his eyebrows, nodded at Rozanov, and then his eyes turned with puzzlement to Dmitry. Rozanov began to laugh. He said, 'They were right about you, after all. You were a child genius, a walking computer. Yet in the age of a pocket calculator, what a useless skill. What a pity that for various reasons you did not live up to your childhood promise.'

Dmitry felt the anger rise in him. 'On the contrary, this sum was far too easy. 698 is just two short of 700. Multiply 143 by 700 and you get 100,100. Subtract twice 143 – 286 – from this and there is your answer. A child could do it.'

He snatched his coat from the hat-stand, turned and ran straight out of the flat and down to the entrance hall, pursued by Rozanov's almost diabolic laughter echoing down the stairs.

7

THE PHONE on Tim's desk rang and when he answered it was Ingrid, with her cool, slightly hesitant voice, talking as if nothing at all had happened in the weeks since he had seen her. Tim was so taken aback that he agreed to meet her for lunch that very day despite all his intentions, if she had phoned, to refuse to see her. When he hung up he stared at the phone for a few moments, surprised at his reaction. He realised that he now hardly cared whether he saw her or not.

He picked up the fax from Mike Harris in Moscow which lay on his desk. Dmitry Nikolayevich Gavrilov, born 1948, Archangelsk, educated at Moscow State University, degree in nuclear physics, researcher at the Kurchatov Institute, had also worked at the Physico-Power Institute, Obninsk . . . Mike added that this information wasn't up to date, because Gavrilov wasn't at the Kurchatov Institute any longer, he had checked that. He suggested Tim contact the IAEA if he thought that he had worked there.

Tim thought, on reflection, that this was puzzling. Why had neither Dmitry nor Katie said when they had their conversation the other night that he was a nuclear scientist himself? Why had the suggestion that scientists might sell their services abroad made him so angry? Or perhaps it was obvious, perhaps someone in his position would be over-sensitive to the issue. He wondered how he had ended up here. Had he married Katie for a passport to the West after his spell in Vienna, rather than return to his disintegrating country? He supposed it was very possible. In which case . . . he wondered whether it had been, for Gavrilov, partly a marriage of convenience. He wondered whether there was a way he might find this out.

He put the fax in his file on nuclear issues, and with an effort turned his mind away from this particular problem to today's news story.

Ingrid was a little late for lunch, as usual. Tim had suggested a new restaurant near the ITN building, which had plain wooden tables and the kind of spartan vegetarian menu which Ingrid would approve of. He saw her walk through the door; she looked just the same; tall, slim, stylish, as collected as ever. He rose when she came in and she kissed both cheeks, slipped into the chair opposite him and regarded him frankly. She said, without any preliminaries, that when Tim had refused even to talk to her about what had happened (in case he didn't remember, his exact words when she told him she had met someone else were 'Right, fine,') she had decided the only thing to do was walk out and not come back. She said she realised now that this was cowardly. Tim, unable to admit that he had not even heard what she had said to him, had said, 'Right, fine,' because he thought she'd just said she was going out, simply nodded. She went on to say that she'd been having an intense affair but she didn't think her lover was going to leave his wife and she wasn't sure what would happen. She didn't regret anything she had done, but was sorry about the way she had treated Tim. She said it had been immature and cruel and she had wanted to apologise.

The waiter came and they ordered; then Tim said, as casually as he could, that he didn't really mind, that it didn't matter anyway now because he, too, had met someone else.

Ingrid looked slightly disconcerted. She put out her thin, nervous hand and lifted the glass of mineral water. 'Have you?' she asked him. 'Is it going all right?'

'Well, it's not really going yet at all, really . . . she's married too.'

Ingrid laughed, a little bitterly. 'It's not your landlady, Katie, is it?'

Tim, not wanting to admit that he was this transparent, found himself denying this. He munched his way through his plate of veggie burger and mashed potato while Ingrid seemed defeated by her salad. He couldn't think of anything to say. He asked, more for the sake of breaking the silence than from real curiosity, 'What does he do? This man of yours.'

'He works for the Foreign Office.'

'Doing what?'

'I don't know, exactly. A desk officer, something to do with the Middle East I think.'

'I see.' Tim couldn't really understand why Ingrid had wanted to see him. He had assumed that she might have regretted walking out and wanted to see if he wanted her back, but that wasn't it at all. Tim began to feel restless. 'Look, I'm sorry I can't make this a long lunch. I'm rather busy at work . . . I'm probably going to Moscow in a week or two . . . It's really good to see you, I'm glad you decided to get in touch, but I can't see things going back to how they were . . .'

'No; no, of course not. I wouldn't have wanted it to.' She said this hurriedly, as if she wanted to make it clear that wasn't why she had come. 'I just wanted to . . . well, sort out unfinished business.'

'Well, there isn't much to sort out . . . only the question of the rent you owe me.' Tim felt a small sense of triumph as he saw her flinch at this remark; he knew she probably couldn't afford to pay it and that this would hurt and humiliate her. Ingrid stared at him for a moment, then said, coldly, 'I'm sorry, I thought that it was right for us to stay friends. That was naïve of me.' She took a card out of her bag and slipped it to him. She said, 'Here's my new number in case you need it for anything. Otherwise don't bother.' She stood up. 'I'll send you the rent. And don't worry, I'll pay for this on the way out.'

Tim reached into his pocket to get out his wallet but she'd already left the table. He watched her go to the till and settle up;

then she went out of the restaurant without a backwards glance. Tim watched her go; for a moment he felt a sharp pang of regret, wondering for an instant whether he hadn't missed out on something. Yes, perhaps they could have become friends. Then he dismissed the thought and drained the remnants of fruit juice in his glass.

He went straight back into the office and put a call through to the IAEA in Vienna. He asked to speak to their press officer, who had just taken up his post, a Norwegian called Wahren. He asked if a Russian called Dmitry Gavrilov had worked there, perhaps one or two years ago.

'Well, I don't know . . . that was before my time. If you hold on I can check for you.'

Tim held on. After a few moments Wahren came back on the line and said . . . 'Yes. He was here, as you say, in 1990, '91, just for one year.'

'What position did he hold there?'

'He was in the Department of Safeguards . . . His exact position is not listed, probably he was some kind of consultant . . .'

'And he was only there a year? Isn't that unusual? I thought they all had three-year contracts.'

'Yes, that is usual.'

'Do you know why he left?'

'I think perhaps he left for personal reasons . . . why do you want to know?'

'I'm trying to contact him. Do you know where he is now?'

'I'm afraid for security reasons we can't give you any information on that. But I assume he returned to Russia. Many of the scientists we have here are from the major institutes . . . I am sure it would not be too difficult for you to trace him.'

Tim thanked him and hung up. Unhelpful bastard. Resigned for personal reasons . . . that was slightly intriguing. It could mean anything, including a dismissal. Still, there was a limit to the amount of work time he could put in to satisfying his curiosity about Gavrilov. He had other, more urgent things to do . . . He'd let it rest for now.

◆

Dmitry knew that the moment was approaching when he would have to tell Katie that he was planning to go abroad. He had tried to raise the issue several times, but each time his courage had failed him. Now he stood by the window, coffee in hand, looking out over the garden. The weather had suddenly turned warm; the early sun shone on the damp grass and lit the new green shoots. Anna was eating her breakfast; Sasha, lying on the rug, was temporarily contented. Katie was making Anna's packed lunch. It was very quiet and still, unusually so, and he felt as if they were all waiting for him to speak out and ruin everything. But there was nothing for it; he had to do it. He said, very quietly, 'Katie . . . I need to go to Moscow for two or three weeks.'

Katie had not been expecting anything like this. She looked up, suddenly, her mouth falling open. 'When?'

'Well . . . at the end of next week.'

Katie asked, 'But why so soon? Why didn't they give you more notice? Is this connected with this UN thing?' She looked harassed, searching around for Anna's lunch-box.

'Yes, it's to do with the new START treaty, dismantling nuclear warheads . . . I have to go to this big meeting.'

'As a translator?'

He must be very careful what he said, give as few details as possible, so he wouldn't be caught out later. 'It's more than a translation . . . they want me to draft this part of the report.' He hesitated. 'And there may be other meetings.'

'You mean, you'll be away again? How often? How long for?'

'I don't know, exactly. I'm sorry. But it is work.'

Katie said, 'Of course you must go, but I wish you'd told me earlier it would involve so much travel . . . why didn't you talk to me about it? I thought that was the whole point . . .'

Dmitry didn't understand what she meant. 'The point of what?'

'Of marriage.'

He turned away, confused, wrong-footed.

Anna must have heard them; she suddenly came and put her arms tightly round him, saying she didn't want him to go away. She turned her face up to him, clinging to him. He lifted her up and kissed her nose. 'Oh, it won't be for long,' he said, smoothing her hair, 'I'll get you a present, a chess set of your own perhaps, or a Russian doll.'

Katie seemed exasperated. 'Anna, get your coat. We're going to be late. You don't want a late mark, do you?'

That evening when the children were in bed they sat down at the table to work out their finances. Dmitry told her that he was expecting some more money from Geneva to be paid into his account next week. The payments he'd received already had made a lot of difference; they were paying off their debts. Katie came and sat beside him, leaned her head on his shoulder, but he didn't look at her. He had not anticipated how much lying to her would distance him from her. He no longer wanted to talk to her about anything of importance; he felt a need to avoid intimacy. He was afraid that if she looked him right in the eyes she would see that he was not being honest with her.

There were bills to pay. Dmitry picked up the phone bill, and without thinking queried some long calls she had made during the day. Katie snapped at him. 'Look, I'm trapped here all day with Sasha, if I didn't talk to someone I would go mad . . .' she paused and ran a hand through her hair. 'Look, Mitya, we have to talk, I can't carry on as we are. What's the matter with you these days? You've got some work now, you should be glad. Instead you seem so negative about everything . . . All right, things are difficult now, but why can't you look forward? Things will get better . . .'

Dmitry felt his heart beat faster, suddenly afraid that this was it, she was seeing through him, she would start to ask him all the questions he was dreading. He felt a need to block it off. He opened his mouth and found himself saying, 'Get better? On the contrary, everything, all over the world, is going to get a lot worse, can't you see . . . this is just the beginning.'

Katie jumped to her feet. She said, 'I can't deal with you, your Russian pessimism, your paranoia, it is suffocating me.' She flew upstairs. Dmitry sank his head into his hands for a moment; he wanted to go and comfort her, and yet he was afraid. He followed her, undressed, sat on the bed beside her watching her brushing out her thick hair. He put his hand on her shoulder. He said, 'Katie, please forgive me. I wish things could be otherwise, I wish that I could make you happy. I . . .' he stopped. He wanted to confess everything to her, but he couldn't. What would she do? No, it was impossible.

She put down the brush. She asked, 'Do you?' She turned to face him; she was angry, her face was hard; but when she looked at him it softened. He pulled her towards him and she came willingly, letting him kiss her, putting out her arms to embrace him. She knelt, leaning her head against his chest, her face hidden from him by her hair, and then, deliberately, placing her legs on either side of his, she lowered herself on to him. She was wet, but not very wet; he did not go in easily, and when he entered her she gasped and cried out. She said, 'That hurts . . . no, please go on . . . I want you to hurt me.' He said, concerned, puzzled, because she had never asked this before, 'Why do you want this?' and she replied with unusual vehemence, 'Because then I can hate you.'

◆

Tim was obsessed with his report. He had little over a week before he went to Moscow, and the pressure was building up all the time. He kept a huge book about nuclear physics on his desk, and in any spare minute that he had, he dipped into it. He was surprised to find that the principle behind an atomic bomb was so simple and well-known; almost any physics graduate could do it. The problem of course was how to get hold of the fissile material. There were two main routes to building a bomb. The first was the uranium route, which needed uranium enriched up to at least about 80 per cent. You could also make a bomb with plutonium, which could only be obtained from used fuel from nuclear reactors. Using plutonium was less attractive because it was more difficult to obtain, and it was also far more toxic and radioactive.

A voice in his ear said, 'Tim,' and he looked up sharply. Rowley had come and sat on the edge of his desk with a memo in his hand. 'French television apparently showed a short clip of film of what was believed to be a transaction to sell highly enriched uranium in Moscow . . . can you follow that up? Is your ticket booked?'

'Yes, for next week.' Tim looked at the memo. The film had been shown on FR3, the French equivalent to Channel 4. He nodded his thanks to Rowley's retreating back and immediately rang Paris, finally managing to speak to the man responsible for the report. He said he had bought the film of the transaction from Russian state television. He had the name of the woman who had researched the item, Larissa Sukoruchkin.

Tim pulled out his file and added to his outline for the piece. He planned to find some nuclear scientist who would talk, preferably to say that he had been offered work abroad or that he would take it if he was. He would want to talk to one of the military officers in charge of nuclear warheads, who he knew would say how safe they were, and contrast this with some expert who would say they weren't. Then there were the experts in Vienna. Tim reached for another thick, turgid UN report. The IAEA in Vienna had been set up partly to police nuclear installations world-wide to ensure nuclear material was not diverted from power plants into military use. The more he thought about it, the more intrigued he was to think that Gavrilov had worked there. He thought that he would try to talk to him again tonight.

When he rang the bell and asked Katie if he could talk to her husband she looked bewildered. She said, 'Oh, how silly, I'm sure he would have helped you, but . . . he isn't here. He's in Moscow himself. He went this morning.'

Tim stood on the step, hesitating only for a second. Maybe

she could tell him something useful. 'Look, if you're on your own, why don't you come down and have supper with me this evening. We could leave the doors open and you could pop upstairs to check the children.'

Katie looked at him for a moment, wiping floury hands across an over-large stripy apron. 'Oh, Tim, how kind of you. That would be lovely.'

She came down at eight. He had rushed around the flat tidying and arranging things for the first time since Ingrid had left, and decided to cook something simple and safe rather than trying to impress her with a culinary expertise he didn't have. She sat opposite him in his tiny kitchen while he nervously stirred the spaghetti; he had given her a large glass of wine, and he noticed that she sipped it very slowly. She was wearing a thick grey sweater and black leggings, which didn't suit her because it emphasised how thin she was, and seemed to magnify the dark circles under her eyes. She had pinned her hair up and wore dangling earrings that emphasised the length of her neck. He was pleased that she had done something about her appearance in his honour. He thought it was a promising sign.

'How long is your husband away for?'

'Oh, I don't know . . . two or three weeks.' She looked at him and smiled, but he thought it seemed a sad, uncertain smile. He decided that the pasta must be done and strained it, and carried the plates through to the table at the end of the living room. He thought he could have done a bit more with the room but then, from what he had seen, she wasn't exactly a tidy person herself.

She started to eat, dabbing at the mound on her plate delicately with her fork. Tim poured himself more wine. He started with a safe subject, asking her about other people they had known at the BBC and filling her in on his more recent history. Katie listened, but said little. He sensed her sadness or depression and finally he steeled himself and said, 'I get the impression . . . forgive me if I'm wrong . . . that you're not entirely happy.'

Katie looked up sharply from her plate. Then she half laughed and said, 'Well, you find me any couple with financial worries and small children who are having a good time.'

'Yes, I can see it must be difficult.'

Perhaps Katie read something in his expression because she said quite sharply, 'Look, Tim, just to make it clear in case you're misunderstanding things . . . I'm absolutely committed to the marriage. I'll admit things are difficult now but that's not the point . . . besides, there are the children. Anna's lost one father . . . I couldn't go through that again.'

'It still doesn't quite answer my question. I asked if you were happy.'

'Marriage isn't just about happiness.'

'No, I'm sorry, it was a naïve sort of thing to say. I haven't ever been married, so I wouldn't know.'

'Tim, you don't know anything about our relationship. You don't know what we've been through in order to be together.' She paused. 'I love him, Tim, if that's what you want to know.'

He looked at her. He realised suddenly that she was very fragile; that she was very fragile; that she was about to cry. He realised that he had struck a nerve, and he suddenly felt guilty about it. He had been indelicate; he shouldn't have asked so soon. She ate slowly, hesitantly, as if she was forcing herself to but wasn't really enjoying it. He asked, 'Is the food that bad?'

'No, it's very good, really . . . it's lovely to have someone else cook for me . . . you just gave me rather a lot.'

'Perhaps you'd like some fruit.'

'No, Tim, I'm all right. Perhaps a bit later.'

Tim stood up from the table and Katie sank back on the black leather couch, a hideous thing which the previous tenant had left behind. Tim put on some soft country and western music, a new band he rather liked, sat down at the other end of the couch and looked at her. She emptied her wine glass and suddenly laughed; she looked much better, more like the old Katie he used to know. She gave him a slightly coy glance and said, 'I hope you're not going to try to seduce me.'

Tim feigned a look of surprise. He said, 'Well, it did cross my mind . . . but I didn't think there was the slightest possibility that I might succeed.'

She didn't reply, and a silence fell. Tim offered Katie more wine but she shook her head. He said, 'Katie, I was doing some research, the other day, looking at some IAEA documents, and your husband's name was there . . . I didn't realise that he's a nuclear scientist.'

'He was,' corrected Katie.

'Well, was . . . He was at the Kurchatov Institute, I gather, before the IAEA.'

'Yes, that's right.' Katie was looking at him, guarded, cautious.

Tim tried to sound casual. 'What was his position at the IAEA?'

'He was a consultant. I don't know exactly, Tim. I can't remember the details.'

'But why did he give it up? That must have been a good job for him, in the West, a UN salary . . .'

Katie sighed. 'He was very disillusioned with it all, I think he saw too clearly how the safeguards programme had just become a cynical exercise . . . and then he met me. He just wanted to get out, to come to England, we both did.'

Tim thought he might not get another chance to raise it, so he pressed on, 'But what was his subject, exactly? Reactor physics?'

'No, uranium enrichment.'

A faint thrill of surprise, of excitement, went through Tim. He was, frankly, surprised that she had told him. He said, he couldn't help it, 'Oh, I see. Sensitive stuff.'

Perhaps Katie instantly regretted what she had said; she suddenly looked away from him. 'Look, I'm not defending him, Tim, I was never in favour of nuclear energy myself, at all, when I was young, you know that, but he's not worked on anything military, if that's what you're wondering . . .'

'No, no, I wasn't thinking that, but, anyway, there's no difference, is there? The technique is the same, whether you want uranium for fuel or bombs.'

Katie said, 'I know that. But he didn't exactly have any choice about it, did he? In Soviet Russia at that time, they selected children with the right abilities, they sent them to specialist schools, chose what areas they wanted them to work in. Anyway, if you're interested, you should talk to Mitya about it, not me. I don't know anything about all this stuff.'

'Well yes, I would like to talk to him. I'll ask him when he comes back. Or perhaps I can look him up in Moscow, if you tell me where he's staying . . . Do you want me to take him anything?'

'Take him . . . what kind of thing? Well, I suppose you could take him a letter, but . . . he'll only be there three weeks, I don't think there's any point in sending a food parcel or anything like that, if that's what you meant . . .'

Tim laughed. He said, 'Well, you could give me his number, anyway.'

Katie said, 'He's staying with someone who isn't on the phone, but he did give me a number where I could leave a message. And there's his sister's number, I could give you that. If you come upstairs for a moment I'll give them to you.'

They went up the stairs together. With the children asleep, the room was quiet and peaceful. Katie found the address book and wrote down the numbers for him on a piece of paper. She stood in darkness, illuminated only by the light of the desk lamp, and Tim found himself staring at the back of her neck, at the downy hair and the smooth curve of her shoulders, and was almost overwhelmed by the desire to kiss her. She turned to him, and he saw that she saw it, and he thought too, from her expression that she didn't mind; that she was enjoying the fact that he was attracted to her. This impression lasted only for an instant; she stepped backwards, away from him, and he restrained himself, afraid he might upset her.

He said, 'I'll pop up and see you before I go.'

'All right Tim, thanks, that would be nice.' She seemed to

have retreated now, was suddenly distant, preoccupied. He wondered if he had made a mistake, had misjudged her, but anyway, it was too late; the moment had passed. He said, almost as an afterthought, 'You don't think they mind, do you? Him running round loose with what he must have in his head?'

Katie looked at him, her lips slightly parted. She said, with a slight wildness in her voice, 'Who's they, Tim?'

'The authorities. In Russia. The . . . I don't know.'

She stared at him, aghast. He could see what she was thinking. He could see that he had worried her, had frightened her, more than she would admit. He wanted to unsay what he had said, but of course he couldn't. Katie turned towards the door, said 'Thank you, Tim, for the supper.' Tim didn't want to leave her but he knew he had to. As he went out he caught a glimpse of her standing in the middle of the room, burying her face in her hands.

8

'WELCOME to Libya.'

The Director of the Nuclear Research Centre at Tajura, Dr Abdul Masoud, was waiting for him on arrival. He held out his hand and shook Dmitry's, and they stood in the courtyard under the dazzling sun. Dmitry held up his hand to shield his eyes. The brightness of the sky above him was so intense it could hardly be called blue.

In the centre of the courtyard, surrounded by greenery, stood a huge sculpture of a metallic atom resting on top of a stone crescent. They stood in front of it and Masoud insisted on photographs being taken, despite Dmitry's protests. They walked over to the main building. Above the front entrance was a slogan in Arabic, saying, Masoud explained, 'The Revolution Forever.' On the wall, to one side, he saw a representation of the periodic table. He couldn't help reflecting that it was this table, a stroke of genius by his countryman and namesake, which had first aroused his interest in science and started him on the path that had lead to him studying nuclear physics. It was the beauty of nature's fundamental structure so logically ordered that had entranced him then, and fascinated him still.

Beyond the complex of buildings stood a high fence and a gate. A tank was parked by the gate; special forces with khaki-coloured berets prowled the entrance with their submachine guns and bayonets.

He was taken on a tour of the facilities. Masoud was clearly proud of everything they saw. The water was provided by a reverse osmosis desalination plant. The buildings had been built to withstand a sizable earthquake. He was taken round the reactor building – the 10-megawatt research reactor supplied by the Soviet Union. In the reactor hall he could see the seals, cameras and other equipment which showed the centre was under international safeguards and inspected regularly. The reactor ran on 80 per cent enriched U235 fuel rods, which is why, he was told, they were anxious to develop their own uranium enrichment programme rather than relying on supplies from Moscow. Dmitry noticed that the reactor was covered by a sliding steel protective slab, and that the casks of used radioactive material from the reactor bore IAEA seals.

Then they showed him round the research laboratories, computer rooms and library. Though he had known the facilities were good he was surprised at just how good, and at how much expensive Western equipment there was, computers and electronic equipment from Switzerland, and instrumentation from the US. It was more modern and far better equipped than the research institutes he'd worked in previously in Russia, places so secret they didn't even appear on maps. The normality of it all reassured him.

At the end of the afternoon, they showed him the café, the medical centre, and his quarters. They took him to his room and he sat there on the edge of the bed, exhausted and bewildered. He looked out of the window. The plant was surrounded by a high fence and a radiation protection zone which was thinly wooded, perhaps irrigated by the water from the desalination plant. He could see the trees stretching away far into the distance.

So here he was, imprisoned in his air-conditioned room, like an alchemist of old or a princess in a fairy tale locked in a tower and forced to spin the dull straw into gold. His room was a simple grey box, with a bed, a cupboard, a desk and chair, and a small bathroom. On the empty bookshelves were a copy of the Koran and Gaddafi's Green Book. Unlike the other buildings, this accommodation block seemed cheaply built, and nothing in the room was quite right; the desk rocked, the bed creaked, the door caught on the floor and closed only with difficulty, and the curtains did not quite cover the window.

The sun was sinking lower in the sky but its heat could still be felt through the window pane. Dmitry lay down on the bed, trying to overcome the lassitude which gripped him. He took off his shoes and they dropped on to the floor with a hollow thud. He stared up at the ceiling; there was a grey box on it, in which a red bulb dimly glowed. He wondered what it was; whether behind it there was a camera, looking down at him.

The thought disturbed him; abruptly he leapt to his feet. He showered, shaved, dressed, then went out and walked across the courtyard to the canteen.

◆

He slept surprisingly well. In the morning after he'd showered and shaved, taken his time over coffee and a roll, he walked along the corridors, past the emergency evacuation signs in both Russian and Arabic. His technician was already waiting for him in the lab and stood up when Dmitry came in.

'I've been waiting for you.'

'I'm sorry. Have you finished the inventory?'

'It's all here.'

The first few days would be spent in unpacking and checking all the equipment he'd requested. His technician, Djambul Suzarbayev, was an enthusiastic young man from Khazakstan, who had formerly worked at a uranium enrichment plant in Russia. He made a good impression on Dmitry; he seemed clever, and inventive. He was honest, too. He said straight away that he doubted Dmitry's project would work and made a joke of it. Suzarbayev told Dmitry that he was a Muslim, but if so he didn't seem to be a particularly devout one; he was also quick to laugh at the more bizarre aspects of the Libyan regime. He pointed out to Dmitry how much better it was working here than in Russia; at least here you got paid properly.

Dmitry ran through his proposal. The first step would be to check all his calculations on the computer; this he hoped would confirm that he had achieved a quite remarkable accuracy. Next they would have to construct the test cell and measure the degree of separation. If this was too low, they would have to find ways of improving on it. Thirdly, and this would be the trickiest bit, they would have to find ways of reliably isolating the fraction richest in U235 so that this could be pumped on to the next unit. Then they would need to construct a small cascade, perhaps of a dozen units, before proceeding to construction of any kind of facility. Dmitry thought it would take much more than two years.

He didn't intend to be around here for that long.

He felt that his mission was hopeless. There was nothing here that he had seen that the Russians wouldn't know about already. He did not see any foreign personnel. No one else spoke to him about what they did and the compound was tightly guarded. But he must try to do something to justify his trip.

Walking down the corridor, he passed a room on his right, where on the first day he had caught a glimpse of filing cabinets and piles of papers on shelves. On impulse he stopped and tried the door; it opened and he went in. There was no reason why he shouldn't, no one had told him not to. It was not locked, after all.

He looked through the files. Many of them were old, dating back to when Tajura was set up. He carried on for some time, sliding open the drawers, flipping through the files, looking for anything that might be of interest, anything that might not have been declared to the IAEA.

Something made him look up. On the wall, above the shelves, he saw an electronic eye or camera. It seemed to be looking straight at him. He casually replaced the file he was looking at, and left the room. A guard passed by him as he closed the door; Dmitry smiled at him but he did not respond.

He returned to the lab. He felt increasingly uneasy. Why had he done this? There was no point. Why should he put himself at risk in this way for Rozanov? He wasn't even likely to learn anything useful.

At the end of his trip, which was meant to be his first, Masoud looked in to see how he was doing. 'How is it going? Is there anything you need?'

Dmitry handed Masoud a list. He said, 'I want to begin with three units, slightly different in design, because I am not sure exactly . . . Here are the specifications.' He had thought, before he came here, that he would make errors in them, so that the equipment the Libyans ordered would be useless, because he assumed this was what Rozanov would have intended, but in practise he found he couldn't do this. It wasn't just because he thought that this was risky; it was also because he realised that he believed in his experiment and wanted it to work. He realised that he had entered into his role; that he was becoming what he feared.

'First, we need these cylinders to be material resistant to UF6, which may of course alert the manufacturers to their potential use . . . but they won't be able to make head nor tail of it. This bears no resemblance to a gas centrifuge. Also the fluorocarbon seals, then the vacuum pumps . . . all these things, as you know, are in the IAEA's trigger list, but I suppose you know how to get around it . . . well, you just put something else on the shipping documents and hope nobody is going to check anything.'

He looked at Masoud who did not react at all. He said, 'As for the UF6 itself . . . I gather you have a supply.'

'Absolutely. That is no problem.'

'And these tuning forks . . . they will have to be very precise

. . . well, no one will know what these are for. Perhaps you could say they are for some special musical instrument you need to extol the virtues of your leader.'

Masoud grinned. He took the papers and laughed. He said, 'This is excellent progress, wonderful . . . we have bought ourselves little short of a genius. You know, Farzad had some reservations, after he met you, but I think he was wrong . . . I think we are going to get on very well together, you and I.'

9

M OSCOW was hot, dusty, humid. Grey thunderclouds hung over the apartment blocks and distant cooling towers and near the entrance to the metro station rubbish blew about the streets. Everyone complained about the rubbish; this was new, ever since Yeltsin had decreed that street traders should be allowed to set up wherever they wished.

Tim had been met at the airport by Mike Harris. He was an old Moscow hand, had been in Moscow for the BBC in the fifties, been expelled and finally allowed to return last year. He was jaundiced and tired. He talked as he drove, about the disastrous state of the country. 'Don't you have any illusions about things getting better here, now communism's gone. The problems are just so huge, so enormous, they don't even know how to begin to solve them. Let me tell you right now; Russia is finished.'

They were driving round the ring road; huge rusty lorries thundered in both directions and at the side of the road, at every petrol station, were enormous queues. As they drove in to the centre Mike Harris pointed out the landmarks, and, near the office, the tall spire of the Hotel Ukraina looming out of the heat haze just across the river.

Mike told him what they had been able to set up so far and gave him a desk with a phone in the corner.

'How's your Russian?'

'Practically non-existent.'

'That's all right. We can provide you with an interpreter if you need it . . . Alya isn't in right now but she's at your disposal.'

Tim's first contact was the woman who had supervised the filming of the supposed dealer in highly enriched uranium. Her name was Larissa Sukhoruchkin and she now produced her own programme for Russian State television. She said that she was very busy but that she would meet him to talk about it further. She could see him that evening. She gave him her address near Taganyskaya metro but said that, since it was so difficult to find, she would meet him in the underground station, at the top of the escalators under the big dome. She said it was the exit on Zemlyana Val, but it wouldn't give this name on his map because, like many other streets in Moscow, it had been re-named.

Tim left the office with Mike at seven and they walked together to the metro station. Near the entrance snaked a long line of people selling things; cheap cigarettes, drink, sometimes displaying just one item, perhaps a bag of flour or a pair of shoes, offering anything they had for a bit of extra money. They passed a market being packed up; trays of tomatoes, potatoes, fruit. Tim said, 'There doesn't seem to be any shortage of food.'

'No, but the curious thing is, there are these stalls everywhere and you never see anyone buying anything. They say the stalls are controlled by the mafia and they keep the prices too high . . . I don't know why. Most people just can't afford it.' They had reached the entrance to the metro; Mike left him there. 'You go in to Park Kultury and change to the circle line. I'll see you later.'

Tim walked through the gates and the wind hit him, that and a peculiar smell he could not identify. The price of a token had just doubled, the third rise in a few months. A train was waiting and left at once; the metro, at least, was still efficient.

At Taganskaya three lines converged and he thought he would get lost. The dome, however, was unmistakable, huge and elaborately carved with a painting on a dark blue ground showing a red flag and fireworks. Little stalls clustered beneath it selling books and magazines. Someone took his elbow; he turned around.

Larissa was thin and pale with fair, crinkly hair cut short; she seemed nervous, but took hold of his arm with surprising force. 'You are Tim Finucan?'

He shook her hand. She looked at him, appraising him. She said, 'We can go to the Kosmos Hotel, if you like. That is where the man in question hangs out. Of course, because I was involved in the film . . . I'm not sure if I want to be seen there. But I've cut my hair . . . also I have some dark glasses.' She looked at him sideways as they started down the escalator. 'It might be dangerous, you see.'

Conversation on the metro was difficult because of the noise of the train, but Larissa told him a little of the background to the story. The dealer operated out of the Kosmos hotel, like a lot of the black marketeers, together with prostitutes and other members of Moscow's new low-life fraternity. Larissa was not sure that he actually had much of the material he was supposedly selling. She had a long list of substances he had offered for sale, including foetal material, and military equipment. Although the film which she had taken had been used on French television to illustrate a programme on the sale of nuclear materials she personally didn't think he was selling uranium at all, more likely Red Mercury. Had he heard about Red Mercury?

Tim said, 'Only vaguely. I was told it didn't exist.'

Larissa laughed. She said this was a headache for those who had been trying to follow the movement of nuclear materials after the Soviet Union had broken up. Across Europe there was a whole network of people – mostly criminals, in fact – offering this mysterious substance for sale at enormous prices, up to $300,000 per kilo. Red Mercury was said to be a highly explosive substance – chemically mercury antimony oxide – believed to be a vital ingredient in detonating certain types of Russian nuclear warheads. International bodies such as the IAEA were claiming it was useless and much of what had been offered on sale was useless too.

The problem was, said Larissa, that those who had so far been arrested for selling Red Mercury had also been trying to sell small quantities of uranium or plutonium.

Tim asked, 'But this guy who we're going to see, Grebishev . . . if they know who he is and what he's doing, why haven't they arrested him?'

Larissa looked at him, clearly uncertain whether he could really be naive enough to ask that question. She said, 'One possibility is because they are waiting to see if he will lead them to something bigger. I am sure they are watching him, of course. But also he is very powerful and he has many friends . . . Half the mafia are paying the police and as far as we know the KGB too . . . don't ask for anything to make sense here. Look, we get off now.'

Tim followed Larissa off the train. He wondered how he would manage to find his way without her. She let him draw level with her and went on talking. 'He is not, of course, the only one. I could give you other names . . . There are plenty of people who, if they could only lay their hand on the real stuff, would be quite willing to sell nuclear material into the hands of anyone who is able to pay for it.'

They came out of the metro beside a huge titanium obelisk, a monument to Soviet space flight. Larissa put on her glasses as she emerged into the open; she looked at Tim and said, 'What do you think? They are very stylish, they were very expensive, they are of Western make.' As they crossed the huge square, heading towards the vast semi-circular modern monolith that was the Kosmos Hotel, she pointed out a large gateway in white stone behind which lay pavilions, sculptures and statues to their left. 'That is the USSR Economic Achievements Exhibition,' she said, with that bitterness Tim was to hear so often. 'Well, since we have no economic achievements, maybe they are going to knock it down now.'

They entered the hotel lobby and Larissa led him through to one of the bars. It was dark and crowded and there was a dreadful band playing. Larissa said, 'Buy me a drink. I don't mind what I have. They only take dollars.' She went and sat down while he ordered two beers and carried them to the table. Larissa was putting on some bright red lipstick. With the lipstick, and the glasses, she looked quite different.

She smiled at him and sipped the beer. 'Don't look round, please,' she said. 'He's behind me. By the bar. He is balding, wearing a dark suit . . . there is a man next to him in a grey jacket.'

Tim said, 'I think I see him.'

Larissa leaned forward. 'He conducts his business here quite openly. Do you have the recorder? If you go up to the bar and get some more drinks you can record his conversation. Maybe there will be something interesting. You are English, so he'll think you can't understand anything . . .'

Tim got up, fiddling with the tape recorder in his pocket, switching it on. He went to the bar; you had to wait a long time to be served. He gave his order, trying to speak Russian, because he knew his Russian was so bad that nobody who had a better grasp of the language could imitate it. The bargirl repeated it in English. Grebeshev glanced at him, obviously thinking him of no consequence, and continued with his conversation.

The bar-girl came back. Tim, to prolong the exchange, ordered something else. She went away again. He stood, staring into space. Larissa, in the corner, didn't look round. She was clearly afraid of being spotted. Tim leaned on the bar. A blonde woman came up, eyed him, then looked at Grebeshev, who suddenly went off with his companion to another table.

When Tim sat down Larissa asked, 'Is that enough? Do you want to go?'

They finished their drinks quickly and left the hotel; Tim insisted on getting a taxi. In the back of the cab Tim got out the machine to check that it had recorded. Larissa took it from him and listened. She pulled a face, either at the poor quality of the recording or at what he was saying. He asked, 'What –' and she cut him off. 'It's very boring . . .' Then she held up her hand. 'Let me listen.'

As they drove along, the light from the street-lamps flickered across her face. The pale light seemed to emphasise the white skin and the high cheekbones, the lack of any spare flesh on her. She said, 'He is saying . . . he says he has the real thing. 25 kilos, 90 per cent enriched. He says he can prove where it came from, from Sarov, Arzamas 16 . . . then the other man asks what is the price. He says, there is no price, it's priceless, and he laughs.'

She started up the tape again . . . Tim could hear the laugh, the same laugh he had overheard at the bar. Larissa paused the tape again and turned to Tim. 'He says he is taking offers . . . he says, if your government is interested . . .'

'Then the man asks where the material is and he says, don't worry, it's quite safe. He asks if there are any guarantees . . . then I can't hear this, wait a minute . . .' she wound back the tape and listened again. Tim could hear his own voice ordering the drinks. She shook her head . . . then she went on. 'He asks how they get it out and he says, don't worry, there's no problem, you just drive it out in the boot of a car – now what's happening?'

The taxi had stopped. The driver got out; he opened the bonnet. Larissa sighed. She listened to the end of the tape and slipped the recorder in her bag. She said, 'That's it. You must have the luck of the devil, you hit gold the first time . . . I don't know if you can use it, it doesn't prove anything.'

Tim said, 'Who was the other guy? I should have looked at him more closely. Grebeshev said, "Your Government . . ."'

Larissa wound down the window and exchanged some words with the driver. She said, 'The idiot . . . he has run out of benzene.'

'Benzene?' Tim, not concentrating, was nonplussed for a moment. 'Oh, you mean petrol.'

'Yes, exactly. Petrol. Benzene. Come on, let's get out and go by metro . . . it's not so far away.'

Larissa left the taxi driver standing bewildered by his car and they walked down the side of the long avenue. Traffic roared past them; Larissa walked fast, determinedly. Tim said, 'But that can't be right . . . 25 kilos. That's enormous . . . that's more than enough to make a bomb.'

'Yes, of course . . . but that's how they operate. The other man asks for a sample and they can produce that. Then they take some money against the real thing and it doesn't materialise . . . but they've still done pretty well out of it.'

'Don't they ever get shot?'

'Yes, of course, several people have been shot. But Grebeshev must come up with something at least part of the time; otherwise he can't still be in business.'

Someone was walking along behind them, at a distance of about twenty feet. Tim glanced round, saw a youth in a bulky jacket. He suddenly felt very vulnerable, walking down the dark avenue, with long distances between the big buildings and nobody much in sight. He was relieved to leave the vast thoroughfare and plunge down into the warm depths of the metro.

At Taganskaya station Larissa paused as they were crossing one of the bridges over the track, resting her arm on the stone balustrade as she adjusted her shoe. From the bridge Tim could see over the tracks down to the end of the platform where, above the dark mouth of the tunnel, a digital display clocked up the number of minutes and seconds since the departure of the last train, a time which was seldom more than three minutes, and, in the rush hour, often only a minute. The clock stood at 1.23.

Then everything happened in an instant. He heard running footsteps behind them and turned to see a young man grab Larissa's bag and, with a fierce shove, propel her against and over the balustrade. Her body lay on top of it, her head flung back, her long white throat exposed; he saw her hands flailing; somehow he grabbed her; another woman by his side reached out and seized her arm. There was confusion, shouting, two or three people ran after the youth, others stood around while Tim helped Larissa back on to the bridge where she sat trembling on the floor. As she did the train roared into the station, an implacable mass of solid steel, rushing under the bridge beneath them and coming to a halt with a harsh, metallic scream.

Larissa sat with her head in her hands. The woman who had helped her stood, issuing a torrent of invective at whoever was listening; Tim could imagine what she was saying, how bad things were getting, how nobody was safe these days. After a minute or two Larissa got to her feet. She swore. She had lost her glasses; they must have fallen on to the track below. Fear gave way to anger; she was furious about the loss of her bag and everything that was in it; she said it would take days to get back some of the information and some names and numbers she might never get again.

Tim said, 'Come on. Let's not stay here.' He held her hand; it seemed quite natural. As they went up the escalator she said to him, 'That was not just anybody, you know that, don't you? They thought I had been taking more film . . . They were watching me, following me. They meant to stop me . . . It is just the same, we are still all afraid . . . first it was the KGB and now it is the mafia.'

There seemed a strangeness in the light as they glided up the escalator; perhaps the lights were dimmer than Tim expected, perhaps fear had also altered Tim's perceptions. Larissa was shaking. She said, 'Will you come with me back to the flat?' He said, 'Of course.' She looked at him and smiled. Perhaps she hadn't smiled at him before; he hadn't noticed that her upper lip came up very high, exposing the gum line, nor that her teeth, like those of so many Russians, were mottled grey and marked by poor diet and poor dentistry. It didn't make her any less attractive; perhaps it was just that he felt protective, but he suddenly wanted to kiss her.

They came out of the metro into the square and walked down the hill in the warm night. They turned off the main road and into the side streets. Two men were coming up the road behind them; Larissa didn't say anything but she glanced around once and Tim knew that she was frightened. They came into a square surrounded by old apartment blocks; in the centre stood a small white church. There were lights on inside it; Tim could hear, very faint on the night air, the eerie sound of high-pitched singing. His hair almost stood on end.

Tim said, 'Let's go inside.' Larissa nodded. She said, 'There's a service now on Wednesdays.' Surely, if someone was following them, they would be safe in a church. They entered by the door and stood at the back. A mass of candles gleamed in the darkness; the congregation, mostly old women with headscarves, stood dotted around; there were no chairs. Tim stood near the door, holding Larissa's arm, and no one came in after them.

The service seemed to be going on behind the highly decorated wall of icons; he heard a priest chanting in a deep bass voice, and occasionally a chorus of high, ethereal voices. The singers were not good, there was a roughness in their voices, but it seemed overpoweringly mysterious and exotic all the same. Tim looked at Larissa, but she pulled a face; she clearly wasn't moved at all. The women crossed themselves; the singing reached a crescendo and the gold doors opened and a priest in white popped out, carrying something on a plate.

Larissa whispered, firmly, 'Let's go. There's a door on the other side.' They walked across the courtyard, past a group of youths smoking, down some steps and into a dismal entrance. Battered mailboxes lined the wall inside the doorway and the stairwell was filled with rubbish. Garlicky smells from a restaurant next door hung heavily in the air.

They went upstairs. Larissa's flat was on the fourth floor; a huge, reinforced door yielded to a sequence of locks. Inside, she banged the door shut with relief. They were in a different world. The flat had bare, polished wood floors, walls of glass shelves, a large table of bleached wood and a modern, open plan kitchen. Tim walked round and stared admiringly.

'We've just moved in,' said Larissa. 'Are you hungry? I'm sorry about your tape. I should have put it in your pocket.'

'Yes,' said Tim, who had been thinking the same thing, 'I know.'

'Do you want something to drink? Coffee? Tea? A glass of wine?'

'Wine would be very nice.'

'My husband is back later,' said Larissa, pouring him a glass of red Georgian wine. 'He's in Nizhny Novgorod, you know, used to be Gorky.' She sat opposite him. She said, 'I'm sorry, I am really frightened. These people mean it, they're not just playing games. I can't help you any more, it's too dangerous for me, I don't think I can see you again. But if there's anything you want to know, if I can help at all, please ring me at work.'

◆

In the morning Alya from the Channel 4 office rang to say that she had managed to arrange an interview with Gennady Federov, the scientist whose name had been quoted in a small paragraph in *The Times* in London. They were to meet at eleven. She said that she would meet Tim at the metro at Park Kultury at ten and they would go from there.

The address he had been given, like most Moscow addresses, he was to discover, wasn't easy to find. They went first to the Kurchatov Institute, past the big iron gates and the bronze bust of Igor Kurchatov standing on a patch of straggly grass outside. Down a side-street they found one of the apartment blocks used by staff from the Institute, and, unmarked by any sign or visible number, a white door. Tim pushed it open and they found themselves in a corridor piled high with books, packing cases and stacks of papers. They were shown by a secretary into a room and offered tea. It was mint tea, from mint grown in her grandmother's garden, she explained, and Alya translated. They sipped it in delicate china cups and waited for Federov to arrive.

'Actually it's rather rude of him,' said Alya, tapping her watch, 'He is rather late.' She glanced around her. Tim tilted his head sideways, trying to read the spines on the covers of the books, which mostly seemed to be works by Marx and Engels. He asked, 'What is this place?'

'It was the Communist Party library,' said Alya. 'Now they are clearing it all out and throwing it away.'

A young man appeared suddenly in the doorway and stared at them. He had dark, untidy hair, was scruffily dressed, and slightly plump with a pale, unhealthy-looking complexion. There was a pause, in which no one quite knew how to proceed; Tim had expected someone older, but Alya asked a quick question and then said, 'This is him.' Tim shook hands. Federov nodded and did not look him in the eyes; he gestured for them to sit down at the table.

'So,' said Federov, with obvious irony, 'Another Western journalist.' Alya translated. The conversation went backwards and forwards between them, very slowly, very stilted. Tim explained what he wanted. Federov sat, expressionless, then nodded and began to talk. Tim asked: 'I saw you were quoted, in a London paper, saying that two of your colleagues were approached by the Libyans.'

'Yes, this is true . . .'

'How?'

He looked blank. Tim said, impatient, to Alya, 'Ask him; by letter, by telephone . . .'

'On the international circuit, at conferences . . . I heard this from them personally.'

'What were they being offered? What was their area of expertise?'

'They were experts in reactor design.'

'Can you give me their names?'

'I would not like to give their names.'

'And they said no.'

'Yes, of course . . . for the moment. But consider the situation for most of us here, with prices rising, and problems in getting the equipment needed to do their work. Actually, I did them a favour, because after these reports appeared our salaries were increased from 1500 roubles a month to 4000, so it was quite good for us I think . . . even though we can't of course manage on 4000.'

'Would you be prepared to appear, on Western television, saying this?'

Federov looked uncomfortable. He spread out his plump, pale hands somewhat helplessly and said, 'I would rather not.'

'And you don't know if any others have been approached?'

'No. I believe there have been others.'

'I have been given various names of scientists who I might be able to contact . . . for instance, Vassily Kunitsin . . .'

'He is working here. I don't know anything about it. You could ring him.'

Tim glanced at Alya. He could see that she, like him, realised there wasn't much point in prolonging the interview – Federov was not what he wanted. He asked, as a final question, out of curiosity, 'There's someone else I wanted to contact in Moscow . . . he used to work here. Dmitry Gavrilov.'

Federov frowned. 'He is not working here now. He went to the IAEA in Vienna.'

'Yes, but he's left there now. I was told he was in Moscow.'

'I don't know then.'

'But you knew him? Did he . . .' Tim didn't know quite how to put this . . . 'Have a good reputation?'

Federov became a little more talkative. 'Oh, yes, well I knew Mitya Gavrilov a little, I would recognise him if I met him again . . . he was very conscientious, hard-working, came to the party meetings, didn't say very much. I don't think he was very happy.' Federov smiled for the first time in the whole interview. 'I believe he had awful trouble with his wife.'

'What kind of trouble?'

Alya, not understanding the reasons for his digression, translated the question, eyebrows raised. Federov shrugged. Then he said, 'Mind you, he has a sister . . . I met his sister once. She is a paediatrician. She works in a clinic somewhere in the north, near Babushkinskaya I think. She would know where he is.' He got up, glanced at his watch, indicating that enough of his time had been wasted.

As he and Alya walked out along the red corridor, past a room where a massive marble bust of Lenin sat disconsolately in a corner, Alya said, 'So he didn't give you any names. Well, either he was not being level with you, or he has not been reading the papers, because their names were published in *Izvestia* only this morning.'

10

'THEY won't give any interviews.' Alya put the piece of paper with the scientists' names on Tim's desk.

'You've spoken to them both?'

'To Petrovsky, yes, and he says no. And the other one, his assistant said he won't talk to the press. I'm sorry. They are very sensitive.'

'They didn't ask for money? Did you offer any?' It was becoming the thing these days for people to ask Western journalists for hard currency when granting interviews.

'They didn't ask and I didn't offer. I think that would have made it even worse.'

Tim sighed. He said, 'Alya, there's one last thing; I wanted to get in touch with Dr Gavrilova. Could you phone for me and see if you could make an appointment?'

◆

The hospital was, as Tim had expected, a miserable place, a monolithic slab of concrete on a wide boulevard in the northern suburbs. Worn lino covered the floor and the air smelt of what seemed to be a mixture of disinfectant and urine. At the reception he had the greatest difficulty making himself understood; he thought, I should have brought Alya with me. He was told to go upstairs and sat on a bench in the corridor for perhaps half an hour. Nobody came. A woman was wheeled past on a trolley, still wearing a thin blue summer dress, blood trickling between her thighs.

Tim got to his feet, found a nurse and discovered he was on the wrong floor. He was taken downstairs and again sat for a long time outside an office. Outside the window tall trees heavily in leaf obscured the view and cast a dingy greenness over everything. A woman carrying a sick-looking child came and sat beside him; the child started to cry, then began to cough, a deep, unhealthy sound. Tim turned his head away.

The door opposite opened and another woman and child came out, and behind them a woman in a white coat who he knew at once to be Dr Gavrilova. She was very tall, thin and angular, had soft, fair hair pulled back from her face in a kind of bun. She had the same high brow and broad mouth as her brother, but her features were much finer and her nose was flat, almost oriental. Her skin was very pale, even paler in this grey-green light, and she looked tired and harassed, but in spite of this she was a striking-looking woman.

She looked at the woman with the child and then at Tim. She said, in slightly halting English, to Tim, 'I understand you wanted to talk to me. You are a journalist from London? You want to make an interview?'

'Yes. But that's not why I'm here . . . I'm a friend . . . I live in the flat underneath your brother's.'

'Ah.' Her face lightened; her eyes shone for a moment. 'You have brought me something from Mitya? A letter . . .'

'No . . .'

'Come in . . . Sit down.' She said something to the woman in Russian who nodded resignedly and Tim felt the briefest pang of guilt, knowing that she was going to have to sit there and wait because of him. He followed Dr Gavrilova into her office and sat on a chair. The room was stark and bare, with a few tired-looking posters on the walls; light filtering through the trees flickered on the dusty walls. She sat and looked at him, eager, expectant.

Tim said, 'Actually, he's not in London at the moment, he's over here; I was hoping you would be able to put me in touch with him.'

'Mitya? Over here?' she frowned, puzzled. 'When did he come? I didn't know . . . he has just arrived, perhaps?'

Tim said, 'Two weeks ago.'

'I see.' She looked down at the file she was holding in her hands; a lock of fair hair broke away from the bun and fell in front of her face. He sensed her puzzlement, her disappointment. He began to feel more than unkind. He went on, 'So he hasn't contacted you?'

'Me? No, no he has not . . .'

They looked at one another. There was an uncomfortable silence. She asked, 'You are here on business? You are writing about Russia?'

'I'm making a television programme.'

'On health?'

'No, not on health . . .'

She looked at him for a long moment, as if trying to work him out. 'Look, I would like to talk to you, but this is not the place. I have people waiting . . . perhaps we can meet later. If you are a friend of Mitya's, I would like to invite you to my apartment . . . Please ring me later, this is my home number. Excuse me, I must see my patient now.'

◆

In the morning Tim heard that they had secured an interview with General Berov, Chief of the 12th Main Directorate, the defence Ministry responsible for the transportation and storage of nuclear warheads.

General Berov stared at them from over his imposing desk. He was in his fifties, grey-haired, a solid tank of a man. Perhaps he didn't always wear his full military regalia, had just done so for the cameras. He wore a grey shirt and tie under a grey military jacket with gold leaves on the collar, gold stars on the shoulder and a pocket thickly embroidered with medals. The interpreter was going through the questions with him.

It went exactly as Tim would have expected. Berov leaned across the desk, his heavy hands folded, cleared his throat, and began: 'All nuclear weapons of the former USSR are under centralised control. There is complete safety. It is the same as before; there is no danger.'

Tim asked whether any of the reports of uranium and other nuclear material being smuggled into the West had caused alarm for those in charge of nuclear weapons.

'Of course we are concerned, but no military material has been involved. There has been no weapons grade uranium nor any quantity of plutonium. You need a minimum of 15–25 kilograms of weapons grade uranium or 5–10 kilograms of plutonium to make an atomic bomb. The quantities which have been procured are just a few grams, perhaps from universities, from research establishments where there is no tight security. Security in all military installations is very strict and there is strict inventory control . . . any loss or theft of nuclear material could not go undetected.'

Tim asked, 'What about the possibility of warheads themselves being stolen?'

Berov smiled. 'Again, this is absolutely impossible. To begin with, bombs are fitted with safety triggers that disarm or destroy them if they are detached from the launch system. All warheads are under the tightest security.'

Tim went on, 'But we have heard that the pace of nuclear disarmament has caused a problem in the dismantling and storage of nuclear warheads . . . That storage sites are filled to capacity . . .'

'This is not a problem. We have plenty of storage sites.'

And so it went on. They filmed for twenty minutes, but probably would only use two short clips. As they set up the cutaways of Tim to film at the end, he could see the translator joking with Berov. He laughed, shrugged, made expressive gestures with his hands; Tim doubted that the man believed a word of what he'd said.

When they'd finished Mike Harris came up to him, looking gloomy and waving a sheet of paper. 'By the way, if you were hoping to get a look at some military installations, you can forget it. We'll have to use that tired old footage of the missile silos . . . Look at this . . . the Western press has just been issued with a new directive that no journalists are allowed to visit any military sites. Well . . . how about a drink?'

◆

Tim stood in the centre of the bare hall in Lubyanka metro with the crowds rushing past him. He had arranged to meet Olga Gavrilova and go back to her apartment. It was ten past seven; he began to get agitated, fearing he would miss her or that she wouldn't come. Another train rushed in, the third or fourth he had watched. Then he saw her, walking towards him; she looked cool and attractive in a white top and trousers.

Tim said, 'Well, this is a funny place to meet . . . one can't help thinking of the KGB upstairs . . . what do they call themselves these days?'

Olga looked at him, amused. 'Oh, they have some new name and they published it in the papers, but nobody can remember it so we just go on calling them KGB.'

They took the train heading north-east. It was too noisy to talk on the train but once they were out in the fresh air she began to explain about herself.

'I am divorced from my husband,' she said. 'I have two boys, but they are in the country with my mother-in-law. It is much easier living there, especially in the summer. We have so many problems here, now there is the problem of crime, and of course my salary buys less and less. I envy Mitya living in the West . . .' she looked at him sideways, obliquely, almost furtive. 'What about you, Tim? Are you married?'

Tim was somewhat disconcerted by this directness. 'No,' he said, 'No, I never have been.'

'Perhaps you are too handsome; probably you have had too much choice,' said Olga. Tim, not knowing how to reply to this, fell silent. They walked two or three blocks to the apartment building, surrounded by tall trees through which the wind was streaming. At first he thought it was snowing, despite the warmth; then he realised it was seeds from the poplars which drifted through the air and covered the ground in white. Olga wrinkled up her nose. '*Pukh*,' she said, 'What do you call it, fluff? It causes many children to have bad asthma.' They trudged up six flights of stairs in the dank, ill-lit interior; as Olga slipped the key into the lock, both of them were out of breath.

She brought them drinks, blackcurrant syrup which she had made in the country, a glass of wine each, and plates with open sandwiches of red caviar and ham with salad. The glasses were tall, of coloured glass, and the plates had once been fine with gilded edges but were now old and faded. She opened a box of delicate Russian cakes. Realising the cost and effort that must have gone into procuring this, he was more than grateful.

Tim helped himself, and she watched him. He had a curious sensation, a feeling of unease, as if he were under observation, as if she was not used to being with a Westerner and wondered what he would do. He thought for a few minutes that she was not going to eat at all, and this made him uncomfortable, but after a while she reached out and took a sandwich. He noticed her hands, sensitive, but strong, capable of being both sensual and cruel; definitely a doctor's hands, he thought.

Tim asked, 'Is it very surprising then that you haven't heard from your brother?'

Olga sighed. She said, 'Well, you see, I have to explain first that there was this problem between us . . . my husband and he, they did not get on at all. By the time we were divorced Mitya and I had not seen much of one another for some years . . . and then, he was living abroad.'

She was pensive for a moment. She said, 'Well, it is very sad. Mitya and I, our relationship was very . . . special. Because we had a difficult childhood, you know, with our father dying so young and mother ill, we were like this – ' As she said this, she clenched her hands together with the fingers intertwined. 'We did everything together, as children . . . he was always in trouble, but I forgave him everything, even this.' She pointed to her nose, to the flat bridge. 'He made it like this. I was hiding under the bed, and he jumped on it, and it broke, and my nose, too, was broken . . . well.' She shrugged. 'He was my older brother, he was so clever, and he always looked after me, protected me . . . I adored him. So you see, it hurts me so much now that I know so little of his life . . .'

It was hot and stuffy in the room; Olga perhaps noticed this as well, for she stood up and went to the window to open it. At once the sound of the wind in the trees and the distant sounds of children playing entered the room. She came back and sat down again opposite him. 'Well, you asked me a question. Although there have been difficulties between us, it would not be like him to spend time in Moscow and not see me. So, I don't believe that he is in Moscow. Maybe he is somewhere else in Russia, but then I would expect him at least to phone me . . . and you see, there are also my boys. He would love to see the boys. Did he tell you exactly what it was he was doing here?'

'His wife said he was looking into his finances and also attending some meeting to do with de-enriching uranium . . . you know, re-converting material from redundant warheads or something.'

'He was coming here to work?' Olga seemed surprised.

'His wife told me he was just trying to find out about it.'

Olga frowned. She said, 'I see. Well, I can make some enquiries. I can ask some people . . . maybe somebody will know something. I can ask an old friend of Mitya's, he may know . . .' She looked up and then said, directly, 'So you have met his wife?'

'Yes.'

'Is she . . . sympathetic? She is a nice woman?'

'Yes . . . yes, very nice.'

'He was married before you know . . . his first wife, what a disaster, she was no good for him . . . you think he is happy with

. . . it's Katie, isn't it?' She hesitated, uncertain of the pronunciation.

'Yes, that's right . . . well, in as far as one can tell . . .' Tim didn't know what to say. He felt awkward; her slightly naive questions, which would have been put more delicately if she had a better grasp of English, were too direct to evade easily.

'And the baby? Little Sasha? I would love to see him. I have a photograph . . . he looks like Mitya, I think. Please, help yourself.' She picked up one of the glasses of wine and drank. 'So, Mitya is over here and you are trying to get hold of him. Why?'

'I am doing some research . . . about the dangers of nuclear proliferation . . .'

'Oh, that.' She seemed not at all interested. 'Do you not have some number to ring him?'

'His wife gave me a number, but nobody replies. Here . . .' and he pulled out his notebook with the scrap of paper in it.

'Let me see.' Gavrilova took the paper and then jotted down the number. She said, 'Maybe I will try. Where are you staying? Can I contact you? Perhaps, if you have time to do some sightseeing, I can show you some of Moscow, maybe at the weekend?'

◆

She rang the following night.

'Is that Tim?'

'Yes, it is.' He liked the way she said Tim, with the long, liquid Russian 'i'.

'It's Olga. Listen, I talked to Galya Petrovsky from the Kurchatov Institute and he will see you. He says that if you ring him he will arrange it. You will need to take an interpreter because he says his English is very bad.'

Tim said, amazed, 'But this is one of the people I wanted to talk to.'

'Very good. I have not seen him for some time, but he said he would see you, as a favour to me, as long as you are not going to misquote him.'

◆

Books and papers lined Galya Petrovsky's small study. On the desk in pride of place stood a small personal computer, something he was extremely fortunate to have, he said, showing it to Tim with considerable pride. Petrovsky's hair was thick and greying, and there was a slight tremor in his hands and voice as if he had aged before his time or had endured some illness or trauma. He said, 'Sit down.' There was only a tiny space on an armchair in which to sit and Alya sat there. Tim perched himself on a corner of the desk.

Petrovsky looked at them both. 'I knew Mitya Gavrilov some years ago, when he was at the Kurchatov Institute, not very well, but I know his sister and her family, so I agreed . . . well. What is it exactly that you want to know?'

Tim explained, through Alya. Petrovsky nodded. He said, 'I was approached by the Libyans at a conference in Helsinki at the beginning of this year. They asked me if I would be interested in working for them at a salary of $2,000 a month.'

'What did you say?'

Petrovsky smiled. 'Of course, I said no.'

'Why?'

Petrovsky sighed. He said, 'Let me explain. As you know, in the past there was only one way we could go abroad, on an official visit. We at the Kurchatov Institute have been very privileged, we could travel abroad, and therefore we have many contacts in other countries which now some scientists are trying to exploit.

'Now, with the new political situation, there are new ways of travelling, working in such places, officially . . . plenty of Russian scientists have worked in Libya. The Kurchatov Institute helps to get permission to go . . . its something like an agreement between the scientist and the Institute making the journey abroad possible and then the scientist can return to work here.'

Petrovsky paused to offer Tim a cheap Russian cigarette; Tim declined. Petrovsky lit up, puffed out a dense cloud of smoke which filled the tiny room, and continued. 'Now of course this is not a problem with some kinds of work, but here at the Institute there are still areas of secret work which might be another problem entirely. Nowadays of course its possible to go abroad on your own, at your own risk . . . I don't know what the attitude of the secret services would be to this. I wouldn't like to try myself. And besides . . . things are not so bad here as people say, and I believe, not immediately, but in a year or two, they will get a little better.'

'Would you be prepared to talk to me about this for British television?'

Petrovsky thought for a few moments. Then he said, 'If you do it with the back of my head so I am not facing the camera and don't give my name . . . then, OK, I will do it.'

Tim smiled. 'That's great . . . we can also disguise your voice so it can't be recognised.' He sat back in his chair. He asked, 'Your position is clear enough, but what about others . . . do you think they will be tempted?'

Petrovsky smiled; for all his former reluctance, now that Tim was there, he seemed eager to please. He said, 'Oh, I imagine . . . there will be a few. The foolish ones, perhaps, who can't foresee the consequences.'

'What consequences?'

'Well . . . you can imagine no one is very keen on their going. For example, KGB . . . this is a big concern of theirs.'

'Have the KGB been in touch with you about this offer?'

'Of course.'

Tim was silent; Petrovsky did not elaborate. He stubbed out his cigarette and looked at Tim, hesitated, as if not sure whether to say something or not. 'I understand,' said Petrovsky, suddenly leaning forward, 'That you wanted to get hold of Olya's brother, who is meant to be in Moscow. She said you told her he was going to work on some new programme of uranium de-enrichment. Well, that sounded odd to me, so I have made enquiries, and indeed there is this project, but I can assure you he is not working on it, and the man in charge there has not spoken to him. I haven't said this to Olya, and I think it might be wise if you didn't tell her, because there is something else about this which I don't like.

'The man who approached me, in Helsinki, the Libyan scientist, he had a list. He showed it to me and asked me if I knew any of the people on it and where he could contact them . . . I asked one or two and they said they were indeed approached but none of them have gone along with it. I told this to the KGB when they asked me what had happened.'

Alya translated, quickly, in a low voice, as if she too was suddenly caught up in the tension; as if she too expected something startling.

'There was one thing I didn't tell them, because I have a soft spot for Olya, and I know she idolises her brother . . .' Petrovsky paused to light another cigarette; he did this slowly, because of the tremor in his hands. Tim held his breath; he thought he could see what was coming, but couldn't quite believe that it was true.

Petrovsky inhaled deeply and let his breath out with a long sigh.

'One of them was Mitya Gavrilov.'

◆

It was Sunday, the dead day for a journalist abroad, when nothing could be accomplished. Tim lay in bed till late, thinking through the implications of his discovery. Why sampling the sights of Moscow did not inspire him he couldn't say; he had never enjoyed tourism. Lazily he picked up the phone and slowly dialled Olga's number. The phone rang seven, eight times . . . he thought with disappointment that she must have gone to the country or that he'd left it too late and she had already gone out.

She picked up the phone; she sounded breathless. For an instant he wondered if there was someone there with her.

'Tim!' she exclaimed. She sounded delighted, as if he were an old friend.

'I wondered if you meant it. About sightseeing today.'

'Yes, of course. I will meet you. What do you want to see?'

'Oh the usual things. Red Square, St Basil's, the Kremlin, Lenin's tomb . . . is that too boring for you?'

She laughed. 'No, I would enjoy it.'

They met by the kiosk which sold tickets to St Basil's. Olga led him into the dusty, dry interior. She explained that had been made a museum in 1928, and consisted of seven separate churches built around a central one. He had imagined it as splendid inside, with high ceilings and large spaces; had not expected the tiny rooms, the rabbit warren of little labyrinthine passages, the aura of decay. Despite the beautiful painted walls the place had a dark, primitive feel about it, an unholy feel, somehow.

Olga bought him a little painted egg at the exit and dropped it into his hand. It was a typical Russian gesture of generosity; he would have liked to buy her something, but he had been afraid she would misinterpret it. He said, 'No, really, you shouldn't have,' but she simply smiled, amused, and turned her head away from him. There was something imperious about her; she wrong-footed him. She wanted to keep the upper hand; she wanted it to be her who was in control, who set the tone.

They walked down the steps and into the bright sunlight. Suddenly she seemed playful. She said he must be a proper tourist and made him pose with her for a photograph in front of the cathedral and queue up for Lenin's tomb.

The long queue moved rapidly. In less than ten minutes they were at the entrance, walking in under the blank eyes of the young soldiers. He wondered why people were going; perhaps, like him, just out of curiosity, to see the man before he was removed and buried in some obscure place. They filed through the cold, black marble mausoleum in silence, past the body or the effigy, whatever it was. Tim thought, well, I've seen him. They went out again into the sunlight.

'I came once before, with Mitya, when we were children,' said

Olga. 'I asked my mother, why is he so small?' and everyone turned and said, 'Shhhh!' Mitya was very frightened, I remember, in case they took me away.'

As they crossed the huge expanse of Red Square, Tim asked, 'Did it bother you? His work? You chose to do something very different.'

'No. Why should it bother me? So many people work in the nuclear industry or in the military towns, it is normal. I respect his decision. It was a good career for him, until . . .' she paused. In front of them, a large lorry lurched to a halt and men started to unload crates of Coca-Cola and lemonade, selling them to passers-by. Tim wished that he had brought his camera. Olga looked at him and smiled. Then she shrugged, as if to say, well, this is what it has all come to, Coco-Cola for sale in Red Square.

'Until?' Tim prompted, trying to bring her back to the conversation.

'Until he went to England,' she said, simply.

His guidebook told him there were three cathedrals, two churches and a museum inside the Kremlin and that afternoon they saw them all. They took it slowly, walked and sat in magnificent splendour under the gilded onion domes, and hardly spoke to one another. A sober mood seemed to have come over Olga. When they left he said he would like to invite her for a meal but she said it was too expensive. He tried to insist but she would not be moved. She said with a laugh that they could go to Mac-Donald's and Tim said he hadn't come to Moscow to go to Mac-Donald's.

Then she asked him to go back with her for supper in her apartment. She asked it almost shyly, and then added, quickly, 'Or maybe you have better things to do.' Tim said, 'No, of course not, I would love to . . .' and then he said, perhaps a little rashly, 'You fascinate me.'

He was afraid for a moment that she would think better of her invitation; she looked slightly shocked. Then she laughed. She said, 'Please, Tim, it's not wise to say things like this.'

'Why not?'

'Because . . .' she hesitated. Then she said, 'Anyway, I will take no notice . . . I have been warned about Western men.'

Olga said she needed to buy some eggs. They went to several shops, all a great distance apart, but there was something wrong in each of them; there were no eggs, or the queues were too long, or the eggs were too expensive. It was hot and dirty, the wind blew dust in their faces, all the distances were vast; Olga was irritated, and Tim began to feel oppressed. He said that if she liked he could buy eggs in a hard currency shop to save them time but she dismissed this and he could see that he had offended her.

Finally she gave up and said they would have something else.

They took the metro to Preobazhensky Ploschad. Olga sat with her eyes closed, her hair coming loose, her face looking lined and tired; but her white shirt still seemed miraculously as clean and neat as when they had met that morning. In her apartment she told him to make himself comfortable and he sat on the sofa with his feet up while she cooked some pancakes filled with vegetables which were delicious.

They ate and drank some wine. They didn't say much, but she looked at him often and smiled. It was a knowing kind of smile, and Tim felt utterly confused. He couldn't make Olga out, received such contradictory signals from her, was aware that he half expected to end up in bed with her and wanted to very much. What was he doing? He sat on the sofa, alongside Olga, and felt this almost conspiratorial rapport with her. How could he feel so attracted to her, when half the reason for doing this, half his desire to prove his suspicions about Gavrilov were right and to expose him, was to win over Katie? He felt as if somehow Gavrilov was exerting some extraordinary influence on him, and that here he was, doubly, trebly betraying him, seeking not only to uncover him but also to seduce first his wife, and then his sister.

Tim said, 'It's very odd about your brother. He couldn't be working on something military, could he? Something secret?'

'Mitya would never work for the military. Anyway, he has been in the West, he is suspect. They would not employ him.'

'Isn't there some way you could check if he is here?'

'He's not here. I have rung several friends . . . he hasn't contacted them. You said he wanted to make some arrangements for his finances so I rang the bank where his money is deposited, and I asked if they had contacted him recently; you know, this is not difficult, because they know I am his sister and I also had some small amount of money in this bank. He has not been in touch with them.'

Olga went on, in a quiet, efficient voice. 'This number you gave me, it's a message service. I left a message and no one rang back. So then I rang the message service to ask if they are taking messages for my brother and they said no, they haven't heard of him.'

Tim said, 'I don't understand.'

'Are you sure his wife told you he was here? You didn't make a mistake?'

Tim said, 'His wife saw him off on the flight to Moscow two weeks ago . . . He told his wife exactly what I told you, there can't be any mistake about that. Why would he lie about it, do you think?'

Olga put down her glass. She seemed distant now, untouchable. She looked at him coldly. 'There is something behind all this, isn't there? That's why you came to see me. You are making some kind of investigation into my brother.'

Tim tried to backtrack, but sensed it was too late. 'I knew your brother was a nuclear scientist and I thought he might be able to help me, give me some contacts . . . I told his wife I'd look him up. I promise you . . . that's all.'

'No, that isn't all. I have been very stupid.' She sounded alarmed, frightened, almost. 'I don't like it that you are here, asking me such questions. Tim, I trusted you because I thought you were a friend of his but now I see that it is not like that at all.'

She was almost panicky. She pushed at her hair with jerky movements, glanced nervously about, then got to her feet and walked across the room, her arms folded across her chest. She said, 'I am sorry . . . I think you had better go.'

Tim could see that there was no point in staying; he picked up his jacket and went to the door, but his feelings of regret were so strong that they made him turn back. He began, 'I'm sorry. You have got it wrong . . .'

'No. I don't think that I have got it wrong.' He saw a tear glint in her eye. 'Please, don't ring me again, don't try to see me, it is finished.' She came towards him and abruptly shut the door. He stood on the dark hallway, where the walls were painted a deep smudgy, blue, and felt a chill pass through him. He was more and more certain that he was right about Gavrilov but at the same time he felt uncomfortable about what he was doing. He realised that he was going to hurt people, people that he liked; he couldn't work out for a moment whether he was using them, exploiting them, or whether, in the end, they, like everyone else, had a right to know the truth. This was all right in theory, but when he thought of Olga, the hurt look in her face and her broken illusions about her brother, and then of Katie's reaction when he told her, he wondered if it was worth it.

11

KATIE sat by the window, reading. She looked weary, her head bowed over her book. In the evening light which filtered through the grimy glass her face looked pale and unlovely.

Tim stood in the doorway, watching her. She'd left the door ajar and he'd walked in without her knowing. The room was full of drying washing; the plates had not been cleared away after the evening meal, and there were children's toys scattered all over the floor. Tim felt uncomfortable, wondering what to tell her, and how to tell her. He knocked on the door and she looked up with a nervous start, relaxing when she saw that it was him.

She stood up and walked to the fridge. 'Hello, Tim. Do you want a glass of wine?'

'If you're having one.'

She poured the wine out and handed him the glass. 'How was Moscow, then, Tim? How did it go? Did you see Mitya?'

Tim circled the room, tensely. 'No, I didn't see your husband, but I did meet his sister, Olga. She was quite helpful, in fact.'

'Oh, yes, what was she like?' Katie's face became animated, seemed curious; she had told him she had never been to Russia, never met any of Dmitry's family. Tim produced the photograph of them in front of St Basil's. They stood close together; Olga, tall and smiling, had her head on one side, grinning at the camera.

Tim said, 'She was great. I liked her a lot.'

'And her children?'

'They were in the country. Look, Katie, she said . . .' He paused, as if uncertain how to put this: 'She said she hadn't heard from Mitya at all and she was very surprised to hear he was in Russia.'

Katie didn't react to this at first; she sat on the sofa and looked at him blankly. 'But you tried to contact him?'

'Yes, but the truth is, Katie, it's rather odd. I couldn't find anyone who knew where he was . . . I rang the number you gave me but it wasn't anywhere . . . it seemed to be just a message service. I left various messages and so did his sister but no one ever called back.'

'I see.'

'Are you worried?'

'Worried? No, not really . . . He's called me, twice. He didn't talk for long, its expensive . . . but he said everything was going well.'

Tim sat down opposite Katie and pulled the chair in closer to her. 'Katie, his sister phoned several of his friends and they said they hadn't heard from him. I also asked about this meeting you mentioned and it seems something like that exists but no one had heard about your husband having anything to do with it . . .'

Katie was defensive. 'Look, I didn't want you to make a big thing out of it . . .'

'I'm sorry, I didn't want to worry you . . . I'm just telling you why I couldn't contact him.'

Katie abruptly turned away from him. 'Look, it's not important. Thanks for trying, Tim, anyway. I expect he'll call me later.'

She clearly expected him to go; Tim gulped down the wine. He said, 'Well, let me know if you need anything. I'll let you know when my report's going out.'

◆

Katie sat up in the chair, biting her fingernails, waiting for Dmitry to ring as he had promised. Tiredness came over her in waves, and her body ached as if she had flu, her neck was stiff, and her eyes felt hot and dry as if she had a fever. She was angry that he should call late, depriving her of sleep. It was all very well for him, she thought, he could come and go as he pleased, not telling her anything, while she was stuck here with the mindless boredom of nappies and housework and walking back and forth from school; in fact she doubted if she'd had more than an hour on her own since Sasha was born.

The phone rang and she answered at once. It was Jenny, asking if she and Anna wanted to go over for tea after school the next day.

'Yes, that might be nice . . . but I'm sorry, I can't talk now, I'm expecting an urgent phone call.'

Jenny apologised and hung up at once; Katie hoped she'd not been rude. She thought that Tim had probably got things wrong, but all the same, she was anxious, she needed the reassurance of the expected phone call, and was afraid that if the line was engaged he wouldn't call back. As time went by, and he didn't phone, she couldn't help worrying; it must be midnight in Moscow by now. She paced up and down, and when at half past nine the phone rang Katie snatched it up; Dmitry's voice came over clearly, and relief flooded through her so strongly that she had to sit down. He asked, matter-of-fact, 'How are you? Are the children in bed?'

'I'm all right. We're all fine. Where are you?'

There was the slightest pause, and then he said. 'Where I said I'd be.'

Katie said, 'But you're not in Moscow.'

'No, I'm not in Moscow, at the moment . . . what is this?'

'Well, where are you? Why can't anyone get hold of you?'

'I'm sorry . . . I am calling you now. You sound upset. Is anything the matter?'

'No, but it could be the matter. Supposing I needed you urgently and I couldn't get hold of you? I want to know exactly where you are and what you're doing. Nobody seems to be able to get in touch with you. Tim said – '

Suddenly the line went dead.

Katie stood, staring at the phone. She put the receiver down and sat, heavily, on the sofa. She thought that it must have been the Russian phone lines and expected him to ring back, so she stayed there, waiting; after a few minutes she could stand it no longer so she got up and began to walk around the room; then she went and boiled the kettle; made some tea; sat and drank it. By this time she knew that he was not calling back. She thought, have I offended him? Should I have been less angry? Was it because I mentioned Tim? Are the lines so bad that he can't get another one?

She went up to bed but knew she would never sleep. She felt sure that something was wrong. She felt guilty now that she had given Tim those numbers in Moscow; she realised that he might have set something in motion through his inquiries that might cause difficulties for Dmitry. He had asked her to be cautious with Tim and she had thought only of the fact that he might be jealous, had disregarded the fact that Tim might be dangerously inquisitive. What did she know of the pressures that might be put on someone in Dmitry's position? She had been stupidly, thoughtlessly naive.

All kinds of thoughts went through her mind; that the authorities might put pressure on Dmitry to stay in Russia, that he might not find it so easy to be back there. She felt she must speak to him that very moment, that she must tell him that she loved him and wanted him to come back quickly, that she was afraid of what might happen to them. She tossed and turned in the crumpled bed, still hoping that the phone would ring again, yet somehow knowing that it wouldn't.

◆

Tim woke from a deep sleep to the sound of the phone. He reached out his arm, picked it up, glanced at the digital display on the clock radio and saw that it was nearly three o'clock. A quiet, distant voice said, 'This is Mitya Gavrilov. Please can you go upstairs and get Katie down to talk to me? I'm sorry to bother you, but I can't get through to her and it's urgent.'

Tim said, 'Yes, hold on.' He put the receiver down and put on his dressing gown over his pyjamas. He assumed that Katie's phone must be out of order, or that one of the children had left it off the hook, or perhaps, that Katie had rowed with him and taken the receiver off herself. As he went upstairs a thought occurred to him; he had a recording device attached to the phone which he had on occasion used for interviews. He had bought it cheaply in the Tottenham Court Road. Its use in these circumstances was, strictly speaking, illegal, but he switched it on, hid it away under the bed, and went up to knock on Katie's door.

After a few moments she came down and opened the door, white-faced.

'What's happened?'

'It's all right, it's just your husband on the phone.'

She looked at him for a moment with a strange expression on her face, then she went on past him down the stairs. He followed her, closed the front door of the flat, and showed her where the phone was. He could see her in his bedroom, her back towards him, her hair falling forward over her face, her whole bearing that of someone trying to talk in privacy. He went into the kitchen to wait and put on the kettle. He could hear her, talking quietly, angry, but controlled. The noise of the kettle starting to heat up obscured her voice. Finally she hung up. She came to the doorway. She said, 'Thanks . . . I must go back to bed.'

Tim stood in the doorway. 'Is anything the matter?'

She made a movement to duck past him but he didn't give way. 'Nothing . . . nothing . . . he just couldn't get through. He was worried . . . Perhaps our phone is out of order . . .'

'I could try your phone for you now if you want to test it . . .'

'Oh, the morning will do. I'm sorry, Tim . . . I'm half asleep.'

'Are you upset?'

'No . . . yes . . . a little . . . I just miss him.'

Tim would have liked to have touched her, to have put his

arm around her, comforted her, but he couldn't; it was the wrong moment. He asked, 'Are you sure I can't offer you anything?' and she said, 'No, I have to go, Sasha might wake up.' He said, 'Shall I call by in the morning?' and she nodded. He followed her to the door. She hesitated for the tiniest moment; then she said, 'Thanks, Tim,' and went upstairs.

Tim went back into his room, rewound the tape, and listened.

He heard Gavrilov's voice, quiet, subdued, as if he didn't want to be heard, and dim noises in the background. 'Katie, please, I have to tell you something. This is very important. I'll be back next week. If I phone you, please don't ask me anything. Just talk to me normally, don't ask me any questions. It's very important, I have to ask you to trust me; I will explain it to you later; do you understand?'

Then Katie, puzzled, shaken, 'Mitya, what is this, I don't have the slightest idea what you are talking about.'

'It doesn't matter, I am just asking you, I am appealing to you, to do what I ask. I don't want to have to explain, to justify myself, anything, just now. I want you to trust me. Will you do this for me, Katie?'

'I don't understand what it is that I'm agreeing to.'

Gavrilov's voice sounded as if he were trying to explain to an awkward child. 'I am in a rather awkward situation . . . I will explain when I come back. I will ring you, and just talk to me, about ordinary things, the children, please. And for God's sake don't tell this to Tim.' His voice changed now; it became softer, more intimate. 'I have to go now. I think about you all the time, Katie. I wish I was with you. I want to touch you . . . I want to fuck you, actually. Do you miss me too?'

And Katie's voice, suddenly softer, too, 'Yes, of course . . . I wish you were home, I'm worried, I don't understand . . . but please, ring me . . . Please take care.'

'There's nothing to worry about. If you like I'll ring you tomorrow night.'

'Yes, please do.'

'By-ee.'

'Mitya . . .' But he'd hung up; the tape ran silent. Tim stopped it, wound it back, sat there, thinking. His chief emotion was one of anger; that Gavrilov should manipulate Katie's emotions in that way. Also, he had heard that sudden intimacy; 'I want to fuck you, actually. Do you miss me too?' 'Yes, of course . . .' It made him feel suddenly isolated, shut out. He thought that perhaps he had under-estimated the strength of their relationship, hadn't seen the clues because he hadn't wanted to. He slid the tape-recorder back on the floor under the bed, took off his shoes, and lay down. Katie wasn't likely to tell him much, now, he could see that. Perhaps if he were to tell her what Petrovsky had said, prove that Dmitry had lied to her . . .

He reached out for his notebook. As he pulled it out of the drawer, a piece of paper came with it, a fragment of Ingrid's last essay.

He read: Basilius Valentinus, a Benedictine monk and alchemist from Thuringia, used a mixture of antimony and mercury to create the Red Elixir.

The Red Elixir. Red Mercury, or mercury antimony oxide. Tim stared at the piece of paper in complete amazement.

◆

Katie was waiting for Dmitry at the airport.

She had promised to take Anna as well instead of getting a baby-sitter, a mistake perhaps, because it was late, and she was very tired. The arrivals board announced the flight from Moscow had landed, but the baggage wasn't in the hall; she knew there would be over half an hour to wait. Sasha cried, and Anna, despite being told not to a dozen times, still insisted on running round in circles and rolling on the floor.

When Dmitry appeared Anna ran for him, reached up her arms. He lifted her so easily, swung her around, then came to

Katie. They kissed; he held on to her tightly, pressing her against him; his smell, the strength of his body, the intense look in his eyes, was the same. All Katie's anxieties vanished in an instant; he was obviously delighted to see her.

Anna was tugging at his arm. 'Did you bring me a present . . . let me see . . .'

'Yes, just a minute, give me a chance . . . you can open it in the car.'

Dmitry looked tired but insisted on driving. Anna was occupied with her Russian doll, opening layer after layer with delight; Sasha complained in his car seat. Dmitry reversed the car out of its space in the car park and had to slam on the brakes to avoid colliding with a passing car; Katie put her hand on his arm, said, 'I can drive if you like . . .'

'I'm fine.'

It was raining; Dmitry switched on the wipers. Katie turned to look at Dmitry; he looked healthy, almost tanned. She asked, 'Was it sunny in Moscow?'

'Hmmm?' Dmitry was miles away; he hadn't heard her. She repeated, 'In Moscow? Was it sunny?'

'I didn't spend much time in Moscow . . . the weather wasn't bad . . . actually I spent most of the time in Novosibirsk.'

'Why?'

'That's where this meeting happened.'

Katie didn't know what to say. She asked, 'Was it sunny there?'

Dmitry turned and looked at her. She couldn't read the expression on his face at all. 'What is all this sudden interest in the Russian climate?

'I just thought you looked a bit tanned, that's all.'

'Well, yes, it was quite sunny . . .' They halted at the traffic lights and he turned to Anna in the back. 'How is school?'

Anna didn't answer. She was looking out of the window, very sleepy. Katie asked, 'Did you see your sister?'

'What?' He was startled, crunched the gears as he accelerated forwards. 'No . . . no, I didn't. I didn't have time . . . I was hardly in Moscow, and she was in the country . . .'

'Tim was in Moscow last week. I gave him your sister's number.'

Dmitry looked distracted and the car swerved fractionally in the fast lane. 'You did what? What did you do that for? Did he call her?'

'Yes, he met her, actually. I just thought it might be helpful for him, to know somebody there, that's all . . . did I do the wrong thing?'

'What was Tim doing there?'

'Some stolen uranium story.'

'Did he turn up anything?'

'I don't know. I don't think so.'

Dmitry said, 'I shall have to phone Olya . . . she will have been very upset to hear that I had been in Russia and not contacted her.'

They were silent; Anna had fallen asleep. The rain was falling harder; Dmitry had to slow down. Katie said, 'So what was all the secrecy? I didn't understand what you said on the phone . . . you frightened me.'

'I'm sorry, it's hard to explain . . . The situation there is very strange, it's difficult to know what you can and can't say . . .'

'Tim said – '

'What did Tim say?' He didn't try to conceal the irritation in his voice. Katie suddenly thought better of saying anything. What could she tell him; that Tim had gone round Moscow asking questions about him? He would be furious, probably rightly so. Anyway, what did Tim know about anything? Probably he had spoken to the wrong people, he'd only been there a week, he didn't even speak much Russian. She had to trust Dmitry, if she was going to go on living with him; she didn't believe he would lie to her directly. She let it go; she simply said, 'Tim said things were very difficult there.'

'You need him to tell you that? Anyway, don't worry, there's no need . . . I probably won't be going back.'

Katie looked at him. She felt sorry for him; she sensed that he shared in his country's humiliation and that he must have been quite shocked by what he had found. She said, 'You don't have to talk about it.' He looked at her, put out his hand and put it on her thigh; she put her hand on his. She said, almost mischievously, teasingly, 'I thought there might be another woman.'

He was startled, and then he smiled. He looked almost happy for a moment. 'Is that what you thought? You are very silly . . . there could never be anyone but you.'

◆

Tim's Russian report was broadcast the week Dmitry got back but, as far as Tim knew, neither he nor Katie saw it. Later Tim heard at work another uranium smuggling story which he thought might be connected to Grebeshev's activities. Two men had been arrested in Vienna with uranium contained in fuel pellets from a Soviet designed WWR 1,000 nuclear reactor. Their correspondent in Vienna said it was all a great joke. The material had been smuggled in through the Czech Republic and the smugglers had been looking for an Arab buyer but, having failed to locate one, had finally succeeded in selling it to an undercover policeman in the Prater amusement park.

12

ROZANOV looked at Dmitry coldly across the table.
He had told them everything he could. Every detail of the layout of the buildings, the computer systems, the names of the staff, any casual remarks he had picked up, especially those made by Suzarbayev, that could be of any interest. He had memorised everything he could, but Rozanov did not seem impressed, and Dmitry could not blame him; there could be little there he didn't know already.

Rozanov turned his cigarette lighter round and round in his fingers. 'Is that all?'

'I think so.'

'When are you expected back?'

'I am not going back. I can't do this. I will learn nothing of any use to you.'

Rozanov raised his eyebrows. 'We shall see,' he said.

'What do you mean, we shall see? You can't want me to develop this technology, can you? I've already done much more than my bargain with you. Anyway, I have decided.'

Rozanov only smiled at him enigmatically.

The meeting was clearly at an end; Rozanov stood up and opened the door for him. Dmitry turned and walked out into the hall and down the stairs, stepped out into the sunlight. The noises of the traffic, of the screeching of a bus's breaks in nearby Baker Street, the sudden strong scent of lilies from a flower stall, assaulted his senses. Everything was too sharp, too clear; then he saw the faint grey dots floating in front of his eyes.

Dmitry took a deep breath, felt in his pocket for his migraine pills, and found he had forgotten them. He made a gesture of acute irritation and went on walking, his head down, concentrating on the ground in front of him. Rozanov's attitude seemed strange to him. Perhaps he had finally realised that Dmitry's intelligence was not much use. It was possible that he had served his usefulness, and now met only with indifference. Rozanov's last words were not enough to frighten him; he felt released. Well, he thought, I too can be ruthless. He had thought of a strategy that might work; he would ring the Libyans now and end this business. Perhaps he need only face one unpleasant scene, and then he would be free.

He rang from a call-box at the station.

'I have to meet you.'

'Why?'

'I have a problem.'

'Very well . . . we can talk about it. Shall we meet where we met before? At, say, six o'clock?'

'It's difficult. I think I'm being watched.'

There was a silence on the phone. The voice said, 'Can you get rid of them?'

'I can try.'

'Do your best.'

They were waiting for him at the bar at the Metropole Hotel and offered him a drink. Dmitry asked for vodka, neat; he drank it hurriedly. His hands trembled on the empty glass.

'We can go upstairs.'

'I would rather stay here.'

'We might be overheard.'

But Dmitry was afraid to go upstairs. They couldn't harm him here, surely, in a public place. He said, 'It's all right.I think I lost them. How can I tell? They are professionals.'

'Who are they?'

'From Russian intelligence.'

'How do you know?'

'Believe me, I know.'

The Libyan looked at him, carefully, thoughtfully, with those hard, black eyes. 'When did you notice?'

'Look, they approached me. One of them . . .'

'His name?'

'What does his name matter? It is hardly his real one . . .' They poured him another vodka and he drank it down. 'Rozanov.'

'Where did they meet you?'

'What does it matter, where? Don't you understand what I'm telling you? They *know*.'

'If you come straight to Libya you will be quite safe.'

'I can't come to Libya. My wife . . . my marriage is already in trouble. Already she thinks I have another woman in Moscow . . . anyway, I have two small children . . .'

'But they are all welcome.'

Dmitry's head was beginning to throb now. 'You don't understand. They won't come, my wife would never come . . . she would divorce me.'

'Your position is very difficult . . . but you have signed a two-year contract.'

'I want to be released from it.'

'I am sure that this will not be possible.'

'It has to be possible. I didn't foresee this . . . I am not expected to risk my life. After all, I'm not being paid that much.'

The Libyan's eyes narrowed. 'If it is a question of money, I am sure . . .'

Dmitry suddenly regretted saying this. Perhaps they would think he had become greedy, had even invented this for the purposes of getting more money out of them . . . He said hastily, 'No, it's not the money. I don't want any more money.'

'Look, don't worry. We can take care of everything.'

'I have to think of my family . . .'

'Yes, indeed, I think you should think about them very carefully, Dr Gavrilov. After all . . . you don't want anything unpleasant to happen to them, do you?'

His words hung in the air long after he had spoken them. It was as if a great chasm had suddenly opened up in front of Dmitry and he stared into it as if from a great height. In an instant, everything had changed. Although he knew the danger he was running intellectually, only now did Dmitry feel and understand the full enormity of the situation in which he had placed himself. He stared at the Libyan's face but saw nothing there to help him, nothing that would lead him to believe he didn't mean it. But still, they could be bluffing; it was easy to make such threats, harder to carry them out. He thought, they can't mean this, I must not give in, I must be absolutely clear. I can ask Rozanov for protection. He said, 'I am not coming. As far as I am concerned, the contract is terminated.'

'I am afraid that this will not be acceptable to my superiors.'

They stared at one another. Dmitry was sweating; he could think of nothing else to say. The Libyan said, 'Your ticket is booked . . . The flight is SU581 to Moscow, on Thursday. Here are the details . . . You will be expected to pick up your ticket at Heathrow. Please don't disappoint us.' He handed Dmitry the envelope and turned and left the bar.

Dmitry sat there, fingering the envelope with growing horror. He found himself outside in the Marylebone Road without having noticed how he had got there. He felt hot, and then freezing cold. The traffic roared past and the fumes caught at his throat. His head hurt so much that he thought he might pass out.

He walked to Baker Street station and phoned Rozanov's message service. He stood by the phone, impatient. Someone else wanted to use it and he rebuffed them, rudely. After a few minutes the phone rang.

Dmitry snatched it up, and said, 'We have to meet.'

Rozanov said, 'Of course,' and named the time and place.

◆

As Dmitry walked down the Bayswater Road on his way to the appointment a bizarre sensation took hold of him. He felt as if he were made of some different substance from everyone else, that he must be standing out from them; as if what was happening inside him was so extreme that it must be visible to the outside world. It was hard for him to resist the idea that the people who passed him on the pavement were looking at him closely, that they turned and stared after he had walked past, that the cars were slowing down as they came up behind him and that people were watching him out of the dark windows of the great mansions. He was able to dispel these feelings only with an effort. He crossed the road into Hyde Park, and walked down to Kensington Gardens. He had arranged to meet Rozanov at the Round Pond; he became more and more agitated as he approached. He sat down on a bench, looking at the dark green trees and the wide expanse of sky above; he thought how unusual it was to see so much sky in London. Grey clouds moved steadily across from north to south; the sun went in, leaving the pond suddenly grey and lifeless. Nannies pushed their babies in pushchairs, a couple of old ladies threw bread to the ducks; the wind, slightly chilly, scuffed the surface of the water, sweeping across the pond, bearing the occasional drop of rain.

Dmitry watched the passers-by carefully, wondering if they were following him. A woman seemed to nod at him as she went past and he wondered for a moment whether this wasn't some prearranged signal. Then suddenly he saw Rozanov on the path in front of him, smoking a cigarette. He was looking up anxiously at the clouds, walking slowly, unhurriedly, with his slight limp. Dmitry rose to meet him and they began to walk, together, around the pond, Dmitry, silent, wondering how to begin, Rozanov silently enjoying his cigarette.

'Well? Why have you asked to see me? Have you changed your mind, Dmitry Nikolayevitch? Have you decided to go back to Libya?'

'They won't release me from the contract . . . they have threatened me.'

'Have they?' Rozanov assumed an expression of concern; but was it his imagination, or did the briefest smile cross the corners of Rozanov's lips for an instant?

'I told them you were on to me. I told them you were having me watched.'

'Did you?' Rozanov looked at him sideways, tossing his cigarette end into the water. 'Well, you are playing a very dangerous game, then. I hope you can handle it.'

'I am not handling it at all. I am going to pieces. Look at me.'

Rozanov did look at him, for a moment; his eyes expressed a faint contempt. Then he continued with his serious study of the sky.

Dmitry grabbed Rozanov's arm and forced him to turn and face him. 'You must help me. You got me into this; all right, I shouldn't have done it, I knew what I was getting into, but I can't go any further. I can't go back to Libya. There must be some humanity in you somewhere, there must be some way you can help us. You said that you would, you told me that you would help me "extricate myself". Those were your exact words.'

Rozanov walked on, pulling himself free. 'Were they? I don't recall. I would be glad to help you, Dmitry Nikolayevich, indeed I wish I could help you, but what can we do? We can try to protect you, but . . . that is very expensive, and as you know, there isn't much money for that sort of thing these days.'

Dmitry made a sound of disgust. 'There is always money when you want something.'

'Well, there is money if we can produce results . . . . but for what you're talking about, round-the-clock surveillance and protection . . . this is not possible. There is no point in our even discussing it . . . I would never get permission from my superiors.'

'But suppose we went back to Russia . . .'

'Even there we wouldn't be able to help you. You would have to take a risk. Maybe it would not be worth it for them to pursue you . . .'

'But you could help my wife and children. You could give them a new identity . . . passports . . .'

'And you would go and live in some remote Russian hamlet . . . do you really think this is possible? Would your wife agree to it? You told me before she didn't want to live with you in Russia . . . come, grow up, be reasonable, Dmitry Nikolayevich. This is just a wild fantasy to help you escape from the painful reality of your situation . . . you would do much better to face up to it.'

The sun had come out, dazzlingly bright. Dmitry stood still, looking at the shadows now stretching out across the grass. What was the force which made him stand and take this mutely? Why did he bother to struggle to remain in control, dignified? He was bigger than Rozanov, he could overpower him easily, he could pick him up and with one thrust throw him into the pond. The desire to do so was so strong that Dmitry had to put his hands in his pockets. He knew that if he lost control, his anger would quickly turn to despair; he was much more likely in fact to weep, and as he thought this, he could feel the tears starting to well in his eyes and had to blink rapidly to stop them spilling down his face, turning his face away from Rozanov for a moment. He must stay calm; he must not react; he must not make a ridiculous scene, it would get him nowhere.

Rozanov said, 'It is a mistake to think that we make choices, Dmitry Nikolayevich. It just leads us to torment ourselves. Isn't it much better just to accept the inevitable?'

Dmitry said, 'You want me to go back, don't you? Why? I haven't produced much intelligence worth speaking of. And my research project . . . it might even work.'

Rozanov lit another cigarette, passing the lighter backwards and forwards across the tip with a caressing movement. He inhaled, turned his head aside to blow the smoke away from them. 'That would be . . . a pity. But I'm sure you can make sure that it doesn't.'

'It's not so easy. Look, if I go back now I won't even be able to pass you any intelligence, assuming I came across anything worth giving . . . I can't take the risk.'

'I have told you, this is up to you.'

There was something about Rozanov's utter indifference which drove Dmitry inwardly wild. He said, 'I would like to kill you.' He hadn't meant to say it; it had just come out, in a perfectly calm, measured voice, and now it hovered there, gathering power in the long silence. Rozanov did not seem to react to it at first; then he said, quietly, 'That would do you no good at all, let me assure you. In fact, you do not know it, but I am protecting you already.'

'What do you mean by that?'

'There are certain people who would like your work to be at an end . . . people who have in fact some other use for you . . . people who are not without their influence. I do not want to bore you with the details, I think you may be able to imagine what I mean . . .' Rozanov looked sideways at Dmitry, and his eyes suddenly appeared soulful and sad. 'You may not believe this, but I do have your interests at heart.'

'What people? What use? What are you talking about?' Dmitry's hands jerked out of his pockets and it was only with a great effort that he kept them away from Rozanov's neck. 'Are you also threatening me?'

'No, not at all. You misunderstand.'

The sun went in again behind a cloud and all the colours faded. Dmitry stopped suddenly and sat down on the nearest bench. He said, 'What shall I do? Please advise me.'

'Well, perhaps this threat is a bluff, Dmitry Nikolayevich. That is a risk you will have to take. Or you can continue with your project. It's as simple as that.' He dropped the stub of his cigarette and ground it into the path with his heel. He looked at his watch. 'I'm afraid I really must go. Do let me know what you decide, Dmitry Nikolayevich.'

◆

Katie knew that there was something wrong the moment Dmitry came home, but he wouldn't tell her what it was. She waited till the children were in bed, till after supper, keeping her patience, hoping that he would say something, but he didn't. He seemed hardly to be conscious of being there at all; she would ask him something and he wouldn't even hear it; he struggled with his supper, forcing himself to eat. Finally he rose from the table and said that he was feeling ill, that he'd had a terrible headache all day, and was going to bed.

Katie followed him. He lay, the covers over him, pretending to be asleep; but she knew from his breathing, from the tension in his body, that he wasn't. She slipped into bed, turning her back to his, feeling the distance between them, and found herself crying; she cried as silently as she could but then Dmitry rolled over and put his arm round her. He said, 'Please don't cry,' and she said, 'I don't understand . . . why won't you tell me what's the matter. Something happened, in Russia, didn't it? What was it? You ask me again and again to trust you, and I try to, but why don't you trust me?'

Dmitry said, 'Because I am not free to give you certain information. You know that; I know you don't like it, but you'll have to live with it.'

'No, I don't. We talked about that, and we decided we didn't have to live with that, and that's why you weren't going to carry on with that kind of work.'

'But it isn't that easy, is it, Katie? There is a lot of information – secret information – in my head which I will carry for the rest of my life. I can't get rid of it. It is part of me; it has made me what I am. Can't you understand that?'

Katie did understand. She understood it only too well; and she had the terrible sense, not for the first time, that because of it he was unknowable, that she would never really fathom him, that she could never be happy with him. She understood, too, perhaps she had known from the beginning, that there was something in him that was attracted to the secret, the forbidden. This frightened her; she felt now that he was involved in something which would bring disaster to them and he would never tell her what it was.

Dmitry, seemingly unaware of her long silence and what it might mean, went on. 'I've tried, Katie, but you can see it isn't working out, I can't just be a translator. It doesn't work. I am not good at it, it makes me miserable. If I could use my knowledge to do something useful . . .'

'Mitya, please, can't you tell me what is going on? Have you been offered some other work, in Russia?'

'No, not exactly . . . I don't know.' He sat up, and ran his hands over his face. 'You can't understand . . . there is no way I can explain it to you.'

Katie sat up and took hold of him, pulling his arms from in front of his face, trying to look into his eyes which he tried to shield from her. 'No, I don't understand. You said things were better, you had this work . . . we got the payment last week.'

'Yes, I know. But it's no good. It's only temporary. I don't think I can go on with it.'

'But why? What is it?'

He didn't answer her. She felt desperate to understand, to get to the bottom of his depression. 'Would you like to go back to Russia? Is that it? Because if that's what you really want, then of course we'll go. I'd go at once, I'd go anywhere, if only it would make you happy.' The words just came out of her, she didn't even know if they were true but at that moment she was so unhappy that she would have said anything to make things work between them.

He stared at her in the darkness. He moved towards her and then seemed to stop himself, said, 'You are too good for me.' She turned and kissed him, small kisses, rapidly, on his face. He said, 'Don't worry, that's not what I want. Don't talk about it now. Let's go to sleep.'

He rolled over and she lay on her side, pressing her back again his body. He must have been exhausted because he slept at once; but she lay awake and fretting for much of the night.

◆

Tim had been avoiding Katie. He had seen her taking Anna to school that morning, had seen how tired and strained she looked; had also seen Gavrilov striding along the street, his head down, muttering to himself and making gestures in the air like a madman. He had seen Gavrilov at the tube station, calling from a payphone; as if by some unspoken agreement they had ignored one another, had avoided their eyes meeting. Now, as he was getting ready for bed, he could hear them upstairs again. When they raised their voices he could hear them quite clearly. He heard Dmitry shouting, 'Don't ask me about it! Please don't ask me! Why can you never leave me alone?'

He heard the sound of something heavy falling on the floor. This alarmed him; he got up from the bed, put on his shoes and went to ring on the upstairs bell. There was a long silence. He thought they wouldn't open it; he wished he hadn't rung. Then Dmitry came and opened the door. He looked at Tim as if he hardly existed, seeming not to recognise him, saying nothing.

Tim said, 'I'm sorry . . . I've run out of milk. I wondered . . .'

'It's half past eleven.'

'I could hear that you weren't asleep.'

There was an embarrassed silence. Dmitry turned and called to Katie, 'Tim wants some milk.' She appeared behind Dmitry, her eyes looked puffy, red-rimmed; her voice, when she spoke, sounded unnaturally bright.

'How much do you want? You can have a whole pint if you like . . . we've got far too much anyway.' She fetched the milk, handed it to him. Tim thanked them and, unable to think of any excuse to stay, went back into his flat. If he had achieved anything by this interruption it was short-lived, because before long the arguing started again.

Tim couldn't stand it. He went out into the garden and stood there in the middle of the lawn, breathing in the sweet, damp air and the heavy scent of the rose which climbed over the neighbouring wall. He glanced upwards; they hadn't shut the curtains upstairs and he could see them, Katie sitting on the kitchen table and Dmitry pacing up and down. Then he suddenly turned and went up to her. He made a move to kiss her upturned face and she turned her head away from him. Then he slipped his hands inside her jumper and she pulled them away. He moved away from her, made some gesture of anger and impatience; then suddenly he came back and with a powerful movement pushed her backwards on to the table. He leaned over her and kissed her; then he took her by her hips and slid her towards him, pulling at her pants and at his trousers.

Tim looked away at once, unable to watch any more; he felt ashamed of having seen them, angry, and half aroused. He went indoors and sat down at the table, listening in spite of himself, but now there were no further sounds from above.

He was aware of a fierce torrent of feelings, following closely one after the other. He desired Katie enormously, more than before; he realised how much he wanted her. He wasn't sure that he had ever felt like this about anyone before. He felt ashamed, wondered if he'd been wrong about her, and wondered what she felt for her husband; perhaps she enjoyed things this way, perhaps she was one of those women who liked to be dominated, though somehow he didn't think so. Or was she simply afraid of him? He felt a deep, primitive anger at the sight of the woman he wanted making love to someone else. He couldn't understand what Katie could find attractive about her husband, he seemed so unpleasant. He thought, I have to get her away from him. He is lying to her, deceiving her, he is up to no good. If I could prove it, if I could be sure . . . that would be the way to get through to her.

◆

'Katie, I want to talk to you.'

Tim had seen her struggling with the pram and the shopping on the steps. He rushed over to help her into the house, unloaded the shopping, and then, because he could see that she was busy and distracted, said: 'Will you come down later, tonight? Please. There's something I need to talk to you about.'

She looked at him, seeming surprised by his urgency, and said that she would.

She came down at half-past eight. It was a hot evening; she was wearing a loose shirt and leggings, and had her hair up, though one strand had come loose and hung down on her neck. She was restless, nervous, and wouldn't sit down. She said, 'I can't be long, just five minutes. Mitya didn't want me to come . . . What did you want to talk to me about? Is it something to do with the flat?'

Tim said, trying not to sound too angry, 'What does it matter if he doesn't want you to come. You want to come, don't you?'

There was an expression almost of despair on her face, as if she knew she could not explain anything. 'I'm sorry, Tim, he doesn't like you.'

'The feeling is quite mutual.'

Katie said, 'Tim, I think you're being very foolish.'

'Am I?' Tim felt he was making a hash of things; he didn't know what to say; he was afraid that he might alienate her completely. 'Why, what's his problem, Katie? Is he jealous?'

'No, it's not that . . . Or then, perhaps it is. Perhaps he has some reason to be.'

'Does he?'

'Well, Tim, you're the best judge of that.'

Tim took in the ambiguity of this remark. Did she mean that she did feel something for him, or that she knew what he felt for her? She turned away from him and began to look at the magazines lying on the table. He offered her a glass of wine but she refused it. Then he took a deep breath and said, 'Katie, I can see you're not happy. I'm sorry, I know it's not any of my business, but I've heard you shouting and you look so miserable . . . he's not drinking, is he? He doesn't . . .' he ran out of nerve. What could he say? Intimidate her? Abuse her?

Katie stared at him, blankly. She said, 'No, of course not. Look, Tim, it's kind of you to be concerned, of course we have problems, but it's not that simple. I think you're making a lot of false assumptions. You don't understand. You don't know what it's like to have children, you don't know what the two of us have been through.'

'Well, maybe I don't, but I can see what you're going through now.'

Katie asked, angrily, 'Is this what you wanted to talk to me about?'

'Yes.'

'I see.' It wasn't his imagination, she was trembling. She was so close, he could reach out and touch her, but he didn't, he dared not. She said, in a softer voice now, 'I do appreciate that you're concerned about me but . . . things aren't as bad as you might think. But I am very worried about Mitya . . . I think he is very depressed.'

'Well, yes, it would seem so. He must be suffering from something, to treat you like this.'

'Oh, Tim, don't be ridiculous. I don't want to carry on this conversation, and I'm going to go now.' She turned away, but he said, 'Katie!' and she turned back to face him. He felt that now he had begun, he had to carry on. He said, 'Look, Katie, I'm at risk of blowing everything, but . . . you're very special to me. I can't bear to see you so unhappy. I think your husband is in serious trouble . . . I haven't told you everything, because I didn't want to alarm you in case it wasn't true, but now I have the evidence . . . Look . . .' and he reached for his notebook.

Katie cut him off at once. She said, 'Tim, you're out of your mind. I don't want to hear this . . . please, I have to go upstairs. The supper will be burning . . .'

'He can switch it off.'

'Tim, really.' The doorbell rang; Katie jumped, like a guilty child. She said, 'It's Mitya.' She went to the door. Gavrilov said, 'The supper's burning and the baby's crying . . . what are you doing? You said you'd be five minutes.' She said, 'I'm coming.'

She turned to Tim. He thought she was going to say something but she thought better of it, turned away suddenly, and closed the door firmly behind her.

◆

Katie lay awake for hours. She had not said anything about Tim's outburst to Dmitry; so now, she, too, was concealing things. She thought that perhaps she had been too open to Tim, had encouraged him. At first she had been flattered by Tim's obvious attraction to her, when it had seemed harmless, but now it had gone too far; she felt furious with both of them, with Tim and with Mitya, and with herself. She was caught between Dmitry's depression and Tim's pushiness and she felt that there were things under the surface she didn't know, she couldn't guess at, and which she was afraid to bring to the surface because of what it might mean for them all. She felt trapped. She imagined walking out of the house, leaving the whole lot of them, of doing something for herself, something ordinary, enjoyable, like seeing a film. She got out of bed, suddenly, grabbing her clothes from the chair.

Dmitry was awake instantly. He asked, 'Where are you going?' She said, 'I don't know, I'm just going, anywhere, out of this house.' Dmitry said, sitting up, startled, 'What do you mean?' He grabbed at her but she evaded him. She ran down the stairs, opened both the inner and outer doors, and ran out into the street. The pavement was damp and it was spitting with rain. She heard Dmitry shout, 'Come back!' and she turned and shouted with all the strength she could muster, 'I – hate – everything!'

She ran down the road in her thin cotton pyjamas, her bare feet slapping on the pavement. She reached the corner, paused, looked back, and saw Dmitry running after her. She ran on again, but as she ran down towards the High Road her confidence began to wane. A drunk across the road stared at her; it began to rain harder. She ran slower, without conviction. She heard Dmitry calling her. By the time she got to the junction she was walking and he caught up with her. He grabbed her shoulder. 'What are you doing?' he said, 'You are crazy, anything could happen to you, like this, you might get killed.'

She was shivering. He put his arm round her, took her hand and led her back to the house. She was crying but he didn't say anything. He led her upstairs, took off the clothes he must have hastily pulled on, and climbed back into bed, pulling her down beside him. He lay still, his hand still holding hers, and neither of them spoke.

She continued to cry, but she cried silently, afraid of disturbing him. She thought, what is wrong with me? We will get through this. She tried to console herself by thinking that if something really terrible happened, for instance, if she woke up in the morning and found that she had cancer, then she would look back and wonder why she hadn't been happy before making this discovery. They were all healthy; the children were well, and Mitya, well, things would surely get better for him in time. She couldn't understand why her throat felt dry, why her head ached, how her heart beat faster than it should have done. Then she realised that these sensations were simply those of fear; she admitted to herself that Tim knew something that she didn't want to hear and that her husband too was concealing something from her.

13

ANNA was late home from school.

Jenny was meant to have dropped her off at four. But now it was nearly quarter to five, and she hadn't done so. Katie tried to phone her, but there was no reply. She tried to ring the school but there was no reply there either, the office was already shut.

She tried to keep calm. Perhaps they had gone to the park. Or perhaps Jenny had forgotten the arrangement. She wished intensely for a moment that she had got to know Jenny better, so that she knew what she might do, where she might go. Perhaps she should go down to the school. But no, the school would have rung her if Anna was still there. She walked up and down, up and down. How long should she wait before doing something?

She was putting on her jacket when the doorbell rang. It was Jenny, with Charlotte; Jenny looked completely distracted.

She asked, 'Is Anna here?'

'No, no, of course not.' Katie instinctively turned and looked behind her, as if Anna might have somehow crept in without her noticing.

'I don't know,' said Jenny, coming in, pushing past Katie, 'I can't understand it. Anna was running ahead of us up the road, she always does, she went round the corner where usually she hides and jumps out at us and when I got there she wasn't there. I looked for her everywhere, then I went back to the school because she had forgotten her coat and I thought she might have gone back to get it, but she wasn't there, so I thought she must have run on home . . .'

'No. No, she hasn't.' Katie felt her voice rising in panic.

Jenny said, 'I'd better go back and look for her.'

Katie couldn't think. She felt her heart start to thump loudly, and she was swamped by a terrible feeling, like the sensation of having forgotten something or left something behind magnified a thousand-fold. She said, 'Which road was it? Where? Which corner?'

'I've already looked. She isn't there.'

Katie stared at Jenny, trying to make sense of what she said. Jenny turned and picked up the phone, calling the police. Katie listened, unable to move, while she gave the details. Jenny hung up. She said, 'They're sending a car . . . It's my fault . . . we didn't come at once because we thought we'd find her . . . it just didn't seem possible . . .'

Katie dashed out of the house and up the road, calling out, 'Anna! Anna! Are you hiding? Come out now!' She realised it was useless; she felt her legs go weak; with an effort she prevented herself from simply sinking down on to the pavement. She kept thinking over and over; this isn't possible. This just isn't possible. In a moment she will pop up from behind a hedge and it will all be a stupid mistake.

Katie ran through all the streets to the school, calling Anna's name. The head-teacher was still in her office; she was extremely concerned and sympathetic but couldn't help, especially as the police had already been called, so Katie turned and ran all the way home again. There was a chance – just a chance – that Anna might have been found by now. As Katie neared the house, she saw a police car come into view and drive up to her.

The driver wound down the window, a policeman in uniform. 'Are you Katie Gavrilov?' He pronounced it wrong but she couldn't correct him.

'Have you found her yet?'

'No, there's no news. If you come back to the house we'll take a statement from you,'

Katie couldn't answer but her face must have told him everything. He spoke into the car radio. He said, 'There's another car on the way. They'll drive around, then, if they don't find her, we'll ask at all the houses.'

When she reached the house she thought that there was just a chance, a faint chance, that Anna might now be there. As she walked up the steps this seemed more and more likely, but as soon as she saw Jenny's anxious face, her hope dissolved.

She sank down on the sofa, exhausted, her breath coming in gasps. A policewoman knocked and came in through the door.

'We're doing a house-to-house. Is there anyone she knows? Anywhere she might have gone? A corner shop? A friend's house?'

'No – not round here.'

'I think it's best if we wait here. Could you make me a cup of tea?'

Jenny put the kettle on. Katie, unable to keep still, jumped up and rang the bell to Tim's flat in case Anna had gone in there, but there was no reply; then she tried the neighbours. She phoned the library where she thought Dmitry was and explained that this was an emergency and asked if they could find her husband, but after she had hung on for nearly ten minutes they said he wasn't there.

Then Katie started to phone all the mothers of Anna's friends from the school who Anna might possibly have gone home with. She dialled the numbers desperately, her hands shaking. None of them knew anything. Sasha started to cry and she sat down and fed him. She was amazed that she could; her whole body felt numb. It was now nearly six o'clock. Katie's only hope now was that Dmitry had left the library early, had seen Anna running along the road, and gone off somewhere with her. It was unlikely, she knew, but it was just possible.

A policeman came to join them. He asked detailed questions about what Anna was wearing, what she looked like, and Katie found some photographs for them, handing them over without daring to glance at them herself. They also wanted information about the family situation, asked whether there had been any custody dispute. Jenny was taken aside and questioned separately. With every moment that passed Katie felt more and more sick. She thought that if this went on for much longer she would die. She remembered something she had read somewhere; that most children who are abducted are killed within a few hours of being taken. She mustn't allow herself to think this. Perhaps Anna had only wandered off, had got lost, and was with some kind person who would be looking after her. But surely, if they found a lost child, they would phone the police? She clenched her hands so tightly that they hurt.

At six-thirty Jenny's husband called and collected Charlotte. Jenny tried to make Katie eat something but she couldn't. She was now worried that Dmitry was also late home. Sasha had fallen asleep; she went upstairs and put him in the cot, not bothering to check his nappy or change his clothes. She started to cry; a terrible pain began to gnaw at her, as if her internal organs were being torn apart; she wasn't sure that she could bear it. She began to rock backwards and forwards. She asked, 'Isn't there something else we can do? Can we put out an appeal? What about the hospitals. Shouldn't we ring the hospitals?'

The policewoman said quietly that this was already being done.

At seven another, more senior, policeman arrived. He sat down opposite Katie and said that a child who fitted Anna's description had been taken into hospital in east London. She was concussed but they thought not seriously injured. He said the child was about six years old, had long dark hair and was wearing a navy blue dress with white spots and black trainers. Katie said at once, 'That's right. That's Anna. Oh, my God.' She couldn't take it in; none of it made sense to her but she had to go at once, had to see if it was really Anna. Jenny said she would stay and babysit Sasha while Katie went to the hospital.

Katie put on her jacket and was rushing to the door when it

opened and Dmitry came in. His face, staring at her, looked white and thin, like tissue paper. 'What's happened, what's the police car . . . ? Are you all right . . . ?'

'Anna's in hospital. They think it's Anna – I don't know. We have to go there. I can't explain . . . please come with me.'

Dmitry grabbed her arm. He said, 'What is it? Is she ill? Was there an accident?' He climbed into the back of the police-car beside her, followed by the senior officer. As the car pulled out the officer explained, 'She was found on the verge at the side of the dual carriageway . . . she may have been struck by a car . . . she is unconscious but the doctor I spoke to thinks there is no serious injury.'

Katie still didn't understand. She asked, 'But how did she get there?' Dmitry said suddenly, 'Oh my God,' and Katie thought for a moment he was going to be sick. His face went bright red, then white, and turned his head sharply to one side, his body hunched over, leaning into the corner. She put out her hand and took hold of his; he didn't look at her, but he held on to her hand very tightly, and this gave her some comfort on the long journey to the hospital.

◆

They stood in a brightly lit corridor while doctors and nurses hurried past. The police officer told them that they would not wait long. He took them into a side room; Katie sank on to a chair and watched Dmitry pace up and down.

The registrar came, a young Asian doctor in a white coat. The few moments before he spoke were agony.

He said, 'You'd better come in and confirm that it really is your daughter.'

Katie grabbed Dmitry's hand and they went in together. Thank God; it was Anna. She looked very small and lost on the large, high bed. The left side of her face was covered by a dressing but Katie could see the deep grazes and raw flesh around her eye, which was puffy and swollen. There was a drip in her left arm.

Katie felt light-headed, dizzy with relief; the moment she touched Anna she felt better. Anything, anything was better than not knowing, not being able to find her. She sat down by the bed and started to tidy Anna's hair, stroke her arm, telling her it was all right, she was there, even though she knew she couldn't hear her; perhaps she was also comforting herself.

The doctor spoke in quiet, confident tones. 'Let me reassure you . . . all the neurological signs are looking good so far. She's still unconscious but she's beginning to lighten and is responding to pain. She probably won't be fully conscious for a few hours . . . she had some nasty abrasions to her left cheek but I don't think they'll scar too badly . . .'

She heard Dmitry saying to the doctor, 'How do you know she'll be all right? If she hasn't regained consciousness . . .'

'We have the X-rays . . . if it is a fracture it is only minor . . .'

A nurse offered them a cup of tea; Katie accepted gratefully. Everyone was very kind. They assumed she would want to stay in overnight, but Katie said she didn't know what to do, she would have to go home at some point because no one else could feed the baby. Dmitry said that she should go home, and he would stay with Anna and phone her when she woke. He put his arms round her and held her, stroking her hair gently with his large hands. Katie looked at him and he smiled. His eyes were open, looking into hers, the pupils wide and dark, and she thought, with a shock, that this was the first smile she had seen him give her for weeks, perhaps months, the first time she felt he was truly giving of himself. She felt as if he had suddenly come back to her.

◆

Dmitry sat in the chair by the bed; he stretched out his legs and tried to sleep but it wasn't possible, though his head ached with weariness. He knew this was no accident, he knew it was his fault, he knew this meant the end of everything for them. As the hours passed Anna became increasingly restless; from time to time she murmured and thrashed her limbs. The nurse came to check her, calm, unconcerned. Dmitry took the child's hand and said softly, 'Anna? Anna? it's all right, Mitya's here,' but he wasn't sure if she heard him or not.

At about one o'clock in the morning she opened her eyes. His voice seemed to calm her, but she didn't look at him properly, as if she was delirious or he wasn't really there. Then she said, 'My head hurts. I feel sick.' Tears rolled down her cheeks. Dmitry asked, 'Do you want Mummy?' but he couldn't go to telephone; she wouldn't let go of his hand.

Anna seemed to sleep for a while; then she woke up and started to be sick. This distressed her and she started to cry; she wouldn't keep still and Dmitry was worried she might injure herself. He pressed the button and the nurse came, then went to get the registrar. Anna began to pick at the tube in her arm with determined, nervous movements. Dmitry took her hand to pull it away and she resisted. She stared at him oddly with her grey eyes and said things which he didn't understand. He was frightened; he wished somebody would come. He was afraid that the damage was worse than they had thought, that Anna might have suffered a brain injury and not fully recover, and that he would never be able to forgive himself for what he had done to her.

The registrar came. He seemed concerned, spoke to her in a firm, urgent voice: 'Anna? Can you hear me? Anna?' He shone a torch into both of Anna's eyes, took her arm and moved it around. Dmitry had to know the worst; he asked, 'Is there . . . brain damage?' The registrar straightened up. 'Vomiting like this can indicate a brain haemorrhage, but I don't think that's the case here . . . I think we'll put a naso-gastric tube down to empty her stomach . . . then she'll be more comfortable.'

Dmitry took Anna's hand and held it while they did this. He wished profoundly there was some way he could take her pain away from her; he was so ashamed of what he had done that he felt he had to deal with it himself and did not want them to go and ring Katie. Perhaps it was also to protect himself, to shield from Katie the full extent of Anna's suffering. When it was all over Anna was calmer; he half lay down with his head on the pillow next to her and talked to her softly, any nonsense he could think of, and eventually she went to sleep. She lay calm and lovely as an angel while Dmitry felt himself condemned to hell.

◆

Katie held Anna tightly in her arms, barely able to let go of her for a moment. When she arrived in the morning Anna had seemed quite all right; she was sitting up in bed and seemed pleased to be the centre of attention. The registrar explained that the police had requested an interview with Anna as soon as she was fit; he thought this afternoon would be all right, and that Anna might even be able to go home the next day.

When the police came to talk to her in the afternoon, Katie went with Dmitry to see them in a private room; he held the sleeping Sasha in his arms. The police had to admit that they were a little puzzled. It was clear that Anna must have been abducted. The hospital had thought that the injuries could have been caused by the child falling out of a moving car. Nobody in the street where she had gone missing had seen anything; there were no witnesses. There seemed to be no clear motive; the policeman was pleased to be able to tell them that, unusually in an abduction of this sort, there was no evidence that Anna had been sexually assaulted.

Katie felt faint for a moment when the policeman said this; thank God, she thought, oh thank God. She felt Dmitry tense, and heard his sudden intake of breath. Then she said, 'But I don't understand . . . why Anna? Will he come back for her, do you think?'

'Don't worry, we think that very unlikely. Abductions by a stranger are usually very opportunistic. He may have been watching near the school, but then saw a child alone, and took his chance. It's most likely that whoever it is will keep away now, for fear of being recognised. He'll know we're looking for him.'

The policewoman said, 'But it is important that we talk to her as soon as possible. Other children may be at risk . . . Her memory may be affected, but she may be able to tell us something.'

Dmitry suddenly became agitated, almost hostile. 'But what is she going to be able to tell you that will be of any use? I don't want her put through a police interrogation . . . She is just a little child.'

Katie put her hand on his arm. She said, 'Mitya, I know it's awful, but it has to be done.'

'No, it does not have to be done. It will only upset her . . . what is the point. We want to take her home.' He said this emphatically; his voice shook; Katie looked at him with dismay. She was disappointed in him for a moment; she looked for him to support her in this crisis and received only his own confusion and distress. The policeman and policewoman were looking at him; she could tell that they thought there was something wrong with his attitude but didn't understand what it was; she saw a look of meaning pass between them.

The policeman said, quite coldly, 'With respect, sir, I understand that you are not the child's father and you have not adopted her. As far as I am aware, you have no right . . . the decision must rest with the mother. If she is happy for us to talk to Anna . . .'

Katie said, 'Please, this isn't necessary. Just because she is not legally his child doesn't mean he has no feelings . . . I know what he means. It may be distressing for her . . . she may not want to talk about it.'

The policewoman said, 'We will be very sensitive. If she doesn't want to talk to us now we will respect that . . . we can always come again later.'

Dmitry didn't say anything. Sasha, who had been sleeping all this time, woke and began to cry. Dmitry stood up and said, 'Whatever you wish . . . You had better talk to her . . . I will take Sasha for a walk.'

'We don't want you to leave the hospital,' said the policeman, 'till we've spoken to Anna. I'll ask someone to accompany you.

I'm sorry, but it's police procedure.'

◆

Dmitry went downstairs, holding the baby across his arm, trembling with anger and self-hatred, aware of the policeman following a few paces behind him. He knew he could not carry on, causing pain and damage to everyone around him, to Katie, who he loved, to Anna, to his innocent child. Of course she didn't understand him; how could she; she did not realise that he was responsible for all this suffering and that he alone held the key to making them safe. He went into the coffee bar and found the payphones, dug in his pocket for some change. He said, 'I have to make a call . . . I need to cancel an appointment.' He knew now that he had no choice, and that the sooner he phoned the Libyans, the better.

As soon as he got through he said, turning to face the wall to avoid the policeman's gaze, 'I've changed my mind. I want to continue with the project.'

'Indeed? That is good news. Excellent . . . the arrangements are all made . . .'

'Yes, but I can't talk now . . . perhaps we can meet and discuss this.' Sasha was beginning to grumble and struggle in his arms. Dmitry pressed his cheek against the warm down on his head. The thought of what he was about to give up made his heart turn cold as ice. He hardly heard the Libyan's voice arranging when and where to meet.

Dmitry hung up. He nodded to the policeman and they went back upstairs. He walked up and down, soothing Sasha, almost giddy from lack of sleep. He sat in a chair and let Sasha rest on his shoulder, his eyes on the door behind which Anna was revealing . . . what? What could she say that would reveal anything worse than what he would soon have to confess to Katie? It didn't matter. Nothing mattered. Soon he would go home, and sleep.

◆

Anna had needed persuasion to talk about it at all. Katie sat with her throughout the interview, reassuring her; Anna addressed herself to her rather than the police. Anna said there had been two men in the car, one driving and the other with her in the back. The car was dark blue. She hadn't wanted to get in, she knew she shouldn't, but the man in the back had grabbed her. She said, 'The man gave me some sweeties in the car. We went a long way. He said we were going home but it was the wrong way.' She couldn't remember what he was wearing. He was wearing trousers. She didn't know what colour. When the policewoman said brown she said yes, but when she suggested blue or black she also said yes. She said she didn't know if they were English, but they didn't have funny voices. Their hair was dark and their skin was light brown. They were not boys but they were not old and they didn't have beards. They were wearing sunglasses. The sweeties had been those little fizzy ones in a packet. She had eaten two packets and they had made her feel a bit sick. When asked if they had hurt her, she said 'No.' Then she said, 'Mummy, I want Mitya.' She couldn't remember how she got out of the car and wouldn't talk about it anymore.

The police got up to leave. They said they would like to see her a few days later, perhaps when she was at home. They suggested Katie should talk to her about it again when she was more relaxed; if she said anything of interest perhaps Katie could let them know. Perhaps she could ask Anna to draw a picture of the car or the men. They said that two men were unusual; these people tended to operate alone. Maybe, they said, they had fallen out, or one had persuaded the other out of it and they had decided to leave Anna by the roadside. It was unlikely that Anna would have been able to open the door herself. They said Anna seemed to have lost the memory of the incident itself but that was normal. She might have suppressed anything frightening that had happened to her but recall it later when the fear had faded.

Katie saw them stop and talk to Dmitry on the way out; saw him start as they approached him and repeatedly shake his head. She went to join him. They were asking him where he had been that afternoon and he said that he had been to the library and then gone for a walk. They asked exactly where he had been walking and he said he had been to Hyde Park. No, he had not seen anybody, he had not met anybody, he had been on his own. He said he couldn't remember exactly when he had left the library because he hadn't looked at his watch.

Katie was frightened for a moment; she wondered if they suspected him, the stepfather. His replies seemed to her confusing and evasive, and this alarmed her, not because she thought he was lying, though this did cross her mind for a brief instant, but because she thought they might mistakenly take some action against him. She also did wonder for a moment whether there couldn't be some strange connection between Dmitry's odd behaviour and what had happened to Anna, though she failed to see what this could be. The police however seemed to be satisfied; they folded up their notebooks and went downstairs. Dmitry turned to Katie and said, 'Anna didn't remember anything.' Despite his flat tone, she took it as a question.

'Two men, perhaps Asian, a blue car, that's all. The police said, two men was unusual. Why, Mitya, why?'

He only stared at her helplessly and shrugged his shoulders.

◆

Katie was at her wit's end. After an initial reaction of relief, of thankfulness, Dmitry seemed even more withdrawn, more upset and anxious than before.

He hung around the house, showing no sign of doing any work or engaging himself in any useful activity. When she asked him what he was doing he simply said that he was thinking, or that he didn't have anything urgent to do at the moment, he was waiting for comments on his draft. Katie wanted to press him further, but realised she didn't have the courage. She knew that something was very wrong but was so in fear of what he might reveal to her that she couldn't ask him at the moment, and she was also afraid of having a confrontation, of doing anything that might further upset Anna, although his withdrawal seemed so extreme that she began to wonder if he was actually ill or having a breakdown of some sort.

About a week after Anna had come home from hospital, Katie finally lost her patience. She came down from reading Anna's bed-time story and found the supper ruined and Dmitry simply sitting at the kitchen table with his head in his hands. When she came down he dropped his arms on to the table as if they were too heavy to hold up any longer. Katie shouted at him: 'Can't you do anything? The carrots have boiled dry . . . didn't you smell them?' He didn't seem to have noticed anything, but looked at her wildly as if she were speaking in some language he didn't understand. Katie rescued what she could of the carrots and potatoes and put them in a dish on the table with the ham. She sat down, facing him, and he pushed his plate away.

'Mitya, you must eat.'

'I can't.'

'We have to talk. I'm so worried about you – you can't go on like this. I think you must be ill . . . you should go and see a doctor.'

'I am not ill.'

'I think you must have some kind of depressive illness, to behave like this. Please, Mitya, can't you get some anti-depressants or something? I can't live with this.'

'For God's sake. What would they do? That is typical of you, to think that some pills will change anything. It is not my mind which is at fault, it is my situation.'

Katie was angry at this injustice to her; surely he knew she saw anti-depressants as a last resort, had deliberately held back from mentioning them for as long as possible. She said, 'And what is it about your situation that is so terrible? Have you lost all your work and can't bring yourself to tell me? Have you got us into more debt? Have you . . .' she cast around wildly – 'Got some woman pregnant?'

He looked at her, open-mouthed. Katie went on, angry, relentless. 'Come on, tell me. Have you got into trouble with the police? Have you –' and suddenly she stopped. Something prevented her from naming the other possibilities which came into her mind – warned her that it was better not to go there. She tried to calm herself, to sound more reasonable. 'Mitya. Ever since Anna came home, you've been like this . . . I don't understand. You act as if she had died, not as if she had got better . . .'

'Yes, I know . . . I can't help it.'

'I thought things were better now. You have some work . . . we have some money. You must tell me, what is the matter with you? You don't talk to me, you don't explain anything. You are shutting me out . . . Don't you see, I feel so lonely.'

He gave a grimace, as though what she was saying physically hurt him, and murmured, 'I'm sorry.'

'Mitya, it isn't enough to be sorry. You have to do something about it. I can't go on like this. I need some support myself. I have Anna, and Sasha, both needing me constantly, I try to help you, and I am getting nothing back . . .'

'I know. I am not much use to you, am I?'

He looked so utterly wretched at this moment that Katie took pity on him. She went towards him and put her arms around him; feeling him soften, she went on. 'You don't confide in me; I wish you would. It would be so much better if you didn't bottle everything up inside you.'

He said, 'But if I told you . . . you could not forgive me.' And then, when she looked at him, startled, afraid, he said, taking a deep breath, 'Katie, I know this is terrible . . . I have something to tell you. If there was any way I could avoid it I would . . . I have to go away again.'

Katie sat down very heavily on the chair next to him. She knew instinctively that something was coming which she didn't want to hear. If she could have stopped the conversation then she would have done, but she could see that it was already too late – and besides, now she had to know. She tried to prepare herself, asking, 'When?'

'At the end of the month.'

'For how long exactly?'

'I don't know. Perhaps several months, perhaps a year.'

'A year? Where? What for? You mean, in Russia?'

Dmitry's voice was very gentle. 'Katie, I didn't tell you the truth. I lied to you last time . . . I was not in Russia. It's the same place as before . . . I am going to Libya.'

It took a few moments to sink in. Katie echoed, 'Libya,' wooden, hollow. Then she got up from the chair. She walked across the room, and the floor seemed suddenly uneven, unstable. She stumbled against the corner of the sofa, turned to face him. He sat there, immobile, his face hanging down, unable to look her in the eyes. Everything suddenly became clear to her, his secretive behaviour, the money from Geneva, his nervousness and depression, the hints from Tim which she had wilfully blotted out. Of course, this was the thing she had most feared. She said, 'I see . . . now I see . . . that is where the money came from. So that's what you have done . . . you have been selling nuclear secrets to the Libyans.'

14

DMITRY stood up, facing her; he felt they were like wild animals assessing one another before a battle. He didn't attempt to deny what she had said. How could he? Now he saw fully the terrible trap that he had made for himself. He didn't dare tell her how it had all happened, how he had been approached first by the Russians, which might have excused him a little in her eyes. Wild scenarios went through his head; that if the Libyans suspected this, they might come and question her; if she knew, they might force it out of her; and then he himself would be dead, or worse. He must let her think the very worst of him; that was the only way. Katie had turned white now, she was trembling, and having struck her this terrible blow, he could only stand and watch her suffering.

'Mitya . . . How could you? Have you gone mad? After everything you you've said, everything you've done . . . at the IAEA, and afterwards . . . I believed you, I trusted you, and now . . .'

'We had no money – ' He was going to say more, but she stopped him.

'And what else would you have done? Would you have robbed a bank, would you have murdered someone . . .'

Dmitry circled round her, trying to calm himself. He said, 'Katie, please, don't be too hard on me. It was not entirely my own doing . . . I have tried to get out, but . . . they have a way of trapping you.'

'What do you mean? They tried to blackmail you? What with?'

'Oh, you can imagine, Katie.'

'They threatened you?'

'Yes, that of course . . . and other things.'

'What other things?' Katie was by now on the verge of hysteria; he could see her distress growing by the moment. 'What things, Mitya? Tell me, for God's sake, tell me.'

Dmitry turned his head away from her. She rushed over to him, grabbed his head, and forced him to look at her. Her fingernails pressed painfully into his face. She shouted, her face ugly with despair, 'I want the truth, Mitya; tell me the truth.'

Dmitry said, 'Haven't you guessed?' and then Katie said, in a much calmer voice, letting go of him, 'Anna.'

He could say nothing. Katie went on, quite calmly, 'I see, so it wasn't some random child molester, was it? Now I understand. That is what has been the matter with you, isn't it. They did it, and it was your fault. Isn't that what happened?'

'Yes.'

'And all this time, when I was thinking, and wondering – you knew. You *knew*!' He had never seen a look like the one she gave him now; he saw that she was struggling between two extremes of feeling, of love and hate. She would have forgiven him anything, probably, as long as he had not put her children in danger; that was the one thing he knew she couldn't live with. Suddenly she hurled herself down, flinging herself forwards on to the sofa, and howled in a terrible, desperate voice, 'Oh, my God, what have you done to us?'

She went on sobbing and crying out, her hands in front of her face. Dmitry went over and tried to pull them away but she resisted. He said, 'Please, Katie, stop this, I can't bear it, let me talk to you, please, look at me,' but she only said, over and over, 'No.' Great sobs shook her body. Dmitry held her, despite her struggling against him, and he too began crying, the tears flowing freely from his eyes and pouring down his face faster than he would have thought possible. She opened her eyes and looked at him, but it was even more terrible to look into her face than it was before; her whole body contorted and she began to sob even more desperately. She tried again to get away from him, turning in his arms, rolling down on to the floor, but he hung on to her, gathering her close to him. He was so strong, there was no way she could physically resist him; he pressed her close to his chest and she hung there, her tears soaking his shirt. She struggled again and he abruptly let go over her, and watched her crawl along the floor, curl herself up into a ball. Dmitry left her and sat woodenly on the sofa, waiting for her to stop crying. He sat and waited for a long time.

Finally she sat up, struggling for control. 'I can't do anything . . . . This is too terrible. I don't know you, I don't know what you've become . . . I feel as if you've killed me.'

He opened his mouth to speak to her, but no words came.

She said, 'This has to end. You've put us all in danger, me, Anna, your own son . . . I can't go on with this.'

She sat on the sofa next to him, her hands in her lap, struggling to stop crying. He saw that there was no way back from here, and that for her sake he had to end everything, decisively, at once. He tried to talk calmly, to make practical arrangements. 'No. Of course you can't. I have thought it all through . . . you must write to the lawyer and ask for a legal separation. Just wait another month, till I get my permanent residency here . . . I will agree to whatever terms you want. I'll make sure that there is enough money for you, I'll have it paid regularly into our account. I'll go to Libya till my contract runs out . . . while I am working for them I will have no contact with you or the children. That way you will not be in any further danger. You must tell nobody about this. When the contract runs out . . . when I come back . . .'

'If you come back.'

'Well, if I come back, then . . . then we can meet and talk about a final agreement, a divorce if you want one, access to the children and that kind of thing.'

Katie trembled from head to foot. The word 'divorce' seemed unbearable to her. She asked, 'And there's no other way out of this?'

'There is no way out.'

Katie said, 'I should have known, back in Vienna . . . there is something wrong with you. You were always too secretive. It's like an addiction. And then like all addicts, in the end you have to destroy yourself, and not content with that you have to pull everyone else in with you . . .'

'Yes,' said Dmitry, heavily, staring at the back of his hands, which now seemed foreign to him, as if they were someone else's, 'Yes, perhaps it is like that.'

'Well,' said Katie, 'I shall never sleep, but even so, I have to go to bed.'

He followed her upstairs. They undressed, in silence, and Katie lay down on the bed. Dmitry said, 'Do you want me to sleep downstairs?' but she shook her head. He didn't think he would be able to sleep either, but he did, almost instantly. He was woken later in the night by her crying. He put his arms around her and held her tightly. She clung to him as if she was afraid of drowning; then she took his hands and placed them on her breasts; still sobbing, she came on top of him and guided him into her and then began to make herself come over and over with sharp, desperate cries. Then they went on, obliterating everything else in the flood of sensation, until finally, exhausted, moaning, Katie begged him to stop. Then she said, 'I don't understand . . . why is sex so good with you? If it was not for that . . .'

And Dmitry said simply, 'It's because we love one another.'

She said, 'Then why? Why wasn't that enough to satisfy you?' and she began crying all over again with as much anguish as when she had first started. And then she stopped suddenly and looked at him, asking, 'How shall we tell Anna?'

◆

Anna didn't understand what he was saying. They both sat, either side of her on the sofa, and tried to explain, that Mitya had to go away and work abroad for a long time, and that he would not be able to visit them. She asked at once, 'But you will come back?' and Dmitry, because Katie had insisted that they didn't lie to Anna and betray her trust, couldn't answer her. Katie spoke up for him, unable in the end to inflict so much pain, saying, 'Well, we hope so, let's see what happens.' At first Anna couldn't take it in, had refused to believe it; but when she saw that they were serious she said, her voice rising to a wail, 'But I don't want Mitya to go away. I want him to stay here and be my daddy!'

Katie looked at Dmitry with the expression of a tigress ready to kill. He said, helplessly, unable to endure Anna's distress, 'It isn't because I don't love you, Anna. I don't want to go . . . I am doing it because I have to.' Anna turned and ran upstairs, sobbing loudly, and Katie ran after her. Dmitry sat and stared at the floor. His own grief seemed pitifully inadequate in front of hers. He wanted to howl in shame and rage, to shed tears as they did, but his frozen frame would not respond.

◆

He met the Libyans once more at the Metropole Hotel. 'I want to go as soon as possible, tomorrow, the next day. I don't want to go via Moscow . . . its all a farce anyway, if I'm being watched, they'll know what I am doing . . . book me a flight straight to Malta.'

Hattab nodded. He cleared his throat; they both faced the bar, not looking at one another. He said, 'I understand that there was a regrettable accident with your little girl. It occurred to me that you might think . . . I can assure you that this was not anything to do with us.'

Dmitry stared at him, uncomprehending. There seemed such sincerity in his voice, his manner, that Dmitry was completely confused for a moment. But if they were not responsible, how could they know? The piped music in the background jangled his nerves. It even occurred to Dmitry for a moment that this might have been some further convolution in Rozanov's diabolical scheming, but he dismissed this thought as soon as it came. He looked at the Libyan; well, why shouldn't he lie, like this, with a smile, to get what he wanted?

Dmitry said, 'I don't want to discuss this . . . it is quite irrelevant. As a matter of fact, I am separating from my wife . . .' He wanted them to think that he no longer cared about his family, that they could not be used to threaten him. He had thought through all the things he could say to them and come up with only one, but this lie was harder for him than all the others. The words he found shocked him with their intensity. 'I have utterly repudiated her . . . she has been unfaithful.'

How could he say this? It was a terrible thing to do, to blacken Katie's character in this way; he did not believe that she could ever betray or hurt him. He thought how different she was to his first wife, who had been unfaithful not once, but many times, who had gone to bed with other men for no other reason that he could see other than to hurt him; he tried to imagine to himself that he was talking about Masha, not Katie. He couldn't shake off a superstitious feeling that by saying these things he might make them true, that he would be suitably punished for his terrible lie. The Libyan, as if embarrassed at this personal revelation, held up his hand. He said, 'I understand.' He ordered another drink. 'Of course, you could always arrange for your children to come with Libya, if not now, then later . . . do you have them on your passport?'

Dmitry shook his head; for an instant he wondered if he hadn't made things still worse for himself; he could see them making arrangements for a child abduction. Everything he said, every lie he invented, seemed to further twist the knot he sought desperately to undo. He said, 'No, they belong with their mother. The boy is a small baby and the girl . . . she is not even my child. What matters is that I now no longer have to spend time in London with them. I can come to your country and dedicate myself entirely to my researches . . . please arrange everything as quickly as you can.'

The Libyan rose. He said, 'Please wait,' and went out to the telephones. He came back after fifteen minutes and handed Dmitry a slip of paper. 'You are booked tonight, on a flight to Malta, at three a.m. Your ticket will be held for you at the airline desk. Someone will be there to meet you and take you on a boat to Tripoli.' He paused. 'Don't worry, everything has been arranged. We shall send a cab for you at midnight.'

◆

So now there was no time left; just an hour until he had to leave. He'd packed his suitcase, a big old leather one that belonged to Katie, the only one they had which was large enough. Dmitry sat at the kitchen table. The clock ticked, it seemed, interminably slowly; it was impossible to say anything. Katie moved silently around the room, picking things up off the floor, putting them away, folding the heaps of crumpled washing into neat piles, one for her, one for Anna, one for Sasha. From time to time she glanced at Dmitry, he could feel her eyes rest on him, but he couldn't look at her.

The clock struck eleven. Dmitry leaned forward and put his head on his arms. On the radio they were playing some baroque choral music, the voices rising high in a chorus of gathering intensity. Dmitry couldn't listen to it; it implied the existence of beauty, of hope, of certainty in the world, from all of which he felt he had utterly isolated himself. Katie must have felt the same, because she suddenly switched off the radio. She gathered up the dry washing and went to the bottom of the stairs. She said, 'Please, Mitya, please, come upstairs now.'

'What is the point? The taxi is coming in half an hour.'

'But at least then I can be close to you.'

He looked up at her, then; it was as if for an instant she was offering him an alternative to damnation. He got up from the table and followed her upstairs. They lay on the bed, close to one another, holding one another, but did not make love.

At midnight the doorbell rang. Katie moved to get up, but Dmitry said, 'No.' He kissed her and she pulled him close to her so that he had to tear himself away. He stood and looked at her for an unendurable moment, understanding and feeling her pain and not being able to comprehend how he had come to inflict it, the one thing in the world which he would have done anything to avoid. Then he turned away and ran down the stairs.

◆

Tim, still awake, drew back the curtain. He saw the taxi, the rain falling, a man taking Dmitry's heavy suitcase, and Dmitry's agonized glance back at the upstairs window before he climbed into the cab. He heard the slamming of the door and saw the raindrops glittering in the headlights as the taxi drove away.

He didn't know why he had this strong impression, but he somehow knew that Gavrilov had gone for good.

◆

Tim hadn't seen Katie for some time. Since she had told him about Anna's accident he had deliberately kept his distance from them, and particularly he had avoided Dmitry, who had seemed to be at home all the time. He had talked to him once briefly on the steps when he was letting himself in, and heard that Anna was back at school and doing well; he had left a card for Katie but felt that he shouldn't intrude.

But in the morning, as soon as he heard Katie moving round upstairs, he went up and rang the doorbell.

She opened the door and stood looking at him, blinking. She said, dully, 'Oh, hello Tim. Have you run out of milk?'

Tim was taken aback. She looked terrible, with uncombed hair and red-rimmed eyes, and it was the first time she hadn't seemed at all pleased to see him.

'I hadn't seen you for some time . . . I thought I'd say hello . . . see if you were all right.'

She said, 'Come in . . . I'll make some coffee.' He followed her up the stairs and into the kitchen. All her movements seemed slow, listless; she moved carelessly, nearly chipping the edge of the coffee pot on the tap as she rinsed it out, seeming to have difficulty in opening the packet of coffee. Sasha sat gurgling in the highchair, sucking on a half-eaten tangerine.

Tim asked, 'What's the matter?'

Katie said, 'Mitya and I have separated.'

Tim said, 'Oh, I see.' Then he said, 'I didn't know.'

'No, of course not. How could you know? He only left last night.'

'Where to?'

'Oh, I . . . I don't know.' She poured boiling water on to the coffee; her hand was not quite steady. Tim wanted to offer to help but couldn't, quite.

'You don't know where he is?'

'What? Who?' She hadn't been listening. Tim said, 'Mitya.' It seemed odd to use his name, or at least, that familiar form of it, because he despised him; but it would have seemed artificial here to call him anything else.

Katie said, 'I don't want to.'

'Don't you?' He was standing close behind her, near enough to touch her. She poured milk into the coffee and turned to look at him, offering him a mug. Was it hostility between them, or something else? Were they, then, intimate enough to be angry with one another? Katie handed him the coffee. She sat down. She said, 'Tim, don't ask me these things, please, not now . . . I am so miserable.'

Her lips trembled; she was going to cry; with an effort that was obvious and painful to him he saw her force back the tears. Tim said, 'But isn't it for the best? That you've split up. I've heard a lot through the floor, you know. I've heard you both shouting and you crying as if your heart would break. I never understood why you stayed with him when he made you so unhappy. What kind of a hold has he had over you?'

Katie turned her head away. She put her hand across her forehead to shield herself from his view. He said, 'Katie.' She looked at him. She was crying, now. He went and put his arms around her and she turned her head into his shoulder. He said, 'Look, Katie, I want to help you. I really care about you, you know that, don't you. I can't bear to see you unhappy like this. Is there anything I can do for you?'

'Oh, Tim, I don't know . . . . everything is such a mess.' She wiped her tears away clumsily with the back of her hand. 'Tim, I'm very fond of you, but I can't . . .'

'You can't what?' He kissed the back of her neck and she didn't resist. She turned round to face him and he took both her hands in his, looked at her in the eyes, and said, 'You look so beautiful when you cry.' She stared at him wildly, stood up, pulling her hands away from him, and went over to the window; he could see that she was trembling. She said, in a shaky voice, 'Please Tim, can't you see? Please don't do this, you're making things worse for me.'

Instantly he knew he'd gone too far. She was too upset, he mustn't take advantage of her in this state. 'I'm sorry, I'm not asking you for anything, Katie, I just wanted you to know how I feel. What I'm trying to say is, if there's anything you want me to do for you, you can ask me, I won't mind . . .'

Her voice was very quiet, controlled. 'Well, right now, Tim, if you don't mind, you can go downstairs.'

He hesitated, uncertain, unsure whether she really meant this or not; then he decided he should take her at her word. He was upset, but not too downhearted, by her reaction; he was determined that in time he would convince her, would win her over; he was sure she was attracted to him, was held back only by a sense of guilt. He felt no guilt at all about his feelings for her, did not feel that he was unfairly making use of her misery. After all, he thought, I have been waiting for a long time.

PART TWO

1

THE HEAT from the ground struck Dmitry like a physical blow as he stepped out of the building. The late afternoon shadows fell heavily across the courtyard; the plants hung limply in the dusty garden. Even the Libyans said that it was hot.

From the moment he arrived back in Libya he had decided he would get on with his work and not think about anything else. His work was the one thing that kept him sane. Shut up in his room, he made hundreds of calculations. Half the time they were irrelevant to his work, he just followed the chain on, seeing where it would lead. Perhaps the abstraction of numbers was his only way of resisting a reality which was intolerable to him.

The project was going well. He could do exactly as he liked, follow his instincts, make short cuts, take risks in a way he would never have been allowed before, and it was paying off. He only had ask for something and it was his. He and Suzarbayev had set up the first test cell, had run the experiment and the first measurements of the degree of separation had been higher than he had anticipated. Suzarbayev had looked at him with complete astonishment.

'This thing is working.'

'I told you it would work.'

Still, promising as this was, it was only the beginning. They had been lucky so far, but the main problem would be how create a pressure variation in the gas to allow the lighter particles containing U235 to be pumped off. In fact, this preliminary promising result might go against him, encouraging Masoud to press for him to try to set up a small cascade before he was really sure that he had sorted out the problems.

When he began to think of Katie and the children he simply stopped himself, then and there, by an effort of will. They were part of another life, distant and unattainable.

However hard he tried to resist it, he was aware of a black mood lurking under the surface, a lack of energy, a feeling that nothing mattered. Perhaps it was simply when he was tired. Or perhaps it was on days when there was nothing much to do, when he was waiting for equipment to be procured, times when, in the ordinary way, he might have had time off. On these days he would try to work, but the numbers on the page would seem meaningless to him. He found himself staring at them blankly, unable to understand how anything so abstract could have any bearing on observed reality. On one of these days, in a desperate attempt to occupy himself, he went down to the lab, took out his notebook, and began to check the results again.

Suzarbayev stared at him across the workbench. He was struggling to loosen some small screw but for some reason was having no success. He said, 'It's getting dark. Why do you work so hard? Why don't you take a break? Let's go into Tripoli tonight and see if there's any fun.'

'You told me there was nothing to do in Tripoli.'

'Well, that's true, but . . . at least it's a change of scene. There's an Algerian pizza place I went to once . . . we could walk around, take a look at things . . . you haven't even been in to Tripoli.'

'That's because you did such a good job of putting me off.'

'Look, come on. I'm going. I'll get a driver . . . we're not prisoners, you know. It's just my luck they assigned me to work with you. Nobody else takes their work so seriously, and they're the ones who want . . .'

Dmitry looked up. 'Want what?'

'Oh, you know . . .' and Suzarbayev mimicked an atomic explosion with his hands.

Dmitry suddenly put his notebook away and got to his feet. He handed Suzarbayev the heavy Swiss army knife which he carried in his pocket. He said, 'Try this.' Suzarbayev looked at it, examined it appreciatively, used the blade to work the screw loose. He handed the knife back to Dmitry. 'Do you always carry this?'

'You never know when it might be useful. Come on then, let's lock up, and you can introduce me to the delights of Tripoli.'

◆

The car drove along the coast-road. They had the windows open; the moon's reflection was gliding over the dark water and the night air was hot and clean, blowing from the sea. Dmitry felt as if he had been lifted out of time, that the days and weeks no longer had any meaning, and that he would be quite happy if this journey lasted for ever, leading nowhere, so that he could just enjoy the sensation of the car speeding through the warm darkness. The lights of Tripoli glowed ahead of them, and beyond that lay the darkness of the sea.

They found the Algerian pizza place Suzarbayev had talked about and had a passable pizza with de-alcoholized beer. They wandered through the streets, past dusty shops, building sites, large impersonal modern buildings, giant posters of Gaddafi, down to the harbour. Containers lay carelessly as if abandoned on the jetty, in the distance a few military boats lay in the dull oily water. Along the front dusty palm trees rustled their leaves in the evening breeze. Looking along the front Dmitry could see an echo of Tripoli's former splendours in the faded white villas lying behind their white-walled gardens. Traffic scorched noisily up and down in the hot night.

Suzarbayev led the way to the Libyan Palace Hotel, a massive, ugly building with its silver sign drooping from the facade, like faded tinsel. Inside, the hotel had a kind of shabby splendour, with its mahogany chairs and tattered antique carpets. To the left, behind a glass screen, was the bar, serving coffee and soft drinks. Dmitry ordered two orange juices while Suzarbayev sat by the potted palms on a cracked leather armchair.

As Dmitry waited at the bar a man came to stand beside him, brushed against his sleeve. The man ordered a drink; his Russian accent was unmistakeable; Dmitry turned to look at him. A slightly startled look passed over the man's face, as if he recognised him; he said, 'Excuse me,' in Russian, took his own drink and shot away from the bar as if Dmitry was contaminated.

Dmitry carried the orange juices to the corner where Suzarbayev was sitting smoking a cigarette. He eyed the drink with disgust. 'The Libyans, they all drink at home, they have cupboards of alcohol stashed away . . . this is just to torment foreigners.' Then he said, 'I saw you talking to Dorokhov.'

Dmitry hesitated before asking, 'Who?'

'You heard me. Dorokhov.'

'The man at the bar? You know him?'

'Only by sight.' Suzarbayev was looking at him in a way he didn't like; tense, suspicious. 'I know who he is. He's from the embassy. A KGB type.'

Dmitry swallowed the orange juice. It was too sweet, sickly, with an artificial taste to it which stayed in the mouth. What was the natural thing to say? He was worried, now. Dorokhov had seemed to have recognised him; perhaps he'd been told that he was here in Libya; or perhaps it was simply that, looking at him, he'd known at once that he was Russian. Or perhaps the meeting had not been coincidental; perhaps it had been deliberate, a brush contact, perhaps something had been passed to him. Certainly it could look that way to Suzarbayev.

Dmitry felt, almost without realising it, in his pocket. He saw Suzarbayev looking at him and felt suddenly hot with confusion. Suzarbayev's face was blank, impassive. 'I have no love lost for these people, Mitya. You're not messing around with them, are you? Because if you are, you must be crazy.'

Dmitry said, 'Is that what you think? Just because . . .'

Suzarbayev said, 'Keep calm. They are looking at us.'

Dmitry said, 'Come on, let's get out of here.' When they emerged from the air-conditioning into the hot darkness Dmitry felt himself shaking. He said, 'Why did you say that to me, in there? That was pure coincidence, seeing him, I had no idea who he was. Do you really think that I am passing information to them? I would have to be insane. Look, if that was the case they would hardly approach me in a public place . . .'

'Wouldn't they?'

Dmitry felt his heart beating in his chest almost painfully, so acutely was he aware of the danger he was in. He felt as if fear must radiate from him palpably. He and Suzarbayev walked, aimlessly, through the empty streets, heading towards the shore. Dmitry said, 'This is incredible. You think I would have anything to do with those bastards? Don't you think I have spent my whole life trying to avoid them . . . ?'

Suzarbayev laughed. 'You chose the wrong profession for that.'

Dmitry had no idea what to say. It was ridiculous that this chance meeting, this meaningless little incident, should threaten his security so totally. He didn't trust Suzarbayev; he imagined he might mention this incident to someone, who knows what for. He had no idea what Suzarbayev's motivations were; whether he was simply here to earn money or whether he felt loyalty to the Libyans. After all, he was a Muslim. There was, after all, no reason why he should favour Dmitry over them; he had frequently told him he had no love lost for the Russians. Dmitry tried to keep calm. He said, 'Look, what is this? I don't like this conversation. You are imagining things, you are reading something into this for some reason I can't fathom. You are making too much of it.'

Suzarbayev said, 'On the contrary, I think it's you who is over-reacting.'

They began to walk, slowly, along the sea-front. The sea was black as ink. Suzarbayev grinned, patting his arm. 'Look, I am your friend, Mitya, you idiot. That is why I am having this conversation with you. That is why I am warning you.'

'Well, no warning is needed.'

'Look, I'm no fool. I know you have been looking into things that are not strictly your concern. I've noticed the questions you ask . . . So far I've told no one.'

'What do you mean, so far?' asked Dmitry, stopping, suddenly angry. 'What is this, Djambul? Are you threatening me?'

Suzarbayev did not reply. Dmitry thought, it doesn't matter, this will all blow over; he saw that everything he'd said had made it worse. They walked on in silence. Dmitry tried to dismiss the incident, but the more he thought about it, the more worried he became. He felt trapped, he felt a sudden tide of panic rise in him. If Suzarbayev said anything, if the Libyans suspected that he'd passed information on to Russian intelligence, God knows what they would do to him. It didn't bear thinking about. It might be better to be dead. He looked up at Suzarbayev, walking jauntily along, seeming quite unconcerned, looking out towards the sea. And then a terrible idea seized him, took hold of him in an instant; that he could kill Suzarbayev, and be safe.

Instead of immediately dismissing this thought, Dmitry found himself actually thinking about it, beginning to think through how it could be done. He had the knife in his pocket. He could throw the body into the sea; maybe it wouldn't be washed up for a while. It could have been a common murderer or thief; unless, of course, there were few thieves in Tripoli. It was not the sort of city where crime could flourish – perhaps that was too implausible. But what of himself? Could anyone suspect him of such a thing? He had no idea. He put his hand into his pocket, to feel for the knife, to be sure it was there. He had no idea how to kill someone with a knife, nothing beyond a brief army training years ago. You needed to cut a major artery. He could cut the throat, but he knew even as he thought of this that he wouldn't be able to do it. He thought he might be able to stick the knife in Suzarbayev's chest. But then, how much strength would he need? Was the blade long enough? Besides, it might hit a rib. He might not inflict a fatal wound first time, and then Suzarbayev would struggle. Dmitry stopped dead in his tracks, overcome by the horror of what he was thinking.

Suzarbayev was looking at him. He asked, 'Are you all right?'

Dmitry walked on in an instant. Suzarbayev's voice brought him suddenly back to reality. 'Yes; yes, something just occurred to me, about the experiment; let me think a moment.' He took his hand out of his pocket; Suzarbayev's bright, lively eyes stared into his, as if they could read his thoughts. He said suddenly, 'Let's go back. There's nothing here . . . you were right about this place.'

They walked away from the deserted shore. Behind them the moon, as if it too had wearied of their conversation, slipped slowly below the horizon.

◆

The fragile peace of mind which Dmitry had felt since his arrival in Libya had vanished in a moment, puffed away like a thin mist at dawn. He was constantly tormented by the foolishness of what he had done. He couldn't understand how Rozanov had put him in this position, how he could have failed to see how his plan would inevitably backfire. He had produced little intelligence of any real value; instead of this, he was willingly conspiring in the very project he was supposed to be preventing. He didn't understand; he couldn't penetrate the mystery of Rozanov's intentions.

Now, at night, he couldn't stop himself from thinking about Katie. He lay awake, in his cold, sterile, bare room; sometimes he had to get up and read or try to work to take his mind off her. He thought of Anna, of her pale, frightened face, saying 'I want you to stay and be my daddy.' That had been the worst, the most unforgivable betrayal. He rolled over in the bed, unable to stop thinking about it. Sometimes at nights he sat and drank, glass after glass, from his seemingly limitless supply of vodka, anything to blot out the agony of his situation. He stayed awake till nearly dawn, then slept for two or three hours before dragging himself to the lab to struggle through the day. He was sure that they were watching him constantly. He was aware that he did not look well; that his work was obviously suffering. Masoud did not say anything, but he could sense his concern. Suzarbayev seemed to have noticed his change of mood; where before he had sought out his company, now he avoided him.

This went on for several weeks. Dmitry thought that it would have been an understatement to say that he was depressed. His existence had simply become so painful for him that when he thought about dying it seemed to him that this would be simply a relief. He walked around in a constant state of mental anguish. He carried out his tasks mechanically, because he had to, to keep up a front, but he derived no pleasure from anything. Now they had hit problems with the experiment. Although the measurements they had taken showed a high separative index, in fact the small size of the system, made necessary by the high frequencies involved, meant that it was proving more difficult than he thought to siphon off the different fractions. His mind wrestled with the problem at one level, frustrated, angry, while the other part of him said, 'This is good. This means that it will never work; you have sold them something useless after all.'

Adding to his distress was the fear that Suzarbayev had reported his suspicions and that at any time the Libyans might decide to question him about it. Even if they didn't, it meant they would be very careful with him, to deny him access to anything he might want to know; in other words, he would be blown, useless, finished. The whole thing had been hopeless from start to finish. What was the point of struggling on, of doing anything?

He was crossing the courtyard one morning, looking at his shadow moving before him in the harsh light of the sun, when the idea came to him with blinding clarity, like a blaze of light itself; that he could kill himself.

He jumped with astonishment at the thought. It was almost as if someone's voice had whispered in his ear, a soft, sinister voice, like that of Rozanov; he shook his head as if to dislodge it. As soon as he had this thought he knew it was the answer. The thought of suicide had crossed his mind before, in moments of despair; but this time it was different. This was not an emotional decision; it seemed to him that this was the only, the obvious, the rational solution. But how to do it? The most pleasant way, the way that he would prefer, would be to get some drug, perhaps some sleeping pills. He was not sure how much he would have to take, how he would get hold of them, whether in doing this he might give himself away. There was no way he could get hold of a gun; he couldn't throw himself from a high building. He didn't want to bungle it; he had to get it right first time because he knew he would never have the courage for a second attempt, and who knew what the Libyans would do if he tried and failed.

But then, he had the knife. He could cut his wrists. It wouldn't be difficult. He could do it tonight. He would do it tonight. There; it was decided. That was the end of it.

He continued with his work, going through everything methodically, making sure he did not behave in any way that was unusual. He ran through the problems with Suzarbayev again, tried to see if he would come up with any solution; but Suzarbayev clearly had nothing to contribute. At the end of the day he left the laboratory and went out into the sunshine. A wind was blowing from the sea; everything seemed unusually sharp and clear, the sounds separate and distinct, the light seemed to have a peculiar quality of clarity about it. He went back to his room and sat on the bed. He thought at once about Katie. He couldn't do this without saying something to Katie; it would be too cruel. He had to say goodbye to her; he had to explain in case she was otherwise left wondering whether he was alive or not, or in case she found out what happened; he knew she had been brought up as a Catholic and that she would have a particular horror of suicide. He went and sat at the table, took out his pen, reached for a sheaf of papers and began to write.

He wrote: 'My beautiful, my beloved, my dearest Katie.'

His hand shook; he was convulsed, suddenly, with anguish; he couldn't write this. He thought of Katie, he could see her face so clearly, remember the scent of her skin, the sound of her voice; he could almost hear her voice now, begging him not to do this. He shut it out, forced himself to carry on. He wrote: 'Everything has gone wrong; I am out of my depth. I have tried everything I can to retrieve this situation but this is the only solution I can think of. I am doing this to spare you any further pain, to ensure your safety, for Anna and Sasha, to take with me this knowledge I possess which can do so much harm.' He stopped again; he realised he had not said what 'this' was; what could he say? How could he put it? What was the point of trying to soften the blow? 'When you read this letter I will be dead. In this act I am seeking redemption not annihilation. I am doing it because I believe it is the only solution to this mess which I have created. I know that you have always loved me; I can't bear to think of what I have done to you. I know that once you have got over the shock you will be happier without me. Please, my love, be happy.' He had to wipe the tears from his eyes to stop them wetting the page. 'I offer no excuses for what I have done but please believe me when I tell you that I have not been as corrupt as you must think. Try to remember the good things that have been between us and not the pain. You know I do not believe that anything will follow death but we have had our moments of bliss, you and I, and these I believe will be eternal. Look after yourself and the children. I love you all. Mitya.'

He did not read it through. He knew he mustn't look at the letter, must not redraft it; it was not a work of art, and besides, he didn't think he could read what he had written. He was afraid that it would sound cheap and that he would feel diminished by it. If he read it again he would want to change it; he could think of a thousand different words to say but in the end it would come to the same thing. It would do; it was done. Now he had to get it to her. He would have to find some way of posting it that would mean it would not be intercepted.

He stood up, sealed the paper into an envelope and slid it into his jacket pocket. He would go into Tripoli. He would go to one of the international hotels and find someone going back to Europe who would mail it for him. He would be watched, of course; it would be difficult to do, but surely, possible.

He took out the knife and felt the blade. It was blunt; he had never sharpened it. He thought, it would be easier with a razor blade. He told his driver he wanted to go into Tripoli.

In the bar of the Libyan Palace Hotel he sat at a table and waited for someone to come and serve him. A waitress came from the bar to take his order. She was tall and slim, with honey-coloured skin and golden eyes. When she smiled at Dmitry he saw that her front teeth were slightly too far apart, but this flaw only added to her attractiveness.

He ordered his drink. She walked back to the bar, her hips swaying. For a moment, Dmitry felt a twinge of desire, as if some force of life was struggling to come awake in him. The waitress came back to the table and smiled at him, a knowing smile, as if some understanding lay between them. She placed his drink carefully on the table. 'Let me know if you want anything else,' she said.

The bar was crowded, and after a while a man came and sat beside him. They began to talk. The man was Danish, he worked for the UN; he was flying back to Geneva in two days. This was perfect. Dmitry asked if he would take a letter to post to his wife and the man said, 'Sure.' Dmitry thought he could see the waitress watching him from the bar. He felt suddenly uneasy. He glanced down at the pile of UN papers and documents the Dane had left on the table, including a report on the status of women in Libya. Instead of handing it to him, which he thought someone might notice, he placed the letter carefully on top of the report. He said, 'It's my wife's birthday. You'll post it directly, won't you?'

As the man nodded Dmitry suppressed all thoughts of what would happen when Katie got the letter. He stood up to leave, and saw the waitress start to approach him from behind the bar. For some reason, he felt uneasy. He hurried out into the street, walked past a string of meagrely stocked shops; in one window unopened boxes were piled high, in another a dusty mannequin leaned disconsolately against the window. He found a pharmacy, went inside, walked down the brightly lit rows filled with shampoo, soap, toothpaste, cosmetics, hair dye. The absurdity, the vanity of the world struck him suddenly and for a moment he felt like laughing. He had assumed that his driver would stay in the car, but as he reached out for a packet of the old-fashioned oblong razor blades he saw the driver coming in through the door and glance towards him. Had he been asked to keep an eye on what he was doing? Dmitry picked up a packet of shaving cream instead and stared at the instructions. It was ridiculous; surely the driver wouldn't suspect or report anything; but he felt acutely, transparently vulnerable, as if his thoughts and intentions must be obvious to anyone.

Dmitry bought the shaving cream and left the blades; he thought that he would use his penknife after all. They returned to the car and sped through the darkness along the corniche. He looked at the lights shining on the dark water, the moon sinking low towards the earth and its reflection breaking up into slabs of light on the sluggish waves. Dmitry found that he was thinking about Katie after all. He wondered how long she would be faithful to him, after his death, whether she would marry again, and if so, who. He thought of her, lying beneath him, naked, her skin flushed a rosy pink, asking for more, please, more . . . he cut off such thoughts instantly, it was like a door slamming shut.

At Tajura there was one last thing he had to do. He was tired; it was dangerous; perhaps it would be a mistake. He crossed the courtyard, heading for the laboratory. The moonlight cast long, strange shadows over the plants in the courtyard; the water trickled gently, that sweet, luscious sound in the desert; the wind rustled in the leaves of the tree. At the entrance to the building the guard stared at him, curious. Dmitry's heart began to pound; he thought they might not let him in, might question him as to what he was doing.

The guard recognised him and let him in.

The building was in darkness. He went into the lab, put on the light, switched on the computer screen. He often worked late, not usually as late as this, but there was no reason why anyone should think it strange; it was only his own sense of guilt. He began to call up the files, and then to delete them, one by one. At first it pained him to do this, to destroy the work he had so laboriously created, but it had to be done. After a while, as again and again the screen flashed up, delete Yes/No? as if it questioned his own determination, he felt a sense of savage satisfaction, like the child's pleasure in destruction. As he did this he could almost hear Rozanov's fiendish laughter, goading him on.

He knew as he did this that he was not entirely obliterating what he had done. Perhaps the information, at least some of it, existed somewhere on back-up tapes which the Libyans would surely make. Further, until the discs were overwritten there was information there which could be retrieved. He was only making it more difficult for them; and there was a chance that they would not be able to get it all back. He went on, doggedly, file after file, to the end, then sat back, giddy and relieved.

Next he unlocked the filing cabinet and began to go through the paperwork. Most of it was a mess, scribbled notes, half-formed ideas; he wondered if anyone would be able to make sense of it. He took file after file, put the paper in the sink. He found a bottle of alcohol-based cleaning fluid, soaked the paper, and tossed in a match. The flames shot up; he stood ready with a cloth.

He heard the footsteps of the guard coming along the corridor. In haste, he threw down the cloth. The flames extinguished themselves; there was a smell of burning. The guard opened the door.

Dmitry sat by the bench in the brightly illuminated lab. The guard looked at him; he spoke no Russian or English. Dmitry spoke barely a word of Arabic. The guard raised his eyebrows, sniffed the air; Dmitry grinned. The guard shrugged and went away again.

Dmitry felt that he had done enough. He left the lab, locked the door behind him. He went back, across the moonlit courtyard, to his room. He shut the door and leaned against it for a moment. So, this was it; there was no point in delaying any longer; he had to do it.

He sat on the bed, his limbs heavy, exhausted. So, he was going to die. He did not believe that there was anything to follow; if he felt no hope on earth, how could he have hope of heaven? He tried to think, for a moment, of nothingness, but realised he couldn't; what he imagined was a black, velvety darkness, and darkness had colour, texture. He realised that his heart was racing, that his hands were damp with sweat, that his breathing had quickened. He must not think about it; if he thought at all, he would be lost. He went over to the cupboard, took out another bottle, wrenched off the top and poured himself a vodka. He drank it, poured another, and drank that too. It didn't make him feel any better and he didn't want to get drunk; maybe if he did he wouldn't be able to steel himself to go through with this. He put the bottle back in the cupboard.

He went into the bathroom. He knew, he didn't know how, that you were supposed to cut your wrists under warm water; perhaps it was to ease the pain, perhaps to encourage the blood to flow. He thought he would do it in the bath, but he couldn't face the idea of taking off his clothes, of dying and being found naked, nor could he see himself getting into the bath in wet clothes. Perhaps the basin would do. He ran the hot water into the basin. Then he went to get his knife. He ran his finger again along the blade. He supposed that it would do. He felt a momentary sense of nausea; he wiped his hand across his forehead.

He thought he heard again that whispered voice behind his ear, crackling like a radio, saying, 'Go on, do it.'

There was a sharp knock on the door.

Dmitry's heart leaped and landed with a heavy thump. He decided he wouldn't open it; whoever it was would go away. He stood, frozen, making no sound, but the knock came again, louder. Who was it? Perhaps they would break the door down. He called out, 'Yes? Who's there?'

'It's me, Djambul.'

Dmitry hesitated. He put the knife down on the table, opened the door. Suzarbayev stood there, the catalyst of his decision, grinning in blissful ignorance. Dmitry knew he should have said, 'Go away; I'm not well.' But he couldn't.

'I had an idea. About the withdrawal pipes . . . can I come in?'

'What? Yes . . . yes, come in. I was just going to bed . . .'

Suzarbayev sat at the table, picked up a pen, began drawing a diagram. Dmitry stared at him, unable to understand. What was Suzarbayev doing there? He had never come here so late before. Why did he have to sit here listening to this trivia? He knew he should tell him to stop, but he didn't want to do anything which seemed odd or out of character, so he endured him a little longer. Suzarbayev got to the end of his explanation. He handed the paper to Dmitry. 'What do you think?'

Dmitry stared at the diagram without seeing it. He said, trying to put some enthusiasm into his voice, 'I think . . . well, it might work. Very good. All right, we'll try it tomorrow.'

'Are you all right? You're looking a little pale.'

'I know. I'm getting a migraine.' Why didn't the idiot go? He could see he wasn't wanted. Suzarbayev hovered in the room. He asked, 'Do you mind if I have a drink?'

'A drink? Why not, of course, a drink.' Dmitry opened the cupboard again and took out the vodka bottle. It was nearly full. He said, handing it over, 'Go on, take the whole bottle . . . I won't be needing it.'

Why had he said that? He realised at once that it was a mistake. Suzarbayev was looking at him most oddly; yes, definitely, oddly. He said, hastily, trying to take hold of himself, 'I'm drinking too much. I've decided to stop . . . go on, take it away.'

Suzarbayev held the bottle awkwardly, then put it down on the table. He still hovered, as if he was aware that something was badly wrong but didn't know what it was or what he could do about it. Then he said, reluctantly, 'I'll go then.' As he turned, Suzarbayev saw the knife lying on the table. His hand went out to rest on it. He asked, 'Do you mind if I borrow this?'

Dmitry could stand it no longer. He said, 'Yes, anything, please take it, but please go . . . I am not feeling well.' Suzarbayev picked up the knife and put it in his pocket, said goodnight, and closed the door.

Dmitry sat down on the bed. His whole body shook; he was almost delirious with a mixture of relief and dismay. He started to laugh. So Suzarbayev had taken away the only instrument he had to kill himself. He was undone; all his effort had been for nothing. Some other, more painful kind of sacrifice was to be demanded of him. In the morning he would have to explain the problem of the burned notes and deleted files.

Then a horrible thought came into his mind. He wondered, with a sudden start, if Suzarbayev had realised what he was thinking; was that why he had hovered in the room, had taken the knife? No, it wasn't plausible; no one but a madman would imagine such a thing. He wiped the sweat from his forehead. So, he wouldn't do it after all. He had been a fool to think that he could have done it in any case. When it came to it he lacked the will.

He thought of the letter to Katie. Even now he could probably stop it. He could ring the hotel. Or he could ring Katie and tell her to tear it up without reading it. No, he couldn't do that; the phone would be tapped, and they would wonder what was in the letter, and that would endanger Katie. No, the letter was a problem. Anyway, he had written it; he had meant what he said. He broke out in a fresh wave of sweat; again he heard a whispered sound in his ears.

He looked around the room. He looked at the tumbler; it was made of that unbreakable glass which breaks into small fragments. Then his eyes fell on the vodka bottle, which Suzarbayev had inexplicably left behind. He poured a last glass and knocked back half of it; then he took the bottle into the bathroom, emptied what remained in it down the toilet, and, holding the bottle by the neck, smashed it against the tiled floor. Shards of glass flew everywhere. He looked down at the jagged, savage edge, and for a moment felt sick. He went back to the basin, ran his finger over his wrist, wondering how tough the skin was, how much pressure he would have to exert, where the arteries might lie. He felt the water; it was too cool; he ran some more hot into it.

He turned his left hand over and looked at the blue veins under the skin. He rested the sharpest section of the glass against them; then suddenly he turned away. It was as if another voice in his head said 'No;' a female voice, a voice like Katie's. He walked back into the bedroom and sat on the bed. He couldn't do it; he was a coward; it wasn't even so much that he was afraid to die as that he couldn't inflict pain on himself. Then he thought, the letter. I have to do it because of the letter, Katie will get it anyway, she will think I'm dead, so I must be. I have decided; this is the best thing. Come on, get on with it. The longer you prolong it the worse it will be.

He drank a final gulp of vodka, went back into the bathroom and stared at his face in the mirror. He caught a shadow in the darkness behind him, a shape reflected in the glass. A feeling of horror came over him. He thought he saw, in the distance, the outline of a figure. It came closer, and he saw it was Rozanov. What was he doing here? How was it possible? He knew he ought to turn his head and look, but he was frozen with fear. He felt a terrible, overwhelming sense of evil. It was insufferable. Whatever happened, he must not let Rozanov reach him. He must do it, now. He took up the broken bottle again, poised it above his wrist, took a deep breath and with a savage movement slashed downwards and across with it.

2

THERE was instant, acute pain. This startled him; somehow he had not expected that it would be so bad. He cried out, watching the blood spurt out rapidly and turning the water instantly a bright red. He transferred the broken bottle with difficulty to his injured hand and forced himself to make another deep cut. That wrist, too, was bleeding, less profusely than the other; the glass fell from his hand and he leaned forward over the basin.

He looked up at the reflection of his face in the mirror; he thought, how strange, I can watch myself die. Seconds passed in which nothing seemed to happen; he remembered with horror how as a child he had imagined the long fall from the top of a high building. He felt sick; he thought, oh, this is horrible, how can I have done this, if only it could be finished already. He felt dizzy; water was slopping over the edge of the basin; there was a gory mess on the floor. He could feel that he was about to faint; he let himself fall back on to the floor and sat there, his eyes shut, his head falling forward, moaning softly, feeling the blood running out of his arms like water.

He heard the door open. He heard voices, raised, agitated, arguing in Arabic. He rolled over on to his side away from them, but he could feel them pulling at him. One of them was angry, shouting, slapping his face. Two men pulled him back into a sitting position; he did not resist; he had no strength; or was he secretly relieved? His head span and he felt them tearing at his shirt, using the cloth to try to stem the blood. He heard himself say, 'No, no;' protesting feebly, but none of it seemed quite real to him; only, as he lost consciousness, he felt a dim, gnawing feeling of humiliation and despair.

◆

He was lying on a hard surface. His wrists were bandaged and there was an intravenous tube in his arm. His head felt muzzy, as if he had been drugged. Someone was standing next to him, carrying on a conversation in Arabic. He thought, Where am I? I have botched even this. What are they going to do to me now? He was afraid to open his eyes too wide in case they saw that he was awake.

Now he could hear that some kind of argument was going on. He opened his eyes as tiny slits. Across the corridor he could see Dr Masoud arguing with two other men. Even without under-standing a word Dmitry knew that they were arguing over him. Twice the men made moves toward him and twice Masoud pushed them back. Dmitry shut his eyes again. Then somebody took hold of his arm, and a voice asked, in English, 'Are you awake? Your wrists must be stitched. We are going to give you a general anaesthetic.' He felt the rushing sensation as the anaes-thetic spread through his body.

It felt as if no time had passed. He opened his eyes. He was in a dimly lit room, a hospital room, illuminated by a pale, impersonal light that seemed to have no direct source. Two men stood by the door, on either side, like guards or executioners. Dmitry tried to sit up; he felt dizzy and nauseous. He forced himself from the bed and half sank, half fell, to the floor.

His arms, he saw, were bandaged, and he wore some kind of long smock. He looked up at the men; one of them nodded at the other, and then went out.

Dmitry leaned against the end of the bed. This was not what he had wanted; was what he had been most afraid of. Through his action he had revealed himself, the fact that he didn't want to work for them, in fact, that he would rather die. He didn't know what they would do to him, what possibility of escape he would now have. He tried to move, but couldn't; he felt pinned as if by a sharp sword in the deepest pit of hell.

The door opened and light shone in from the corridor. Then the light went on above him, dazzling him.

A doctor in a white coat was looking down at him; because the light was behind and above him, Dmitry could not see his face clearly. The doctor asked, 'How are you feeling? Try to sit up on the bed.'

One of the men took Dmitry's arm, to assist him, but Dmitry, filled with panic, resisted. The other man grabbed his other arm and they pulled him backwards. Dmitry used all the force he had to try to break away but he was weak and they easily overwhelmed him.

They manoeuvred him into a sitting position on the edge of the bed. The doctor moved round, into the light. He spoke softly. 'Do you know who I am? I – '

Dmitry interrupted, trying to put as much irony into his voice as possible. 'Yes, I know. You are the devil, and have come to take my soul.'

A look of extreme alarm, of horror almost, crossed the doctor's features. He said something in Arabic to another man who had appeared in the room, and he came forward, holding something in a metal dish.

The two men tightened their grip on Dmitry, pinning his arms to his sides. He watched the doctor prepare a syringe, then come forward, putting his hand on Dmitry's arm. He began to talk to him soothingly, but Dmitry was afraid of the injection. He said, 'Get away from me,' but the doctor carried on. Dmitry protected himself in the only way he could; he gave a violent jerk, bent his head down and sank his teeth into the doctor's arm.

The doctor cried out and the syringe flew out of his other hand and went spinning across the floor. One of the men grabbed

Dmitry's head and pulled it backwards while another put his hands tightly round his throat, forcing him to let go; they pushed him roughly back on to the bed.

Dmitry looked up, breathing heavily. He wasn't sure if the salty taste in his mouth was blood or sweat. The lamp above the bed glared fiercely down at him, making him blink.

Out of the corner of his eye, he could see the doctor rubbing his arm. He called out again and Dmitry heard some more footsteps come into the room. He said something sharply but the men did not, as Dmitry expected, strike him. Instead they changed their positions, and four of them leaned over him, holding him down on the bed so that he was totally immobile.

The doctor addressed him in a soft, soothing voice. He said, 'Dr Gavrilov. It is all right now. Don't try to say anything; we understand. Listen to me. You have been under great stress, you are ill, and we are going to help you to get better.' Dmitry felt that he should resist the voice, that it was some kind of trap, but it was so soft, seductive, caring, that he couldn't; instead it was a relief to give into it.

The doctor's voice continued as he rubbed alcohol on to Dmitry's upper arm and then pricked him sharply with the needle. 'It is important that you rest. I am giving you something now that will make you sleep for a long time. Don't worry, everything will be all right; we are looking after you now.'

◆

He woke in a white room. He drifted slowly to wakefulness, his mind relaxed, unhurried. He lay in crisp white sheets, cool and smooth to the touch. The room was square, with white walls, a white marble floor, and thin white curtains were stirring at the window. The curtains moved gently back and forth, as if the window was drawing breath. Occasionally they fluttered as a draught from the fan which was spinning on the ceiling shook them. It was very quiet in the room, except for the hum of the fan and some distant sound which he was not quite aware of but which nevertheless had a curious effect on him, as if he had been here before.

Dmitry lifted his head from the pillow. Next to the bed stood an elegantly carved chair and a small table. Across the room, a man who had been sitting on the chair stood up and went out. After a minute or two he came back and stood by the door, silent, attentive; when he saw Dmitry lift up his head he carried a tray over to the table. The man nodded, smiled politely, and went out.

The smell of fresh coffee reached Dmitry's nostrils and he slowly sat up. He was wearing a white nightshirt of thin, soft cotton. He moved slowly, gingerly, not sure what his body was capable of doing. His wrists were still bandaged and there was a mass of bruising on his arm. He wondered, in a disconnected sort of way, where he was, how long he had been there, what drugs they had been giving him. He wondered if he had been questioned under their influence, whether he would remember if he had.

He swung his legs over the side of the bed and reached over for the coffee-pot. His hands felt clumsy and stiff and his body curiously light and powerless. He wondered if he had been given tranquillising drugs and was still under the influence of them. He poured out a cupful of the thin, black, steaming fluid, tasted it gingerly; it was very good.

He slowly sipped the coffee, ate a fresh bread roll, admiring its open texture and yeasty taste. When the cup was empty he stood up and walked to the window. The top of the window was open, but there were bars outside. Suddenly he realised what the sound was that had so affected him; they were by the sea, and the sound of the waves came to him very softly on a light breeze. Beyond the white stucco walls of the house lay a long strip of white sand and then the sharp blue of the flat, calm sea. He stood and stared at it. There was nothing else; only, in the distance, a wire fence, in front of which a soldier with a rifle across his shoulder was patrolling up and down.

Dmitry crossed the room. He felt dizzy; he had to pause to

steady himself. There was a small mirror; he stared into it. He looked different. They had cut his hair short; his face looked thinner. He opened the cupboard; some of his clothes were there; folded, clean, pressed. The belts from his trousers were missing; he felt through the pockets but they were empty. There was no watch; he didn't know what the time was, though from the angle of the sun and the freshness of the air he imagined it was morning. He wondered whether to put on his clothes and try to go outside. He assumed he was a prisoner; but he had no intention of trying to escape. He simply wanted to see where he was, to step outside into the sunshine for a moment and look at the sea.

He dressed, and tried the door; it was not locked. He stepped out and walked quietly down the corridor and into the hallway. A man was sitting on a chair, watching the door; Dmitry assumed he must be a guard. He heard steps coming up behind him and turned; Dmitry recognised the doctor who had been at the hospital.

Dmitry had the feeling, looking at him, that he had seen him again, in between, as in a dream. He had an impression of snatches of conversation, of a gentle voice piercing through clouds of confusion, of being locked into some kind of mental combat with him, but these felt like fragments of distant memories from a long way back.

The doctor was young, in his thirties, with a long, narrow face and fine nose. His eyes were very dark, his nostrils flared like a horse's, and he had thin, sensitive hands.

He looked at Dmitry intently, shrewdly, as if he were looking right into him. He said, in a pleasant voice, in fluent English, 'I am Dr Senussi. How do you feel?

'I'm all right.'

'Please, sit down.'

Dmitry sat down on a cane sofa, and the doctor sat beside him. Dmitry had to turn his head away from his gaze.

'You seem much calmer now. You have slept a long time.' He hesitated for a moment. 'Do you still think I wish to harm you?'

Dmitry turned to look at him. Dr Senussi's eyes, though shrewd, were kind. There was a softness in them. All the same, he could not bring himself to trust him. He answered, 'Yes.'

Senussi sighed. He said, 'I'm sorry, but we had to keep you under sedation. You realise that you have had a mental breakdown, I'm afraid, quite a severe one. I assure you we will not harm you; on the contrary, we are here to help you.'

Dmitry didn't want to listen; he felt awkward and ashamed of himself. He asked, 'May I go outside?' He saw the doctor glance at the second man, then he said, 'Of course. Please,' holding out his hand in the direction of the door.

The glare of the sunshine hit Dmitry like a wall of light; also the sound of the sea, the breeze, and the salt smell. He took a deep breath. The verandah outside led down straight on to the beach; he stepped on to the sand, feeling the warmth slip in between his toes. The sunlight glinted on the surface of the calm sea in a myriad startlingly bright points of light. He sat on the steps; Dr Senussi came and sat beside him. It was very quiet.

'What is this place?'

'It's a holiday house. You are here as a guest until you are recovered. We have chosen it because there is nothing to disturb you, it is well guarded so you are quite safe. You have nothing to worry about. Trust me.'

Dmitry shook his head. 'Why should I trust anyone?'

Senussi said, in a quiet, even voice, 'This is part of your illness, a kind of paranoia . . . we must all trust something or we will go mad.'

They sat in the shade, staring at the sea. From time to time Senussi asked him a question, and Dmitry answered cautiously, anxious not to give anything away. After an hour or two Senussi retreated and they brought him lunch, kebabs and salad; the guards stood in the doorway while he ate; perhaps they were afraid he might stab himself with the thin wood skewer. When he had finished Senussi came and asked if he could come inside so that he could examine him. He was polite, deferential. Dmitry sat on the edge of the bed while the doctor took his temperature, his pulse, and removed the bandages to look at the wounds on his wrists. Senussi said, 'They will heal well. Of course, you damaged the tendons, but you have had some surgery to put that right . . . it's not been badly done. Well, we will have to see. Move your fingers. Good.' Then he asked, softly, 'What made you do this to yourself?'

Dmitry didn't answer. Again, he felt an acute, a nauseating stab of shame. Carefully, the doctor re-bandaged him. His touch was gentle, relaxing; Dmitry found he didn't want him to stop. Perhaps the doctor sensed this; he said, 'If you don't want to be alone, I can stay with you for a while. Perhaps you would like to talk? I should explain to you – I am a psychiatrist. I know that in your own country psychiatry does not have a good reputation, but I studied in London. Believe me, it would do you good to talk.'

A voice interrupted him, calling from down the corridor. Senussi said, 'Excuse me,' softly and went out. Dmitry could hear voices down the corridor, then Senussi returned and said, 'Dr Masoud is here to see you. I am against this, but he insists. If you want, I will tell him you are not well enough.'

Dmitry stared at Senussi. At the mention of Masoud's name a feeling of dread came over him, he couldn't say why. Then he thought he might as well know the worst. He said, 'I'll see him.'

'Very well. I will allow you five minutes. Come.'

Masoud was sitting in the hallway, drinking coffee in a little gilded cup, which he placed on a tray beside some delicate, spicy cakes. Masoud helped himself greedily, brushing the crumbs from his full lips. When he saw Dmitry he rose to his feet; he spoke quickly, as if his speech had already been prepared. He said, 'I must apologise for not offering you help before, Dr Gavrilov. We did not realise that you were so unstable. Of course we realised that you had been under strain, but we did not foresee that you would do something so desperate. I should have seen the way that things were going; Suzarbayev said himself he thought that you were ill. I should have had a proper talk before now; I regret very much that I postponed it. Are you able to talk now?'

Dmitry said, very quietly, 'What about?'

'Listen,' said Dr Masoud, in a calm voice, sitting down on the carved chair, and indicating for Dmitry to sit next to him, 'I don't know what you imagine, but we are not as stupid as you suppose. We have been aware, of course, that you have been in contact with Russian intelligence in London. We expected them to approach you. We realised that you would go to some efforts to obtain intelligence but, well, let us say we were keeping a close eye on you. I can assure you that most of the information you have passed on is completely useless.'

Dmitry shut his eyes; he let his hands fall apart in a gesture of helpless passivity. He thought, then it's all over, it was over before it had even begun. He was surprised that he wasn't more affected by this realisation; perhaps it was still the effect of the drugs.

'I think that you have allowed yourself to see everything out of all proportion, Dr Gavrilov. I am sure that once you have rested here, had time to reflect, you will realise this. Your fears are completely unjustified. You simply have to fulfil the contract and then you are free to go home; you have nothing to fear from us.'

Dmitry thought he saw a way to get out of this. 'But I will be no use to you. I am mentally ill.'

'Senussi thinks this is only temporary. You have been put under intolerable pressures by these intelligence people on both sides. You should know, Dr Gavrilov, never to get mixed up with this kind of thing. You and I, we are scientists. We should stick to that.'

Masoud poured himself another cup of coffee from the elegant silver pot. 'I can assure you that no harm will come to you, or your wife and family. I have had assurances on that. I have no sympathy for these people. So many times they try to force people into doing what they would do quite willingly given a free choice, don't you agree, Dr Gavrilov?'

Senussi came and looked meaningfully at Masoud who rose, offering his hand to Dmitry, who refused it, not wanting to seem to have agreed to anything, and ashamed of displaying too openly the bandages on his wrists. Masoud left. Dmitry found himself trembling; Masoud's mention of his wife and children had suddenly reminded him of the letter to Katie. The instant he recalled it he did not know how he could ever have forgotten it; the recollection made him feel quite sick, and he knew he must address it with the utmost urgency.

He turned to Senussi. 'I must telephone my wife.'

Senussi was apologetic, but firm. 'I am afraid that I cannot allow you to use the phone.'

'It's very important.'

'I'm sorry, it is not possible. Please wait for me in your room.'

'Then it's as I thought. I am not a guest, as you said, but a prisoner.'

'Not at all. You are a patient; that is different. Please, come with me.'

Dmitry knew there was no point in protesting; he thought he must stay calm, he must do what they wanted. He allowed Senussi to take him to his room and at his request lay on the bed while Senussi went to fetch something. But it was no use; he could not forget about the letter. He was beginning to fully realise the terrible thing that he had done. Katie would have the letter; Katie would think he was dead. The cowardice of his action suddenly came home to him. Why did the thought of Katie reading that letter affect him so much? She would have gone through as much pain reading that letter had he really been dead; it was just that he wouldn't have been there to think about it. He had been so full of his own pain that he hadn't been able to imagine hers. The very thought of what he had written in the letter consumed him with shame so acute that he writhed inwardly.

Senussi returned with one of the guards, who stood by the door. He had a tray in his hands which he put down on the table. On the tray were a glass of lemon tea, a bowl, some tablets, an ampoule containing a straw-coloured liquid and a sterile syringe.

'It's time you slept, now. I would like you to take these tablets. And I need to give you another injection.'

Dmitry was deeply suspicious. At the sight of the syringe, his heart started to beat faster and his mouth went dry. He had a fear of his mind being altered, of being turned into some kind of passive zombie like those he had once seen in a Russian mental hospital. 'What drugs are you giving me? I need to know what I'm taking before I agree to it.'

Senussi nodded. 'Yes, of course. These are anti-depressants. This will help you sleep. And this is what we call a major tranquilliser. It will act quite quickly. You will find that it relieves your feelings of anxiety, so that your body feels calm. It will not stop your obsessive or paranoid thoughts, but it will dull them, making the mental pain easier to bear.'

'You have got it wrong. I am not paranoid. I am anxious because I need to know . . . I wrote to my wife, telling her . . . did they find the letter . . .'

He stopped himself abruptly. He was muddled. He had wanted to know if the letter had reached Katie or if they had intercepted it, but now he was afraid that because he had mentioned it he had put her in danger. Was this what Senussi meant by paranoia? The doctor was looking at him, seemed to see his distress; his eyes seemed kind, full of genuine sympathy. He said, 'I'm sorry, I don't know any details, I don't know about any letter. Why does this matter to you now?'

'I have to tell her I'm all right.'

Senussi put a hand on his arm. 'Let us talk about this in the morning . . . You are becoming agitated. I warned Masoud that it might not be a good idea for him to talk to you today.' He turned to the guard and snapped a few words at him, and a second man came in through the door. They stood there, waiting; Dmitry fought back panic. He protested, 'But I need time, to think. You cannot keep me doped for ever.'

Senussi sat down and faced him squarely. 'I'm sorry, but you must understand your situation. You have had a severe depression, and, even more worrying, a psychotic episode. Without the drugs, your symptoms would return.'

'And if I don't agree to take them?'

'I'm afraid I will have to administer them forcibly. In your own best interests, I must stress.'

Dmitry could see that argument was useless. He began to tremble; he was angry with himself, at his body for letting him down in this fashion. He walked to the window and then back again, trying to regain control. The palms of his hands felt sticky and his heart began to jump around wildly. He felt dizzy and sat down again on the bed.

Dr Senussi's voice was soft but firm. 'Listen to me. You are exhausted. You cannot think straight when you are exhausted. In the morning, you and I can go for a walk together, we can talk things over. You can tell me what you are worried about. This is why everything has got out of proportion for you, because you have not talked to anyone about it. Now, please, let me give you this injection.'

Dmitry reluctantly inclined his head.

◆

Katie picked the letter off the mat with the rest of the mail. She looked at the envelope with puzzlement; it was posted in Geneva, with a UN stamp. She went into the kitchen, put Sasha down on the mat with some toys, and opened it.

At first she could not understand it. She read the letter several times, hoping that somehow she could assemble the words differently, that they would reveal, on close inspection, some other meaning, but this eluded her. Finally, there could be no doubt. For a few minutes she was surprised that nothing extraordinary seemed to have happened; her heart was still beating quite normally, there was music on the radio, Sasha was reaching out his hand for a piece of fluff on the carpet.

She dropped the letter down on the table, stood up and went to the door. A feeling of terror began to grow and grow inside her. She didn't know what she could do, but she knew she couldn't be alone; she could not be here on her own with Sasha. She realised that she wasn't in control of herself; she would frighten him, might hurt him. She rushed to the telephone, but she knew she couldn't ring her family; she couldn't ever hope to explain it to them and in any case she had vowed she'd never ask them for help. She thought of some of the mothers from school, but she knew they wouldn't understand either, not even Jenny. Then she thought of Tim; it was still early, he might still be in the flat. She banged on his door; it opened; she went in. The window was open, the radio on, but Tim was not there.

Katie struggled to think clearly. He couldn't have left for work so early, and he wouldn't have gone leaving everything like this. He must have gone up the road to the shop. She ran out on to the pavement. It was a moist, warm day; earlier it had been raining but now the sun was coming out. She ran up the road to the newsagent on the corner. As she reached it Tim came out with some milk and a newspaper. He looked at her, his smile slowly fading and being replaced by a look of horror. He said, 'What's the matter?' but Katie couldn't speak. Tim took her hand and led her back to the house; she stumbled through the front door and handed him the letter. It didn't matter that Sasha was crying; he would have to cry; she couldn't stop him, she knew that in a minute she would start to cry herself and then there would be no stopping her. Everything seemed focused on this moment in time, on Tim, holding the letter; she hoped that perhaps he would read it differently, though she saw already from his expression that this was not the case.

◆

When Tim had read to the end of the letter he sat, stunned. He looked at Katie and didn't know what to say to her. Until this moment, he realised, he had never really thought of anything from Gavrilov's point of view, had never seen him as a real person, who thought and loved and suffered; the letter expressed such agonizing thoughts that they burned themselves into his mind; he could not imagine, himself, ever feeling such things. It was quite unimaginably dreadful, a human life gone, wasted. Katie suddenly spoke. She said, 'It was posted a few days ago, in Geneva. Do you think it is true? Do you think that – he must be – '

She turned away, took three steps across the room, and then flung herself forward on to the table. The noise she made was hardly human. Tim sat and watched her, unable to react; Katie's cries, and the howls from the baby, made him feel close to panic. He picked up the baby, ran upstairs and put him, protesting, in the cot. Then he ran downstairs. 'Katie, Katie, please, don't make that noise; here, let me help you.' He put his arms around her and held her against him, trying to offer support but sensing that this was the not the kind of grief for which there could be any kind of comfort. He said, 'Katie, is there anyone I can ring? There must be someone who could come and look after the baby for you.'

Katie simply stared at him, white-faced, utterly distraught. Tim glanced again at the letter. He wondered if it was genuine or if for some reason someone had made him write it. It didn't sound like the kind of note anyone would make anyone write. He looked at the envelope; it had been posted in Geneva. Then he looked at the letter again. At the top, with the date, he now noticed, it said: 'Tajura.' Tim knew what that meant. He felt a curious sensation on re-reading the letter; a sense almost of triumph, because he had been right, and also because the obstacle between him and Katie had been removed.

Katie lay down on the floor and started howling. Tim knelt over her, soothed her hair, but it made no difference; she was completely out of control. She sat up suddenly and said, 'I can't breathe, I can't breathe.' Tim held her by the shoulders, shook her, trying to remember what you should do. He said, 'Stop this, stop it, you are hysterical, you must stop.' Katie said, 'I am trying to stop,' wrenched herself away from him and flung herself face downwards on the carpet. Tim didn't know how to cope with this. He said, 'Katie, I shall have to get help. Shall I call the doctor? Do you want me to ring your parents?'

At this Katie sat up, made an effort to control herself. She said, 'No . . . please don't call them. I don't want to see them, they would be pleased . . . they hated him.'

Tim said, 'You'll need help with the children. Can they go somewhere? You need someone to be with you. I think I should call the doctor.' He thought they might be able to give her a sedative, something to calm her down. 'Or what about Jenny?' He stood up to go to the phone but Katie suddenly grabbed him and said, 'Tim, please, don't . . . It's too much to ask. I can't let her see me in this state. I would rather be with you.'

It was very still in the room. There was no sound; upstairs, the baby must have cried himself to sleep. Katie's shoulders still shuddered, but she was now calm. She looked beyond tears. Tim sat on the sofa beside her and put his arm round her shoulder, gently stroked her head. He said, 'That's all right. I'll stay.'

He sat beside her, holding her hand. There was no point in saying anything; Tim just sat, and waited. After a while Katie said, 'I have to know, Tim, if it's really true. What if someone made him write it? What if he meant to do this, but didn't? – There must be some way to find out. Do I contact the Russian embassy? How do I find out what has happened to . . .' she was crying again – 'his body?'

Tim said, 'We have someone in Tripoli. I could ask him if he knows anything.'

'I'm sorry?' She looked bemused.

'The letter says, Tajura. Do you know what that is?'

Katie was staring at him wildly; he took hold of her again,

pressing her head against his shoulder and feeling her sobbing breaths. Tim was wondering what he could do with this information. It was the first actual case he had come across, where it could be confirmed that a Russian nuclear scientist, an expert in uranium enrichment, had been working for a foreign government. He, too, wondered how they could confirm that he was dead. Somewhere like Libya, it would be easy for a body to be disposed of, for the government to claim that he had never been there . . . Unless, of course, there was another reason for the letter. Tim said, voicing his thoughts, 'Perhaps it's not how it looks, Katie, perhaps there is a reason . . . perhaps he wanted people to believe that he is dead.'

Katie sat up. She pressed her hands against her cheeks. She said, 'Tim, don't do this to me . . . don't try to give me hope. He couldn't have written me such a letter and not have done it, how could he?'

Tim took her hand. He said, 'You love him, don't you? Why?' and she said, 'I don't know . . . I don't know.' Tim had thought for a moment that Dmitry's death might make things easier for him with Katie, but now he saw that it would make things more difficult. He stood up and drew the curtains. Warm sunlight suddenly spilled into the room. He said, 'Perhaps there is some way to find out . . . I could work this into a news report, or perhaps sell the story to one of the papers . . . this might force someone to give out some information, to confirm or deny . . .'

Katie said, 'No. No, Tim, no . . . If you do this, and he isn't dead . . .'

'Yes, I know.' It would be like signing his death warrant. Tim looked at Katie; her face was blotchy, pale, almost ugly. Tim saw that he had to make a choice, between her trust in him, or getting his story. He said, 'I will try to find out for you, Katie, carefully, discreetly. It might be possible . . . It might not be advisable for you to make enquiries. It might have the same effect . . . you might alert people, and then . . .' He put his arms around her. He said, 'Will you trust me with this, Katie?'

'Oh, Tim, I have to trust you . . . who else do I have?'

He embraced her, held her close to him for a long time. Then she said, 'I have to ring my mother. I'll ask her to collect the children.' Tim passed her the phone; she dialled the number with shaking fingers. Tim held her all the time she talked. She told her mother she had flu, and asked if she could collect Anna from school and take both the children for a few days.

Tim could hear her mother's voice dimly, saying it wasn't very convenient, they had some do at the Golf Club.

Katie's voice was pleading. 'Mummy, this is an emergency. I can't manage. I can't get out of bed. I've never asked for anything like this before – ' her voice trembled. Tim could hear her mother reluctantly agreeing. Katie hung up, and started crying again.

'I must pack some clothes for the children. They'll be here after lunch.'

'I'll help you.' Tim went upstairs and Katie shoved some clothes at random into a large cloth bag. When they went in the baby's room he woke up and started crying; Katie held him to her, rocking him. Tim found Anna's toothbrush and her teddy. All the time she moved around, Katie went on crying.

When her parents were due Katie made him go downstairs. 'I don't want them to see you. They'll ask questions . . .'

'Does it matter – ?'

'You don't know them.' She insisted that he left her. Tim hovered on the stairs down to his flat. He heard the car arrive, the doorbell ring, and Katie's mother in the entrance hall, asking her if she had seen a doctor. He thought that Katie looked ill enough to convince anyone.

Katie's mother said, 'Why don't you come with us. I don't like leaving you alone. Aren't you still feeding the baby yourself?'

Tim's heart sank for a moment, thinking she would go. Then he heard Katie say, 'Only at bedtime . . . he will take a bottle. I want to be alone, honestly. I'll be better on my own. If I come with you the children will just want me all the time.'

Tim looked out of the window. He saw Katie's mother carrying the baby to the car and her father waving. As soon as they had gone he ran upstairs.

Katie was sitting in the middle of the floor, shaking her head. Tears kept washing down her face.

'I can't bear it, Tim,' she said. 'I just can't bear it. Help me, Tim, please help me.'

◆

That evening she asked Tim to spend the night with her because she was afraid to be alone. He lay on the bed beside her, chastely; if she was aware of his desire she showed no sign of it. The first three nights he shared her bed he made no move towards her but on the fourth, when he put his arms around her and began to caress her, she did not resist him. After a while he said, 'Is this all right? I don't want . . .' and she said, 'Oh yes, please, go on, it's all right, I want to.' He was very tender with her and she seemed to be enjoying it but afterwards she cried. He didn't know whether it was with relief, disappointment, guilt or simply the release of emotion.

In the morning she seemed guilty. She said, over breakfast, 'Tim, this isn't fair on you. I need you now, I like you, I care for you, but I can't feel anything . . .'

He tried to reassure her. 'Look, it doesn't matter. I want to be with you.'

'But why, Tim? Why me? Look at me . . . I'm a mess . . . I feel I'm just making use of you.'

'Well, I'm quite happy to be used.' He kissed her cheek. He was not alarmed; he had her, now, and thought that it was only a matter of time till she got over this and came to love him. 'Look, I've got to go to work now . . . I'll ring you. And I'll do some shopping on the way home.'

◆

The children were due back that morning, but Katie felt she couldn't cope with them. More than anything, she wanted Anna not to know, not until she was absolutely certain; it was still possible that somebody had made Dmitry write the letter or that he had somehow been reprieved. She needed more time; she rang her mother and said that she was still unwell, and begged her to keep the children till the next day.

Alone, she sat and brooded; finally she felt she had to do something. She rang the Russian embassy in London, anonymously, to ask if it would be possible for them to trace her husband, a Russian, in a third country and, if he had died, whether this would have been reported to the embassy there.

The official told her off-handedly that this would probably be possible, but when he asked for the name and further details she was afraid to give them and rang off.

At half past six that evening, just when she was beginning to expect Tim home, two men came to the house. When she opened the door she knew, even before they spoke, that they were Russian; it must have been something to do with their faces or the cut of their clothes. The older man, grey-haired and in his fifties, said he wanted to talk to her about her husband; he was inside the door before she could protest. She followed them into the living room.

The Russian spoke without finesse, with the authority of someone who is used to getting answers. 'Have you heard from your husband since he went abroad? Has he telephoned you? Do you have any letters?'

'No.'

'Please don't lie. We know you telephoned the embassy this morning. Why?'

'I wanted to know where he was.'

'It was more than that.'

She turned her back to them. 'I wanted to know if he was alive. I don't want to talk to you, whoever you are. Please leave me alone. If you don't go I will call the police.'

The younger man, at a nod from his superior, went to the telephone and with a violent jerk pulled the lead out of the socket on the wall. Then he turned to the desk in the corner. It was locked. He asked her for the key and she pointed to the mantelpiece. She watched him take the key and open it and start to go rapidly through the papers, examining each item before discarding it on the floor. Katie, fearing that they would take the house apart, said, 'There was only one letter. It's upstairs, I'll go and get it.'

'We'll get it. Where is it?'

'In the drawer by my bed.'

The younger man went upstairs and she heard him clump across the bedroom floor, and the sound of things being roughly moved around. In a few moments he returned; his superior took the letter from him and read it without any change of expression in his face.

'You've heard nothing since?'

'Nothing.' She experienced a moment of inner panic; if she had heard anything she would have said the same thing, to protect him; why should they believe her? What might they do? For a moment she understood what it must feel like to live under a regime of terror; to know that there was no one she could turn to for protection. Her heart thumped, her mouth went dry, and she glanced repeatedly at her watch; if only Tim would come home, he was due back any minute . . .

The Russian refolded the letter and thrust it into his inside jacket pocket. Katie watched him with horror. She leapt forward, putting out her hand instinctively, wanting to hold on to this one last thing of Dmitry's. She pleaded, 'Please, don't take the letter.'

He ignored her, as if she hadn't spoken. 'What about money? You are still receiving money?'

'From a bank account in Switzerland.'

'Let me see.'

Katie fetched the file with her bank statements. She asked, 'Do you know where he is? Do you know if he is alive?'

The man didn't answer her. As he thumbed through the papers she heard the outer door bang and Tim's footsteps in the hall. The Russian handed her the file, looked up, startled, as Tim came in.

Tim's face blanched with anger. He looked at Katie and then at the two men and demanded, 'What is this? Who are you?'

'Tim.' Her voice was low, warning him. The Russian put a card on the table and said, 'If you do hear from him, call me on this number.'

Tim saw them out. He didn't ask her anything; like her, he must have guessed who they were. Katie was still numb at the loss of the letter; she was trying to work out how they knew.

She turned to Tim. 'They knew I'd called the embassy . . . but I didn't give my name, I didn't say who it was, what country, anything . . . how did they know?'

Tim sat next to her and took her hand. 'It's all right, you didn't give anything away. Obviously, your phone is being tapped.'

She turned and stared at the disconnected phone in disbelief.

'But if they know . . . why did they come here? Why take the letter? What is the point?' She felt herself trembling.

Tim stroked her shoulders. 'Did they threaten you?'

'Not directly.'

Tim asked her to tell him everything that had been said. They went over it several times. He said, 'I can't make it out. Of course, they are on to him, but why, it doesn't make sense . . .' He paused and took her hand. 'You haven't had any other contact with him, have you?'

'No – of course not.'

Tim stood and shook his head. 'I know there's something wrong with this, but I just don't know what it is.'

◆

The following afternoon, Katie's mother rang to say she was setting off with the children. She told Katie she was concerned about Anna. She cried a lot, and resisted sleep; then she had bad dreams and woke up, sobbing and calling out for Mitya. Her mother said that Sasha too had fretted constantly and that it was all too much for her to cope with. When Katie rang off she felt angry and upset; she had to get outside, go for a walk. There was sunshine between the clouds and the air was warm.

At the top of the road, when she turned the corner, she passed the Catholic church. It was an ugly Victorian building which she had walked past many times without ever being tempted to look inside. She saw the door was open, and cautiously looked in; she thought someone might be there preparing for the evening mass. But the church seemed empty.

On impulse she went in and walked over to the statue of the Virgin in the side chapel, where half a dozen candles were burning on a metal stand. The statue was a plaster one, with a silver crown on her head, and a sweet, delicate expression on her face. It was so long since she had prayed, and she did not know what to say. The words came back to her from her school-days, 'Holy Mary, Mother of God . . . pray for us sinners, now and at the hour of our death.' Was Mitya dead? It was worse because it was not completely final, because there was still the smallest possibility that he was not. How could she bear it? She took a candle and lit it, held it up, said 'For Mitya,' and when she said this, she could not hold back the tears; they washed down her face and her breath came in great, gasping gulps. Her body was shaking and she knelt down, thrusting her arm into her mouth to block any sounds from escaping. She didn't want to see anyone; she didn't want anyone to try to help her, least of all a priest.

She thought she heard a sound from the back of the church and turned and ran to the entrance. Outside, it was very bright. The sun had come out from behind the clouds and fell warmly across her back. Dizzily, she sat on a low stone wall. A little breeze stirred her hair and a plane passed slowly overhead, etching a long white line across the blue sky. Against the church wall, a late rose bloomed. She felt a moment of complete stillness. Somehow, she knew she could bear it; for the sake of her children, she would have to. In some way, she was comforted. She knew that inside the church the candle would go on burning, a wordless prayer that would continue long after she had left.

◆

Senussi said, 'Let us walk by the sea.'

It was possible to walk for miles along the beach. They would go in the morning, when the sun was low, and the sand was still cool beneath their feet. Dmitry enjoyed these walks, part of the unvarying routine of his day. He would wake, breakfast, walk, swim, have lunch, then rest; later in the afternoons he would read or play cards with Senussi or one of the men he took to be guards. He began to take a simple pleasure in physical things, in the food, which was very good, in the sensation of the sea and the sun on his skin, in the patterns of light and shadow which the sun cast across the sand and the glinting of the light on the surface of the sea; sometimes he would paddle in the water, or fall asleep in the evening on the beach like a child, lying down in the warm sand.

Dr Senussi would come with him, on his own. Though he looked for signs of surveillance it seemed to Dmitry that they were alone, and that the doctor was taking a tremendous risk, because of course it was possible that he might become violent again or try to get away; but perhaps they trusted the drugs to keep him compliant or knew there was no escape from this place.

He wrote to Katie saying that he had been ill, that he'd had a breakdown but was receiving good treatment. He said as little as he could because he knew the letter would be read by the Libyan intelligence service.

Senussi took the letter and said, 'I can't promise that it will be posted.'

'Why not?'

'It is not up to me. It is for others. It may be thought that you are safer here if certain people think you're dead.'

Dmitry understood at once that this would be in the Libyan's interest. He realised that they wouldn't post the letter and resigned himself to this in silence.

Senussi always tried to talk to him on these walks, to draw him out, but Dmitry resisted. He could not believe that he was talking to him as a therapist, that what he said would not be reported back, to people who might be able to make use of it. Nonetheless Senussi continued to ask questions, always gentle, always respectful. Dmitry had come to like him, to depend on his calming presence; he realised more and more that he was a highly intelligent and sensitive man.

Often they walked in silence, but this morning, for the first time, Dmitry felt impatient. He felt, suddenly, that he wanted things to be resolved; it was he who initiated the conversation.

'I would like to come off the drugs.'

'All in good time.'

'I think this is a good time . . . I am feeling much better.'

'I am not convinced of that. I have already reduced the dose. If you came off the drugs completely, you might feel worse again.'

'I would like to know that for myself.'

'I understand your distrust of these drugs, but I can assure you that they were necessary in your case. You are responding very well, much better than I initially feared.' He paused. 'I would feel happier about stopping them if you would agree to any other therapy.'

'You want to psychoanalyse me.'

Senussi smiled. 'Well, let's not put it like that. Let's just talk about things a little. As I've said, this is part of your problem, that you don't talk. Often these barriers which we put up to protect ourselves then serve to prevent help from getting in when we need it later on.'

'What do you want me to talk about?'

'Well, you could begin with your childhood.'

'Why do you want to know about this? It will not be very relevant for your superiors.'

Dr Senussi sighed deeply. He said, 'I have told you before, I am not here to interrogate you. I am a doctor, I will respect medical confidentiality.'

'I am sure it is all very fascinating for a psychiatrist, my feelings for my mother, the impact of my father's early death, my relationship with my sister . . . but none of that has anything to do with this.'

'Doesn't it?' Senussi turned, staring out to sea. 'Often the seeds of a breakdown like this are sown much earlier. And this is not the first time you have felt suicidal, is it? Have you ever actually tried to take your own life before?'

'No.'

'But you have thought about it?'

Dmitry sighed. Did it matter, what he said? Perhaps he wanted to understand, himself. He did not see, thinking about it, how distant memories could reveal anything that would be of use to anyone. They began to walk again, and Dmitry began to cast his mind backwards, to all the periods of depression in his life. He remembered sitting outside his father's room when he was dying, shut out, and afraid. He remembered his mother's inconsolable sobbing, and a dim lamp burning on the table; he and Olga, huddled in bed together, clinging to one another for comfort. Then he recalled one winter, a time of intensely bitter cold, and the ice patterns on the car windscreen as he drove along a stretch of road . . . Suddenly, almost without realising it, he began to speak aloud. 'When I was working, somewhere in Russia, it doesn't matter where . . . every night I would drive home to my first wife along this long, straight road. There was a huge tree by the road, and every night, when the headlights lit it up, I would think, all I need to do is to pull the wheel a little to the right, just a few centimetres, like this, and I would go off the road into the tree and be killed. It would take just a few seconds; and every night, I was those seconds from death. Why didn't I do it? What was it that stopped me from doing it? I came so close. Even now I don't understand.'

'You were unhappy at the time?'

'My marriage was breaking up. My wife was unfaithful . . . we had no children, she didn't want any. My job was tedious, all research was blocked, we were enduring the political stagnation of the Brezhnev years . . . what was there to look forward to?'

'Still, you didn't kill yourself . . . . and there were things to look forward to.'

Dmitry said, bitterly, 'Yes, I had a second chance . . . and look what I have done with it.'

'We all tend to repeat patterns.'

'It gives me no comfort to hear you say that.'

'Still, you survived that depression, and there is no reason to suppose you will not survive this one. You do not seem suicidal now.' He paused. 'Will you try again, do you think?'

'No. I don't want to talk about it; really, it's over. I am not going to try again.'

They had come to the limit of their walk, up by the cliffs; Senussi turned, they stopped and looked at the sea, then began walking back again. Their shadows stretched before them and the sun, getting hotter, burned on their backs. Senussi said, 'You sound so confident. Why is that?'

How could he explain? Dmitry felt changed. His attempt to kill himself had been a final attempt to force events under his control, to assert himself in the face of everything that had happened to him. He no longer felt any desire to do that. Ever since, as a young man, he had chosen to work with nuclear energy, his life had been compromised. He could see that now. He could not go back and change the past; he had to go on as best he could. He sat on the beach, watching the sun sparkle on the moving surface of the water, and thought, it doesn't really matter what I do. Just give up, go with it, do what is expected of you. After all, wasn't this what he had done for most of his life? Just now it was enough simply to exist; he felt as if he had never felt sensations so acutely before. He had not thought he could survive the torment he had been through but now he felt almost happy. He turned to the doctor suddenly and smiled, letting the soft sand run through his fingers, and blessed the fragility of emotion which gives both an edge to bliss and the knowledge that there is an end to pain.

3

KATIE sat at the kitchen table and watched Tim work, a pile of papers and his laptop in front of him. He told her he was compiling a list of reports for his editor on Libya's mlitary procurement; of the involvement of British companies in setting up a chemical weapons plant, of a missile site in the Sahara, of a known German missile technician working in Libya, of Ukrainian customs officers seizing a consignment of rocket propellant bound for Tripoli. He had tracked down an agent for an Anglo-Russian pump venture and established that they were supplying vacuum pumps for Libya, though they strenuously denied that these were for use in nuclear installations. Tim was planning a trip to Libya at the end of the month. This filled Katie with anxiety.

From time to time Tim looked up at her and smiled. He had practically moved in, though Katie concealed the extent of their relationship from everyone, especially Anna. Tim worked late and came home long after the children had gone to bed, and in the morning Katie woke Anna, gave her breakfast and took her to school before Tim was up. In spite of this, Anna seemed to realise something was going on, and she seemed uneasy in his presence.

Katie knew that what she had done would be considered shocking and that nobody would sympathise with her, not her parents, who thought Dmitry was working in Russia, and certainly not the few friends she saw in whom she confided little.

She knew they wouldn't understand that she had to be with someone otherwise she would fall apart, and she had to keep going because of the children. She felt that a man's presence there protected them. Besides, sex was like an anaesthetic, an opiate, it was the only thing that could make her forget everything, even if only for a few moments.

Tim stood up, went and poured a glass of red wine for himself, and a smaller one for Katie. As he put it on the table next to her, he leaned over and kissed the back of her neck. She looked back at him and smiled. He went back to his work and they sat in a companionable silence. She was grateful that he never demanded much of her; in fact, he seemed not to like too much display of emotion, and while, normally, this would have bothered her, now she felt relief, worn thin as she was by too much feeling.

She was writing to her bank. Tim had advised her to set up her own account and transfer money from the joint account to make sure her money was secure. She was puzzled because the money was still coming in at the end of the month; she had wondered at first whether this might mean that Dmitry was still alive, but Tim had pointed out that he could have arranged for money to be transferred monthly from some other account and that this might carry on till the money ran out. She hadn't dared to ask a lawyer what the legal situation was, what proof they would need of death, and anyway she was fairly certain Dmitry hadn't made a will; it was better not to raise the issue. And if he wasn't dead? What would happen then? She had no idea.

Tim had asked to look at the bank statements, had queried whether there was any way of finding out more about the account from which the money was paid, but Katie said it was a numbered account in Switzerland and she had no further details. Tim had also asked about some money which had come from a different bank in Geneva but Katie told him she thought this was for some translating he had done for an international organisation. Tim tried to find out more but failed. He'd asked, 'Don't you mind where the money's coming from?' and she had said, defensive, 'No, we have to live.'

But she had minded. How could she have blamed Dmitry for what he had done, when she was living comfortably off the proceeds? Tim's remark angered her, because it had hit a nerve. But she felt it would be even worse to take money from Tim and put herself further in his debt.

Katie finished the letter, signed it and sealed it in an envelope. She handed it to Tim to post. It was quiet in the room; she reached out and took his hand. She asked – she hadn't dared ask him before – 'Tim. About this trip to Libya . . .'

'Yes, it's okay. It's all set up.'

'How long will you be away for?'

'Not very long. A week or two, maybe . . .'

'Oh, Tim, don't go.' She had wanted him to go, at first, in case he found out anything; but now she thought it might make things worse for all of them, including Dmitry if he were alive.

Tim pulled his hand away from her. 'Katie, I can't not go now, it's all set up, I'd look an idiot, I've been pushing for it. Look, I know what I'm doing, don't worry. I know exactly what I can and can't do. They can't do anything to foreign journalists, it's too risky . . . they don't want any further international action. Besides . . .' and a trace of exasperation came into his voice, 'I thought you wanted me to go.'

Katie was ashamed, but she couldn't help herself. She realised the superficiality of her relationship with Tim compared to that she'd had with Dmitry, but she knew she needed him. She thought back to those dreadful last days before Dmitry left and knew she couldn't have carried on much longer. Perhaps the relationship would have ended anyway, perhaps it was impossible to live together, feeling as they did. Every time she thought of it, those scenes played in her mind as if they were happening all over again, and she had to stop herself. She clung to Tim as the only thing which stood between herself and despair. She hesitated, and then said, 'I don't want to lose you too, Tim.'

He looked at her for a long time. 'Don't worry,' he said, 'It isn't going to happen. You're stuck with me; I'm here for good now.'

◆

Dmitry was back at Tajura. To his relief when he returned neither Masoud nor any of the others ever referred to what had happened; even Suzarbayev made no mention of it. Dmitry went back to work as if there had been no interruption. Most of the material which he had deleted from the computer had been reinstated and it took him only a few days to restore the rest. The new vacuum pumps had arrived, via some Anglo-Russian joint venture, and Suzarbayev had already installed them with his own modification to the withdrawal system.

About a month after he came back they had a trial run of the first cascade. Suzarbayev was in the lab with him now, checking the readings. He said, 'This is excellent. They will be very pleased.'

Dmitry sat on the side of the bench. He said, 'At this rate they could have a bomb inside five years.'

'Are you worried about that? Don't think about that, it's not on your conscience. They have enough for that already.'

'I'm sorry?' Dmitry was so startled he nearly fell off the end of the bench.

'It's in the next block, upstairs. It came from Sarov – from Arzamas 16. How exactly they got it I don't know. I think the Russian government are so embarrassed they won't admit to it.'

Dmitry kept his voice as casual as he could. 'How much do they have?'

'They have 25, 30 kilograms, 90 per cent enriched. More than enough to build a bomb.' He laughed. 'That'll have the Yankees running.'

Dmitry simply stared at him. Then he said, 'I don't believe you.'

Suzarbayev turned around. 'Oh, it's true,' he said, 'I've seen it.'

They broke off abruptly as there was a knock on the door. Dmitry opened it; it was Senussi. He came to see Dmitry once a week, not for any formal therapy, because Dmitry had refused this, but simply to talk with him. Dmitry knew that Senussi had been asked to monitor his mental health but he did not resent this, looked forward every week to their conversations. They had discovered a mutual passion for Bach; Senussi had found Dmitry a portable cassette player, and every week brought him a new recording he had dubbed from his collection. This week he had promised to bring the six suites for solo cello, recorded by Rostopovich.

Dmitry, Senussi, and Suzarbayev all stared at one another awkwardly. Then Dmitry said, 'Excuse me,' and walked out into the corridor to join Senussi.

They stepped into the courtyard. There was a powerful smell of plants in the sun, of lavender and rosemary. Dmitry was silent, feeling no impulse to say anything; this was a curious feature of their relationship, the fact that Dmitry felt as comfortable with him in silence as in conversation. Senussi suggested they went to the canteen and had something to drink.

Dmitry took an espresso coffee. Senussi pointed to the small cup with its inky, poisonous liquid. 'It's bad for your migraines.'

'I haven't had a migraine for months.'

'Perhaps you have no more need of them.' Senussi produced two cassette tapes and slid them over the table. He said, 'I have brought these for you. Please keep them as a gift. You will enjoy them – they are sublime. May it be that in happier times they will remind you of me.'

Dmitry was moved by this statement and didn't know how to respond. It had been Senussi's kindness, he felt, that had helped him more than anything, more than the drugs or the enforced rest. He took the tapes and slipped them into his pocket, saying, 'I shall treasure them.'

Senussi drained his own cup and pushed it away from him, produced a long, thin cigarette and turned it over in his fingers. He cleared this throat, hesitated as if he were about to say something difficult. 'I have been told that as you do not need any more treatment, there is no need for me to come and visit you again.'

Dmitry said, 'I'm sorry.'

Senussi said, 'I too am sorry that we cannot meet again. I must make it clear that this is not my wish. I still think that you are . . . vulnerable. I have warned them of this.'

Dmitry looked up at him. He realised now that the doctor really meant this; that Senussi had his orders and could not overturn them. He realised that he was, in fact, very upset. He saw that Senussi's help was like a lifeline to him, and its withdrawal, in combination with the information he had just received, was deeply disturbing to him. He was distracted; he was thinking about what Suzarbayev had let slip, whether there could be any reason why Suzarbayev had told him what he had. Had he simply let it slip out in an unguarded moment, or had he told him deliberately, thinking he would pass it on? Would he tell others that he had let him know? Would that compromise his own position?

He needed something desperately to do with his hands; impulsively he put out his hand to Senussi and said, 'Give me a cigarette.' As he took the cigarette he could see his hand tremble; he looked at Senussi and laughed. 'Too much caffeine.'

Senussi's eyes narrowed just a fraction. Dmitry could feel them resting on him, looking far beneath his skin; he would not be fooled for a moment. Dmitry turned and looked out of the window. Senussi went on softly, 'In particular, I have warned them there is a risk of a relapse six to eight weeks after stopping the medication. You should be aware of this, yourself.'

Dmitry said, 'It must be nearly six weeks.'

'Exactly.'

Dmitry looked away. A guard came over and stood behind them; Senussi, perhaps realising that all hope of meaningful conversation was at an end, rose and held out his hand.

'I must go,' he said. 'It has been a pleasure . . . I wish you well.'

Dmitry took his hand and held it for a moment firmly. He realised that he would never be able to express his gratitude, but that Senussi would understand it anyway. Senussi turned and walked away; Dmitry sat down and stared at his empty coffee cup. This did not make sense. Why, if they were concerned about his mental state, would they do this to him?

He went back to the lab, looking for Suzarbayev. But Suzarbayev was not there.

4

DMITRY noticed that security at Tajura had increased. There were more guards patrolling, more tanks outside; now there was someone standing outside the laboratory, and the block itself was more heavily guarded. When he went to ask Masoud where Suzarbayev was he was told simply that he had been assigned to another project. When Dmitry protested, Masoud said that there had been a breach of security and that Suzarbayev was suspected.

He had a new technician, a young Libyan who did not speak Russian but had excellent English. He wore thick glasses, seemed arrogant and was not particularly competent, and Dmitry immediately suspected that his main purpose was not to work but to keep his eye on him. He did not know whether Suzarbayev might have confessed to them what he had told Dmitry and that therefore Masoud knew that he knew.

Dmitry found he could not concentrate on his work. He went to Masoud and asked if he could see Senussi. Masoud put his work down on his desk, took off his glasses, and gave him a long, penetrating look.

'Senussi is not available. If you are feeling ill, we can arrange for another doctor to see you.'

'It must be Senussi. He knows my whole history. No-one else will do.'

'I regret that this is not possible.'

Dmitry did not argue; he knew that he would get nowhere.

He was afraid, for a moment, that something terrible had happened to Senussi and that his asking for him would only make things worse. He felt that they were separating him deliberately from anyone with whom he might confide. The sense of isolation was overwhelming. Dmitry knew now that there was something going on; he became convinced that Suzarbayev had told the truth. Was that why Rozanov had sent him there? Perhaps they knew the Libyans were trying to get nuclear material from Russia. They wanted someone on the spot to find out. Then why hadn't they told him about it? Or did they not trust him? Or were they afraid that if he knew he would somehow give it away? He decided that if he could, despite the risk, he must make contact with Russian intelligence.

Rozanov had told him, before he left London, what he had to do if in any emergency he wanted to arrange a meeting with the residency in Tripoli. He was to call the consulate – from a safe phone – to speak to Andrei in the visa section, to say that Yerenkov needed to collect his passport urgently and would be there at a specified time. They would meet in a certain bookshop. It was up to him to ensure he wasn't under surveillance.

But how was he to do this? There was too much risk. He *was* under surveillance and any attempt to evade it would in itself be suspicious. Even to find a telephone from which to ring the embassy would be difficult. The bookshop might be closed, and he was afraid that so long might have elapsed since he'd been briefed that the meeting place would have been changed or the arrangement forgotten.

He went into Tripoli on the Friday afternoon and told the driver he was going to do some shopping. He knew that many shops would be closed earlier for the midday prayers. The driver pulled over on to an empty building site which was being used as a temporary car-park. Dmitry pointed to a café across the road and told him to wait for him there.

Dmitry wandered down the street. He went to Green Square, walking south down Sharah Mohammed Magarief, towards the post office and the old cathedral. He passed clothes shops, travel agents and an abundance of cafés. Then he turned right and right again into one of the main commercial thoroughfares, past small Arab lock-up shops. He walked fast, mixing with the crowds.

He found a modern pharmacy in a side street and went in. The pharmacist stood behind a counter, staring into space; Dmitry explained, half in English and half in sign language, that he wanted something for a headache. The pharmacist produced a box of pills. Then Dmitry indicated that he wanted to use the phone.

The pharmacist shook his head. Dmitry persisted, offered him some money. Eventually the pharmacist lifted a telephone from under the counter and handed it to Dmitry. He dialled the number he'd committed to memory and a Russian voice answered. He asked for Andrei, gave his message, which meant they would meet in two hours' time. He was afraid that anything shorter would be impossible; perhaps even this was stretching things too far, but he didn't want to hang around in Tripoli any longer than this. He had no idea what the procedure was. Would the person the other end have to seek permission? Would he too need time to avoid surveillance?

The bookshop, Ferghiani's, was near the roundabout off Green Square near Sharah 1 September. He stood by the magazine rack, thumbing through a copy of Newsweek. He tried to stop glancing at his watch, but every so often his concentration would slip and he would find himself touching his wrist. The hour came and went and no one showed. Dmitry began to sweat with agitation. He felt that everyone who went past was watching him and knew what he was there for. He looked again at his watch.

If he complied with the instructions Rozanov had given him, he should wait no more than ten minutes, go away, and try again in two more hours. It might mean that his contact had been

unable to make the time, had perhaps found himself under surveillance. Or it could mean that he himself was still under surveillance, and they knew it, and would then abort the meeting.
How long could he stand in this bookshop, browsing along the
shelves, trying to pretend he was looking for something? His
behaviour was odd; if they were watching him, it would certainly
seem strange, he was so obviously waiting for a contact. But
then, did he have so much to lose by waiting longer? He waited
twenty minutes, then twenty-five, then abruptly gave up and
went out into the street.

It was hotter than ever outside. Dmitry didn't know what to
do; he couldn't easily spend two more hours in Tripoli. His driver
would be wondering what had happened, might even report him
missing. He felt angry, upset at the thought that he had been
exposed to all this stress and danger for nothing. And yet; so far
he was safe. He hadn't made a contact; sitting in a bookshop
looking at your watch might be suspicious, but it was not a
crime.

He walked the streets, confused. Why had they not
responded to his request? Wasn't he important to them? Nothing
made any sense; he felt more and more uneasy. He could wait
another hour and a half, or he could call it off and try again
another day. Perhaps they knew that he had failed to shake off
his watchers, and that was why they not made contact. He
would have to wait, even if it was another week till he had the
chance to come back into Tripoli.

He was walking back towards the café where he had left his
driver when a car flashed past, the brilliant sunshine reflecting
off the metal and dazzling him. He stepped back, into a recessed
doorway; the darkness and coolness gave him some relief. The
dots in front of his eyes became brighter, then more complex, tri-
angles and hexagons spiralling out of one another, white inside
but refracting around the edge to the pure colours of the spec-
trum. After a few minutes the aura faded. Dmitry was already

inwardly tensing himself to meet the headache. He'd felt his trapped anger boiling inside him, but now a feeling of passive helplessness overwhelmed it.

His driver was still waiting at the café. Dmitry stepped into the back of the air-conditioned car with relief. He said, 'Take me straight to Tajura.'

It was the only place now where he could feel safe.

◆

Tim sat in the lobby of the Libyan Palace Hotel, drinking Coca-Cola and wondering how soon he could go home. Tripoli was worse than he had expected. It had been a hellish journey to Libya, by road from Tunis. The van had broken down and there had been problems at the border. The camera crew had arrived in his wake in bad spirits, and then there were all the bureaucratic difficulties. He felt he had got hardly anything they needed; the only thing that had gone right was that they had been allowed a brief interview with Gaddafi. This was something of a coup, because in recent years Gaddafi had become more reclusive, paranoid, and reluctant to appear before the press.

The scene had been a complete set-up for the cameras. They had assembled early in the morning to be taken to some secret location outside Tripoli. Before they left everything was thoroughly searched, cameras were dismantled, film canisters checked. They were driven for an hour by armed guards to the outskirts of Tripoli where Gaddafi was waiting in his tent. A wood fire and camels were on hand, specially arranged for the occasion. Tim found it hard to take it seriously. They were allowed to film the scene and talk to Gaddafi only for a few minutes. Gaddafi, who looked subdued and somewhat aged, no longer quite the handsome playboy, stressed that Libya's atomic energy programme was purely peaceful. Libya, he said, was pursuing knowledge for its own sake. Everything was under international safeguards.

In the afternoon the film crew took some general views of Tripoli, of closed-up shops, affected by the sanctions, of the harbour, of the coast. This was all they were going to get. As to asking any questions about Tajura, or being able to visit it, they met only with blank silence.

On his third day, through another journalist he knew, Tim managed to get an invitation to a reception at the Russian embassy. He wanted to talk to the ambassador, perhaps persuade him to grant an interview outlining Russia's policy on Libya.

Tim moved among the guests, sipping the champagne; it was good to have a drink at last. Tim found himself standing in a group of journalists. Some Russian was holding forth, saying that diplomatic contact between Libya and Russia 'has always been close and productive' and that there was more to be lost than gained by de-stabilising the Gaddafi regime. US policy against Libya in particular was extreme and unfair.

Tim steered the conversation round to nuclear co-operation between Russia and Libya.

'There has been a great deal of co-operation between Western nations and many other Arab states,' said the Russian. 'It is hardly fair to point the finger only at Russia. There have been some exchanges between Tajura, and Russian scientists have worked here, on purely peaceful projects, I would stress.'

Tim sighed. Everybody said the same thing; it was hopeless. He said, 'But there have been some intelligence reports . . . that there have been other scientists working there, let us say, unofficially . . .'

The Russian seemed surprised. He said, 'I don't know of any such reports.'

'But there was one report . . . there was a name. It was an expert in uranium enrichment, working here . . . a Dmitry Gavrilov.'

'I'm sorry, I don't know of this person. If you will excuse me, there is someone I need to talk to over there.'

Tim was left sipping his drink. He felt weary and annoyed; the trip would turn out to be almost pointless. He was afraid that Rowley's prognostications would turn out to be correct; he would have to justify the money somehow; he needed something concrete. At any rate there was no point in hanging around here. He put his drink down and moved towards the door. As he reached it he was aware of someone following him, stepping out beside him, a short man, with dark hair, middle-aged, nondescript.

'My name is Dorokhov,' the man said. 'I couldn't help hearing what you said to the attaché just then. This is a very important subject, worthy of much more attention.'

Tim mumbled a reply; something about the way Dorokhov looked at him made him uneasy.

'You mentioned some intelligence reports. May I ask, do you mean, British reports?'

Tim looked at him, startled. He was quite sure now that Dorokhov was KGB. He said, 'You know a journalist always protects his sources.' Dorokhov laughed, drily. They were half-way down the stairs; in front of them was an empty plinth from which the bust of Lenin had probably been removed. Dorokhov went on, 'So you are writing about this, are you? This man . . . Gavrilov . . . he will figure in your report?'

'Well, yes . . . unless of course he's not here, has gone back to Russia or is . . . dead.' Tim threw this out, rather as a desperate last chance, because he didn't want to feel he had failed Katie completely, that at least he had made some real attempt to discover what had happened.

'Dead?' Dorokhov's face, which must have been trained for impassivity, registered complete amazement and disbelief. He stood still for an instant; then he continued to walk forward, slowly, perhaps anxious not to reach the entrance to the embassy, to risk losing Tim. Tim, now that he had gone so far, and thinking of Katie, asked, 'Well, is he?'

Dorokhov clearly had no idea what to make of Tim or what to say to him. He said, 'You are asking me this question? Why? You seem to know everything yourself.' His eyes were narrow, now, hard, calculating. Tim felt that he wanted to get away at once. It struck him that he had made a stupid error; that Dorokhov might wonder how on earth he knew these things, think that he might be a British spy. This might have the most awful, unforeseen consequences. He said hurriedly, 'Well, of course, not everything . . . if you excuse me, I have to go . . .'

They had reached the door; Dorokhov stood in front of him, blocking his way. He said, 'Well, perhaps, tomorrow, everything will be known. Yes, well, that's very possible. It has been a pleasure to meet you, Mr Finucan.' Tim felt a shock when he heard him use his name. Dorokhov put out his hand and Tim shook it, and found it hard as steel.

◆

Dmitry's car was mired in traffic on the corniche beside the harbour, heading for Tajura. The sun was sinking low in the sky and in the distance he could hear the sound of the muezzin calling people to evening prayer. The sound touched some nerve deep within him; what could it be like to have such faith in God that you could speak of him like this? He lowered the window to hear the sound more clearly and, as he did so, saw a motorcycle drew level with them. It came so close, weaving through the narrow gap between the vehicles, that he felt it touch the car; he felt the slightest impact as it passed. He caught a glimpse of a taut, set face under the rider's helmet; then the motorcycle swerved abruptly in front of them, on to the hard shoulder, where it accelerated away at great speed. Some instinct alerted Dmitry. He shouted to the driver, 'Get out!' and flung the door open, running as fast as he could between the traffic and on to the side of the road.

There was a bright flash. He was sitting on the tarmac, looking at the car, except that it was not a car any more, the front was a crumpled mass of metal and the bonnet was ablaze as if a fire had been lit under it. He caught a glimpse of the driver, and didn't want to look; he swivelled his head away and instinctively passed his hand in front of his eyes. People were running past him in all directions, abandoning their cars, fleeing for safely. One or two of them were bleeding, holding hands to their heads, others were screaming and waving their arms. He scrambled to his feet, but he couldn't balance properly; he wandered aimlessly up and down the pavement, in front of the crowd which was rapidly gathering, aware that they were staring at him; then he went back towards the car, unable to leave the scene, mesmerised by the flames. The crowd gathered round him, all talking at once, pointing; he followed their gaze and saw for an instant the outline of the driver in the fire, like a charred stick.

This vision was so terrible that he couldn't think straight. It could have been him in the car; it should have been him. It must have been a bomb. They had tried to kill him. A policeman was running along the pavement, shouting at the passers-by to step back. He addressed Dmitry in Arabic, then, when it was clear he didn't understand, in English. He asked, 'Were you in the car? Please, come here.' His voice sounded as if he was a long way away.

Dmitry heard the police siren, then another; an ambulance arrived; Dmitry sat down suddenly on the pavement, shaking violently all over. With every moment that passed, as the realisation of what had happened hit him, he became more and more panicky. A policeman had knelt down and grabbed hold of him and was asking him questions, but he sounded faint, like a radio turned down too low. Dmitry shook his head; he didn't understand, he couldn't even work out what language he was speaking. He felt something wet dripping down his face, he felt his forehead, which he now saw had blood on it. There was blood coming through his sleeve, too, but he couldn't feel anything, he couldn't understand whether he was hurt or not.

He heard more sirens now, and the crowd was pressing in on him. The policemen took him by the arm and helped him into the back of an ambulance. Dmitry didn't want to go; he didn't want to admit he might be injured. He kept saying, over and over, in English, 'I'm not hurt, leave me alone,' but nobody took the slightest notice.

◆

Tim heard the dull thud of the explosion in the lobby of the hotel but it was some minutes before he realised what had happened. Lewis, one of the cameramen, ran into the lobby and started picking up his things, surreptitiously, anxious to avoid the gaze of the minders who went with them everywhere. 'Quick, Tim, there's been a car bomb, on the corniche . . . come on, let's go the back way.' They ran through the hotel kitchens, past puzzled chefs, assaulted by the smell of frying meat and the sound of clattering saucepans. Outside, in a side-street, they found a taxi. The area near the bomb had been cordoned off and there were police and soldiers everywhere.

Lewis managed to get some shots of the smouldering wreck-age, crouching down and filming between the legs of the crowds to try to avoid a confrontation with the police, who would almost certainly confiscate the film if they saw him. Tim managed to find someone who spoke English, who told him that the ambu-lance had just left for the hospital. He said that the driver of the car had been killed but the passenger, it was remarkable, had seemed almost completely unhurt, but had been wandering up and down the pavement in a state of shock.

Tim didn't think it would be any good, but he thought he might try to go to the hospital and have a look. Lewis said he would come with him.

The nearest hospital was a red brick building near the city centre. An armed man stood at the gate; Tim said he needed to see a doctor urgently, he showed his international press card; finally the guard made them fill out a form and waved them in. They walked down the hospital corridor; nobody stopped them. Tim asked for casualty and a doctor pointed back the way they had come.

They came to a room full of people waiting on long benches. As Tim walked in and moved along the wall, scanning the weary rows of faces, he saw and recognised Gavrilov. Tim knew it was him at once even though he looked different – his hair was much shorter, he was thinner, and his face looked gaunt. It gave him a shock; this was too much good fortune, he couldn't believe his luck. Gavrilov was sitting, staring straight in front of him, with blood smearing his face and staining his white shirt. As Tim started to move towards him a doctor came out of a side-room and nodded at Gavrilov, who stood up and followed him inside.

Tim sat down on one of the chairs, Lewis beside him. Tim said quietly, 'You'd better go back to the hotel . . . I'll stay here and catch up with you later.' Lewis nodded and left. Tim, impatient with waiting, wondering how long he would have to stay, and hoping no one would realise he wasn't injured and had no right to be there, stood up and walked past the open door. Gavrilov was sitting on a chair, his left arm bared; a doctor and nurse were extracting tiny bits of glass and metal. As Tim stood in the doorway, Gavrilov looked up and saw him.

It was extraordinary. Though Gavrilov must obviously have recognised him at once, and though he could not possibly have expected to see Tim here, he did not betray that he knew him with the slightest change of expression on his face. Tim dropped his gaze; he moved away; he went and sat down again among the waiting people. They were sitting, some hopelessly resting their heads on their arms, some moaning, mothers holding grubby-looking children and old men sitting in attitudes of despair. Tim looked at his watch impatiently. He waited well over half an hour; then Gavrilov came out of the room, walking slightly unsteadily, his arm bandaged, a small dressing on his head. He hesitated, looked around the room and along the corridor, and then came and sat down on the vacant chair next to Tim. He didn't look at Tim, he made it look quite casual.

He looked at his watch. The glass was broken; he held it to his ear. He said to Tim, again without looking at him, 'Do you know what the time is?'

'It's just after four thirty. Were you in the car?'

'Are you real?' Gavrilov reached out suddenly and took hold of Tim's arm, then withdrew his hand sharply. He said, 'I was in the back. Why are you here?'

'Looking for you.'

Gavrilov did not react. Tim went on, still looking straight ahead, 'How did you get out. How . . . ?'

Gavrilov made a gesture as if to say, how can I explain it? He glanced sideways at Tim, he looked tense and nervous, and every so often he gave a little shiver, as if he was cold. He said 'There is something I must tell you. I am going to give you some information. Memorise it, don't write this down, anywhere. Don't phone with this, don't send it by courier, go yourself; I'm sure you will know who to talk to. If you don't want to take the risk you'd better get up and go now.'

Tim said, 'I'm listening.'

Gavrilov spoke in a low, hurried voice. 'Libya has somehow imported about 25 kilograms of highly enriched uranium, stolen from the Arzamas 16 facility in Russia. One of my technicians, named Suzarbayev, has seen it. I am convinced this is true because there has been extra security at Tajura since it arrived.'

Gavrilov looked down at the floor. He said, 'The Russian authorities may deny it.' He paused and said, as if Tim needed this spelt out to him, 'If this were true then Libya would be in a position to make a bomb.'

Tim said, 'OK, I understand,' and Gavrilov said, 'Then go.' Tim hesitated; he suddenly felt enormous pity for Gavrilov. He said, 'Can't you get out? I was talking to a woman in the hotel. Her husband was Libyan, had abducted her children and brought them over here. She had come over from Malta, without a visa, in a fishing boat; she said it was easy.'

Gavrilov turned and looked at Tim as if he had taken leave of his senses. Then he turned away as a doctor came and handed him a packet of tablets and then pointed along the corridor. Tim felt awkward; he was acutely aware of what Gavrilov would feel if he knew that he, Tim, was Katie's lover. He wanted to offer him some crumb of comfort; he said, 'Katie . . .' He was going to say something like, sends her love, but it sounded so trivial that he couldn't say it. 'She wanted to know if you were all right.'

An expression of pain shot through Gavrilov's face and he

struggled to speak. 'Tell her . . . even though I know it is all finished . . .'

He stopped, abruptly. Tim could see a man approach and come to stand by the wall. Gavrilov stood up, moved towards him and they walked together towards the door. At the entrance a second man stepped forward, fell in beside him, escorting him along the corridor.

Tim stood up and followed at a discreet distance. He went down to the entrance where, through the glass doors, he saw them open the car door for Gavrilov. There was something about the way they half helped, half pushed him into the back seat which seemed utterly hostile and contemptuous. Tim was suddenly filled with fear. They behaved as if they had arrested him; Gavrilov, too, had looked frightened. It occurred to Tim that they might suspect him of knowing what he knew, that they might interrogate him, and that Gavrilov might tell them that he had told Tim. All these thoughts flashed through Tim's mind in an instant. He knew that if what Gavrilov had told him were true then what Tim knew was enough to have him arrested, questioned, killed . . . he must get out at once.

Tim was light-headed, his heart beat faster, he felt hot and cold, exhilarated, more alive than he had ever felt. He took a taxi back to the hotel. It was as if he was moving in a film, every action, every movement, seemed calculated, unspontaneous. He went up to his room and put a call through to London.

Rowley answered the telephone himself.

Tim said, 'Look, it's a waste of time my staying here any longer . . . I think I've got everything I need. I've got a terrible toothache, I need to see a dentist, could you ask Sarah to make an appointment for me? I'll get the boat to Malta tonight if I can get a ticket . . .'

Rowley was too experienced to ask him any questions. He said, 'Very good, Tim, we'll expect you shortly. Take care.' Tim went down to reception and asked them if he could get a ticket.

He made a big deal about the toothache, about not trusting Libya dentists. Lewis said that it was all fixed, the boat left that afternoon, they had just two hours to wait.

Tim sat down in the hotel lobby, and waited.

◆

They drove Dmitry back to Tajura in silence. He could not understand exactly what had happened. Who could have planted the bomb? The most obvious explanation was that it might have been an action by the Israelis or the CIA, who had somehow found out that he was working in Libya. But how had they timed it? No-one knew he was going to Tripoli that day, they would have needed time to prepare.

Of course, the Russians knew what he was doing, knew the time of his appointment. But this chain of thought was so horrific that he didn't want to even contemplate it. Could they have decided that he was useless to them, worse than useless, so that they had decided to abort their plans and end his life? Could this be possible? He broke out in a cold sweat.

Dr Masoud was waiting for him at Tajura. As they crossed the courtyard towards the accommodation block, Masoud expressed his concern that they had not given him adequate protection. From now on, he would forbid Dmitry to leave the centre. He said that everything he needed could be provided there.

Dmitry locked the door to his room and lay on the bed, exhausted. He wanted only to sleep, but he slept fitfully, jolted awake at midnight from a strange half-dream. He dreamt he was a star, falling into darkness, consuming itself with heat and fire. He stood up and went to the window, looked out at the moon hanging brightly in the sky over the reactor building. He thought, this cannot go on. I have had enough. Somehow I am going to get out of here, go home, see Katie and the children. He felt as if there must be some hidden reason behind his miraculous escape. He was convinced he wasn't meant to die, that there was something he had yet to do; it was as if there was someone or some-thing directing his destiny, who, like a good torturer, time and again pulled him back from the brink.

5

TIM crept up the stairs and into the bedroom. Katie was asleep, curled up with her arms around a pillow as if to comfort herself. She breathed slowly, deeply, silently. He lay down beside her, gently so as not to wake her, and then, unable to resist, touched her face with his hand. She opened her eyes; there was a moment in which, startled, she didn't recognise, didn't react to him; and then she sat up suddenly, jolted into full awareness, clutching the sheets tightly around her.

She said, 'You come back early. Did it go all right?'

'Yes, fine.'

He kissed her and she responded, but she did so cautiously, slightly guarded, as if she didn't want either to reject or encourage him. He thought he knew why; that she wanted to ask about her husband, but didn't quite dare, so soon. Tim felt a rush of irritation. He didn't want to talk about it, now; he would rather just make love. He would rather Katie didn't care.

She was looking at him, her lips slightly apart, her eyes fixed on his face, expectant, half hoping, half fearing the worst. Tim thought he should get it over with. He said, 'Katie, I met your husband. He's alive. He's still working at Tajura.'

She almost jumped at this and stared at him, her eyes wild, her hand outstretched. She said, 'I don't understand. You mean, you actually saw him?'

'I was sitting right beside him.'

She was confused. She couldn't take it in. Her hand went up

to smooth back her hair in nervous, quick, jabbing movements. Then she smiled; she laughed; she wrapped her arms around her knees and clutched them tightly. She asked, 'Did he say . . .'

'We couldn't talk. I didn't want anyone to know that I recognised him. It was like that.'

Katie said, 'I see.' But he thought she didn't see. Her face was suddenly strained and anxious. 'Where did you see him?'

Tim said, 'There was a car bomb in Tripoli – '

'Yes I heard. It was on the news. I rang Rowley . . . he said you were all right.'

'Did they mention any names? Did they say who was in the car?'

'No. Why? You said Mitya was all right – '

'Yes, he was, he was fine. Just a few cuts from flying shrapnel, that's all.'

She fell silent. Tim got up from the bed, took off his clothes, then sat down beside her, naked. He said, almost brutally, sensing her withdrawal from him, 'Well? Are you glad he's alive? Are you upset? Does this change anything?'

'Tim, I don't know . . . how can you ask me that, now?' She was watching him, nervous, tense, still fiddling with her hair. He put his arms round her, wanting to be close to her, but though she held him she hid her face from him, burying her head in his shoulder.

Tim said, 'I think Dmitry was meant to be in that car, that he was the target. I don't know how he can have got out unhurt, but that's what happened. I saw him at the hospital, afterwards. I'm sure the bomb was meant for him.'

Katie was absolutely still, holding on to him.

Tim was thinking, wondering what to do. He had spoken to his editor on the phone on arrival at Heathrow. He had the car bomb story and the Gaddafi interview, and that in itself was enough to justify getting home quickly – they would show the film today. But Tim didn't know what more to reveal. It was impossible to broadcast the fact that Libya had stolen uranium from Russia without some proof or back-up. Anything like this which involved the intelligence services, which might prejudice their own or police operations, couldn't be used. But someone must be told. Gavrilov had said, I am sure you know who to tell, possibly without realising the irony of it; it might be clear in Russia, but Tim had no idea.

It was an unwritten rule for journalists never to get involved with the intelligence services. If you were known to pass them information, or if you did a favour for them, then your work was compromised. But in this case he didn't see that he had any option, because of the nature of the information and because of what Gavrilov had risked in telling him. Of course he could speak to his editor, Rowley, who would know who to talk to. But he didn't want to talk to him in case he decided to release the full facts.

He knew that Katie would not agree to him revealing Gavrilov's name. Of course he could do this without telling her, and face things afterwards; but he couldn't bring himself to do this. Perhaps he should explain to her how important this was, discuss it with her first, persuade her to agree. It was going to be hard, but he thought he should try.

'Katie, I need to talk to you. This report I'm doing – '

'Tim, not now. I can't think. I thought he was dead and now I know he's not – '

Tim looked at her, and felt a moment of real anger. 'What do you want? Do you want me to go? Do you want me to sleep downstairs?'

'No, Tim, don't do this now. Of course I want you to stay. Please don't . . . Oh no, there's Anna.' The child's forlorn wail came from the other bedroom and Katie rushed away to comfort her. Tim could hear Anna asking, 'Who's there, Mummy?' and her reply, 'It's just Tim, from downstairs.' Then she closed the door. He sat on the edge of the bed, listening to the murmur of her voice and then her singing to her daughter in soothing tones. Her words were like a slap in the face; the whole situation was beginning to get on his nerves. Her reaction to his news showed that she clearly hadn't got over Gavrilov, though he couldn't understand how she could possibly have any genuine feelings for him after what he'd done. And it wasn't easy being with her children, especially when she tried to downplay his relationship to her with Anna. He felt she was over-protective of them and that this made it hard for him to get to know them, though in truth, he really wasn't ready to be a father, least of all to someone else's children. And this wasn't the kind of relationship he'd imagined with Katie either.

Katie came back into the room and lay down on the bed, turning away from him, and pulling a pillow over her head. Tim put out his hand to touch her and she didn't respond to him; but then she didn't actively reject him, either. He lay down beside her and moved close to her. He felt her breathing deepen as she fell asleep and he inhaled the subtle scent of her skin. He still desired her so much. Yet he had to admit how disappointed he was with the way things were going. He thought of how she never wanted to meet any of his friends or colleagues and how she always seemed to keep part of herself aloof from him. Often, when he made love to her, he thought she was pretending to feel pleasure. And now, this relationship was even interfering with his work. He had this great story and he couldn't use it because of her. He had to convince her that this was the right, the only thing to do. He would try again tomorrow. He had to persuade her that her husband was a criminal and that he needed to be exposed.

◆

Tim said he would take her out the next evening to celebrate his coming home and her birthday, which he had missed when he was away. He'd bought her some earrings from a jeweller near the news building in his lunch-hour, long, dangly ones with a yellow-gold stone at the end – citrine, the jeweller had said it was. In the end the meeting about Libya had gone on longer than he'd thought, and he'd had to phone ahead to tell Katie he'd meet her at the bistro where he'd booked a table.

As he expected, Rowley had put him under pressure to name his sources. For a moment he'd been tempted to confide in Rowley everything he knew, but he was afraid of the repercussions. He knew he'd have to come clean with Katie first, even though he feared her reaction. She was waiting for him when he got to the bistro; she jumped to her feet when he arrived and he could see she was pleased to see him. He was also glad to see that she had made an effort to look good. She was wearing a dark silk dress and wore her hair up in an elegant chignon; she'd put on a little eye-shadow and lipstick, just enough to emphasise her pale skin and full mouth.

They ordered and he chatted about work, and Katie told him about her continuing difficulties with her parents. Tim said he'd like to meet them but she said she couldn't do that, yet, they wouldn't understand. Then he gave her the earrings. She opened the box and gave a little exclamation of pleasure, and put them on straight away. The earrings danced as she talked and sparkled in the candlelight on the table. They were very pretty; he couldn't have made a better choice.

'They suit you.'

'Oh, Tim, they're lovely.' She leaned over the table and kissed him on the mouth.

Over coffee, Tim thought that it was now or never. He drew a deep breath. 'Katie, this report I'm putting together. This time I am going to have to give his name. Otherwise the whole story is watered down, it won't mean anything. I don't think it matters, now, not after this; you can see what it means, can't you? The people who really want to know already know.'

Katie's face went hard. 'Anna doesn't know. My family don't know, friends, mothers at school . . . if it's on television, in the papers . . .'

'Yes, Katie, I know it's hard, but those aren't important reasons. People have a right to know the truth, especially about something like this.'

Katie came straight back at him, her voice high-pitched, angry. 'No, you're not interested in the truth, Tim. Do you think you really know the whole truth in any case? What you're interested in is your reputation, in getting a good story.'

'Katie, that isn't fair.'

'You can't do it. You can't do this to us. It might kill him.' Katie was getting agitated; people were turning round and staring at them. 'I can't believe you're asking this. Tim, you realise, that if you release his name it's all over between us, don't you?'

Tim shook his head. 'Katie, we've just been over all this, that it's my job, that I have a moral duty . . .'

She jumped up from the table, grabbing her bag as if she was going to leave. 'But we're not talking about some abstract moral issue, are we? We're talking about destroying my husband. If you do this thing, Tim, I swear to you, it will be the end of us. It will be worse than that. In fact, if you give his name . . .' her voice died away, as if she didn't dare to say what she might do to him.

'For God's sake, sit down, keep your voice down, please, don't make a scene.' He thought she was going to walk out, but then she sat down again; he saw that she was crying. Tim didn't put out his hand, didn't try to touch her. He said, 'I don't understand you. Why can't you be angry with him, hate him for what he's done?'

'I do hate what he's done, Tim. That doesn't mean I hate him.'

'You are so bloody understanding.'

'No, it's you who don't understand. It couldn't happen to you, could it? You live in nice, safe England. You know nothing that could be a danger to yourself. You won't get hurt, whatever you do to others.'

Tim thought, as she said this, that it was not quite true. He had known, himself, the last few days, what it felt to have a secret that endangered him, a secret that even now he needed to pass on. But he saw that it was no use arguing with her. He had to decide; he supposed he had no choice. He realised that he couldn't give her up, not now. In any case, it would be too cruel. He said, 'All right, I understand, if you feel like that I'll keep his name out of it, I promise. I'm sorry, I shouldn't have mentioned it. Now I've ruined the evening.'

'No, Tim, you haven't ruined it. I'm sorry too.' Katie seemed to make a great effort to control herself. She wiped her eyes, smiled her beautiful smile, and stretched her hand out to him across the table.

◆

'I'm sure you know who to tell.'

Tim sat in front of the editing screen, paused the tape; he couldn't get Gavrilov's voice out of his mind. It seemed to mock him, reproach him for his delay. An idea had suddenly come to him; on impulse he picked up the phone and rang Ingrid. She answered her telephone immediately, was startled when she realised who it was.

'Tim, How are you?'

'I'm fine. Ingrid . . . I hope you don't mind. Your boyfriend, in the Foreign Office. Do you still see him?'

Ingrid's voice was cautious, puzzled, 'Yes. Why?'

'I need to ask someone . . . you said he was quite senior. What is he?'

'He's a desk officer, for Saudi.'

'Would he talk to me?'

Ingrid sighed. 'I should have known you had some reason for your call . . . Tim, you don't change. No, I don't think it's a good idea.'

Tim put on his warmest, his most charming voice. 'It's very important, Ingrid. If it wasn't I wouldn't ask you.'

Ingrid didn't reply for a few moments, as if she was weighing it up, trying to make up her mind. 'All right, I don't suppose it can do any harm, I'll give you his office number, and you can ring. Here it is . . . Just say you're a friend of mine, he doesn't know about you . . . his name is James Markham.'

'Thanks, Ingrid, I'll see you sometime, yes?'

'Is that really all you called for?'

'I'm in a hurry now, I'll call you another day . . .' But Ingrid had already hung up.

Tim dialled the number she'd given him straight away. A voice, smooth, well-modulated, said, 'Markham.'

Tim said, 'Ingrid gave me your number. I'm a friend, a journalist, from Channel 4 News. Ingrid thought you might be able to help me . . .'

'You should ring the Press Office.'

'No, this is something else. I need to talk to someone. It's a rather delicate matter, but I have some information which I feel should be passed on to someone who would know what to do with it. I thought you might know who I could talk to.'

There was a long pause, a very long pause. Markham said, 'I see.' Then he asked, 'Ingrid suggested that you ask me?' There was a slight emphasis on 'Ingrid.'

'Yes.'

'You'd better give me some details.'

'I've just come back from Libya. I have some very sensitive information . . . I'm afraid I don't really want to say any more on the phone.'

'Yes, yes, I see, of course not, I understand. I'll have a word with someone . . . you will probably get a call in the next day or two. I don't think there will be any need to talk to me again.'

◆

At ten that night, when Tim was sitting on the sofa, his arm round Katie, watching the news headlines, the phone rang. Katie picked it up. Tim could hear Ingrid's voice from where he sat; she sounded angry and upset, hysterical, almost.

Katie handed him the receiver with an odd look.

Ingrid said, 'Tim, I was an idiot, to give you James's number. I didn't know what he did, but he assumes that I did and now he's had to report that there's been a leak, his cover's blown . . . Now it's all come out, about his affair with me . . . anyway, he's broken off with me.'

Tim couldn't follow all this, not at first. He edged away from Katie on the sofa, turned his back to her, said to Ingrid coldly, 'I'm sorry, I don't understand.'

'Don't you? Can't you see what I'm saying? Obviously, James is an intelligence officer. I had no idea, you of course had no idea, but he thought you did and now you've blown it. You have completely screwed things up for me, do you understand? Just because you had to know something for some stupid story . . . You don't care who you fuck up as long as you get what you want, do you? Well, I hope one day you suffer . . . I hope you really suffer, you stupid bastard.'

She hung up. Tim looked at the phone, startled, put it down. Why had she turned on him like this? He couldn't understand why she had felt the need to talk to him like that. Katie was looking at him, puzzled, nervous. 'What was that?'

'Ingrid.'

'Yes, I know, I heard . . . I thought you never spoke to her.'

'I don't.'

'Then what was it about? She sounded pretty angry. Anyway, how did she know you were on this number?'

Tim started. He said, 'I really don't know. I called her from the office. Maybe they gave it to her.' He knew he hadn't given the number to her, or to Markham either. Tim walked across the room, agitated. He said, 'Katie, it's just some stupid thing she thinks I've done, some misunderstanding . . . It doesn't matter. Anyway, it's nothing . . . don't look at me like that. You know it was all over months and months ago, you know that . . . she means nothing to me.'

Katie's voice was shaking with anger. 'I don't like to hear you say that, Tim. It frightens me. You lived with her for two years, didn't you? You used to be crazy about her, you told me. If you can get over her so quickly, what's to stop you turning round one day and saying the same thing of me?'

◆

The call Tim was expecting came in the morning, in the office, at about eleven. It was a woman, young, well-spoken. She said, 'Your friend James said you have some information which might be of interest. Do you think it would be an idea to get together and have a chat about it?'

She suggested they meet for tea at the Savoy. When Tim came in she was already there; she lifted her hand and gave a little wave as he approached. She introduced herself as Susie. She was slightly plump, with mousy hair, cut straight, and subdued office clothes; she was the kind of girl Tim imagined would have been a school prefect or even head girl; organised, competent, slightly bossy.

After they had ordered, made small talk, and the waiter had come with the tea, she said, 'Well, perhaps you'd better tell me what it is you've got.'

She watched him, and listened. There was a kind of attentiveness about her, a shrewdness in her glance, which he had missed at first. She nodded her head, made polite noises, asked him one or two questions, to clarify or explain.

It did not take long. At the end she said, 'You've thought about this a great deal, obviously. There isn't anything else at all, that you've left out?'

'No . . . I don't think so.'

She asked for the bill and paid it. She smiled, stood up, slipped her bag over her shoulder. She said, 'Well, it was very nice to meet you, Tim. It's been very useful to talk to you, I think you decided to do exactly the right thing. Of course we have all this area pretty well covered, but it's always nice to have confirmation . . . We've got your number if there's anything else we need.' And that was it.

Tim walked to the bus-stop. It was raining and he didn't have his coat. He felt let down; that this was all it came to, after all his stress, anxiety, excitement, soul-searching. He supposed she was exactly the kind of person they would employ; anonymous, ordinary, instantly forgettable. She would have had the right values too; loyalty to the school, loyalty to one's country. It made you a bit sick.

He wondered what they would do now with the information. It was quite possible of course that they would do nothing, that it was all being dealt with already, that they knew everything, and that what he had told them was not of much interest after all, except perhaps, as she had hinted, to confirm what they already knew. On the other hand, he thought it could be high level stuff, there could be inter-agency discussions, liaison with the police, with politicians, even with the Prime Minister. He wondered whether they would act, and if so, how quickly.

It took them a week. He and Katie heard the report on the radio in the morning. A US bombing raid had been launched against Libya at dawn, targeting the Nuclear Research Centre at Tajura. Recent intelligence reports had indicated that Libya was developing a clandestine nuclear weapons programme and that there had been attempts to procure fissionable material from the former Soviet Union. The surgical strikes had been extremely effective and the main reactor building had been damaged. There was no danger of radioactivity except at a local level.

At the first phrase of the report Katie's hand shot out and knocked over the coffee pot. The dark liquid spread across the table, soaking into the dry toast and over yesterday's newspaper, and began to drip down on to the bare wood floor. Katie and Tim looked at one another over the wreckage of their breakfast and neither of them spoke a word.

6

THE SOUND of the explosions startled Dmitry out of a deep sleep. Even in his shocked, confused state, as the room rocked and he felt the concussion, a sound almost too loud to hear, he knew what was happening. He lay in bed, rigid, unable to move; there was another impact, then another. Instinctively he rolled over on to his face and pulled the covers over him. Perhaps there were six impacts in all, some of them so close together as to be almost simultaneous. This was followed by the sound of the plane engines shrieking into the distance; there was a moment's silence, then an alarm bell sounded.

At first Dmitry could not move. He felt as he had done as a child, woken in the middle of the night by a thunderstorm right overhead. He was afraid that if he moved, if he looked around, something terrible would manifest itself; that he might even discover he was dead. Then he heard voices shouting outside and sirens sounding, and the noise of engines. Cautiously, he shifted in his bed. Nothing happened. He swung himself out of bed and went to the window. One of the bombs had hit the main building; flames were streaking up, and black, acrid smoke was streaming from the roof. Dmitry wondered if they had hit the reactor; he wasn't too concerned, it was a small one, and the chances were that there would not be much release of radioactivity even if there had been a direct hit and the containment breached. People ran in and out of the buildings; a second, louder alarm sounded.

Dmitry pulled on his clothes, rushed down the corridor and out into the cool of the morning. He stood by the wall, unnoticed; someone was pointing an inadequate hose at the main building; the water on the flames fizzled and hissed pathetically.

He looked up. After the deafening sound of the bombs and the jets that dropped them, there was an eerie silence in the skies. The technician appeared at the door, half dressed, his hair standing upright. He had completely lost his cool, and his taut, fanatical face was twisted up with anger. 'Those bastards, the Americans! They think they can do what they like, that they own this fucking planet!'

Dmitry felt quite calm, detached, though he was sure it wasn't over yet. He said, 'I'm going over there to see what the damage is.'

'Are you crazy? They hit the reactor. The place could be radioactive. And what if they come back and hit us next time?'

Dmitry said, 'We shouldn't panic. There's no need.' The Libyan stared at him, shocked and confused. They turned to watch the army trucks arriving, the soldiers looking helplessly around while the fire spread. Then, as they watched, there was another explosion, from inside the reactor building; then a third and fourth, like aftershocks; Dmitry felt a faint but definite tremor in the ground beneath his feet. He stood rooted to the spot, suddenly terrified. A second explosion could be far more serious; it could mean that the bomb had damaged the reactor and let it run out of control, and now there was a more dangerous, nuclear explosion.

How could he tell? That was the terrible thing about radiation, you could neither see it, feel it, hear it, smell it. Radiation might be pouring out into the air at this very moment and no one would know about it; certainly not the soldiers struggling to put out the fire. It would be like a miniature Chernobyl. An emergency alarm sounded, a louder, higher note. Someone started to shout orders through a megaphone, perhaps ordering an emergency evacuation. Dmitry dashed at once back inside the building. His mouth was suddenly dry and he could feel his heart racing. He wanted now to get away; he must, at all costs, get away from here.

He went back into his room. From his drawer he took out his radiation badge and a jar of white potassium iodide tablets; he read the label and swallowed the correct dose. Outwardly calm, he took some clothes and folded them carefully into his suitcase, wishing he had something smaller to put them in. He picked up the suitcase and walked swiftly down the corridor. At the door the technician tried to pull him back and he wrenched himself free. Outside, in the dazzling sunlight, Dr Masoud stood with an army colonel, ordering the reluctant soldiers to go back into the building to check what had happened to his colleagues who would have been on duty. Masoud told Dmitry that the bomb had cut off the electricity supply, that the emergency generators had not cut in, and that he believed there must have been an explosion inside the reactor because the control rods could not be lowered. He said to Dmitry, 'Get indoors, there's no need for you to risk yourself. The Colonel here is leaving immediately for Tripoli. You can go with him.'

The colonel put a hand on his arm and walked him back towards the laboratory block. Dmitry shut the door behind him with relief and stood in the dim, unlit corridor. The colonel took Dmitry into an office, sat at a desk, and began telephoning. Outside, Dmitry could hear the sound of engines revving, of sirens, of raised, frightened voices, while here, inside, it was very quiet and the colonel seemed to be quite unperturbed, making his telephone calls.

Dmitry walked up and down in the little room. Perhaps too many dreadful things had happened to him and he was unable to react; he felt very calm, detached, and his mind seemed sharp and clear. The colonel looked up and waved his arm towards a chair; Dmitry sat down. He flipped through the piles of paper on the desk in front of him. There was a list of sites where various parts of Libya's nuclear programme were situated; personnel lists; files of orders; in fact, everything Rozanov could have wanted. The colonel didn't even seem to notice what he was doing so he took his time to go through them, memorising what he could.

The colonel hung up and stared at Dmitry, his face blank, oppressive, as if he was wondering what to do with him. In a flash an idea came into Dmitry's head. He said, 'The highly enriched uranium. It's stored here, in this building . . . surely you should remove it?'

The colonel turned his black eyes to look at Dmitry. He must have thought that if Dmitry knew of this he must be in the trusted core of staff there, the inner circle who knew about these things. He said, 'Yes, of course, you are right, that is a priority.' He picked up the receiver again and punched out a number. There was another long discussion, in Arabic. He hung up, got to his feet, said, 'Please wait here,' and went out.

As soon as the door closed Dmitry picked up some of the papers on the desk and stuffed them into his suitcase. He didn't know what made him do something so dangerous; perhaps he was careless of his life because of the radiation, who knows, he might have received a fatal dose already. Dmitry went to the window. Outside, an ambulance was standing near the reactor building. There was no sign of Masoud. The smoke drifted over towards them; even through the closed window Dmitry could smell the smoke. He started to sweat. He thought, the colonel doesn't understand, why don't any of them understand. We must get out of here.

When he opened the door he saw the colonel coming back along the corridor. He beckoned to him; they went out of the back door. A jeep was waiting for them, its engine running. Soldiers struggled to load a wooden box into the back. There was a strange smell in the air, not just of smoke, but an almost metallic smell; this alarmed Dmitry because he knew it might mean the presence of ionising radiation. He said to the colonel, 'Please, let's go, quickly.'

The jeep lurched forward. Dmitry watched in astonishment as they drove past the tank and a couple of armoured vehicles and passed through the gates alone. He felt in his pocket and took out the radiation badge; it had turned dark blue. Well, that was to be expected; it would have darkened at a much lower level than he had probably been exposed to, way below what was needed to cause any immediate effects. He felt light-headed and giddy for a moment; he looked sideways at the colonel; he appeared cheerful enough.

Dmitry glanced round and looked at the box. He asked, 'Where are you taking it?

'To the military headquarters in Tripoli. Where I will also take you.'

Dmitry did not know what might happen to him there. He thought they might question him to see if he had revealed anything he knew which might explain the attack. He imagined the kind of interrogation they would give him, and felt an overwhelming need to escape. He leaned forward and took the colonel's arm. 'Look, I am not a prisoner. I am a scientist . . . Don't you realise that we have been exposed to radiation? Look,' and he showed him the badge. 'I insist you take me to a hospital in case I need treatment.'

'Dr Masoud told me there was no danger from the reactor. Anyway, I have been told I should keep you with me.'

'We should both go to the hospital as a priority. Don't you understand – '

The colonel swivelled round in his seat. 'Okay, we will deliver this stuff, then I will get someone to take you to the hospital.'

Dmitry turned round and looked again at the wooden case in the back of the jeep. He realised that he had a chance, an extraordinary and unforeseen opportunity, to get away. The driver didn't seem to be a soldier and as far as he could see, he wasn't even armed. The only thing that stood in his way was the colonel. He could even get hold of the uranium. But this was ridiculous.

What was he thinking? Even if he did, what would he do with it? Take it out of Libya single-handed? It was absurd.

The sun was well up now; it was beginning to get hot. They drove fast, through orchards and olive groves; they passed some army vehicles travelling in the opposite direction; otherwise, the road was empty. Then they heard the sound of an aeroplane circling overhead. The colonel asked the driver to pull off the road and stop the jeep; in the sudden silence they heard the droning of the engines. Dmitry asked, 'One of ours?' but the colonel indicated for him to be silent. He sat, his head craned upwards, and Dmitry thought, there, this is my chance. But he couldn't do anything; he couldn't move. If he made an attempt against the colonel and failed he was done for.

The moment seemed to last forever, while Dmitry struggled with himself; should he act, or shouldn't he? The bright sun illuminated everything with extraordinary clarity; he looked at the gun gleaming in the colonel's belt; if he could just get hold of it . . . Dmitry saw his chance slipping away from him. He couldn't act; it was as if his limbs were paralysed. Then, just as the colonel turned to indicate to the driver to continue, Dmitry found that his body leapt into action, striking the colonel as hard as he could with his fists and pushing him forwards out of the jeep.

He leapt down on top of him but the colonel was already reaching for his gun; Dmitry kicked at him, leaned over to snatch the gun himself; both of them were snarling like animals. The colonel now had grabbed Dmitry's arm; they were both kicking, grabbing, punching, both of them uncoordinated, both desperate. Dmitry had pulled open the leather strap over the holster and the gun fell out into the dust. Dmitry had his hand on it; the colonel stamped on it; Dmitry, dizzy with pain but still managing to keep going, launched himself on top of the colonel and punched him in the stomach.

All the time the driver simply sat, watching.

Dmitry had the gun now. He picked it up, backed off, aimed it at the colonel, released the safety catch. His hand was agony; he wondered if any of his fingers were broken. The colonel lay in the sand, his hands shielding his head, awaiting his execution. Dmitry knew that he should shoot him, that there was no way he could risk leaving the colonel alive to explain what had happened, but he couldn't do it, not like this, not in cold blood. He cursed himself for starting something he couldn't carry through. When moments passed and nothing happened, the colonel slowly, anxious not to provoke anything, got to his knees. He turned his face to Dmitry, his dark eyes pleading.

Dmitry turned to the driver, pointing the gun at him. He said, 'Tie him up.' The driver did what he was told; Dmitry supposed that no one argues with a madman with a gun. There was a rope in the back of the jeep. The colonel lay face down in the earth and the driver tied his legs and arms behind him. Beyond the road was a ditch and then there were olive groves. Dmitry made the driver drag the colonel into the shade.

Dmitry tested the ropes. He was afraid of several things; that the knots would be too tight, the colonel would not be found, and he would lie there and slowly die from thirst. Then he was afraid that the knots would be too loose and he would soon be free and raise the alarm. Why had he even begun this? Long shadows from the early sunshine slanted under the olive trees. Dmitry ordered the driver back to the vehicle.

The driver knelt on the ground, terrified, making no move. Dmitry was aware of him watching as he turned and took a toolbox from the back of the jeep, extracted a tyre lever. The wooden container was clearly marked with a radioactivity symbol and securely pad-locked. It would be far too heavy to lift. He used the tyre lever to force the box open. The bars of uranium lay inside in a thick layer of lead. There were six bars of the silvery grey metal, lightly covered with oxide as if they had been dusted with a thin layer of flour. Dmitry lifted the bars out, one by one, examining them carefully. They looked like uranium, a dull grey metal; they were heavy enough to be uranium; with the edge of the tyre lever he scraped at the surface and found that, sure enough, the tiny scrapings ignited spontaneously in the bright air. He turned his head away so as not to breathe them in. He was convinced. He was not afraid to handle the bars; he knew that pure uranium is not highly radioactive; the alpha radiation it emits could not penetrate even the dead outer layer of skin. He tried to assess how much material was there, whether there was enough to form a critical mass on its own or whether it would only go critical in a bomb assembly surrounded by a neutron reflector. For a bare sphere of uranium, the critical radius would be about eight or nine centimetres and the critical mass about 52 kilograms; in small bars of uranium 235 with linear dimensions like these, the chain reaction would simply damp out. Nonetheless, he was careful to wrap the bars in his clothing and pack them as far apart as possible inside his suitcase.

Dmitry straightened up. A sudden cool wind blew at him from out of the desert. He felt utterly deserted and alone. Now he had burned his boats; he had only one thought, and that was to get out of Libya. He turned to the driver. He said, 'There are fishing boats, boats who will take people to Malta or Tunisia . . . where do they go from? Can you take me? And get off this road.'

The driver stared at him blankly; he spoke little English, didn't understand. Dmitry, holding the gun, pointed to the driver's seat and he scrambled in. Dmitry rummaged in the front; there was a map. He showed it to the driver, pointed to a road running along the coast. He drew a picture of a fishing boat, fish, and drew a line to Malta. The driver suddenly nodded. He turned the vehicle and headed back along the road, driving much faster than before.

There was very little traffic. Dmitry thought that they were too conspicuous, was afraid all the time that someone would stop them. In the aftermath of the explosion, he imagined he would have some time before they realised he and the colonel were missing. The driver pointed ahead; they were approaching a small fishing village. The white buildings were huddled down by the sea; on the front the fishermen were refolding their nets.

Dmitry asked the driver to turn off the road and they left the jeep hidden behind the ruined wall of an old house. He put the gun in his pocket but let the driver know he would use it if he had to. Then they walked down to the village. People looked up and stared as they approached. The driver stopped outside one of the houses near the water and stepped in through the curtain of pink plastic strips which hung in the doorway.

The curtain rattled as they passed through.

They stood in the dark interior. A middle-aged woman came in, looked surprised to see them, at Dmitry so large and foreign-looking, clutching his heavy suitcase. The driver asked her something and she went out at the back. Dmitry thought that he could easily betray him, have asked her to go to the police, but knew he was unlikely to because he knew that Dmitry was desperate enough to kill and that he had a gun. It was cool in the room but he was sweating. The driver too was nervous; he kept touching his lips with the tip of his tongue; sweat beaded his forehead.

The woman came back and offered them a drink. They sat at the little table and drank some herbal drink in chipped glasses. The woman put out some little pastries; Dmitry, not knowing when he would next have a chance to eat, forced himself to eat one. A fly darted backwards and forwards across the table; in the distance a radio was playing some kind of Arab music, interspersed by a loud voice which sounded as if it were exhorting people to work harder, no doubt to help the revolution or some such nonsense.

Dmitry sipped the tea. It tasted faintly unpleasant; Dmitry thought that it might make him sick.

Nausea is the first symptom of radiation sickness.

Dmitry pushed this thought aside as soon as it had come to him; he would not allow himself to think of this. The door at the back opened and a grizzled man came in, in a tattered shirt and short trousers. The driver pointed to Dmitry and spoke, in Arabic. The fisherman nodded, turned to Dmitry, and said, in broken English, 'I am Nabil. I cannot go to Malta today, I have not enough petrol. I can go to Zarzis.'

'Zarzis?'

'Tunisia. Much nearer. You pay me dollars two hundred, now, I take you.'

Dmitry nodded. He took the money from his wallet and handed it over. Now he saw another problem; what should he do with the driver? If he stayed behind, as soon as they were at sea he would tell the army or police. Dmitry either had to kill him or take him with him. He said to Nabil, 'He comes too.'

'Two people, three hundred dollars.'

Dmitry shook his head. He didn't want to part with everything he had; he would need some money in Tunisia. He opened his wallet, took out another fifty dollars and some dinars, saying this was all he had. Supposing he refused to take them, just because he was short of fifty dollars? Would he then have to take the driver somewhere and shoot him after all? Nabil took the money, fingered it, and nodded. He took them out of the back of the house and down to the sea.

He felt, waiting as the fisherman prepared the boat, as if everyone was staring at them, even though there were only a few fishermen in sight. The boat was small and sleek with a metal hull, a small cabin and an outboard motor; it bobbed up and down on the surface of the water and a strong smell of rotting fish came from the nets. Dmitry again felt slightly nauseous. He wished that he could shower, change his clothes. He wondered for a moment whether to wash in the sea but he couldn't risk leaving the driver or the suitcase even for a moment.

Nabil said, 'Come.' The driver, realising that he was expected to come too, began to protest. Dmitry gave him a look which silenced him instantly.

They sat on the cross-pieces inside the boat. The floor was swilling with sea-water and seaweed and some dead fish which stank appallingly. Nabil fiddled with the engine – Dmitry thought his luck was against him when it failed to start, but after a few minutes it reluctantly spluttered into life. Once Nabil had manoeuvred clear of the shore and powered up to full speed the noise was deafening; conversation would be almost impossible. This was a relief to Dmitry, because he didn't want to risk the driver talking to Nabil. As they got out to sea the breeze sprung up and buffeted him; the vibrations from the engine penetrated deep inside him, seeming to jangle his bones and jar even his teeth in their sockets. His hand still hurt and was badly swollen; he wasn't at all sure that one finger wasn't broken, it was so painful when he moved it. But perhaps this was the least of his problems. He had very little money; what was he to do in Zarzis? He felt suddenly exhausted. Hunched beside him, the driver seemed to fall asleep.

The sun was right overhead now; there was no shade, it beat down on him relentlessly. He thought again of the colonel, lying underneath the tree. He glanced down at his arms, which seemed to darken even as he looked at them. A terrible thought struck him and he pulled back his sleeves, but to his relief there was a sharp mark where the cuff fell; this was not, then a nuclear tan, caused by radiation that would have penetrated the thin fabric of his shirt. And the nausea, which he now felt more strongly, that could easily be a mixture of stress and sea-sickness.

The situation he found himself in was beyond anything he could have imagined. He wondered what he could do with the uranium. It occurred to him that the easiest thing for him might be to just throw it overboard, bar by bar, and let it be lost forever at the bottom of the sea. But they were still within sight of the shore; they would still be in Libya's territorial waters, Gaddafi's infamous 'line of death.' Perhaps they would be able to recover it. In any case, to discard it was impossible; it went against all his training. You did not just release nuclear materials into the environment. They could be dredged up by a trawler, could get into the food chain. Besides, his whole career had been dedicated to the production of this priceless substance. It was unthinkable. No, he had to somehow restore it to the proper authorities.

He looked up at the sky. He expected to see a spotter plane along the coast, or naval boats, patrolling, but there was nothing. Perhaps it was better not to look; he could do nothing about it. He wondered how long it would take before they put out an alarm. Perhaps they would expect him to go to Malta, not to Tunis along the coast; perhaps once they were in Tunisian waters they would be less able to act.

The afternoon passed; the sun slipped down into the sea. It became cooler, but Dmitry could feel his face and the back of his neck were burnt by the sun. The coast was closer now, bending round to the north; as it got dark the lights along the shore became visible, from little towns or villages, and then, right ahead, the brighter lights of some bigger conurbation. Nabil pointed, and said, with satisfaction in his voice, 'Zarzis.'

They landed at a jetty in the fishing harbour, among a clutter of brightly-coloured boats. Large empty oil jars were stacked up along the quay with huge crates of fish. Again, there was the stench of fish, so strong it almost made Dmitry retch. He wondered if there would be any officials patrolling the harbour but he didn't see any. The driver stayed sitting where he was; he spoke to Nabil and indicated that they would go straight back to Libya. Dmitry let him go. He wondered what the driver might say and whether Nabil might come back and report him, but he heard the sound of the engine fading as they headed right out to sea. He took his suitcase and walked up the quay in the darkness, cursing its weight.

To the right of the port lay a long expanse of beach, shining whitely in the moonlight. Dmitry went down, took off his clothes and plunged briefly into the sea. The shock of the water revived him; he washed his hands, his hair, rubbing his body, washing off any traces of dust. The bruises on his face and his fingers from his struggle with the colonel smarted painfully. He waded out of the sea and sat naked on the beach, waiting for his skin to dry, then took a clean set of clothes out of his suitcase and put them on, burying the others in the sand. He checked the gun to see how many rounds were left, then put it away in the suitcase.

The sea lapped gently on the beach, made little gurgling sounds. He was so tired that for a moment he wanted to sleep. He forced himself to his feet, and walked towards the front; along the shore the lights of the big hotels gleamed. At last, he was back in civilisation. He looked in his wallet; he had about 50 dollars, but he did have his old credit card. He peered at it in the light of a streetlamp and saw the date had expired.

He picked up his suitcase, and went to find the bus to Tunis.

7

'TIM, is there any news?'

Katie was waiting for him by the door. She had put the children to bed and was standing in her dressing gown, her hair unkempt, and her face a harsh chalky white. Tim had been dreading coming home, had put it off as late as possible; now that he was here, he didn't know what to say to her.

The news that day had been full of the usual reactions to the US raid. The US justified its action, backed up by the UK, and there was condemnation from the Arab states and, more mutedly, from Russia. There were articles and reports speculating on Libya's nuclear potential; Tim had been working on this all day.

He went over to the kitchen and poured himself a drink. 'The Libyans haven't released any reliable casualty figures. They are exaggerating, apparently, they say hundreds of people have been admitted to hospital and villages near Tajura have been evacuated but our correspondent here thinks that's not the case.'

'You're talking like a news report. What about Mitya? Did you ask? – '

Tim took a deep breath. How was he to break this to Katie? There was no easy way – perhaps better just to come out with it. 'There was one CNN report which said that a number of nuclear scientists known to have been working at Tajura had probably been killed in the bombing. But it's only guesswork at this stage, Katie. There's nothing definite.'

But Katie, having only just adjusted to the fact that Dmitry was alive, could not deal with this new blow. She was awake all night in great distress and at Tim's insistence went straight to the doctor in the morning to ask for tranquillisers. Tim waited with Sasha till she came home but then she clung to him and begged him not to go to work and leave her on her own. Tim was beside himself.

'Katie, I have to go. You don't understand, it's my job. For God's sake, there's a briefing at the Foreign Office with Douglas Hurd and I have to be there at eleven.' He pulled Katie's arms off him and stared down at her pale, blotchy face. He said, 'I've already taken too much time off for you. If you can't be on your own you have to call your parents. I can't help it. If I don't go in I'll get the sack.' He felt trapped, desperate, not knowing what to do with her; he began to regret that he had ever started a relationship with her. None of this was what he had bargained for. He had become involved with Katie thinking of her as she used to be, a warm, capable, lovely woman, but now instead he found himself saddled with a nervous wreck.

◆

There was a cheap overnight bus from Zarzis which left at nine and deposited Dmitry in the centre of Tunis at six-thirty the following morning. He decided to avoid the airport and catch a ferry; it would be easier, more anonymous, to travel by sea.

He took a taxi from the bus station to the port, where, feeling dizzy with hunger, he bought a roll and a kebab to eat. He stood in the hot, stuffy office, in a small queue, shuffling the suitcase across the floor as he inched forwards. He had managed only the briefest sleep on the bus; now, he felt exhausted. In his rusty French he asked for a one-way ticket to Marseilles. The official nodded. 'You are not French? May I see your passport? You have a visa?'

Dmitry knew at once that the man was going to be difficult. Sweat broke out on his forehead and he wiped it with his sleeve.

He said, 'No, no visa . . . I have residence in Britain, look, it's here in my passport . . .'

'Let me see.'

Dmitry handed his passport over. The official examined it suspiciously. He looked at the page with the British residency stamp, frowned, flipped through the other pages. He picked up the phone and began a conversation about visa requirements for Russians. Then he put down the phone, frowning, and said, 'You have no entry visa for Tunisia. This is very irregular. Of course you should have been stamped on entry . . . besides, you have a Soviet passport.'

'You are right. I have a passport for a country which no longer exists. This too is no doubt irregular.'

The official looked at him for a moment and suddenly laughed. Dmitry laughed with him; the ice was broken; perhaps, he thought, this would do the trick. The official continued to study Dmitry's passport. Then he shrugged and handed it back.

'I'm sorry, I cannot help you. I think you will have to contact your embassy or the aliens' office in Tunis to sort this out.'

Dmitry threw up his hands in hopeless protest and went out. He stood in the bright sunshine outside, looking around for a taxi. He asked the driver to take him to the Russian Embassy but when they pulled up outside the ugly white building they seemed to be too early, the iron gates were locked and barred. He tried to work out what to do. He should wait and then go in and hand the uranium over to them. But that would mean handing himself over to them too. What would they do with him? He had no idea. Dmitry looked around across the street to where a blue car was parked, with two men sitting in the front. Dmitry immediately said to the driver, 'Drive on, drive on.' Of course, the Libyans would be expecting him to go there. He was convinced that they were waiting for him, that if he went and stood at the gates, or rang the bell at the closed doors, he would be shot. He couldn't risk it. He had one over-riding desire now, to get back to London and see Katie.

'Where's a good hotel?'

The taxi driver began to reel off a list of names; the Sheraton, the Hilton . . . Dmitry said, 'Try the Hilton.' The driver swung the taxi round. They seemed to be going a long way, right out of town; Dmitry's heart sank, it was going to be expensive, and there was this problem with money. Dmitry fished in his pocket for his last few dollars which were mercifully enough. He declined help with his suitcase and walked into the lobby.

The air conditioning hit him with a cold blast; he realised his shirt was damp with sweat, that he felt dizzy and sick again. He stood still for a moment or two. He was convinced that people were staring at him, that their eyes were following him as he walked across the large expanse of the entrance hall. He knew he looked terrible; in a place like this he was conspicuous. He thought that he must go and tidy himself up. He fought down the sudden nausea which swept over him.

He burst into the men's cloakroom, rushed over to the wash-basins, leaned over and was violently sick under the appalled gaze of a man in an elegant suit. Dmitry turned on the tap, rinsed out the basin and then splashed his face with cold water. His head throbbed; perhaps it was just a migraine. Or perhaps it was just the cheap kebab he had eaten at the port earlier . . . He straightened up and looked at himself in the mirror. There was no denying it; he looked dreadful. Somebody would throw him out of the hotel. He glanced round; he was now alone. He took out his shaving things but it was not easy to make a good job of it because of the bruises on his face and his swollen, painful fingers.

He straightened up, dried himself and went out into the lobby. He went to the bar at the back and ordered a mineral water to drink, sat and sipped it on the terrace. He stayed there for a long time; people started to arrive for lunch. His nausea had now completely vanished; he felt light-headed and dreadfully hungry and thought that perhaps he should try to eat.

He looked around for a waiter. A German couple were sitting at the next table, a man of about fifty and his slightly younger wife. He could over-hear their conversation; a holiday couple, reading their guidebooks, planning a trip to Carthage. He sat in the cool breeze under the sun-umbrella and watched people going about their ordinary business, while here he was, with enough highly enriched uranium to make an atomic bomb in his suitcase, and for all he knew every major intelligence agency in the world on his heels. What was he to do? He could go to the British or the US Embassy. But what would they make of him? They might arrest him for terrorism. They might hand him over to the Tunisian authorities and he could be imprisoned here – he couldn't imagine that their jails were pleasant. No, it would be better to take it back to London to the Russian Embassy there. He must ring the airport and find when the next flight to London was. They would do that from the desk. But here was the terrible thing; he hadn't the money to pay for it. He hadn't even the money to pay for a night at this hotel. Then there was the problem of his passport. He was afraid that he would be on some wanted list, might be stopped by the police. They might notice he had no entry stamp; his luggage might be searched.

He looked again at the couple at the next table. The woman had bleached blonde hair, obviously dyed, and was slightly over-weight; the man seemed bored with their conversation. Dmitry could, he supposed, rob them. He could go up to their room and see if they had left any money there. Their key lay temptingly on the table; perhaps if they got up for a moment, went to the bar, he might be able to take it . . . He tried to read the room number on it but the tag was the wrong side up. He looked at the man again. If he took their money, he could also take the passport . . . he might get away with it. The man was tall, about the right age . . . it might do at least to get out of Tunisia. Surely they never looked carefully at passports when you were leaving? With a German passport he could take the first flight, anywhere in

Europe. But supposing its theft was immediately discovered? The man would alert the police immediately. It wasn't possible. Unless he could persuade the man not to go to the police. How? Threaten him? Bribe him? Knock him out? But then, his wife . . . no, it didn't work.

The waiter came to the next table and Dmitry hailed him. He ordered a sandwich. His mouth felt dry and after one bite he had no appetite, but he knew he had to eat. The woman at the next table glanced at him without any interest. Then, as he looked at her, an idea came to him. It seemed insane; it was a plan of utter desperation, but once it had occurred to him, he couldn't shake it out of his head. He went over it again and again, testing it, trying to see if there was any flaw in it, but he couldn't find one. The couple had finished their drinks; they got up from the table and went in through the doors. Dmitry stood up, holding his half-eaten sandwich and still carrying his suitcase, and followed them into the lift. They stood, close to one another, avoiding one another's eyes. The woman pressed the button for the seventh floor and Dmitry, on impulse, the fifth. He got out there and strode quickly up the next two flights. He could see the couple along the corridor, standing outside their room. They opened the door, went in, and he heard it close.

Dmitry's heart started to beat very fast. He thought he could never go through with this; then he thought that he had to. For an instant he remembered Rozanov's mocking laughter and he felt a sudden desire to prove to him that he could carry out this plan. He unlocked his suitcase, took out the gun, and slipped it into his pocket. He locked the suitcase again, walked down the corridor, and, taking a deep breath, knocked at the door. There was a long pause. He thought, supposing they don't open it. Then I will be saved; then I will not have to do this. He felt as if by doing what he planned he was putting himself beyond any moral acceptability, cutting himself off from all ordinary human feelings and becoming, in his desperation, something he despised. He heard a voice inside the room, footsteps, and then the man say, in poor French, 'Who is it?'

Dmitry hesitated. What was 'Room service' in French? *Service de chambre*? Would they even know, anyway? He spoke the words, loudly. There was another brief pause; then the door opened. Dmitry immediately stepped inside, forcing his way past, and pushed the door shut behind him. He turned the key and put it in his pocket. Drawing the gun, he stepped back against the wall and looked at them. The woman's face turned white under her tan; the man, too, blanched and stepped backwards, putting out his hands in front of him, palms upwards. The woman sat down heavily on the side of the bed; he saw her look at the phone. Dmitry said, in German, 'Don't even think about it.'

The man said, 'What do you want?' His voice was hoarse. He glanced at his wife; they both looked terrified.

Dmitry said, 'I want money. And I want your passport.'

The man looked almost relieved at this. He said, 'Yes, of course.' He reached for his jacket, which hung from the back of the chair, and dug into the pocket. He pulled out notes and travellers' cheques. Dmitry said quietly, 'Put it on the table.' He checked the money; about 500 deutschmarks and some local currency. 'Now your passport.'

The German placed it carefully on the table. Dmitry snatched it up, examined the first page. Friedrich Gunter Gottlieb of Frankfurt, businessman. Aged 48 years. Height 182 centimetres; ten centimetres too short, but still, tall. The photo was not too bad at all, he thought; I might get away with it. He slid the passport into his pocket. He looked at the two, frightened faces but he felt no pity for them because he was as desperate as they were. He was afraid that something would go wrong, that there was some small detail that he hadn't thought of, or that they would panic and force him to some drastic act.

He said, in a quiet, low voice. 'I am going to tell you the truth. I find myself in a very serious situation. I am an agent of a foreign power, and I have to get out of this country immediately. That is why I need your passport. But this is not enough. If I leave you now, you will go to the police, and this passport will be worse than useless. So I have to take you – ' and here he looked straight into the woman's face – 'with me.'

It took a few seconds for this to sink in, then she turned with a rapid movement and looked at her husband. He could see that she was trembling. Dmitry pressed on, now looking at Gottlieb, adjusting his grip on the gun as he spoke.

'I would advise you very strongly against going to the police. You are under surveillance, and if you take any action other than those I instruct you to, I can assure you that you will not see your wife again. We have agents everywhere – ' Dmitry paused for effect – 'and I can assure you that things have not changed quite so much as you might imagine.' He could see Gottlieb trying to work him out, trying to place the accent in Dmitry's voice, an accent which must confuse him because, though no doubt there were Russian sounds or inflections there, he had learned his German in Vienna and had a good ear for languages. He was beginning to warm to the part now, it seemed to be going all right, he sounded convincing, he thought they believed him. He turned to the woman and said 'And for you, the same thing. If you try anything, something very unpleasant will happen to your husband. I can assure you that if you both co-operate no harm will come to you.'

Gottlieb said, quickly, eagerly, 'Yes, of course. We understand. We will do exactly what you want.'

Dmitry half sat on the little table; the whole situation seemed unreal; he was gaining confidence with every moment. He said, 'Once we have arrived at our destination your wife will be free to ring you. You can do what you like, then. You can go to the police, then, of course, but since this is a matter which involves the intelligence services, all you are likely to get out of it is hours of detailed interrogation and no action that you will ever see.'

He watched their faces; they seemed to accept what he told them; what else could they do? 'Now,' said Dmitry to the woman, 'Ring the desk and ask them for flights out of Tunis to London tonight.'

There was one to Paris in the afternoon, connecting to London, and one direct flight later to Heathrow. Dmitry asked if there were seats and was told there was no problem. He asked her to book two seats in the name of Gottlieb.

He said, 'Have you money, traveller's cheques, a credit card? You will need to pay at the airport. I want you to pack, now. Take those things, a change of clothes, whatever you need. Come on, hurry.'

She did as he asked, packing neatly as if from habit, folding up her blouses and pressing them down, glancing from time to time nervously at her husband. When she was ready she kissed her husband's cheek, suppressing tears, and walked across the room where Dmitry opened the door for her. She walked ahead of him down the corridor; in the lift she stood opposite him, staring at the floor. He sensed her revulsion; it both angered and reassured him, because he could see how afraid she was. For once his appearance worked in his favour; if I were a better-looking man she would not be so afraid of me, he thought.

They took a taxi to the airport. She sat, silent, at the other side of the car. Dmitry said, suddenly, in a low voice, 'Let me see your passport.' She handed it over. He looked at it; her name was Gertrude. She was a teacher. He said, 'Gertrude, you are my wife. We've been married a long time, so we don't have to talk too much, we don't have to be overly affectionate, but you must not look hostile, you must not look frightened. You must not do anything which will attract attention to us.'

She nodded.

'Tell me, where do we live?'

She gave him an address in Munich.

'Do we have children?'

'Two boys.'

'How old are they? Their names?'

'16 and 14. Berthold and Horst.' She looked at him. 'It's because of them . . . please don't harm us.'

'I have no intention of harming you,' he said, and then, with a touch of harshness, 'Unless I have to.'

He felt for the gun in his pocket. Somehow, before they checked in, he would have to get rid of it. It would be better to do so before they got to the airport. But he didn't want Gertrude to see him dump it; he wanted the threat of it as long as was possible. He glanced at her; she was looking fixedly out of the window. They were in the long road approaching the airport. He took out the passports and pretended to examine them; then, as they turned a corner, he dropped them on the floor. She looked at him; she watched as he leaned down to pick them up and deliberately looked away. He bent down to retrieve the passports and as he did so surreptitiously deposited the gun in the pouch behind the driver's seat.

The airport seemed crowded with holiday makers. They walked past the jasmine sellers; Gertrude stumbled alongside him, her face white, and he wondered whether ever afterwards she would associate the smell of jasmine with fear. He took her to the ticket desk, whispering, 'Don't look like that . . . you have had a holiday. You are happy. Smile.' She nodded, but she looked close to tears; her smile was a travesty. She looked so pale and fearful that Dmitry was convinced she would give them away.

The airline agent checked their booking and made out the tickets. Gertrude took out her credit card and he stood, nervous, while she signed. The agent said, 'Excuse me a moment.' She went back into an office. Dmitry thought Gertrude might have signed wrongly to attract attention to them and went hot and then cold all over. Gertrude too was frightened; he could see the sweat dampening her blouse; her face was white and tense. Dmitry whispered, 'What is wrong? If you –' but the woman came back, handed him the tickets and told them to go to the check-in desk.

Now he would have to check in the suitcase. He was fairly confident that it would not be scanned here, or that if it was, the metal bars would arouse no suspicion. When he saw the suitcase vanish on the conveyor belt Dmitry felt first acute anxiety and then relief. They negotiated passport control without a hitch and sat in the departure lounge. When they went through the metal detection gate Dmitry saw that Gertrude was puzzled; she was clearly wondering what he had done about the gun, but she said nothing to him.

They sat down. Dmitry wondered what the procedure would be if they searched the baggage prior to loading it. He assumed that they would call him. It was impossible to relax. Gertrude sat next to him, her back straight, trying to read a book; he watched her read the same page over and over again. Dmitry couldn't stand her tense, terrified expression; it made him angry because he couldn't afford to let himself feel sorry for her. He said, 'You are too obvious. Try to relax. Would you like me to get you a drink?'

'I want to go to the toilet.'

'On the plane.'

'I need to go now.'

'You will have to wait till you are on the plane.' He looked at her fiercely; he had to conceal from her the terrible truth that he was absolutely powerless and that if she chose to give him away there was nothing he could do about it. On the plane she insisted again that she had to go to the toilet so he went and stood outside. When she came out he grabbed her wrist to keep her with him and peered inside. She asked, 'What are you doing?' and he said, 'Just checking.' He thought he had seen a film sometime where someone left a message in lipstick on the mirror. He let go of her hand; she went and sat down. She said, in a low voice, 'I don't want you to touch me. I can only stand this if you don't actually touch me.'

They sat in silence. As soon as he sat down, Dmitry realised he had a new problem; he was so exhausted that he might fall asleep. The noise and vibration of the plane were soporific; he'd hardly slept for over 40 hours. If he fell asleep surely he would notice if she climbed or leant over him . . . but he couldn't risk it. He turned to her. He said, 'Talk to me.'

This seemed to fill her with new horror. 'Why? I can't. There's nothing to say.'

The stewardess came with drinks. She asked for a Campari and soda; he had coffee. He was trying to think ahead, now. He thought she might try something at Heathrow. She might be afraid that he would break his word, that instead of releasing her he would take her off somewhere and kill her. Perhaps he should try to reassure her. He said, 'At Heathrow, I will enter the country on your husband's passport. Once we're through customs I will give it back and you will be free to go. You can telephone your husband to say you're safe but you should not attempt to contact the police for 24 hours. After that you are both free to do what you like – though I advise you to do nothing, just in case. Do you understand that?'

'Yes.' She looked down at her lap; he could not read the expression on her face. She asked, suddenly in a low voice . . . 'Please, tell me . . . it's not drugs, is it? You don't want me to carry something through for you?'

'No, it's not drugs.'

'You look ill. Can I give you anything? I have some paracetamol in my bag . . .' she drew out a bottle and handed it to him. He looked at the bottle carefully, tipped the pills into his hand, and held them out to her. He said, 'Take one.'

She looked at him, alarmed. Then she took one and swallowed it with her Campari. He watched her for a few moments and then took two himself. He tried to relax, to ease his headache. He started; he must have fallen asleep for an instant. The plane sounded different; perhaps the engines had altered or the air pressure changed. Gertrude hadn't moved. He wondered how long he had been asleep; whether there had been time for her to have said something to the stewardess. He put his hand on her arm. She froze; she looked at him, there were tears in her eyes. He said, 'Gertrude, I asked you to talk to me.'

'I can't. I'm very tired . . . I'd like to sleep.'

'All right, then, sleep.'

They completed the journey, in silence; she, no doubt feigning sleep, while Dmitry had to force himself to stay awake.

◆

As they left the plane the air hostess hoped they'd had a pleasant flight. Dmitry strode down the long corridor, Gertrude walking meekly by his side. They joined the immigration queue, Dmitry, for once, on the EEC side. He handed Gertrude her passport. He said, 'I'll be behind you. Don't do anything; just look bored. Wait for me the other side.' He took her arm to prevent her bolting; she let him hold her, unresponsive, stiff. She went ahead of him; there was a moment when he thought she might say something to the officer but she must have thought better of it and walked straight through. Now it was his turn. He stepped forward, handed over the passport and let his legs bend at the knees very slightly to reduce his height. The immigration officer looked at the passport, at Dmitry, at the passport again, then back at Dmitry's face. He said, 'You had an accident?'

Dmitry put his hand up to feel the bruise. He said, 'A robbery.'

'I'm sorry to hear that, sir.' The officer still hesitated, holding the passport. Dmitry turned towards Gertrude, standing with her back to them, a few yards away. He tried to subtly imitate a German accent. 'Fortunately they didn't hurt my wife.'

This seemed to dispel any doubts the officer might have had; he handed the passport back to Dmitry and he walked through.

Only now that his heart slowed down did Dmitry realise how fast it had been racing. He felt his shirt was damp with sweat. He hurried after Gertrude who was now striding straight ahead. They took the escalator down to the baggage collection area and sat on a bench. Gertrude stared ahead as if she didn't belong to him. Dmitry thought she was probably calculating how she could get away. But now, he had other worries. Looking up, he couldn't help noticing a man staring at him from across the room. He felt a wave of heat sweep over him. Had the Libyans tipped somebody off that he was on the plane? Perhaps they would try to take his baggage or somehow intercept it . . . perhaps they had men working on the staff at Heathrow airport . . .

The carousel began to move. Dmitry pushed his way to the spot where the luggage came down; there was no way he wanted anyone else to get hold of his suitcase. A few people stared at him coldly as he pushed his way to the front and heaved the battered suitcase on to the floor. He glanced around for Gertrude and saw her snatching her own suitcase off the carousel.

He went to stand beside her, and handed her the German passport. 'Remember what I said. They are watching your husband in Tunis.' She nodded and backed away from him, then turned on her heel and began to walk quickly towards customs. As he followed, she increased her pace. He thought, if only she concentrates on getting away from me, doesn't stop to tell anyone, it will be all right. He rounded the corner. She walked ahead of him, glancing neither to left or right, heading for the exit. He followed slowly, trying not to hurry, keeping his eyes fixed ahead, deliberately not looking at the customs officers. He had never been stopped in customs before; it was going to be fine; any moment now he would be through.

Then a voice came from his left, 'Excuse me, sir.' He knew the voice was speaking to him but he ignored it; then it was repeated, more loudly. Somebody was moving round in front of him. He had to stop. The customs officer smiled politely, coldly. He said, 'Could you just come over here a moment, sir?'

The hall span round. Dmitry stumbled, collected himself, tried to look calm. Taking a deep breath he hoisted the suitcase in his hand and walked over to the bench.

8

'PUT your suitcase on the table.'

Dmitry lifted up the heavy case, trying not to make it seem too much effort.

'Where are you coming from, sir?'

'Tunis.'

'What were you doing there?'

'A holiday.'

'May I see your passport?'

Dmitry hesitated, then he handed over his own Soviet passport. The customs officer looked through it. He said, 'You have no entry stamp today. You have British residency . . . but your residency is about to expire. The immigration officer didn't query this?'

'This is my temporary residency, for one year . . . I applied for permanent residency, it should have come through, it is automatic, my wife is British. You can telephone her if you need confirmation. You must realise it is a complicated situation with my passport. For some reason I have to go to Moscow to get a Russian Federation passport . . .'

The officer continued to study the passport. 'You have no Tunisian stamps either . . . however, you were recently in Libya. May I ask what you were doing there, sir?'

Dmitry said the first thing that came into his head. 'I was acting as a business consultant.'

The customs officer nodded to the man standing next to him and went through into a room at the back. He was gone for some minutes. When he came back he said, 'Would you mind opening your suitcase, sir?'

Dmitry stared at him, not making any move. The officer hesitated. He asked, 'Did you pack it yourself, sir?'

'Yes.'

'There's no reason then to suppose that there's anything in it that would interest us?'

'No.'

'Then would you mind opening it for us, sir?'

Dmitry had no idea what would happen to him if he admitted what was in it. He thought the best thing might be to ask to see someone from the intelligence services, to make a clean breast of it and throw himself at their mercy, but he was afraid to do this. He supposed that British intelligence might contact the KGB, but this might not help him; they might deny all knowledge of him. He might be accused of smuggling, might be made an example of. What could he say? Even now he might be lucky and get away with it. Would they even know what the metal bars were? Could he pretend that they were simply lead? He said, to gain time, 'I've lost the key.'

It sounded ridiculous as soon as he had said it. They were tense, uneasy, looking at him; it was obvious that this situation worried them. The officer said, 'May I remind you that it is an offence to obstruct a customs officer in the performance of his duty. We want to have a look inside your suitcase. If you're not prepared to open it we shall have to do it ourselves. You can always make a claim for any damages.'

One of the officers muttered something to the other and he went away. The first put out his hands to try the locks on the suitcase and the second suddenly said, with an edge in his voice, 'No. Don't.' They looked at one another. Then they turned to Dmitry. The first one said, 'I'm sorry to inform you that you are under arrest. Please come with me. You carry the suitcase.'

They took him to an interview room. It was hot and airless and the light was too bright. Somebody came to search him; they took photographs and fingerprints. When he asked if he had the right to see a lawyer they said this could be arranged, they would call a duty solicitor, but at this time of night it would take some time. He also had the right to inform his embassy of his presence there but again, this would have to wait until the morning.

The officer who had made the arrest sat down opposite him and looked at him across the table. He was young, with a pale, eager face and large dark-framed glasses. He said, 'It will be easier for us all if you co-operate. You have the right to silence, but if you do not explain yourself it will not look good for you and may stand against you if you have to go to court. We are just trying to establish what you are doing here . . . we want to know what it is you are carrying in your luggage that you don't wish to reveal to us.' He turned to one of the other officers. 'You can take it to have it scanned now.'

They went out with the suitcase. Dmitry fidgeted helplessly. He felt angry, impotent; he had so very nearly made it. He wondered if Gertrude had phoned the police; if so, he was undone. He put his hands over his face to shield his eyes from the fluorescent light.

Another man entered the room. He introduced himself as George Bradman, Assistant Collector for Her Majesty's Customs and Excise. He was middle-aged, had a pleasant face, and an air of authority. He went quietly over the same questions as the others; what had he been doing in Tunis; in Libya; what was he carrying in his suitcase; why was he obstructing them. When Dmitry did not answer satisfactorily he looked increasingly worried. He was coldly, impersonally polite. The official returned. He said, 'We've put it through the scanner . . . there are some opaque objects, possibly metal bars, possibly explosives . . . what looks like a cassette recorder and earphones . . . It doesn't look like a bomb, but . . . shall we open it or do we need to call in the bomb disposal people?'

Bradman considered for a moment, then he said impatiently, 'Yes, yes, I think in this case the whole works, Special Branch, the security services . . .' he kept his eye on Dmitry as he said this. 'I don't like the look of this. Perhaps you should also get through to security and have them evacuate the terminal . . .'

Dmitry had been sitting stunned while all this went on, simply not knowing what he should do. Now he realised there was no point in holding out any longer. 'I'm sorry, this is all pointless . . . Where is the suitcase? Why are we making all this fuss about this suitcase? Look . . . Bring it here and I will open it for you.'

Again, there was an exchange of glances. The Assistant Collector nodded. One of the officers went and got the suitcase. It was too heavy and bulky to lift on to the table; Dmitry bent over and fiddled with the lock. His hands were trembling; they couldn't help noticing. The officer next to him suddenly put out his hand and pulled his arm away.

'No. Don't do it.'

Dmitry turned and stared. The second officer said, 'It's OK. I've seen the X-ray. If its material for a bomb, it's not wired up.'

'These explosives can be tricky.'

'OK, we'll go outside.'

They left him to open the case. They must have watched him through the one-way mirror; after a few minutes, they came back in. The Assistant Collector came over and started to search the suitcase gingerly. He took out the cassette recorder, the shaving bag, which he examined thoroughly, and began to feel through the untidy, crumpled clothes. He lifted out the pile of documents, gave them a cursory glance; then he found the six metal bars. He lifted one up, weighing it in his hands. He said, 'Good lord, this is very heavy. It looks like lead.' He turned to the other officer, who took it from him. 'It feels too solid to be hollow.' He turned to Dmitry. 'What is it?'

Dmitry opened his mouth but found himself unable to answer.

Bradman turned to the man standing behind him. 'Mayhew. I want you to get on to the Foreign Office . . . . and you'd better ring Harwell . . . someone should take a look at this . . .' He replaced the ingot on top of the clothes in the suitcase and looked at Dmitry again. He pulled the chair up close to him and stared at him, his face far too close. 'Why don't you explain yourself? We are going to get to the bottom of this sooner or later. You are an intelligent man, you must realise you will be kept here until we do . . . if you could just explain, Dr Gavrilov, what this is all about.' He broke off suddenly. 'Are you feeling all right?'

Dmitry loosened his tie and leaned backwards, away from Bradman's oppressive stare. The atmosphere in the room was hostile, overwhelming; he felt light-headed. He said, 'I'm sorry . . . I'm feeling dreadfully ill. My head . . .'

And now there was a subtle change in the room, from animosity to the faintest touch of fear. Bradman got to his feet. He said, 'I think we'll get a doctor to check you over.' He walked across the room, and as he went, used his foot to flip the lid of the suitcase shut. He pushed it into the far corner of the room and came back. He said, 'You can see what we are thinking . . . a Russian, without entry stamps, coming via Tunis from Libya, with something suspicious in his luggage . . . what is this man? Is he a terrorist? Is he, perhaps, involved in illegal trade? Could this be, for example, something . . . nuclear?'

Dmitry looked up sharply. Bradman seemed to recognise that he had got somewhere near; he pressed on, his voice icy. 'Those bars I handled . . . tell me what they are . . .'

Dmitry finally confessed with immense relief. 'They are highly enriched uranium. I brought them from the Nuclear Research Centre in Tajura.' He paused. 'I did this for my own country – and for the West.'

'I see.' Bradman nodded, then turned to the other officers. 'You've touched this – go and wash your hands. You, take over while I do the same.' Dmitry sat and watched them go, completely detached. From somewhere far off, an alarm bell sounded.

When they came back in, Dmitry said, 'It's all right, it's not dangerous. It's not highly radioactive. You are in no danger . . . I would not have allowed you . . . I have handled it myself . . .'

'Yes, and you are feeling ill. We can't simply take this on trust. Suppose you are lying, and it's something worse? Has this uranium, for instance, been irradiated? Where does it come from?' Dmitry could sense Bradman's suppressed alarm. He said to the others, 'Get it taken out of here and get it stored safely. Get immediate advice . . . you had better retain anyone from the airline who might have been in contact with this stuff . . .' He turned back to Dmitry. 'You will be facing a number of criminal charges, carrying radioactive material on to an aircraft, smuggling prohibited goods into the UK, obstructing customs officials, and that's just to begin with . . .'

◆

It was a long night. Three men sat with him in the interview room; more stood guard outside. The men did not say who they were and Dmitry didn't need to ask. They were very skilled. They asked difficult, probing questions. They asked for details, then more details, and they did not give up until they had everything they wanted. By now there was no point in telling them anything other than the whole truth, and this they extracted from him, layer by painful layer, even the things he would rather not have told them. Afterwards he was exhausted. He did not exactly feel purged; instead, he felt empty and abandoned. They took him to another room and told him that the doctor was ready to examine him.

The doctor was cold, clinical and thorough. He said that he thought that Dmitry was mainly suffering from exhaustion but that as he had been exposed to radiation he ought to have certain tests done, and he could arrange for this when he knew where Dmitry would be staying. The doctor said that he had obviously received a low enough dose to escape immediate effects but it was possible his white blood count would fall and that he would be vulnerable to infections. Perhaps out of kindness, he didn't mention the long-term effects. He wrote out a letter of referral to a private hospital and suggested he contact them to make the appointment as soon as possible.

Bradman returned to see him in the morning. He said that they were making further enquiries, but they were not bringing any formal charges at the moment. He must present himself at Holborn Police Station at 9am on Monday morning, but now he was free to go.

Dmitry stared at him in disbelief. 'What do you mean, I can go?'

'What I said. The door is open.'

'Why?'

Bradman shrugged. 'Orders from above.'

One of the interrogating officers put Dmitry's wallet, keys, and pocket diary on the table, together with his shaving bag and the money he had stolen from the German. The officer told him they would be holding on to his passport. Dmitry picked his things up, bewildered. At the door, he turned and said 'I have no sterling. Is there somewhere – ?'

At this the officer grinned. He said, 'There's a currency exchange in the main terminal; it should be open by now. But just in case, if it helps, I'll give you the tube fare into town.'

◆

He sat on the underground train into London, wondering what to do now, where to go. He sat with the commuters, going about their everyday business, reading their papers and listening to their walkmans. Dmitry felt he had only the most tenuous connection with them, as if he inhabited some other, parallel universe which enabled him to see but not to feel or touch them; he had the feeling too that if he spoke, they would be unable to hear him.

On reflection, thinking about it, he realised that it was not so odd that they had let him go. Either he was telling the truth, in which case he had done them a favour, or he was lying, was a black marketeer or double agent, in which case they would be watching his every move, waiting to see if he led them to any contacts he might have. He thought he had better go to a hotel. He wanted to wash, to sleep. Then he would ring the bank. He would ring Geneva, see if he could get some money transferred; then he would ring Katie. At the thought that he was so near, could see Katie and the children, he began to tremble.

He found a cheap hotel in Gower Street, Bloomsbury. When the woman at reception asked for his passport he told her he was a British resident and that his passport was with the Home Office; he registered under a false name and paid in cash for one night. In his room, he drew the curtains and flung himself face downwards on the bed. He slept solidly through the afternoon and then the night. When he finally woke it was eight in the morning and the pale light was coming in through the thin curtains; the rush hour traffic roared below in an endless stream. He ran a bath and soaked in it for a long time; then he shaved and dressed.

He went out, taking his few possessions in a plastic bag, and caught a bus to Piccadilly, found a payphone and telephoned his London bank. They told him there was hardly any money in the joint account and that his wife had transferred it all to her own account, to which he did not have access. He found the number for the bank in Geneva and dialled that. He quoted his number and code word and asked them if he could make a withdrawal and arrange to collect it from a suitable bank in London.

The bank said that this was impossible because, as he could hardly have forgotten, he had faxed them only the day before requesting that he transferred all the money to an account in the Libyan National Bank.

This hit Dmitry like a physical blow. He protested weakly, 'But I never sent such a fax. It's impossible.'

'Does anyone else know the identification code?'

Dmitry tried to remember. He thought back to the bank in Geneva on the Rue du Rhone where he had opened the numbered account. Could Ghesuda have seen it, over his shoulder? He thought perhaps he could. He said, 'But the signature?'

'I'm sorry, no signature was needed. I have it in front of me here, the discharge form which you signed . . . you can write to explain the situation, but – '

Dmitry hung up before he could hear any more. Of course he could have no redress in law; it was hopeless. He felt desperate; what was he to do? He could only manage for a couple more days at most. Not giving himself time to think, he picked up the receiver again and dialled Katie's number.

He heard her voice, casual, unsuspecting. 'Hello?'

He said, 'It's me. I'm in London.'

She said, 'Mitya,' then, for a long time, nothing else. He said, 'I want to see you.' She asked him, 'Why?' He couldn't answer her. She was crying, he could hear that she was crying. She said, 'Oh God, I can't take this. Are you really alive?'

He could hear a child in the background, Sasha, crying, but it was not a small baby's crying any more, but a more complaining kind of sound. Katie said, 'Wait a minute.' He heard her talking to Sasha for a moment and the crying stopped. She came back to the phone and said, 'Where in London are you?'

'In a hotel. I don't want to tell you where. Could you come down and see me?'

'No, I can't.'

'Katie.'

She was silent for a long time. Then she said, 'I'm afraid to. Anyway, I don't understand. How long are you back here?'

'Permanently. Katie, I have to see you. I have no money, no clothes, nothing. I am not well, I have to go to a hospital for some tests. Will you help me?'

She answered, 'I can send you some of your clothes, I can ring the bank and ask them to transfer some money into the account. How much do you need?'

'I don't know.'

'£500? Would that do for now?'

'Yes . . . all right . . . that will be fine. Can't you bring it to me? I would rather have cash. I don't have a card . . .'

There was silence. This was terrible; she would think he had only rung her because he needed money. He said, softly, pleading, 'Katie.'

'Mitya, I'm sorry, but I can't see you. You must understand, that after everything that's happened, it's too dangerous. If you want to see the children I understand, you have that right, I will arrange for it somehow, perhaps some some sort of supervised access, but please don't ask me to see you again like this. I thought it was all over – in fact, as you well know, I thought you were *dead*.'

Dmitry said nothing; the sudden violence in her voice shook him. After a few moments Katie said more softly, 'Tell me where you are. I'll ring the bank straight away and you can go and collect the money. I'll send you the clothes in a taxi later on.'

Dmitry accepted her fear at seeing him. He realised that he wasn't at all sure of his situation; he understood that she might think her line might be tapped, and it was of course likely that he would be followed. He said, 'You told me once, where you were born, don't say the name. Can you meet me there? It's imperative that I talk to you.'

Sasha's crying in the background had reached intolerable levels. Katie said, 'I must go; all right, wait for me there. Give me a couple of hours. I need to find someone to look after Sasha.'

◆

Katie knew where he meant; the hotel on Hyde Park Corner. She had been born, upstairs on the top floor, when it was St George's Hospital, and was surprised that if he needed money so desperately he would be staying in such luxury. She felt the terrible irony as she walked towards it that her life had begun there, and now felt as if it were about to end in the same place. The pain she felt in her heart was overwhelming. Hearing Mitya's voice had taken her straight back to the anguish she had felt in those last few days before he'd left them. She felt sick with anxiety. The leather bag with his things in it weighed heavily on her arm and she felt as if in telling him what she had resolved to say, that there was no going back and they had to finalise their affairs, that she was going to destroy him.

She found him waiting in the hotel lounge, pretending to read the newspaper. When she came in he stood up and they stared at one another. It was so strange for her to see him living, after thinking him dead. He was the same; but he was not the same. He looked haggard, ill, his face was badly bruised, and seemed to have aged several years in the months since she'd last seen him. The moment she saw him he had, as always, this terrible, devastating effect on her; she had to struggle with herself not to abandon all her resolve and throw herself into his arms.

She put the bag on the floor beside the chair and sat down, quickly, before he was able to reach out and embrace her; she folded her hands protectively across her lap. She was uneasy, feeling the falseness of her position, and didn't know what to say to him. She fiddled nervously with the fringes of her fine wool shawl.

'I bought some clothes . . . there are some papers and things, about your residency . . . And your coat, I thought you'd need that. I didn't know what else you wanted . . . perhaps you had better look . . .'

He looked at her intently; she couldn't meet his gaze. He said, 'We don't have to stay here. We could go for a walk.'

'No, Mitya, I don't want to.' She didn't want to be alone with him; she was afraid that there would be some terrible scene or worse, that he would want to kiss her or plead with her to give him another chance and that she might want that, too. Rebuffed, he sat heavily on the chair opposite her. He seemed altogether wrong, out of place, in the grand, expensive room, with its Chinese vases, plush sofas, chintz curtains and Persian carpets.

He asked, 'Would you like some tea? I can ask them to bring some . . .'

'No, it's all right, please don't bother . . . I can't stay long, I left Sasha with a friend . . .'

She sat, helplessly, trying to think of something to say. He asked, 'Are the children all right? Has anyone been helping you . . .'

'Yes, they're fine. We've managed, somehow.' She didn't want to mention Tim; of course she knew she should tell him, but how could she, now? It would be too cruel; she couldn't, on top of everything else that had obviously happened to him, deal him this blow. Dmitry asked, 'Can I see them?' and she softened for a moment. She said, 'Yes, of course you can see them, in time. Anna . . .' and suddenly she found herself on the point of tears. How could she say, 'Anna misses you'? Rather than let herself cry, she instantly became angry; 'I didn't know what to tell her. What could I say? She has been very withdrawn, she has nightmares . . . don't you realise what this has done to her?'

'Katie . . . don't.' He hung his head. 'I am not trying to excuse myself . . . but I need to talk to you. We have to sort everything out . . . what do you want? Do you think there is any chance – '

She didn't want to talk about this; she didn't know what to say. She felt frozen, unable to deal with the confused emotions which were sweeping through her. She said 'Mitya, how can I answer these questions now? I don't know. If you want the truth I'm frightened of you, I'm afraid of being seen with you, God knows what might happen. Our phone has been tapped, we've been watched, the KGB came round to search the flat . . . I can't live like this. It's been a kind of hell.'

'That will soon be over.'

He looked ashamed as soon as he had said this; anyway, she didn't believe him. She asked softly, 'Will it?' She looked at him and he dropped his gaze, staring at the glass-topped table. She went on. 'How could you write me that letter? Don't you realise what I've suffered? How could you let me believe . . .'

'I meant it. I tried to kill myself. It was because . . . it was to make you safe.' He loosened his shirt cuffs and held out his wrists to display the scars. She saw the red marks scoring the skin and felt a moment of pity and revulsion; the anguish he was feeling radiated from him like something palpable. Looking into his eyes now was like looking into a vortex, an abyss; it was like the *liebestod*, love-in-death or death-in-love or whatever you called it in English; she had to save herself.

She shifted backwards in her chair. She said, 'You said you'd been ill. Are you going to see someone? You look terrible, Mitya. You need help . . .'

The waiter came and stood by her elbow, delicately clearing this throat. He asked them if they wanted anything; Katie couldn't tolerate the thought of sitting there, sipping tea, trying to make any kind of normal conversation, and jumped to her feet. There were so many things she wanted to ask him; what had happened after he had written his letter, whether he had been at Tajura at the time of the raid, how he had got away, but she didn't want to ask him now, she wanted to get away as fast as possible. She said, 'I have to go, Mitya . . . look, I'll see you again soon. I will arrange something, with the children, once I feel it's safe for them to see you . . . but you must accept that we can't live together any more.'

He followed her to the door. On the steps of the hotel she felt a sense of panic. She didn't want to leave him; she was afraid that if she left him now something would happen and she would never see him again, and that her last words to him would haunt her forever. She turned to him and said, 'Please, let me know what you are doing . . . will you call me, tomorrow . . .'

'Katie – '

He put out his hand to take hold of her and she jumped away. Her shawl fluttered to the ground and he stooped to pick it up; she turned and started to run so that he wouldn't see her crying. When she got to the entrance of the underground she turned and saw him looking after her, letting the shawl run helplessly through his fingers.

◆

Dmitry stood on the pavement outside the hotel, holding the shawl to his nostrils so that he could inhale the faint trace of perfume. He thought it wasn't possible to feel more desperate. Once again he felt the only thing to do was die. Yet he couldn't give up hope of having Katie; he had to do something, to make his position safe. He went back into the hotel to collect his things, then down to the payphones in the station to dial the number he had used to contact Rozanov.

It was unobtainable. He rang the Russian consulate. He said, 'I want to speak to Gleb Rozanov.'

'There is no one of that name here.'

'He works upstairs. You know who I mean. You must put me through at once.'

'I am not able to do so.'

'I don't have time to play these games. Give me the head of the foreign intelligence service. Tell him it is Dmitry Gavrilov.'

'Please give me your telephone number. Maybe someone will call you back.'

He gave his number and hung up. He waited for a while, but no one called. He rang again and repeated his demand, and again the woman said she couldn't connect him.

Dmitry said, 'Tell him that I have a gun, and that I will come over and shoot myself on the steps of the consulate if he doesn't see me. Then you will have some explaining to do.'

She said sharply, 'Please ring off.'

'I have valuable intelligence from Libya. They will want to hear it.'

'I do not think they will be interested in your intelligence. Don't call again. You are becoming a nuisance.' There was a terrible threat in those simple words; Dmitry felt a chill go through him. The line had gone dead; he hung up. He didn't know what he would do, but he walked through the pedestrian underpass and out of the northern exit, and began to walk all the way across the park, towards the Russian embassy. The trees were beginning to turn, and as he walked, some dead leaves blew along the path. He knew he looked disreputable; he was unshaven, wore his old black coat wrapped about him, and could not suppress the desire to curse out loud. He was aware that anyone seeing him would probably have taken him for a drunk, and yet he didn't care.

As he neared the north side of the park, he stopped. He blinked, passed a hand before his eyes. In front of him, on the path, he saw Rozanov. Behind him stood two thick-set men.

Rozanov turned and walked towards him, the men following behind him.

'Are you armed?'

The two men searched him. When they had finished, they fell back and Rozanov turned and walked beside him. He did not waste any time with formalities. 'What is this information?'

'Did British Intelligence contact you? Did they tell you what I was carrying at Heathrow?

Rozanov lit himself a cigarette with an elegant lighter; he smiled and said, 'Believe me, we know everything. I doubt if there is anything you could tell us . . . This business is closed now. I imagine you want money.'

'But I have done the job you wanted, I have the information, more than you could have hoped for, not just about Tajura, but other procurement . . . why are you not interested?

Rozanov said, 'After the events of the last few days it is probably only of historical importance. By all means, we can arrange a debriefing. I have received permission to make a payment to you if you if you agree to be co-operative . . . the money could be in your account tomorrow.'

'You think you can just pay me off.'

'Dmitry Nikolayevich, don't sound so ungrateful; this is extremely generous. You realise that we could have you killed, indeed that in some quarters this would have been thought the best thing? Consider yourself very lucky.'

Dmitry's voice was icy cold. He saw the whole thing, now. 'You wanted me dead all along, didn't you? That was all part of the plan. I was to be a scapegoat, to show the world what would happen to any Russian scientist foolish enough to go and sell their secrets in the Middle East. You could point the finger at me and say, look, how dangerous this is. This will happen to you, too. You tried to kill me in Tripoli. That was what you intended, wasn't it? Admit it.'

It was the only thing that made sense to him. It explained why Rozanov had expressed no concern that Dmitry had produced so little intelligence, how his warnings that his project was working had not disturbed him. He was never intended to live to complete it. He was to be a sacrificial lamb, whose death would serve to warn others and help prevent the spectre of nuclear proliferation. He wondered for a moment whether, if they had asked him to lay down his life in this great cause, he would have considered it; it was an interesting thought. But one would want to know, to have been given the choice plainly; as it was he felt only betrayal and disgust.

Rozanov, faced with Dmitry's utter dereliction, seemed suddenly to feel a need to justify himself. He turned and waved the two men back, and continued up the path with Dmitry. He said, 'Dmitry Nikolayevich, let me assure you, it was not our idea. These days, we are not entirely our own masters . . . it was a deal.'

'A deal? What do you mean? With whom?'

'With our new friends across the Atlantic, with the CIA . . . it was their idea. To be a warning, as you said. They set it up. I believe they even set up the journalist who was to expose you . . . a pity he didn't do a very good job.'

For a moment the ground seemed to sway under Dmitry's feet. He had distrusted everyone, considered them capable of anything; but even he had not expected this. So everything that had happened, almost, had been planned from the beginning, and he had been the passive victim from the outset. 'And they asked for your assistance?'

'Of course . . . We are co-operating more and more these days. They asked us to find them a scientist, someone the Libyans might approach . . . You seemed the perfect candidate . . . we'd had our eye on you for some time. We needed somebody expendable, someone whose career was finished, somebody who didn't matter . . .'

'Except of course to his wife and children.'

'Believe me, it is not pleasant to make these choices . . . do you think I enjoy it? Dancing to another's music? Wake up. This is the harsh new world in which we live, Dmitry Nikolayevich. As an independent power we are finished. Come, now, you are alive, that is the main thing. In fact, I think you have come out of it rather well. You did us a great service taking this material out of Libya. You showed great resourcefulness – I may even say, courage. The CIA are very pleased with us. If you want to come back to Russia, you know, we can help you find employment. We can get someone to put in a good word for you at the various Institutes.' Rozanov paused. 'In fact, I would advise you to leave the UK as soon as you can.'

'I have no passport.'

'Well, I took the precaution of preparing one for you.' Rozanov withdrew a red Russian Federation passport from his pocket, and handed it to Dmitry, who stared blankly at the double-headed eagle on the front. 'It is in another name, so you will not alert anyone at the airport. We would like a person of your talent back in Russia. Your country has need of you.'

Dmitry made an exclamation of disgust. He was not flattered in the least by Rozanov's words; he had suffered too much, and besides, what use might they want to put him to now? He turned and grabbed Rozanov's arm. 'Tell me, how does it feel, to select your victim, get to know him, prepare him, deceive him, look into his eyes and tell him . . .'

'Mine is not a pleasant job,' admitted Rozanov. He glanced at his watch. Dmitry could see he had nothing more to say, was anxious for this to be over as quickly as possible. For Rozanov, the matter was finished; it was left to Dmitry to see what he could salvage from his ruined life.

Dmitry turned away. He felt an intense desire to put as much distance as he could between himself and this man, to be rid forever of his influence. As he turned, he saw the two men step out from behind the trees. Overcome with sudden fear, Dmitry turned tail and fled.

9

DMITRY ran down to the edge of the Serpentine but nobody seemed to be following him. He turned left and walked hastily, glancing occasionally to right and left, carrying his bag in one hand, the other thrust deep into his pocket. He walked for miles across London, not knowing what to do.

He walked east until in the afternoon he found himself in the City. He went into a pub, sat at the bar, and began to drink. After a few vodkas all he could think about was Katie. He saw now that he had handled it so badly. Why had he not told her when he saw her that he loved her, that she and the children were the only thing that mattered to him, that there was no point at all in him having survived if he couldn't be with her? He had another drink. He was sure that if he could only see her again, explain to her everything that had happened, beg her for forgiveness, she wouldn't turn him away. He would go that evening, now, this minute, take her some flowers. Surely if he went and spoke to her now she would see that he still loved her . . .

He set off in search of a shop where he could buy her flowers or chocolates. He realised that he was a little drunk but this didn't seem important. He hoped that by the time he got there he would have sobered up. It was late now, beginning to get dark, it was nearly eight o'clock and all the shops were shut. It was a heavy, oppressive evening, hot for the time of year, and he thought that it might thunder.

He bought some chocolates from a late-night store and went to wait at the bus stop. The bus was a long time in coming; he went to get the tube at Bank and went to Oxford Circus, hoping to lose himself in the crowds. He had no idea if anyone was interested in his movements, the Russians, British Intelligence, the CIA. And what about the Libyans? Would they be after him? Did they even know where he had gone? He changed tube trains three or four times, at random, always stepping on or off at the last moment as the doors were closing; he didn't think he was being followed, but how could he be sure?

He reached Kilburn after ten. It was late, he knew it was a stupid time to call, but now he was there he couldn't turn away. He was devoured by a need to be with Katie, to touch her, to see the children. He thought they might be watching the house so he went round the corner, to the path that ran behind a car-park and gave access to the rear of the properties; he could get in that way without being seen. The house was in darkness; he felt in his pocket for the keys. He thought he would just go in, look at the sleeping children and talk to Katie if she was awake. It occurred to him as he took out the back-door key that she might have changed the lock but when he tried it the door opened. He stood in the kitchen and looked around. The place looked strangely familiar but also different; it was tidier and cleaner, and the walls had been freshly painted.

He went upstairs, treading softly so he wouldn't wake them, but the boards creaked, sounding unnaturally loud. He stepped into the children's room. Anna was asleep, lying on her back; her sweet face glowed in the light from the night lamp. Sasha, in his cot, had more than doubled in size. He was not a tiny baby any more, he was a boy; his face had filled out and his hair was thick and curly; when Dmitry looked at him he could see something of himself. Staring down at his son, he was amazed. How could he have forgotten, have neglected, this extraordinary gift? He was overcome with love and wonder, and tears poured into his eyes, temporarily blinding him. He wiped them away, recovered himself, and then turned to look into the front bedroom.

He wondered if he should knock; he didn't want to alarm Katie. But then, he would alarm her in any case. He pushed the door open wider and looked into the room. Katie was not alone in the bed; Tim was there beside her. They were lying back to back, touching, close to one another, like a married couple. Dmitry saw them, and he understood. All the strength drained out of him in a moment; he staggered backwards and Katie, sensing something, sat up suddenly. She saw Dmitry in the doorway and gasped; she put out her hand towards Tim, instinctively covering herself.

Tim woke and sat up, startled; Dmitry saw him lean over and switch on the light. They all stared at one another, blinking in the sudden brightness.

Katie leaned over, reached on to the floor, and pulled on her dressing gown. Dmitry turned and stumbled down the stairs and Katie followed, saying, 'Please, wait.' She grabbed hold of him and he pushed her away. She pursued him into the living room.

She stood there, staring at him. He could see both anger and pain in her face. She said, 'Are you mad? Why did you come here? You could at least have warned us, have rung the doorbell.'

Dmitry said, 'Why? It's my house. After all, I've paid for it, haven't I?' He didn't mean to say those words; he realised as he uttered them that they sounded all wrong. He was completely beside himself, stunned with shock and rage. He thought that until this moment he hadn't known what suffering was. He tried to calm himself, sat down at the table. After a pause he said, 'Can I have a drink?'

Katie reached up and opened the cupboard. She took down the half empty vodka bottle, untouched since he left, and poured a glass which she put on the table by Dmitry. She said, 'Please, Mitya, don't get drunk. I couldn't stand it. I can't stand much, these days.'

Dmitry looked towards the stairs. 'How long has that been going on for?'

'Since I got your suicide letter.'

'Not before?'

'No, Mitya, not before.'

Dmitry drained the glass in one gulp. He said, 'Oh God, you could have said . . .'

She turned her back to him, walked over to the sink. She said, 'What did you expect me to do? We were separated. I was on my own with the children, miserable, unhappy. I needed help, just to get me through each day. Then you told me you were dead. How dare you come back, after everything you've done to us, and accuse me of anything?'

Dmitry tried to keep his voice reasonable. 'I am not accusing you . . . I just can't bear it, that's all.'

Katie seemed to have retreated into herself; she seemed fragile, cold, and bitter. 'Well, you'll just have to bear it. Is it so very terrible, compared with things that you have done? And anyway, what about you? Have you been faithful to me all this time?'

This question seemed so senseless to Dmitry that he couldn't answer her. He heard footsteps on the stairs; Tim came in, fully dressed. He went over to Katie and put his arm round her, deliberately, protectively; Dmitry wanted to pull him away but forced himself to stay still. Katie seemed uncertain how to react; perhaps she didn't want to hurt or provoke Dmitry by an open display of affection but didn't want to rebuff Tim either. She looked awkward, uneasy in his presence.

Dmitry remembered the box of chocolates and put it on the table.

Katie's eyes fell on the beautifully-wrapped package. 'What is this?'

'I bought them for you.'

'Oh, Mitya.' There was so much sadness in her voice that he felt tears welling up in his eyes. This was terrible – whatever happened, he must not weep in front of Tim.

He said, 'I need another drink. Can you pass the vodka bottle?'

Tim turned to Katie. 'Don't let him get drunk. He already is drunk, by the look of him. Don't give it to him.'

Dmitry's anger boiled over at the sight of Tim, telling Katie what to do in his own house. 'I am not drunk. How dare you speak of me like this . . . It is my vodka after all, and my glass, and my table.' As he said this he banged the flat of his hand on the table in emphasis.

They both stared at him, aghast. Then Katie turned and went to open the window. It was unseasonably warm, like a summer night. The wind rushed loudly in the trees like the sound of the sea. The breeze was a welcome intruder in the hot, still room, though it brought with it threat of thunder. Dmitry could feel his heart thumping.

They sat round the table. There was a long, long silence in which they heard the clock tick, the dry leaves rustle and the distant sound of a night bus grinding up the hill.

It was Dmitry who broke the silence. 'Katie, I can't talk to you when he is here. I need to talk to you alone.'

Tim said, 'I don't think that's a very good idea.'

'Please don't interrupt me.'

'I am not interrupting you. I think you have a nerve, just coming back here, without so much as ringing the bell . . . I suppose you think you can just come back and be forgiven for what you've done . . .'

Katie put her hand on his arm, restraining him. 'No, Tim, he doesn't . . . but anyway, why shouldn't he be forgiven? Everyone who is truly sorry should be forgiven.'

Dmitry shook his head. 'It would be nice if the world really was like that, but . . . I don't think I can so easily be forgiven. There is no forgiveness in hell, once you are damned, is there, Katie? What did your Catholic teachers say about that?'

'Look,' said Tim, 'We don't want a bloody theological discussion . . . But since you're here, as a matter of fact, I would like some answers to some questions.'

Dmitry found Tim's arrogance astounding. Didn't he understand anything? 'I have answered enough questions. I have nothing to say to you.'

'What I don't understand,' said Tim, ignoring this, 'Is whether Russian intelligence knew all about it, and if so, why they didn't try to stop you. When I talked to this guy Dorokhov in Tripoli . . .'

Dmitry turned to Tim. 'Dorokhov? You spoke to him? When?'

'At the Russian Embassy, the day before the car bomb.'

Dmitry stared at him. What had Tim been thinking of? Now, he thought he could see how all Tim's actions had worked against him. He closed his eyes, then opened them again. He said, very quietly, 'Yes, of course, they knew all about it, because I was working for them from the beginning.'

Tim looked at him, breathed in sharply, then let out a long breath, almost a whistle. For a moment he was silent, seemed at a loss for what to say. Katie looked bewildered. She jumped up from the table. She said, 'I don't understand. You mean you were spying for them, in Libya? That you were a sort of – what do they call them – *double agent*?' She made the words sound absurd, like something out of a cheap thriller.

Dmitry looked at her, saw her struggling to take in this information. For a moment, he felt hope. Would this change her view of him? Would she realise that what he had done was not quite as dreadful as she thought? Would she, now, be able to forgive him? But before she could continue, Tim butted in.

'Let me get this straight. You – '

'You are a journalist. This is impossible. I am not going to talk to you. Haven't you caused enough damage? Don't you see what your blundering around has led to?'

'On the contrary, I thought that was what you wanted. After all, it was *you* who talked to *me*.'

Katie seemed desperate. She put her hands over her ears. She said, 'Stop it, I can't stand this. Don't be too hard on Tim, Mitya. He did agree to keep your name out of the papers.'

Tim added, 'Which, you should realise, I could undo at any time.'

This was too much. Dmitry leaped up, putting up his hand

to strike him, but Katie put herself in the way. She cried out, 'For God's sake, Mitya, don't do this, and you, Tim, shut up!' She looked from one to the other in despair. She said, pleading, 'It's so late . . . I don't think I can take this. Mitya, can't we talk some other time?'

Dmitry could not believe that at this point she could turn him away. He said, 'I can't leave. I have nowhere to go.' He laid his head down on the table, felt the hard wood press against his cheek. The pressure of it was reassuring, convincing him that he was still conscious, that he could still feel something, still connect with physical reality. He knew now that he had come to the end of his strength; he was unable to carry on any longer. He felt as if he might die, as if his body was so exhausted and so grief-stricken that his heart would simply fail to go on beating.

Katie leaned over him, put her hand on his shoulder. He felt the soft pressure of her palm through the fabric of his shirt, and inhaled her unique scent. It was agonising. She said, very gently, 'If you like, if you can't move . . . you could stay the night downstairs in Tim's flat.'

Dmitry turned his head towards her. What else could he do? He raised himself up a little; despair had gripped him like iron shackles, he could hardly move. He said, 'All right.' Katie handed Tim the key from the hook; Tim took his arm and helped him to his feet. He let himself be helped downstairs. As Tim closed the door behind him, he flung himself across the bed.

◆

Katie went upstairs and sat on the edge of the bed, staring straight in front of her, horrified at seeing Dmitry in this state. She wanted to go, now, and speak to him, tell him they could work something out, that he would be able to see the children, and that maybe in the future they would be able to see one another without pain; then she thought that this would make things worse. As she pulled off her dressing gown and lay down, Tim came in, leaving the door ajar so they would hear the children if they woke.

Tim sat down beside her, his hands resting on his knees. 'Why did he have to come here? Is he mad? Doesn't he realise how much it upsets you?'

Katie said, 'Of course he felt he could come, after all, he is still my husband. He has a right to talk things over with me, to see his son . . .'

'What, at this hour? Without asking?'

'He didn't know about us, he thought I would be alone. Why are you so angry? Is it because you're afraid that I still love him?'

Tim put his hand on her arm and she let it lie there, unable to respond. She realised, with a jolt, that she felt revulsion at his touch. She rolled away from him. He leaned over her and asked her, 'But you do still love him, don't you?'

'I don't know, Tim . . . Can love really end?'

Tim lay down beside her, on his back, staring straight up at the ceiling. He said, 'You don't feel the same way about me.'

'No. It's different. But perhaps it's better that way.'

'I don't think so. It wouldn't work out in the long term . . . it's pretty clear to me what you feel. I have to be honest with you, Katie, I see the way you look at him . . . I don't know if it's worth my carrying on with this.'

There was a hardness in his voice that she had never heard before, and she felt panic rising. She didn't want this conversation, not now; if she followed it through to the end she could see herself ending up alone, without Dmitry, without Tim. It had seemed downstairs as if they both wanted her, but, underneath, she saw that it was not like that at all. She could see how fragile her relationship with Tim was and how he was jealous of her feelings for Dmitry; she had sensed also Dmitry's disgust that she had been sleeping with Tim. But could being alone really be worse than what she had now? She knew that, deep down, she was afraid to be on her own, to find out and confront who she really was. She turned to Tim and said, despairingly, putting her arms around him, 'Tim, I need you; is that so very different from love?'

◆

Katie couldn't sleep. At some point in the night, probably at around three o'clock, when her body was at its lowest ebb, she thought she heard the front door catch click and something move on the stairs. She thought at first that it must be Dmitry; she lay still, tense, wondering whether to feign sleep or to get up now and tell him to go away before Tim woke up and there was another scene. There was silence; then another muffled footstep. She heard the door to the other bedroom creak and sat up, alarmed, in an instant; surely he couldn't go and wake the children? She got out of bed on the far side, anxious not to wake Tim, and took two steps towards the window.

The door crashed wide open.

She saw a gun in a gloved hand and a hooded head behind it. She would have cried out but she had no voice. Tim, woken by the sound of the door-handle smashing against the wall, sat up and put out his hand, switching on the light. His eyes, coming awake, registered his fear and horror; he shrank back against the wall, pulling up the sheet as if it would offer some protection. She heard him whisper, 'No . . . oh, no.'

His eyes turned and looked at Katie. Katie couldn't do anything; she was paralysed; her limbs would not move. The man, with a flick of his wrist, indicated that she should move back. Then he turned and fired at Tim, once, twice, three times. The sounds, with the silencer, were muffled thuds; she caught a glimpse of Tim's head, of something strange happening to it, his face suddenly changing, and a spray of blood hitting the wall. She knelt, curling herself up into a ball, hiding her head under her arms. She crouched there, waiting for the shots which would kill her. But they didn't come.

She listened to the long, long silence; then she heard the sound of footsteps going down the stairs.

She opened her eyes. The floorboards gleamed in front of her in the light of the lamp. Nothing moved. She couldn't look at Tim; he might be alive, but she couldn't do it, she didn't want to see. It was better to stay like this and not to see anything. She was aware that she was shaking; perhaps she was just cold. What was she going to do? What if she looked up and found Tim was smiling at her, if this was just a bad dream? Surely if she waited he would get up out of bed, and come to ask her what was wrong?

But he didn't. She opened her eyes and looked up for the briefest moment, but there was only the red stain of blood on the wall and large red splashes on the sheets.

And then she heard more sounds, sounds which filled her with terror; of shots ringing out and echoing in the street outside.

◆

Dmitry had not been able to sleep for long either. He woke in the early hours with a pounding head and dry throat, and lay in the dark on the bed fully dressed, thinking of Katie upstairs with Tim, in bed with him, holding him, perhaps even making love to him. No, he couldn't think of it. Of course he could not complain about it, he had left her, she had the right to look for happiness elsewhere, but still he couldn't endure the thought of it. He blamed Tim; he had taken advantage of her situation, when she was lonely, frightened. He felt violent, murderous thoughts towards him.

He got up from the bed and went to pour himself a glass of water from the kitchen tap, then sat in the living room, staring into space. He thought he heard someone moving round upstairs and then he heard something strange, a dull, thudding sound. Whatever it was, it made him wide awake, his ears straining for any further sound. He realised that he was suddenly, terribly, afraid. He leapt up, and went to open the door into the hallway. Someone was coming down the stairs; not running, but quickly, with muffled steps. Dmitry waited, easing the door off the catch, and then, as he saw a shadow in the hall, he gently pushed it open.

He saw the back of a hooded man holding a gun, removing

the silencer. He knew at once what this meant. As the man opened the front door, Dmitry leapt forward and sent him flying, down the steps and on to the paving stones. The gun fell from the man's grasp, span across the stones and into the hedge. Both of them dived for it. Dmitry got there first, grabbed the gun, rolled over, and scrambled to his feet. The gun, a semi-automatic, felt heavy and awkward in his hand. The man lay on the ground; Dmitry saw his dark eyes turn upwards in dismay, but he felt nothing, no anger, no pity; all human feeling seemed to have deserted him. He knew what he had to do; he slipped off the safety catch, stretched out his arm, and fired without an instant's hesitation, several times. He was not a good shot, and he wanted to make sure; he did not want to risk his own life and besides, he thought that this man had killed Katie. He walked over, looked at the body in the orange light of the streetlamp, saw his open eyes staring upwards and the dark hole in his forehead. Perhaps he was a Libyan, perhaps he had been hired by the CIA. He was, without a doubt, dead. After the deafening sound of the gunfire, everything was very still. Over the road, one or two lights came on in the houses.

Still holding the gun, Dmitry turned and ran into the house and up the stairs, pushed open the door to the children's room and turned on the light.

They were both sleeping, quietly; he could see that they were safe and hear their gentle breathing. He turned off the light and went into the front bedroom, trying to prepare himself for the horror he envisaged. On the bed Tim lay sprawled on blood-stained sheets, his hair a tangled mass of red. Katie was crouched in the corner, her head between her knees, her hands pulling at long strands of hair, rocking herself backwards and forwards and making plaintive, whimpering sounds. He rushed towards her and bent over her, touched her to see if she was hurt, but she shuddered convulsively and pushed him away. He said, 'The children are all right. They're sleeping, he didn't touch them.'

She was so shocked she couldn't speak, her teeth chattered loudly, but she seemed to understand, she nodded slightly. Then, staring at him wildly, she wailed, 'Tim's dead, isn't he? I can't look. I can't look. Oh God, please look for me and tell me if he's dead.'

Dmitry went over to the bed. Tim had been shot, at least twice, in the head. Dmitry put the gun down on the bedside table and picked up the phone. The dialling tone sounded unnaturally loud in the silent room. He said to Katie, 'I think he's dead, but I don't know for sure. Ask for an ambulance. Say he's injured, don't tell them he's been shot.' He dialled 999; it took a surprisingly long time for someone to answer. He handed her the phone and she said, in a trembling voice, 'Ambulance.' He heard a man's voice ask what was the matter and she said, 'Something's happened . . . I think he is dead.' She gave the address. The man tried to keep her talking but Dmitry took the phone from her and hung up and then, in case they called back, took the receiver off the hook.

He turned back to Katie. She was looking up at him, her eyes wide and disbelieving. Dmitry said, very gently, 'No, I don't think there's any chance . . . but it's still the right thing to do.'

He knew they would not have long before the ambulance arrived. He looked across the room. His eyes fell on the gun, lying on the table by the bed. He said, 'My fingerprints.' His mind was working slowly, but still fast enough to fill with fear. He must do something. He picked up the gun and wiped it clean of prints with the front of his shirt. Then an idea came to him and, wrapping the gun with a corner of the sheet, he placed it awkwardly in Tim's limp hand. Perhaps, until they did the forensics, this would confuse them. Perhaps it would stop them immediately looking for someone else.

Katie had put her head between her knees and was shaking now quite violently. Dmitry pulled her to her feet and led her downstairs, stumbling, away from Tim, away from the blood.

She clung to him but Dmitry gently pushed her away from him, down on to the sofa, and, kneeling in front of her, took both her hands in his.

'Katie, I am so sorry.'

'It was you they meant to kill.'

'I think so, yes.'

She gave a strange, convulsive sob. Dmitry put his arms around her and she didn't resist him; then she suddenly cried out and pressed herself against him. She looked up at him, held on to him tightly, saying, 'Oh, Mitya, thank God it wasn't you . . . oh, thank God, it wasn't you.'

They stayed, embracing, for several long minutes. Dmitry could feel the warmth of her body melting into his, and the way she shuddered in his arms.

He said, beginning to panic now, 'The ambulance and the police will be here any minute. I can't stay here . . . Katie, I must go.'

'Go? Go where? Where could you go?'

'I could go to Moscow. Now, this morning, on an early flight. If you didn't tell them straight away that I was here . . . You are in shock, you can't remember anything . . . Just give me a few hours to get away . . .'

'No, you can't go, Mitya. I want you here, now, always.'

He took her face in his hands and made her look at him. Her eyes looked right into his and then she began suddenly to kiss him, quick, passionate kisses on his lips, his cheeks, his eyelids. Tears ran down his cheeks and she licked them away. She said, 'Mitya, I didn't love him, not like you. It was never like it was with you . . . if you had only been there . . .'

In the distance, they heard the sound of the siren. It seemed to come from a long way off, intermittent, growing and then fading in intensity as it passed behind the buildings, but steadily coming nearer. He said, 'There's not much time. You told me, once, that you would come to Russia to be with me if that was the only way to be together. Would you do that, Katie? If I went there, would you come?'

Katie said, 'But I saw him, Mitya. It was self-defence. They couldn't convict you, they wouldn't even bring it to court. They couldn't possibly want to bring it to court. They will believe us . . . If you try to run away they will think you are guilty . . . Mitya, please, stay with me, tell the truth, it will be all right.'

But he knew it wouldn't be all right. How could he explain? His wife's lover dead, several shots in the body outside. Someone could have seen him from the houses opposite. If the dead man were a Libyan or a known assassin he might get away with it; but he might not be. The intelligence services would deny him, they wouldn't back his story; who knows what games they would want to play with him?

He tried to think clearly. The only thing he wanted was to be with Katie. But if he stayed, what would happen? The police would separate them at once, they would be questioned apart to check that their stories matched. Dmitry would be arrested; perhaps the police would be forced to bring a case against him, they might add all the other charges from the airport, he might become a scapegoat after all, be publicly named and humiliated and spend the rest of his life in prison. He wanted to explain all this, to discuss it, make the right decision, but there wasn't time.

He looked at Katie. He felt that his salvation lay only with this person, the one who would always love him whatever he became; his love, his only hope, his angel of redemption. He knew now that she still loved him despite all that he had done, and that there existed in this world a kind of love that could endure through anything, could survive disillusion and betrayal. She trembled in front of him; she looked so fragile, so frightened, how could he turn his back on her? He knew that if he left her she would feel he had abandoned her. His mind was in turmoil, rushing backwards and forwards; he thought that he would stay;

then he thought that he would go; then he thought that he would stay again.

He heard the squeal of brakes outside the house. Blue lights flashed eerily around the room.

Katie let go of him suddenly, said, 'Quick! Go out the back way.'

He grabbed his bag and coat and ran out into the night.